GODS
OF
WILLOW

Amrish Kumar is an entrepreneur who has spent over a decade working in Indian textiles as the managing director of brand 'Ritu Kumar'. His desire to be heard has resulted in him building a record label, an internet film venture and leaving a trail of long suffering friends and family. He has an MBA and is a fellow of the Aspen Institute. *Gods of Willow* is his first novel.

GODS
OF
WILLOW

A Coming of Age Innings

a novel

AMRISH KUMAR

IndiaInk
ROLI
BOOKS

First published in 2022

IndiaInk
An imprint of
Roli Books Pvt. Ltd
M-75, Greater Kailash II Market
New Delhi 110 048
Phone: ++91 (011) 4068 2000
E-mail: info@rolibooks.com; Website: www.rolibooks.com
Also at
Bengaluru, Chennai, & Mumbai

Layout design: Bhagirath Kumar
Production: Lavinia Rao

ISBN: 9788186939970

Typeset in Minion Pro by Roli Books Pvt. Ltd.
Printed in India at Sai Printo Pack Pvt. Ltd., New Delhi.

~

To the women in my life, who assured me that they knew better.
Mother, aunts, cousins and friends. They encouraged me to
keep writing and helped regularly check my own instincts
(or foolishness as they put it).

To the men in my life, who assured me that I didn't know what
I was doing. Father, brothers, lads and uncles. They encouraged
me by finding amusement in all my life's trivialities and endeavours.

Come to think of it, it's amazing this thing got written.

~

BOOK I

BOOK I

CHAPTER ONE

9 March 1998

He woke to the piercing urgency of an alarm clock. The clattering instrument was loud at any time of day, but early mornings' velvety consciousness made its trill almost unbearable.

Making matters worse, his bed had formed the perfect alchemy of comfort. Pillow pushed against the headboard just right, coverings curled around contours and the mattress deliciously cocooned his weight.

A clumsy arm flew out from under the blanket, flailing at the offending object. He questioned the need for torturing himself at this ungodly hour.

A quick calculation ensued – what if he didn't get out of bed?

But in the end, it was hopeless. Just like every other morning, the fog cleared, and he remembered the cause. The reason he would always sling his legs over the side and sit upright.

He hated this moment of inevitability. His obsession with it all.

Obsession is a clumsy, judgmental word. If you are obsessed with something, there is a flaw in your personality; you are hankering to fill a void. You should be counselled, you should look towards meditation, you should do yoga, you should be speaking to your aunty who smoked pot as a twenty-something-year-old. But bravo for acknowledging and accepting your deep flaws. Well done for owning your own limitations and reaching out for acceptance. Friends, people who know your friends, family, extended family and really anyone who knows you exist, now knows that you are flawed. You can be judged with a certification. You and your obsession! Honestly.

For twenty-one-year-old Kabir Menon, cricket isn't merely an obsession. It serves a specific purpose. It is a tool, which helps with mundane cerebral functions required to manage his day. When he lays down to sleep, he imagines playing a match where he is bowling outswingers. First one past the bat, second one... left alone, third one an in-cutter, rapped on the pads, LBW – thanks very much... he's asleep.

Cricket helps him measure the passage of time and hangs smears of memory to his life. He knows he had his tooth pulled out when he was twelve, which resulted in a swollen mouth during the 1992 series played in Australia. To his great joy, he was allowed to sleep in the TV room as the matches started at 4 a.m. in India. He remembers Srikanth pulled Ambrose for a six over square leg while he was in and out of a novocaine-induced fever.

Cricket has formed a crust in some critical neural pathways of his brain. Associations and physical ticks often have something to do with the sport. If you see him walking along, pondering the day, he will most likely be playing a shadow cover drive.

How did this predicament come to pass? It probably has something to do with a little boy's neurological development. What the rhyme did not mention, was that along with snails and tails, little boys are made of an innate desire to belong to a tribe. To immortalize stories told of physicality and competition. This tribalism finds fertile pasture in an adolescent brain. Patterns and colours start forming – the angles created by leg spin, for instance;

the bushy black caterpillar on Javed Miandad's upper lip, the neat hand-stitched seam on a new cricket ball, the rotund shape of Boon or Ranatunga whose generous stomachs looked better-suited to rest a plate of your fried snacks, than on a professional sports arena and so on. These tenacious impressions then hang on to the subconscious like a stubborn tick and you find Kabir, a decade later, doodling the shape of Viv Richards' bat logo whilst in a lecture on Keynesian demand stimulus.

So, early this morning, having dragged himself out of bed, Kabir walked through the neighbourhood bazaar on the way to cricket practice. It was pleasantly cool at this time of day. The freshness of spring had not yet been wrapped in the heat of summer's thronging reverb. Slanted sunlight glinted on the old, black cobbled-stone street. Rhythms of the market were beginning to play themselves out the way they had for hundreds of years. *Doodhwalas* on creaky cycles were off for their morning deliveries. Some stores were being opened; others were being swept. Newspaper bundles had just been delivered to the street-side magazine kiosk and Mian Qadir was waiting for his copy to be cut loose from the plastic tawny thread holding the bulk together.

Mian Qadir never looked less than stately. His slim face, manicured grey beard, tailored kurta and waistcoat were a permanent fixture in this lane.

'Mianji, how clean and starched you look,' Kabir teased with the confidence of an indulged ward. After all, he had known Mian Qadir all his life and took great glee that after a growth spurt at fourteen, he was now four inches taller than this man. Mian remained elegant in aspect and looked over Kabir's cricket whites and university team cap. Even though in principle his clothes were clean and to his size, Kabir managed a disheveled visage. His kit hung off his shoulders as if his body was yet undecided on the shape it must become.

'With great grace and foresight, the Almighty has given me the sense and ability not to offend others with my appearance.'

Mian Qadir's mellifluous voice came from great depths and spoke in honeyed timeless Urdu. It sounded as though there was a cave in his throat where additional chambers could be called upon for use. Passionate about his qawwali, he sported the stained mouth of paan-chewing maestros of this art. His occupation was the proprietorship of Sunshine Bakery and the adjoining Biryani Plaza restaurant – both long-standing institutions, passed on through generations. Where one began early with sugared breads and small glasses of chai, the other would open its simple padlocked façade just before lunch and go on till well after midnight.

Striding into the bakery, Kabir helped himself to a fresh batch of fluffy yellow cake with embedded bits of raisins. Mianji feigned irritation and pulled the boy away from the counter.

'Listen here boy, I know you are not altogether useless, so why is it that your father is despairing of you? Why won't you start studying for the IAS or law like he suggests? You know that the time has come to start thinking about what happens after college.'

'How am I to do all of this, Mianji? I have cricket practice and college exams. Besides, who does IAS anymore? Who wants a government job now? I don't want to spend the rest of my life wearing a safari suit and sucking up to babus.'

Qadir raised his hand to stop the rambling teen. 'Little man, speak to your father. It's only fair to him that he knows you have no intentions of all this.'

'How can I? He won't understand, Mianji. To him it's either the IAS or law – these are the only choices. Now, just because he did not get to go to college and sit the exams doesn't mean that I need to...'

The wheels of Kabir's mind seemed to be turning.

'Can't you speak to him on my behalf?' Kabir was grasping at straws now for any relief from his father's scrutiny. It had become so severe that hearing the latch of his father's door would make him anxious. His sole motivation then became how to get out of the room without being noticed. It all seemed quite hopeless.

'You're right in a way, boy. There are other opportunities in the world for you, which we did not have. But if you think that you won't need to suck up to safari suits, you have a bigger shock coming. Anyway, I will speak to him for you, but you will need to show some purpose in life.'

As with all such conversations, Kabir's mind was beginning to wander. Noticing his waning attention, Mian Qadir cut his losses and diverted his care to the slovenly pace at which his sales staff was attending to a new customer.

The bazaar was waking. Commercialized graphic design avariciously covered every corner of masonry. Advertisements peddling Pepsi, Liril soap and ICICI Bank dominated. In between the garish posters were hints of a more ancient place. Carefully constructed doorways with Islamic arch detailing, remnants of carved wooden balustrades, all mixed in with modern plasterwork and tawdrily painted blocks. Small cubbyhole stores of locksmiths, dentists and knife sharpeners had made way for mobile phone vendors, video rentals and internet cafés. However, the old faithfuls like Sunshine Bakery and Agarwal General Store still anchored the street.

Today was day four of the India vs Australia test match and the Australians were ahead. Naturally, Kabir could not dwell on IAS exams at a time like this. Deep within him a flutter of hope remained – Sachin Tendulkar hadn't come in to bat yet. The tension was making him jittery. It could all be over in a flash if they got him out. That would really ruin his week.

He grew up a Hindu in a community, which was equal parts Muslim, some Christians, and a smattering of Jains and Jews. As a child Kabir was made to bow his head to a small shrine in his home and he now did it as a matter of habit before an important match or exam. The shrine had a small multi-limbed deity surrounded by playing card-sized pictures of gods and goddesses. Each had a specific function, each heroic in posture and larger than life in colour and intent.

But Indian cricket was Kabir's true religion and it seemed destined to provide more pain than joy. Its prophets led their flock up a mountain but never seemed to glimpse any semblance of a promised land. For the rest of his life, he was fated to yearn for the triumph of the team. Its successes were euphoric and cruelly sporadic; its failures were constant and soul sapping.

Kabir sauntered absent-mindedly towards the bus stand to catch the number 13 to college. Hearing his name called out, he swung around. It was Montu – a boy from the neighbourhood, who graduated from the same college two years ago. Kabir groaned as he watched Montu trotting to catch up. It was not that he didn't like Montu, but there was something about him that Kabir just didn't like. Perhaps it was Montu's whiff of condescension at being just a little older.

Montu had recently acquired an articleship at a local chartered accountant's practice. This added to the worldly way in which he now carried himself. He had been given a small square plastic box of business cards with his name printed in a clunky bold type. Mahinder Jain, Junior Officer at Radhashyam Gulshan Chartered Accountants. This was the closest to godliness Montu had ever felt.

Kabir quickened his pace to get away from this forced companionship. Montu managed to catch up to him anyway.

Montu handed one of his business cards to Kabir and ensured he zipped it up safely in the inner pocket of his kit bag.

'No chance today. Day 4 on the Chennai pitch, Shane Warne bowling, we won't even get a lead of 150. Australia will win the match today itself'.

Kabir knew he was being goaded, but it still irritated him. He fought off the urge to respond but the seeds of doubt had already been planted. He struggled to keep his cool and his expression barely disguised his inner monologue.

Knowing the track record of the Indian team, it was a precarious position to be in. But in amongst those doubts was the resurging splendour of – what if they pull it off? But they never do, do they? Was cricket actually making him unhappy? Just when the logical mind was pulling his conscious away from the unease over a bloody cricket match – the pestilent id started imagining a Tendulkar century and a swashbuckling innings from local hero Azharuddin. The possibility of beating the best team in the world was all too much for him to maintain his composure.

'Montu, shut up man,' he blurted. 'We have a real chance today. We are only one wicket down and this team can play spin. We have Azhar to come and anyway a lead of 220 is enough to win.'

He was almost imploring Montu to agree, as though the more support the cause had, the more likely the outcome would be. Montu's slightly sweaty upper lip curled into a smile. Thankfully for Kabir, the clattering metal box came around the next bend and skipping into a run, he jumped into the back.

CHAPTER TWO

The dilapidated wooden shutters were still robust enough to block most of the morning light, but stray orange rays fought their way through the gaps where the slats had withered. In trying to open the windows of this dim room, Barman Choksi stubbed his toe on something that shouldn't have been on the floor. Cursing and now limping, he maneuvered his way to the low-slung sills. All elbows and knees, Barman's movements were neither efficient nor economical. He had real trouble focusing on mundane rituals such as opening windows in the morning. The banalities were taxing, as were most niceties and trivialities. He also had to work at improving his patience. After all, a senior faculty member was required to interact with other people.

Barman had refused to head the history department so that administrative snarlings did not impede his research. His area of enquiry was Hyderabad – from the breakup of the Mughal dynasty till independence from the British Empire. It is not certain whether this enquiry into English occupation had anything to do with his other very British fixations – cricket and democracy. He was both the coach of the college cricket team as well as the faculty in-charge of college elections.

Paradoxically, fate rendered him with an innate sense of style, an effortlessness in presentation. His long skinny arms made kurta sleeves look too short yet stylish. His thick utilitarian reading glasses looked much too modish for an academic. Over the years Barman had had his share of feminine attention, not least from bored wives of colleagues and mothers of students. But mostly he managed to unwittingly dismiss their intentions by being himself. A couple of dalliances had threatened to make tenure with Mr Choksi, but he spectacularly crash-landed those.

Light now streamed into the front room of this university faculty bungalow. As a senior professor, Barman was eligible to live in housing within Sikandra University. The campus had once been the erstwhile forest department grounds. It was converted into the University in the early twentieth century. The bungalows, designed for the heat, had high ceilings and large windows, but the insides were otherwise small and non-descript. A semicircular porch and small yard framed the exterior, which was ensconced within high hedges.

A kettle on the stove whistled and its lid pattered as the water boiled. Barman poured thick, dark coffee, so sweet that one of his exes had once joked that his spoon would stand up straight if left in the cup. He often imagined the standing spoon while stirring his coffee.

On his way out, Barman pulled shut his front door, not bothering to lock it. The campus was safe and there was nothing to steal anyway. The cricket ground was a fifteen-minute walk, but he was running late and considered using his scooter. He almost never used the damn thing because one, he preferred to walk and two, whenever he needed to go somewhere too far to walk, he didn't like to drive. The scooter leant against its stand, a fine layer of dust uniformly shading it in a vintage patina. It was an older machine with a sunken and generous seat, not like the new ones with springy pod-like perches. Barman straightened it and gave the starter a couple of kicks, but there was no sign of life. Sighing at the predictability of it all, he replaced the stand and set off.

Walking gave him space to think. He thought about the book he had been planning to write for the last decade, of the politics amongst the college faculty and of the judgmental looks he got from the neighbour's mother who thought no pious man should be single and living alone at his age. Most of all, he daydreamed about the prospects of the college team.

Thus far it had been a reasonably successful season but they had not yet reached the most important event. The selectors for the first-class team were scouting players in earnest and the Hyderabad State Cricket Association (HCA) was expected to turn up. Barman reminisced about the time young Azharuddin played on these very pitches. It was twenty years ago, but he still remembered vividly the small crowds gathering on dusty grounds to watch the wristy prodigy. When Azhar debuted for the Indian national team, Barman and his friends gathered to listen to the commentary on All India Radio. Televisions were a rarity and thanks to the state's socialist ideals, programmes on agricultural animal husbandry would interrupt the broadcast.

Cricket stars of those days were men of a gentler persuasion. They looked almost embarrassed to be featured in a newspaper advertisement promoting hair cream. But change was afoot. In 1983, Kapil Dev led his mustachioed team to a completely unexpected World Cup win. The sheer gumption of that era was transforming the way India saw itself. In particular, with respect to the white nations; the colonized psyche, if you will. Over the years, India began to win (occasionally). Azhar became captain. His gait changed from an emaciated lope to a muscled swagger. At pre-match interviews he no longer looked like a reluctant youth searching for the closest escape and instead acquired the confident diffidence belonging to this big stage.

Today, Hyderabad's skyline was punctuated with satellite dishes streaming non-stop popcorn content into every home. You couldn't get away from larger-than-life posters of a cricketer or film star selling motorcycles, whiskey, biscuits, life insurance – you name it. An aggressive onslaught on a nation hungry to consume.

Thankfully the campus was devoid of these stimuli. Barman arrived at the ground where the team was trickling in. Despite the morning dew still on the turf, grounds staff were lugging large black rubber hoses to the corners of the field and sprinkling the grass. A booming voice startled him.

Janardhan Seth's small frame was in sharp contrast to the timbre and gusto of his vocal range. The Seths were an institution at the university. They had been groundskeepers for longer than anyone remembered. In his pressed khaki shirt and shorts, Janardhan looked like a military man. His strafing of the grounds men followed a familiar pattern. Every morning he questioned their parentage. What manner of people could give birth to such lazy, good-for-nothing, sluggish men? None of them were born with a backbone and each was to be thrashed (if they did not pick up the pace). The forbearing malis were used to this abuse and their pace of work betrayed no change.

Not only was Seth extremely knowledgeable about the botanical intricacies of his environment but he was also an astute observer of cricket. He took great pride in his work – theirs was one of the best-maintained pitches in the city and certainly looked a lot better than the abomination the national team was playing on against Australia.

Barman walked over. 'Good morning, Seth'.

'The pitch will play quick this weekend. I hear there may be some scouts coming in?'

'I have heard some murmurs, but I need you to get me more information. Your ear is much closer to the ground than mine is.'

Seth didn't turn to acknowledge the deference paid. This was not a case of false flattery – Seth was a person who got things done.

He knew every household in his locality and had connections across the city in offices high and low. His lack of formal education never bothered him; in fact, he saw it as an asset. Managing the complex wheels of the system required skills, which were not learnt in classrooms of colleges such as this. It was no wonder then that he could scarcely hide his condescension of the blunt instruments walking around campus.

Barman often consulted Seth on decisions regarding the players and on machinations on campus. Equally important was that Seth was his go-to-man for all manner of trivialities. If Barman needed help with his gas connection, driver's license, or even get his cable TV installed – Seth inevitably had a cousin or a neighbour or a sister married to the second cousin of someone who knew someone.

But these two men could not be classified as friends. Their differences in upbringing never gave them common ground. They came from very different sides of the track but they had a loyalty to each other. It was a personal kinship. Equal in their minds perhaps, but not to anyone who looked at them.

They continued chatting as they walked up to the nets. Seth suggested they play an extra fast bowler for the game against the Gardens Cricket Club fixture this weekend. They also identified Rana as the one bowler who they thought might catch the eye of the selectors. Some of the other players had a chance, but it was an outside chance. Kabir was mentioned; they both liked the lad, but neither imagined his cricketing career would make it much further. As they walked within earshot of the boys, Janardhan peeled off.

CHAPTER THREE

Cobwebs of waking early were long gone and the morning's vitality crept into Kabir's veins. Mentally he was gearing up to pads up and bat, his favourite thing to do.

The walk from the Sikandra University gate to the ground was under the overhang of large mango trees. The vista had a very 'central India' quality to it – blue skies with wisps of high cloud. Hemmed around the edges of the cricket ground were ancient banyan and peepal trees. The earth had a warm, red tint with a sticky, fertile consistency. This was home.

Nets were erected in the corner of the field and a handful of players gathered around. Kabir met the team with the customary high fives and dropped his kit next to Sareen.

Sareen and Kabir had gone to the same school, had lived down the road from each other and their fathers had been friends. In fact, Kabir suspected that Sareen's father was the closest friend his father ever had.

When Sareen's father died, his mother moved them to his uncle's home. Even though Sareen rarely brought it up, Kabir knew that he hated living with his uncle. For the first few years, Sareen spent a lot of time with Kabir, loitering around the bazaars and staying nights at their home.

Recently, Sareen hung out less often. He had befriended some boys in his new neighbourhood and it was like being in a club of sorts. They would have scheduled meetings where the talk would often move to issues regarding the protection of their community. None of it made much sense to Sareen but he liked being in a fraternity. He had a new audience, one in which he was the funniest guy in the room. Sareen hadn't told Kabir about all this. He had a feeling that Kabir wouldn't understand.

Standing by the nets, Sareen intently watched Rana run up to bowl. Rana was the tallest kid on the team and had already played for the Under-19 team at HCA. His run up was ominous, like the soundtrack when something bad is about to happen in a movie. It was a smooth athletic action, which seemed to involve no effort as it gathered momentum. The final motion was rapid, the energy of the steady acceleration lifting into a rapid crescendo of flailing arms and feet.

For players, the sounds of cricket are critical to the feel of the game. The soft accelerating crush of turf during a bowler's run up, the thud of landing into the stride, the grunt as he pivots muscle and limb into the release and finally the whishing, whirling leather ball hurtling at the batsman. The rhythm of sound and its intensity dictate the psyche of the batsman. If he is able to confront it, half the battle is won. If he is timid or apprehensive, then all manner of doubts creep in and he is in trouble.

Sareen flinched dramatically as the fizzing ball cannoned into the back of the net. He whispered, 'How many eggs do you think he eats in a day?'

'Probably all of them.'

Widening his eyes, pushing his jaw out and hunched with arms on his hips, Sareen looked like Winston Churchill. He called out to Rana, 'Oye mountain, put some effort into it man. What's with the dinky bowling?'

It was evident from Rana's grunts and stares that he was putting all he had into it.

'Rana! My mother could bowl faster than that. No, scratch that, her mother, my grandmother could bowl faster than you AND she has more hair on her arms than you!'

He went on to give Rana a unique set of helpful tips, to the amusement of the boys around. They turned away, hiding smirks, not wanting to give Rana the impression that they were encouraging this. They would have to bat against him at some point.

Kabir noticed Barman coming up to the nets and shushed Sareen.

'Morning, sir. Play starts in an hour. Do you think we will still be in at the end of the day?'

'Let's not worry about that for now, Master Menon. Let's just get through our morning nets without fretting about what we cannot control.' Barman tried to exude calmness, but he too had butterflies in his stomach thinking about the test match.

'Okay sir, just tell me what you think of the Chennai pitch.'

'You mean Madras.'

The practice session went well. The boys were in good shape towards the end of the season. Some of them had really come into their own.

Kabir went in to bat and spent the first few balls trying to get his feet moving. He always struggled early on and took time to get used to the pace and bounce. After he did though, he was a good batsman and had a reasonable, if outside, chance of selection. He coped with Rana admirably, even with his extra yard of pace. By the time Sareen came on to bowl his gentle off spin, Kabir was timing the ball nicely.

As the practice was ending, Barman noticed the new vice chancellor of the college, Harshad Bhosle, across the field. Appointed six months ago, Bhosle had replaced the long-standing Mr Ramaswamy, an institution at the university, who had been at the post for almost two decades. Mr Ramaswamy was of Telugu descent and had retired at the ripe old age of eighty. He cut a striking figure in his pristine white lungi, starched shirt and occasionally white tilak on his forehead. A highly respected and published scholar, he was a freedom fighter in his youth and had seen the birth of the nation. He was committed to academia, but perhaps less in touch with other requirements of the role and of the changes afoot in India. Perhaps it was a reaction to this stodginess that the replacement chosen was almost solely focused on change and not on intellectual rigour.

In Barman's experience, 'Big B' (as Bhosle was referred to by students) did not need a good reason to probe things with his sugary, sticky style. Hidden within these interactions was a sustained tone of censure, so he preferred avoiding them altogether. Hurriedly closing proceedings, he flung some instructions at the group and quickly edged away from the field. This was not lost upon Kabir and Janardhan. Seeing a chance to watch some of the test match, Kabir went after him.

~

An impatience for authority and his deep knowledge of cricket made Barman an appealing role model for Kabir. Barman was his archetype of living life, his cricket guru, the father-figure no father could ever be. Their interaction began, thanks to Kabir's second most prized possession (after his cricket bat), his grandfather's old Nikon F2 which he never left home without. He loved using it and had become quite adept at it. Naturally he began taking pictures of college cricket matches. This appealed to Barman's instinct to chronicle, and Kabir became a self-appointed record keeper. Soon Barman gave him other tasks including the administrative work he loathed doing himself. The boy seemed happy enough to do it. Barman found the boy tolerable company – high praise indeed.

Kabir had a couple of hours before his first lecture and invited himself to Barman's place to watch the start of the test match. As they entered the shabby front room, Kabir busied himself switching on the TV and clearing away some of the files from the coffee table. Barman followed a passing thought into his study where he busied himself in some work.

The match had begun as Kabir took his place on the worn couch. He started organizing piles of photocopied pages into individual sets. These were manuals, rules and guides for voters, candidates and ballot locations.

Barman romanticized the ideal of democracy and elections. His higher education was under the tutelage of enlightened Nehruvian educators. These men marvelled at the bewildering achievement of India as a democracy and Barman's eyes would glaze over every time he spoke of the 'heroic experiment'. So, college elections were the one responsibility he was willing to shoulder.

A loud yelp from the front room shattered the morning quiet. Barman rushed into the front room to find Kabir in distress. Sidhu had gotten out early and their worst fears were coming true. Barman joined Kabir on the sofa and they watched in tense anticipation.

Kabir couldn't sit still for very long. It was all too much. He paced around the room grumbling.

'They have done it again, haven't they? Tendulkar is in early, now he will get one good ball, get out and the rest will fall apart. It's like the rest of them have never played cricket before. I mean, come on! It's useless. We may as well just put it off now.'

A soft knock on the door broke the tension. Janardhan Seth peeked in, his eyebrows raised in enquiry. Barman stood clumsily, knocking over a mug on the table. He set it right, relieved to find it was empty.

'Come in, come in, Seth.'

Janardhan entered gingerly, barely disguising his look of censure as he scanned the disordered room.

'What can I get you? Tea, coffee, water, juice? Wait, I don't know if I have juice, let me check in the –'

'Nothing for me, thank you.'

'Right, right...'

Barman now stood next to Seth, hands loosely on hips, nodding and not knowing where to go next, now that the set of initial enquiries were complete.

Seth spoke softly to break the awkward silence, 'I need to speak to you... privately.' He pointedly looked over Barman's shoulder towards the boy. Barman gestured that they sit outside on the verandah.

Both men took a seat on the curved bamboo chairs, a staple of all outdoor verandahs in this part of the world. Between them was an ashtray on a matching wicker table. Seth perched himself economically while Barman fell into his seat, extending his gangly limbs to their complete length. Pulling out a packet of Gold Flake cigarettes, he offered one to Seth. Smoking was one of Seth's few vices; he accepted and pulled out a matchbox. The ritual of lighting cigarettes and exhaling their first drag was done in silence. Looking into the distance, Seth broke the quiet.

'Professor sahib, I have been hearing that there is some new interest in the elections this year? It seems that the boys standing for election have less to do with the college and more to do with politics.'

A prickly unease crept over the back of the professor's neck. He recalled the strange conversation with Bhosle the other day. The vice chancellor had recommended the aid of a local businessman to help with the candidate selection. Barman found all this quite irregular but had pushed it out of his mind. The politicization of student elections was not new; it had been around for decades, but it was usually restricted to the larger state universities. Barman hadn't even considered that there would be any interest in Sikandra University.

Not wanting to give the impression that these goings-on had escaped his attention, Barman rubbed his chin, 'Yes, there have been some unlikely candidates this year and also some external interest. I had not given it too much thought.'

'The problem, professor sahib, is that this type of thing rots the roots of the tree. Before you know it, you will have all sorts of people getting involved. Soon we won't know where the rot began and who is responsible.'

Barman wasn't altogether sure he was following the intent of this conversation. Was this a warning?

'What have you heard and from whom?'

'In truth, I haven't had anyone come up to me directly to say anything. But yesterday some of the groundskeepers heard that the AVP was organizing some kind of march and that it was to pass through the campus. Also, you know my bhatija (nephew) works for this printing press. He said they had received a large order for posters and flyers from the AVP. The posters were about local college elections and our college was mentioned.'

Barman's mood was progressively dampening, not so much due to the news but more from the fact that he did not know who any of these people were.

'Who the hell is the AVP?'

'It's some kind of a youth organization. They do some public work, like they distribute food to the needy on certain holidays, they have a works programme where they place their young members as apprentices in businesses, and that kind of thing.'

'That doesn't sound so bad…'

'But I think they may have some connection with the political parties as well as the larger unions at Hyderabad University. My bhatija said that he overheard some of their chatter in the shop and it sounded like they were in the mood to create trouble. You must have seen them around; they wear matching khaki shirts and shorts with a sash across their shoulders.'

Barman had indeed seen these kids around. They exuded no threat or menace; in fact, these boys in their ill-fitting garb looked more Rotary Club than Hitler Youth. The girls were in similar coloured salwar kurtas. Barman recalled thinking that it was a breath of fresh air to see them taking part in a cause. Now that he was able to visualize this threat, which to his mind had the look of overweight pre-pubescent kids, he was relieved.

'Oh yes of course, I have seen those kids. They don't look like much, Seth. Why the concern? Do you think you may be overreacting? After all they are kids. Kids say stupid things but they are all bravado.'

Seth pondered this. The two men sat in silence for a moment.

'My father often warned me about it all happening again and I suppose I am hearing his voice in my head.'

Seth knew where to press. An appeal to Barman's sense of historical adventurism solicited an animated response.

'What do you mean by it happening again?'

'Once, many years ago, there was unrest in college. We almost lost everything then. I was a child – I remember my father hiding me in a trunk one afternoon when there were riots in the street. They were burning and looting, and we lived on the edge of campus. It all started with college elections and political parties becoming involved. In the beginning, it was about dispensing patronage and exercising power in appointments of faculty, you know that type of thing. Then it got fully political with the Jan Sangh and the communists who were fighting Indira. There were goondas on the street. The government even sent the army in, and a couple of students were killed. The university was shut down for a full year. When it was re-opened, Ramaswamy took serious action; all the political groups were disbanded and the faculty changed. He was the one who made sure that we never went back to those days.'

Barman knew a little of this but had never heard a firsthand account. He was putting together the timeline of the Jayaprakash movement in the 1970s and the Emergency of 1975. He had no clue that the university played a part in all of this. He made a mental note to dig into the university archives.

'But those were different circumstances, Seth. It is very unlike today. That time it was a large national movement. Today people are more interested in Star TV and some Bollywood bimbo.'

'You may be right.'

Janardhan harboured more than a passing suspicion and Barman knew him not to be an alarmist.

There was a roar of cheer from inside the house. Seth, stubbing his cigarette, turned to look at Barman.

'Well, let's see what comes up. Keep your eyes open, Professorji.

Barman got up with him and moved to shake his hand, but Janardhan had already pressed palms in namaste. He responded awkwardly, unused to this way of sendoff. Kabir came bounding out of the house in excitement.

'Tendulkar is on a roll... He's murdering them, you must come watch, sir.'

When he turned back, Seth was straightening the haphazard bits of furniture on the verandah and making his way out. Remembering the scooter problem, Barman called out to him, asking if he knew a mechanic who could come and fix it. Janardhan's unflappable face fell. He couldn't think of anyone. He looked like he had been punched in the gut.

'It's okay, Seth. Never mind, I will find someone.'

Kabir had a sudden epiphany.

'Sir, sir, I know someone who can fix it. I can get it done super quick and super cheap.'

Barman turned to go into the house as Seth walked away. 'Well, if you can have it back here mended and without punching a hole in my pocket, you can use it when I don't need it.'

Kabir couldn't believe his ears. Having a set of wheels was the greatest freedom he could fathom. His imagination was doing cartwheels at the prospect of it all. Even though all he could come up with was driving his friends up and down university, it was glorious! This news coupled with the morning session of the test match was turning this into a great day.

Tendulkar had come in to bat and all eyes were on the battle between the greatest batsman in the world vs Warne, the greatest bowler in the world. After a quiet, watchful start, Tendulkar unfurled two consecutive cut shots for four. After that he began playing an innings, which beggared belief. He was cutting and pulling the spinners on a wearing track, he was scattering the field and destroying the best team in the world. Both Kabir and Barman were rooted to the spot. Neither allowing the other to move from their position on the couch. It was a superstition that only cricket fans really understand; for each of them, being in this very physical spot was what enabled Tendulkar to bat in this way. If they moved, they would break the spell.

Finally, the match paused for lunch and both realized that they had missed their individual obligations. Barman had forgotten a faculty meeting and Kabir his morning lectures.

Sheepishly, Barman collected his papers to head into the administrative offices. Kabir got the keys and went around the back to the scooter. He unlocked it and wheeled the machine out of the compound.

CHAPTER FOUR

Overlooking a manicured front lawn, Mustafa Reza was waiting in the cloisters of the main university building. He loved sitting here peering at the features of this Indo-Saracenic edifice. Small Islamic arches connected slender gothic columns and it made for an odd, yet not unpleasing effect. The stone-grey corridor remained shaded and was cool to the touch. What he liked the most was not in the building at all but in the varied flowering creepers which covered the exterior and the jacaranda trees which dotted the perimeter. This time of year was spectacular as the trees in full bloom enhanced the structure's old world quality. Buildings and spaces deeply moved Mustafa and from a young age he knew that he wanted to study architecture.

Kind, soft spoken and quick to smile, he was the third member of the KMS posse (as they liked to call themselves) – Kabir, Sareen, Mustafa. They imagined the acronym was well known around college, but nobody else actually referred to them as that. Mustafa was the more artistic and studious of the three. He liked his comic books and loved his English (Hollywood) movies. He was an 80s 'nerd' – *Star Wars, Back to the Future* (Parts 1, 2, 3), *Big, Police Academy*, you name it, he knew the minutia. There used to be a video library of VHS cassette tapes near his home, and he watched these films till the tapes were rubbed raw.

The cloisters was their regular meeting point and today's plan was lunch and then watching the match somewhere for the rest of the day. Mustafa had heard the score and was itching to get to the closest TV. From a distance he heard the faint bleating of a horn and Kabir's voice calling out to him. He picked up his bag and set off to locate the sound. Going around the back, he found Kabir standing with a dull sage, rusty-looking scooter, grinning with all the elasticity his face would allow.

'Can you believe it?'

When Mustafa looked puzzled, one nostril on his rather large nose would raise to a sneer and tilt his large black-rimmed glasses.

'Believe what exactly?'

Kabir launched into a rapid explanation of the day, replete with descriptions of the net session, the test match and then the incident leading to how he was now pushing a dead scooter across the campus. He stopped abruptly, waiting for a reaction. Mustafa's 'buy in' was critical, not only was he the most sensible but his father ran a car dealership and service center, which is where Kabir had planned to take the scooter. Looking decidedly unimpressed, Mustafa walked around it and bent down to run his fingers across a damp, angry-looking rusted smear on the side. He noted that the horn was no longer bleating with any urgency, the draining battery had reduced it to a garbled squeak.

Without a discernable change in expression, he said to Kabir, 'This is fucking brilliant!'

They both burst into rapturous cheers and danced around the scooter hugging each other. As this was lunch hour, students streaming out of the building witnessed this commotion. Most laughed as they passed, others came to enquire as to what was going on.

Together they pushed the scooter out of the campus gate and

stood on the main road leading to the labyrinth that was the rest of the city.

Outside was a different world. The quiet sedate campus gave way to a flurry of sounds and colour. Across the road, festive eateries were filling with students. These were flanked by a row of cigarette kiosks selling a wide range of effects including tobacco, paan, aspirins and pre-paid mobile phone recharge coupons. If you knew the right person and the right password, you could also score some weed. Almost all the kiosks proclaimed '*yeh dil maange more*' (This heart wants more), with Shah Rukh Khan, Rani Mukherjee and Sachin Tendulkar holding sweaty Pepsi bottles. The occasional kiosk rebelled with Orange mobile hoardings.

Mustafa took out his Ericsson to call his father. Still wrapped in protective plastic, the phone looked like a black brick. It was meant for emergencies only. After taunting his son about what classified as an emergency, Mustafa's father agreed to help the boys but they had to figure out how to get the scooter to the workshop.

Despite all the new cars on the roads, of which there were many, you were never too far away from a horse-drawn tonga in Hyderabad. Almost immediately one appeared and after haggling a price, the boys lifted the scooter on to the back. With a click of the tongawala's tongue, the long-suffering mare jerked into a steady amble.

Kabir turned to Mustafa.

'Did you hear of a march or parade being organized through college? Seth came to Barman's house after cricket practice and was saying something about a demonstration.'

'Why did you go to his house by the way?'

'Oh I'm helping him with some of the election stuff and I wanted to watch the match but –'

'Suck up. You know that's not going to get you selected, right?'

'No, but seriously, he was saying something about those guys who roam around in that green uniform, you know, with shorts and a sling.'

Mustafa thought about it for a minute. 'Those guys are a little weird. I have read some of their flyers but they don't make a lot of sense. They come near our bazaars shouting slogans and pissing people off. Have you asked Sareen about it?'

'Sareen? Why should I ask him?'

In matters of Sareen, Kabir felt like he should be the first to know things. He was his oldest friend and was affronted that someone else – even Mustafa – should know anything that he did not. Mustafa was sensitive to this protectiveness and ventured gingerly.

'He has been hanging with people who may be the uniform types. Mianji told me he saw him with them.'

'Mianji? Really? I just met him this morning, he didn't say anything to me.' This was a double betrayal. First Sareen, then Mianji. Why didn't they confide in him first?

'Maybe he did, and you forgot because you were busy sucking up to the coach.'

Kabir punched him in the arm. He knew there was an element of truth in that somewhere, his father often chided him for being distracted and not hearing what was being said. Anyway, he started thinking about a pull shot Sachin had played before lunch and began imitating the swivel.

∼

Mustafa and Kabir sat with Salim bhai, Mustafa's father, in his pristine white office. Dressed as he usually was in his crisp white pathan suit, he camouflaged into his domain. The emptiness of the showroom created an echo – every footstep and dropped pen clattering through the glass and shiny tiles. This surgical whiteness was part of the prefab kit he had received from Hyundai to sell their little bee-shaped cars.

Salim bhai had inherited a modest workshop. Through grit and hard work, he rode the wave of Indian liberalization. One of the first

Hyundai dealers in the city, his business was doing well. The car was the right size and price for the narrow gullies of Hyderabad. Behind the glinting edifice, hidden from the passing eye, was the original workshop. This was the opposite of the front, with no hint of white anywhere. Rather the black, brown and green of a gritty mechanical outfit. Some years ago, a manual had come with clean diagrams of mechanical hoists, uncluttered arm-length storage spaces and safety maps on the walls. But there was never any pretense of it being followed. Here things were much like during his father's day. The place looked like an impressionist version of a greasy landscape. Yet it felt like things got done here. The mechanics wore expressions of slow yet assured competence from years of hands-on tinkering.

Salim called in one of his lead mechanics to banish the 'disgraceful' scooter to a lowly mechanic shop down the road that 'did this type of work'. With customary good manners the boys now sat in front of Salim, who made enquiries after Kabir's family – each member, one at a time, and interjected with a memory of each of them. Under normal circumstances this would have all been fine, but the match had started and the boys were itching to get going. Finally, Mustafa couldn't sit still any longer. He blurted out that they would be next door at a restaurant watching the match and ran out with Kabir hot on his heels.

Salim smiled wistfully as the boys bolted and decided to join them. He let himself out of the back door so that his staff wouldn't notice.

CHAPTER FIVE

It was lunchtime at Sahiba Baig's ancestral home in the old city. Priya, her new friend from college, came over to spend the afternoon studying. Three generations of Baigs met in their small, open-to-the-sky courtyard. A plinth in the middle held a healthy looking tulsi bush, which centered the space. Rooms of the house were set back a couple of feet so that the doors opened into shade. The women had pulled out their pastel cotton kurtas heralding the passing of winters' chill, but the marble-floored courtyard was well shaded and so most had a light shawl draped over their shoulders. In this part of the city, old homes were giving way to large chunky plazas which used every inch of available space. Dismantling these houses had become one of the most lucrative businesses in the city, but thankfully their home had managed to resist this onslaught. Their joint household included Sahiba's parents Masood and Zia, her little sister Ruksana, her brother Arif, her grandmother Bade Ammi and their aunt Fatima. Bade Ammi sat on the armchair in the center and the ladies settled on cots and bolsters around her. The cast today included just the girls and Alya, Zia's sister, who often dropped in for lunch. They relished her company as she brought humour and scandals of the goings-on in the city.

Preparing lunch was taken in turns. Today, Fatima had made biryani with roasted aubergine and raita. This was regular fare and little thought was given to the time-consuming, intricate nature of its preparation. Each home had its own recipe. Fatima added large quantities of mint and coriander to the usual marinade of cardamom, cinnamon, cloves, black pepper, turmeric and other spices. It required her to marinate the chicken overnight; the brightness of the leaves took time to infuse into the meat. She would cook the rice in the morning and add the chicken to it with additional aromatics in an earthen bowl. As was the local tradition, it would include saffron infused milk, ghee, onions and lime-juice, all sealed in with chapatti dough, which would cook for another hour and a half. The aubergine was spiced and cooked over a naked fire to leave the skin crispy and charred. All these flavours and spices were tempered on the palate with a cool mint raita. Just before serving, a tiffin was dispatched to the office down the road for Masood while the women ate at home.

The Baigs were ancestral traders in cottons and silks. Earlier generations had been purveyors of hand woven muslin and raw silk sourced from individual weaver communities. Recent ancestors were savvy in predicting the change in the market and created a *karkhana* (factory) of power loom machines. These now produced cloth with speed and at a lower cost, which lacked the finesse and beauty of the hand woven yardage. However, this new cloth was suitable for stitching into more modern, westernized clothing, the demand for which had exploded across the country in recent times. Being aesthetes of textiles, the Baigs had maintained some links with weavers and traded their wares, but that business was diminishing.

Masood Baig, Sahiba's father, ran the business. He had acquired an economics degree away from home at Delhi University, which exposed him to a more cosmopolitan belief system. He was proud that his wife, Zia, spent part of her time at the office to help coordinate with buyers. The family was seen as progressive and was rightfully proud of their entrepreneurial nature.

Masood encouraged his family to speak English at home and avoided the traditional kameez for a shirt. He believed in dressing like a businessman and not like a trader. Much to his mother's lament, he eschewed the more devout Muslim practices and was partial to the evening scotch and soda.

Lunch had been consumed and the clearing up of plates and utensils was underway. Alya passed around a small, carved wooden box with a burnished copper lid containing betel nut and fennel seeds, the traditional post-meal mouth freshener. Settling herself contentedly against an ample bolster, she picked up the tabloid supplement of the *Times of India*. The front page had a large picture of the three Miss Indias, one each to represent India for Miss Universe, Miss World and Miss Asia Pacific later that year.

'I don't think we are going to win anything this year. These girls are not of the same league of Sushmita, Aishwarya. I mean they are nice, I guess.'

Zia looked over her shoulder, 'But what a beautiful lehenga she has on. Must be Ritu Kumar's.'

'*Haye ya*, they look so good in a classical outfit, don't they? You know those girls win because they look Indian and cultured. I don't know what upside-down outfits the girls in the other countries wear, honestly. Boobs hanging out and everything. You know, Sushmita looked so lovely, people loved her. Aishwarya also – same'.

'She wasn't so modest in the swimsuit round, mami,' Sahiba chirped in. The younger girls giggled.

'Chup oye, child. Sometimes you have to do these things, na? But even then, our girls look like someone you want to bring home. Some of these girls in these American shows nowadays…,' Alya widened her eyes and raised her eyebrows.

She opened the paper to the lavish spread of images from the beauty pageants over the years. Sahiba and Priya peeked over. They perched themselves around her bolster, pushing and squeezing. Now the evaluation began in earnest as the pictures were carefully considered and debated.

Young Khaled, Sahiba's brother, had the misfortune of barging into the gathering at that moment. The jovial tittering fell into a stone-cold silence as they looked at this male intrusion contemptuously. He mumbled a greeting, went to his room to grab what he came for and excused himself. His only succour was a smile from his doting grandmother as he stumbled out. The ladies laughed lustily at their mischief and got back to their conversation.

Zia teased, 'Arrey Alya, on one hand you are proud of these beauty pageants but on the other hand you wouldn't let anyone dress like that in your home?'

Oblivious to contradictions, Alya forged ahead 'Didi, these shows have really muddled our girls! Every day you hear about girls having affairs and divorces. Do you remember any of this happening when we were kids? Incidentally, did you hear about the Kapoors? Their daught...'

Zia cut her off with a sharp look. There were children present.

Sahiba and her sister absorbed it all like hungry sponges. Priya smiled to herself. She had witnessed many versions of this conversation at her own home. In fact, it was being played out in households across the city – 'back in our day "vs" girls these days'. They, the new half-half generation, had spent their adolescence in an older, isolated India, their belief system was born in a more orthodox age. Yet their youth was being lived in a rapidly changing time of global influence and social libertarianism. So, it came to be that half the time they suckled on the opiate of slick international TV of sex, violence and individualism and the other half preferring the desi dramas about family, piety and god.

Bade Ammi had been left out of the conversation longer than she was comfortable. As the long-suffering matriarch, it was her prerogative to hold forth.

'I agree. There is too much aping of the west. I am all for change, but we should remember our own ways. When your grandfather died, things were very difficult...'

Bade Ammi could connect almost any subject to their family history. Interrupting a story about your elders was disrespectful and so, once again, their grandmother was center stage. Not that the girls minded. After all this was their own family's fairy tale, they loved hearing it.

Bade Ammi began retelling the story of when her husband died. Masood had just graduated from college. It was a difficult time, but she managed to hold the family together due to the good nature of the people of the city who helped her.

Ammi's stories were her way of ensuring the family's story, and her own significance in it was drilled into the generations. The girls were fascinated with tales of the city's golden days, 'replete with wealth and grace.' Their grandfather was cast as a handsome 'prince amongst men'.

Zia would listen quietly. She knew of the liberties taken in the re-telling. The truth was a little more pungent. Their grandfather had died from liver disease, a result of a poor diet, his lack of exercise and a socially accepted alcoholism.

As mothers-in-law go, she had always made Zia feel significant and welcome. Zia recalled some difficulties as a new bride but she was thankful for the relationship she now shared with Ammi.

For Ammi it was her own daughter Fatima who was the cause of her concern. Ammi was widowed when the girl was too young to think about marriage. It was the father's responsibility to find suitable matches and Ammi had tried to get Masood to take on this role, but the boy was useless in these matters.

Fatima's great love was the big screen. Despite the flood of new-age content now being piped directly into homes, Bollywood retained its melodramatic penchant and the masses flocked to the syrupy virtue of the three-hour epic romance. Plot lines were a pastiche of Indian virtue winning over the immorality of western ways. Even though Fatima was far too sensible to believe in this over-simplified parody, it gave her an undeniable thrill to watch the 'sentimental homegrown' triumph over the 'evil outsider' love story. Her latest obsession was *Kuch Kuch Hota Hai* (KKHH), a film that had hypnotized Indian film audiences. She had watched it five times already, but these frequent repeats held a secret. Her trips to Regal Cinema were not solitary; a shy skinny courtier had been humming the songs along with her.

Anil Sadhav was far from his home in Central Madhya Pradesh. He followed the righteous path of the 'new India' allegorical journey from birth to exam topper to engineer to IT employee. Fatima met him the first time she watched KKHH – he was part of a larger group of friends. The first thing she noticed was the mop of hair sweeping across his head. He had a kind face with a moustache intended to make himself look older. During the interval they struck up a conversation and she found his quietness assured and calming. Over the last few months, they had been meeting with greater frequency and he had shaved.

Sahiba and Priya excused themselves to study, with little Ruksana in tow, who was enthralled with everything to do with her elder sister. Once in the room, they latched the door and Priya pulled out a little pouch of cosmetics. The girls started trying them on each other and began chatting about *Titanic*, which both of them had recently watched.

'ANY DAY – I would run away from my husband for Leonardo, and I would jump in the ocean,' Priya exclaimed.

Giggling, the girls went on to compare the boys in college and neither of them seemed to have a particularly high opinion of them.

'They all seem like such children, hai na? I wonder at what stage do these boys actually change. At the moment all they are interested in is cricket and Britney Spears. I speak to some of the boys in class and they have nothing to say.'

It hadn't been very long since Sahiba had started talking about boys. She took her cues from what she saw on TV on how to lilt her tone and what to opine on. While undoing her long braid in front of the mirror and fluffing her hair, she arched her eyebrow at Priya's reflection. 'You know who's not a child? Professor Barman!'

They burst into peals of laughter, 'I can definitely see you having little Mr Choksis with him.'

'Shut up Priya – Ruksana is here! She may take you seriously.'

Ruksana was sitting wide-eyed, just happy to be allowed to observe.

'Don't worry, Ruksi. We won't let Mr Choksi seduce our Sahiba. In any case I saw him first... If he even looked my way I would whisk him away for a date.'

'Where would you take him?'

Priya came unstuck with this question. The girls were beginning to discover rules of this newfound maturity. Priya, now with a coating of make up on her face, dropped the pantomime and uncertainly ventured, 'Actually I don't know what you do on a date'.

More peals of laughter and the girls went into a huddle about other critical questions in their new lives. They took turns guessing at what the other girls in their college talk about, what boys look for and other matters of feminine import. They left the more carnal questions for another day given little Ruksi's presence, but there wasn't going to be much studying happening today.

CHAPTER SIX

The day's light was extinguished but for the halo on the tops of trees. What an incredible few days they had been and till this moment Kabir had rarely considered the divine. He could picture Hindu gods standing on clouds, beatific smiles on their faces, radiance around their crowned heads, their many arms akimbo, looking down on him with light shooting out of their palms and the rays touching the top of his head. It reminded him of Sunday mornings as a child when people would be transfixed to the broadcast of the *Ramayan*. An entire country would come to a standstill during that hour of state-sponsored mythology. As he lay back on the grass chuckling, he noted that he was quite stoned.

Just a few days ago, he was sitting glued to the TV with Mustafa, watching Sachin play the finest innings of his life. All doubts and insecurities associated with the Indian team were extinguished as they roared like lions. Much like the mythological conquest of Lanka by Rama's pious army, the Indian team, led by local hero Azhar, defeated the loud-mouthed, aggressive Australians.

Simultaneously, he was beginning to perform well at econometrics which was, till that point, the bane of his academic existence. Spending a little time at the library, being tutored by his friend Aarti had transformed a beguiling subject into a series of patterns. Kabir's mind worked well with visualizations – his comprehension was transformed as Aarti helped him rethink the equations into graphs and rates of change.

The college team won over the weekend and Kabir scored a respectable 34. After the game, the Hyderabad Cricket Association had called a few players including him to a selection camp. He tried to be nonchalant and keep it to himself, but his feigned indifference lasted only as long it took him to bump into the first person he knew.

The KMS posse set out planning travel to and from trials, they were going to be there naturally. Aarti was also very excited, which was nice, but he wasn't sure she even knew the rules.

Most importantly, there was peace at home – his father had uncharacteristically calmed down and made no mention of Kabir's future, his prospects, his attitude. Perhaps it had something to do with the HCA selections or the econometrics results, but whatever it was, Kabir was thankful. Nowadays their time was spent talking about cricket and what was happening at college.

But these were not the reasons for Kabir's spiritual awakening. Divine intervention struck him merely an hour ago. The boys were on the edge of campus at the far end of the main field. Here, the grounds gave way to a grove of tall trees, far enough from the regular paths for the group to look like they were up to no good. In the diminishing early-evening orange glow, the wail of peacocks heralded the end of the day. On Fridays, college kids would gather here and plan the weekend.

Sareen had emptied out a cigarette and was now filling it with bits of weed mixed with tobacco. They sat with their backs to the path so that no one would see them smoke. Sareen lit the joint and just as he passed it, someone called out Mustafa's name. Mustafa slapped Sareen's his hand away.

This is when it happened. Kabir spun around and saw Sahiba for the first time. Sahiba and Priya walked over to them, they seemed to know Mustafa quite well; he had lived a few homes down from the Baigs for years.

As Kabir stared, he felt a yearning, which he was wholly unfamiliar with. Her beauty had jammed his circuit board. Mustafa introduced the girls and they made small talk.

'What course do you study?'

'Do you live far?'

'So you guys play cricket?'

'How long have you all known each other?'

Simple, light inanities became arduous trials. Fear interfered with his neural pathways and he developed a stutter in his speech. Sareen had been affected by a similar predicament and responded to everything they said with a high-pitched giggle. Kabir felt uncomfortable and incredibly uncool, as he stood rooted to the spot. He prayed for this torture to end soon. Thankfully Mustafa did most of the talking and the girls needed to be somewhere and started heading off.

Kabir blurted out, 'Hope to see you soon sometime.'

Sahiba turned to look at him for the first time in earnest and smiled, 'Yeah, see you around!'

As if zapped with a ray gun, his hair stood on end. It was thrilling and unlike any euphoria Kabir had ever felt. Mustafa laughed at the two of them who set upon him with a barrage of questions.

Who was she? How long had he known her? Did she have a boyfriend? And most importantly, why hadn't he introduced her to the group before? Mustafa refused to answer most of these questions, enjoying this sweet torment. Finally, they got around to smoking the joint.

'Kabir you seem smitten boy. What happened to you? "my na..., who, how...,"' Mustafa imitated a clownish stutter. 'I have never seen you like that before. I hope you get better than that, or you will remain a virgin forever.'

Sareen jumped up in proclamation, 'Screw his smitten, I'm completely in love. She will be mine. I am sure of it. It's written in the stars and when you know you know, you know?'

You couldn't help but laugh at Sareen's tomfoolery, its hilarity amplified by the delicious effect the joint was having.

'Sareen, I challenge you to even remember their names.'

'Names are unimportant, when Kama the god of love has spoken and be in no doubt that yes, he has spoken. He has laid out my future and my future is with... honestly, either of the two. Whichever will have me – she is destined for me.'

Turning now to Kabir, Mustafa asked conspiratorially, 'There is little doubt who Mr Kabir has an eye on, eh? But what will happen to poor Aarti's little heart if she finds out her Prince Charming is charmed by someone else?'

Kabir snapped out of his meanderings. 'What are you talking about? That's rubbish, she's just a friend who helps me out with lectures and stuff. She's cool yaar, but it's not like that.'

The expression on the other two faces were clear enough but they seemed to think it wise to drop it. For the moment.

Kabir pushed Mustafa into telling him more about Sahiba.

'What do you want to know?'

'Well, what is she like?'

Seeing his cue, Sareen stepped in to perform. 'Mian Mustafa, what our young sir,' pointing at Kabir, 'and I,' pointing at himself, 'wish to know must be explained in a way our young sir,' pointing at Kabir, 'and myself,' pointing at himself, 'would understand'.

'Would you classify our young begum and her friend as Imran Khan type girls or Kapil Dev types?'

Imran the swashbuckling, handsome, fast-bowler, whisk-you-away-on-his-wild-stallion pathan was the first, and perhaps only, cricketer sex symbol. Girls would fawn over his bulging biceps, his long locks and his international playboy image.

Kapil Dev, on the other hand, looked like the salt of the earth in human form. A makki-di-roti-sarson-da-saag type, with long limbs and dynamic talent, his raison d'etre was to lead misfits who did not think they could win, to victory. Sareen assumed a defiant herculean pose with fists clenched and biceps curled, gazing out into the distance.

Kabir liked this analogy. There were merits to both sides. With Kapil you were likely to find good-natured humour and a rooted strength. With Imran you were looking at adventure and charisma. Where one was likely to gain weight, the other would probably spend all your money. They came to the consensus that a blend of the two would be the safest option, but if they had to choose, they would date one and marry the other.

Kabir plucked one of the tall grasses to chew on as he lay back on the field to watch the last light of day, which is where we found him initially, contemplating the divine.

THE ENGLISHNESS OF IT ALL
Lords 1990, England vs India first test

The young are often predisposed to attach ascriptions of themselves into literature and figures of history, even though they belong not at all to their world. It enhances identity or personality. These days, Kabir belongs to the colours of the Rastafarian flag, the music of Bob Marley and ja peace, love and unity. If someone makes reference to it, he feels a pang of protectiveness, a bigotry to this idea of self he has co-opted.

When he was ten, it was the writings of P.G. Wodehouse and that simpering Bertie with the unflappable Jeeves. For an early teen, these cultural fancies are caught less by conscious choice than by assimilation. Kabir was destined to model these preferences because it was passed on unknowingly through his genes, through the affectations of his ancestors. He grew up with fragments of English culture littered around the house, the

41

books, the TV comedies, the theatre and of course the deference to Lords – the home of cricket.

When India toured England in 1990, the coverage was not televized in India. You would wait for the scores in the Times of India *sports pages*. A few months later, his father picked up a VHS highlights tape on a business trip to London. Kabir watched that video on a loop.

The damp bright turf of the English ground was of a world far away yet one that resided in the shelves at home. Grounds were foreign yet so familiar; they looked so clean, so manicured. It was a BBC production replete with the gentle melody of polite English commentary, measured applause, members sitting on benches in yellow and red striped ties and the pomp of the stately pavilion building in the background.

Graham Gooch made mincemeat of the Indian bowling in that match, scoring 333 runs in the first innings. The Indian team looked like a band of boys, plucked from far-flung districts, without a fashionable haircut between them. They seemed smaller and intimidated by their burly opposition. This was the home of cricket and we were playing our erstwhile rulers. There were glimpses of genius from the talented Indian ranks, Kapil Dev's audacious four 6s in a row to avoid the follow on and the collective first innings batting heroics, but in the end India lost tamely. They were given consolation applause for having 'tried hard,' 'good effort,' 'well played' but it never looked like this talented team could galvanize into a real threat against the mighty English.

CHAPTER SEVEN

The evening routine began once Prem Menon poured a drink. Children would be underfoot until calmed and then the family would listen to the news together. Prem believed in educating his children beyond the narrow confines of academia. So on most days, he would encourage a lively 'debate' on current affairs, literature, music or even the strange drawing little Sakshi had made (of an animal she insisted was a camel). These debates were short, lasting a few minutes; an attempt by an earnest father to inculcate reasoning and introspection. If there was any cricket on, the highlights were mandatory and on weekends they would watch a movie.

Of late, this tempo had changed. As the children grew older, they had people other than their parents to spend evenings with, so debate time became a rarity. Prem grumbled at this evaporating ritual and tried making the fewer debates more meaningful by infusing greater gravitas to the subject. Unfortunately, this had the opposite effect from what Prem intended and the kids preferred avoiding them altogether.

Prem spent his formative years in post-colonial Calcutta where the brown folk replaced the English in their clubs and habits. Even though the Menon surname suggested intellectuals and links with the Kerala coast, Prem only knew of a couple of distant cousins in Madras, where he was born. Their family weren't related to any of the famous Menons. Prem figured their clan had disbursed to be high-browed in other parts of the country. His own social circle included amateur dramatics, Hindustani classical music enthusiasts and an urbane, genteel crowd. He met his wife Radha, in a production of *Taming of the Shrew*. She remembered being charmed by a slim, distinguished-looking man with intelligent eyes and a classic, if not fashionable, style. They courted, fell in love and had both their children in those simpler times. His contemporaries joined large English companies and settled into a life of lunchtime meetings over gin and tonics. Following their path, he abandoned his ambitions in academia and its poor monetary prospects. His mercantile life began in a 'managing agency'. As the name suggested, these companies managed the Indian interests of English multinationals left behind after independence. As a junior manager at Smith and Macaulay, Prem cut his teeth in their engineering and commodity trading subsidiaries, which were born in the river docks of Calcutta.

Due to a combination of mismanagement and the hostile policy environment in India, the administration of his venerated company slowly drove the enterprise into the ground. Other changes were afoot in the city – roast lamb lunches and cabaret were giving way to political rallies and populist governments. Prem ventured into a partnership with one of its suppliers. The next few years were spent in a brutal initiation of the License Raj. He built a reasonably successful business but the rise of the red communist wave in Bengal took on a militant complexion, and one fine day the union shut down their new plant.

Sickened with the hopelessness in Calcutta, Prem decided to leave this city of his youth, the city he loved. The enormous pressures of starting from scratch and maintaining his family hardened his easy-going attitude. On the advice of a friend he moved to Hyderabad and, over the years, built his own trading business. He now made a healthy living, albeit removed from the lofty ambitions he had harbored as a young academic.

The age-old story of fathers and sons was playing out in the Menon household.

Book recommendations for Kabir had changed from 150-page Wodehouse romps to 700-page historical drudgery. This was in line with other changes to do with Kabir. As he had grown older, Prem's need to impart lessons and mould his son's future had acquired a more urgent tone. The catalyst to this change in tone was undoubtedly the fact that Kabir had become an older teenager with no apparent interest in anything, except cricket. When he was at home, he resembled a pre-evolutionary slug draped on furniture but most of the time he was out doing god-knows-what.

Kabir was in awe of his father. His sense of upright decency was ingrained from an early age. He agreed almost entirely with most of what his father said, but when it came to his own development, he wished he could get a little more space. Kabir was nervous every time his father was around, fearing a rebuke was on its way. So he started to hide things in order for them not to become problematic to explain. It wasn't like this before, at one time he would share the goings-on of his friends, his schoolwork – but now he feared Papa would find a flaw in everything.

Prem wished the boy would speak to him more often about what was going on so that he could comprehend it, maybe even be a part of it. Although a man of wisdom, Prem did not have the same tether on his own prejudices that he sought in others. He knew his manner was too hard at times and caught himself becoming more stubborn and taciturn as he grew older. This added tinder to the predictable tension between them.

Today was a relief from these tensions as the family sat huddled around a phone wishing Kabir's grandfather in Calcutta on his eighty-fifth birthday. Kabir wanted to be the last in turn for he had a lot to talk to Dadu about. Once everyone had their say, the family peeled off and Kabir started speaking conspiratorially into the receiver. Sakshi grabbed the phone one last time to say bye, only to be shooed away.

Raj Menon was an easy-going, jovial man who loved to tease his grandchildren. As a young man, he cut a dashing figure as an accomplished sportsman – he played cricket for the top clubs alongside the white men. Not one to suffer fools easily, he carried a brawler's reputation in his youth. Despite this, he had many friends and had become an establishment in Calcutta circles. Between the wars he spent a few years in the British India Air Force after which he ran a business in motor parts. The allied effort to hold off the Japanese created opportunities in North East India and Burma. After the war, their abandoned machinery became valuable. His adventurous spirit got the senior Mr Menon involved in those regions where he found the stuff was available to knock down and trade.

'Hi Dadu.'

'Hi son, how are you? Have you cut that mop on the top of your head?'

'I kind of had a trim, but I like it, Dadu.'

'Well, I guess it's okay looking like a walking broom at your age. As long as you're not trying to impress girls – you should be fine.'

Kabir pondered this for a moment. After all, this man was rarely seen with a hair out of place and happened to be the only person Kabir had seen wearing a silk cravat.

'My hairstyle is cool Dadu, the girls like it. It's what's new these days.'

Dadu chuckled, 'It's nice to have hair, I guess. Now tell me what's happening in life? Are you scoring runs?'

'I got some runs this weekend, missed getting a 50 though. Stuff at college is fine… oh by the way, Professor Choksi offered to lend me his scooter if I got it fixed. So I took it to Salim uncle, you know, Mustafa's father. He's going to fix it up for me and then we are living the dream.'

'Oh good stuff, lad. Best way to break your nut before you get out of college, not that you were using it anyway, right?'

'That thing doesn't go fast enough for me to break my head even if I jumped off it at full speed.'

'Speaking of using your head. Have you started looking at what you are going to get into next year? I know your father is giving you a tough time but he's right, you know.'

'I know, I know he's right. I have to start thinking about it. I don't want to go the IAS route, that's for sure. Nobody in my batch is even considering joining the administration. I don't think law is for me either, I need a little more time to think of what I want to do. Sometimes I envy Mustafa. He has known what he wanted to do from the time he was ten.'

'I think your father has been at the sharp end of lawyers for so many years that he wants you to be able to wield that end. He's just worried about you. Listen, you have always been a smart kid and I know you will be fine. Just don't be a fool, okay? Don't get caught with your pants down. Start somewhere and after a couple of years you can think of what you want to do next. I was thinking the other day, you know your cousin is in Bombay? Why don't you move over there and get a job? It will do you good and you can see a new city, meet new people.'

'Leave Hyderabad? No way, Dadu. My friends are here, there is enough new stuff going on for me to figure something out. I don't think I will ever live anywhere else. Anyway, Bombay is too crowded and smelly, okay for a visit but please...'

They talked a little more about Dadu's F2 camera. There was always a little lesson in these phone calls and Dadu promised him a new lens on his next birthday. Speaking to his grandfather was reassuring. After hanging up he bounded into the living room just in time for the highlights. On cue, Radha Menon rose gracefully from her armchair and left the room. She didn't care to get caught in the crossfire of her husband and son shouting at a TV.

It was the first day of the second test match played in Calcutta. After their defeat in the first test match in Madras, there was always the great danger of the Australians bouncing back.

Kabir had heard the score earlier and for the second time this week, he could scarcely believe what was happening. To better understand the emotions running rampant, we need only to refer to the performance of the Indian team over the last decade. There were fleeting moments of genius, but they would inevitably manage to screw it up eventually. Today, the team seemed to buck this trend. Australia batted first and the Indian bowling attack, scratchy at best, had somehow gotten them out cheaply.

They set themselves up in the TV room, muted the volume and waited for the highlights. Suddenly the cable signal went out, eliciting howls of protest from the boys. Radha, now in the next room, rolled her eyes. Sakshi joined in the fun and started stomping her feet. The men busied themselves in trying to resolve this issue by slapping the TV and wiggling the wire. But these technical, usually reliable solutions, failed them this time around. Kabir deduced that the signal must be out from the cablewala's end. So he grabbed his camera and set off to the shop.

~

Night time, devoid of noise and people, was the best time to walk the city. The streets of this residential colony were partially lit by the odd streetlamp, leaving unclaimed dark spots, casting a mysterious, moody setting. Tall tropical trees, which went unnoticed in the day, became principal characters as they swayed and sighed in the night breeze. Cats played out the dramas of their lives, calling out in greeting and protecting their turf. Whispers of people conducting the rituals of returning home at the end of a full day crept out as you walked past gates and doorways.

Alone with his thoughts, Kabir pondered his next move. There was always an outside chance he would be selected for the HCA team. If that happened then the path was determined – he would play cricket and try to make it to the first XI and then beyond. This was the most glorious option, but it came with a nagging doubt about whether he even wanted this as his future. Shaking it off, he started thinking about the various pieces of advice he had received. He never considered not being able to find something he was interested in. On the contrary, he had a wide range of interests. His affliction was that while he was confident in his abilities, he was simultaneously uncertain whether he could make it on his own. Often, he found himself being led by whomever was advising him at that moment – if his father's banker friend was advising him, he was inclined to agree that finance is what he should do. Or if there was a businessman in the room it would be pharmaceuticals (which he was sure he couldn't spell) or software and the internet, both equally nebulous, mysterious concepts. It was probably the result of a father whose encouragement and censure were uneasy bedfellows.

Kabir became anxious when thoughts delved into these uncertainties. At times like this his mind would move towards that which gave him solace – to adventures with the KMS posse, chats about cricket with Barman and his father's steady hand. Today however, he had a more potent panacea as he thought about his chance encounter with Sahiba. Even though he had barely spoken a word to her, Kabir thought of her constantly. Over the last few days, his mind concocted multiple scenarios, each ending with her falling madly for him. Obviously, he couldn't breathe a word of this to anyone, least of all to his friends. There was the other possibility that she didn't know he existed. Something needed to be done. He needed to find out more about her, maybe even get someone to put in a good word.

As he walked closer to the market, the honking and sporadic flashes of headlights heralded a change in pace. SS Cable was a small 200-square-foot store with a large signboard tucked away in an alley lying parallel to the main market. A narrow gulley rendered the signboard superfluous, easy to miss it if you didn't know where it was. There was little to suggest the nature of business. Inside were a couple of non-descript tables facing the alley. Kabir walked straight through to the back of the shop and slid open a small door into a cabin. The inside was chilled with air conditioning and here sat Sukhbir Singh, flanked by a wall of screens and switchboards. He was a round Sikh man with a bushy beard and a yellow turban. Under the glass-topped table in front of him were a mass of visiting cards and atop the glass were four telephones. He looked flustered and seemed to be speaking on all of them at once. Even before Kabir got his first word out, Sukhbir started berating him.

'Your cable has gone out? Why did you come here, Kabir? You should have called instead. What am I going to do with you standing here on my head? I wish that by staring at your face the wires would miraculously reconnect but till date I have never seen that happen.'

To the uninitiated, Sukhbir seemed rude but Kabir took no offence. This was Sukhbir at his gentlest. Any cable operator who needed to deal with daily complaints of poor reception, additional channel requests, piracy, and so on, was bound to be in a constant state of agitation.

'Sukhbir, it's impossible to get through to your number,' he said pointing to the phones which were all off the hook. 'It's happened twice this week. The match is on! Please can we get it fixed quickly?'

'Yaar, you and your bloody match. It's that damn peepul tree on your street. The branches keep falling off and snapping the cable. Vinod is up on the terrace fixing some of the connections; go speak to him. If he's free he can go with you now.'

Kabir bounded up to the terrace to find skinny Vinod draped on a metal chair, smoking languidly and chatting on his mobile. Waiting for him to complete his phone call, Kabir lifted his camera and clicked a few pictures, hoping the light wasn't too poor. The view was straight out of a sci-fi book imagined many decades ago. Surrounded by a multitude of large satellite dishes, the vista overlooked a sea of terraces of similar three-storey structures. Ever so often there would be another rooftop with similar white disks and on others there were antennae. Spires of mosques and heritage palaces punctuated the scene; some were lit up entirely while others had a simple beacon at the top.

This roof was the nerve cell of the SS cable operation. White disks captured signals beamed down by satellites, which were decoded in the office below and distributed to households within a few kilometers of the store. Like SS Cable, the area had three other operators, each with their own territory. Some element of competition existed, but by and large they kept to their own streets and zones. What amazed Kabir was the sheer jumble of wires thick and thin, entwined like angry snakes. Hitched up to makeshift hooks, these streamed out from the terrace to TVs all over the neighbourhood. Even more remarkable was how Vinod was able to tell exactly which one needed to go where, given that none of them had any discernable markings.

Dealing with Vinod was an art form. The humble technician was low on the pecking order but wielded the power of getting you your fix of cable TV. A complex character, Vinod often bemoaned his job and his position in the cable TV hierarchy, but he took great glee in the sway he held. Kabir went over to him with a packet of cigarettes he had bought for this very purpose and cajoled him into looking at the problem.

Wheels aptly greased, Vinod got to work almost immediately, that is to say after talking about his life for ten minutes. They walked over to the suspected peepul tree and found the wires, which disappeared into its thick branches and emerged taut and unscathed on the other side. Grumbling to himself, Vinod figured the problem was in the office switchboard. This meant having to encounter Sukhbir Singh, something he did not relish doing.

Walking back to the shop, Kabir noticed a news van parked in the middle of the bazaar, which he made a mental note to investigate. Vinod's demeanor changed dramatically as he entered the shop. Supplicant shoulders and an appeasing smile replaced the unbuttoned shirt and the matchstick-in-snarling-mouth swagger. Satisfied that the work would get done, Kabir loped out to investigate what was happening in the market.

~

The van on the street was emblazoned with an Indiworld TV logo, the largest English news channel in India. Outsized graphics of sparks flying and globes spinning covered the entire vehicle. Kabir was staring at the large dish welded to the top of the roof when he was shoved by a couple of burly camera-wielding guys who had jumped out of the back. Intrigued with the goings-on, he followed the 'camera people,' they had now been joined by a few others including an attractive woman holding a mic. Marching into the newly opened Café Coffee Day, they had set up a gaggle of lights all pointing to three frightened-looking students, squeezed onto a small bench. The presenter quickly checked her make up in a hand-held mirror, perched herself next to the nervous trio and barked instructions at no-one in particular while tapping her ear.

'Sound... sound, no sound... can't hear anything. Come on, guys. This is not so difficult. Prakash, are you there? Is the script okay now? Yes? Okay fine. I'm ready.'

Abruptly one man shouted 'Rolling!' and her demeanor changed into a bubbly news anchor. Kabir leaned in a little too close to all the action and he was promptly shooed out of the café – 'crew only'. Walking away, he noticed a couple of men behind the van and trotted up behind one of them.

'Sir. Hi. Sir, yes hi.'

It took a moment for the paunchy guy in a black t-shirt to acknowledge the small voice behind him.

'What is going on here? What are you guys shooting?'

The man appraised him above rimless glasses far too fragile for his fleshy face. Prakash Gawde was an old production hand who had cut his teeth on state-run TV and Indian cinema. Since the advent of newly launched 24-hour news channels, his talents were highly in demand. Gawde had made it up the ranks from a spot boy to a line producer, having worked on all the bits and pieces along the way. Not one of those romantics who began his journey inspired by Satyajit Ray and Kurosawa, he had spent his life shooting gaudily colored ensemble dance sequences with high-pitched music blaring into the set. The type of job didn't matter to him; authority and money were his deciding factors.

The first thing Gawde noticed about Kabir was the F2 hanging around his neck. It was a version of the first camera he had used when he was learning the ropes years ago. Calling him over, he took the camera from Kabir to remind himself of its weight and the mechanical clack and slick on pressing the trigger. Gawde was in a good mood today, willing to indulge Kabir's curiosity.

The crew had travelled to Hyderabad to shoot a multitude of stories – operating on shoestring budgets meant that they needed to get as much content as possible. Today they had pinned some acne faced engineering students who were in high demand as 'techno-coolies' in resolving the Y2K problem. Students graduating from computer studies were being snapped up to be thrown en masse to rewrite millions of lines of code so the dastardly two-digit 'year' didn't cause the world economy to implode and planes to fall out of the sky. Recruiters flocked to Hyderabad, thanks to the thousands of students graduating from the hundreds of new schools set up there. Many of these kids came from modest backgrounds and were earning starting salaries their parents would never dream of earning in their lifetimes.

Yet the treatment of the story was superficial and light on the touch. Gawde had a pulse on what the audience wanted. Less about the gravity of the issue, more about the personal. A voyeurism into other lives.

'What will be the first thing you will buy with your new salary?'

There was a lot of content to make before they returned to Mumbai and given the breakneck speed of these trips, the crew had hardly done any preparatory work. Gawde leaned into Kabir for some local ideas. After considering the question briefly, Kabir had a light bulb moment.

'It's Eid soon and the best thing about Eid is the food. I know all the best places… the local stuff. I can show you around.' Gawde mulled over the idea. It sounded like a 5-minute segment, on repeat, for a week. They would like that back in Mumbai.

'Sounds good, kid. What about college? Any rumours there? Any faculty got any student pregnant?'

Kabir was fascinated. Did this stuff really happen? Was this the stuff these guys hunted down? He wondered what other events of national importance and global scandal were on their beat.

Pulling out the most blasé look in his repertoire, Kabir replied confidently, 'No, not this year, you missed it. It happened and they got married. Now it's happily ever after.'

Gawde smiled. The kid was quick witted. Handing him a mobile number, he told Kabir to call him the next day. Kabir was chuffed at having managed to get himself attached to this crew. He could brag about it. It was so exciting that he didn't think of Sahiba once on his walk home.

CHAPTER EIGHT

Lectures were winding up and students sedately moved away from the central building. Kabir and Sareen were standing on the first-floor corridor, leaning against the banister. Gazing into the courtyard below, this spot allowed them to watch people go by.

Scattered around the path were a group of students in khaki green uniforms with breast badges of different sizes and colours. They were handing out flyers and looked like they had been at it for a while with lots of errant pieces of paper scattered around like confetti. One of the uniformed girls looked up at Sareen who smiled and raised his hand in acknowledgment. In fact, Sareen seemed to know all of them and smiled and waved at several others. Kabir did not recognize any of them.

He observed the 'uniforms' as they made efforts to converse with everyone walking past and hand them their literature.

'Oye, Sareen, I can't figure out if your suited and booted friends are recruiting people or annoying them. What are they talking about anyway?'

'It's about the college elections. We have a candidate who we think will be a good, strong representative.'

'WE?' Kabir looked at him with raised eyebrows. 'I didn't

realize you knew anything about the election, let alone supported a candidate.'

Kabir felt strangely wounded at being left out. A moment passed in awkward silence.

'Here I was thinking you were trying to meet girls in uniform.'

They chuckled and the stiffness evaporated. Kabir put an arm around Sareen's neck and pulled him into a headlock.

'So when are you going to introduce me to your dorky friends then? And when are you going to sell me on this great new leader? What's his name anyway?'

Mustafa bounded up towards them.

'What did I miss? Actually, before you tell me, look what I got.'

He held up a key-ring on his finger with the scooter key on it. They collectively whooped and high-fived.

'So, what were you two talking about?'

'Sareen here was about to tell us to vote for this new leader for the student election, what was his name…?'

Mustafa's face darkened. 'Vote for Samrat!'

Sareen looked sheepish.

For the second time that afternoon, Kabir felt like an outsider. 'Hey, how did you know?'

Mustafa muttered, 'Never mind, we can talk about it some other time.'

Kabir had just spotted a familiar figure exit the building below. Although her back was to them, he knew the gait. The others followed his gaze and noticed Sahiba walking out of campus towards the bus stop.

Sareen and Kabir caught each other's eye, with the idea dawning upon them simultaneously.

Sareen snatched the key from Mustafa and bolted towards the central staircase. It took Kabir a fraction of a second to register and he hotfooted in pursuit, screaming at Sareen to give back the key.

As they got to the stairwell, Sareen swerved sharply and

bounded down two steps at a time. Kabir gathered momentum and grabbed the round edge of the large balustrade, which easily took his weight, swinging himself down the stairs. The speed of the pivot allowed him to catch Sareen at the first landing and he shouldered him against the wall. The impact forced the keys out of Sareen's hand and knocked both of them to the floor. The keys clattered away from them on the landing. Kabir managed to pick them up but as he was righting himself, Sareen threw a foot out. It caught Kabir as he launched forward, resulting in him hopping down the next flight using the banister for balance. Advantage Sareen; he was upright and tearing after Kabir. The penultimate landing served as a platform as there were only a few steps left to the bottom. Here Sareen caught up and as he lunged for the keys, Kabir managed to twist himself away. They collided like billiard balls where Kabir slammed against the banister and managed to stay standing, Sareen flew off the edge of the platform and sprawled out on the grey stone floor. Kabir miraculously still had the keys in his hand. He looked over at Sareen, winced and bolted out the back to get the scooter.

Thankfully it spluttered to life immediately. Kabir opened the throttle. By this point Sareen had gathered himself and intercepted Kabir at the entrance. The anemic acceleration of the scooter allowed him to jump on the back and they were a team again. As they came around the trees on the bend, they noticed a bus had pulled up to the stand. Willing this jalopy to go faster, they kept on their pursuit, but the bus was now pulling away. A low whine emanated from the engine, but they managed to pull up alongside and spotted Sahiba sitting by a window. Trying to get her attention, they called out to her and slapped the side of the bus which was now getting away. Hearing the commotion, Sahiba turned to look back quizzically and saw the two boys on the scooter grinning and waving frantically.

'Hey, how're you doing? It's me, Kabir!'

Puzzled, she half smiled and waved. The boys gave up the chase and stopped on the side of the road as the bus folded into traffic.

Inside the bus, the commotion had caused a few passengers to stand and watch. Embarrassed, Sahiba looked at Priya next to her and they burst into giggles.

CHAPTER NINE

With evening came time to break fast in the month of Ramzan. Mustafa and his parents visited the Baig's home with tiffins. Sahiba and Mustafa were almost the same age but he was closer to the older Fatima. As children, they shared a love of reading and would huddle together, sharing comic books and novels. Sahiba's energy on the other hand was directed towards jumping, running, playing, painting, anything which required physical movement. But all the girls loved Mustafa. His quiet, sweet demeanor made him a favourite, especially with mothers, aunts and grandmothers.

Neither of the fathers was particularly religious, but given the occasion, they held back from sharing a drink till later. Also, the devout Mian Qadir had dropped by with biryani from the restaurant. He would not have taken well to them wetting their beaks in front of him today.

Qadir sat with the elderly Bade Ammi, exchanging notes about the goings-on in the city. Even though he spoke softly, his cultured, classical Urdu could be heard through gaps in conversations. After a short time, he rose with his head bowed, hand on his heart and bid the family farewell. He called Mustafa over to see him out, who followed obediently to Qadir's white Hyundai.

'Why don't you come over to the shop one of these days? There is something I want to discuss with you. Will you come day after tomorrow?'

Without waiting for a response, Qadir settled himself into the car and drove off.

Mustafa walked back into the house to find Sahiba waiting for him by the door. She conspiratorially grabbed his arm and pulled him up to the terrace, away from the others.

'Mustafa, your friends chased me the other day on a scooter!'

Mustafa smiled but said nothing. He knew Sahiba was not really offended or angry. She was making a half-hearted attempt to seem put out.

'Are you not going to say anything? I don't really know those guys, but they yelled out to me while I was on the bus. It was really embarrassing. What are you smiling about?'

Mustafa walked over to the edge of the terrace and looked out at the twinkling city lights before him, giving nothing away. Unsure of what to do next, Sahiba took a beat and came over to stand next to him.

'Are you bothered that they pursued you or that they didn't catch up to you? Because we can fix that.' Avoiding his gaze, she asked, 'Who is that guy Kabir? Have you known him long?'

'One of my oldest friends. We went to school together and he comes over all the time. I'm actually a little surprised that you haven't met him before. He's a good guy.'

'Is that it? Good guy... Your oldest friend and all you boys have to say is "good guy"?'

She did an impression of an oaf with lazy eyes and a thumbs up. Mustafa smiled.

'What do you want to know? Look, he is studying economics, plays for the college cricket team, lives about fifteen minutes away. He likes taking photographs. Like many, he is not sure what he wants to do when he graduates this year. The rest you should figure out yourself. I think he plans to come over on Thursday. Why don't you guys hang out?'

'Hang out? Who said anything about hanging out?'

'Sahiba, please,' Mustafa exaggeratedly rolled his eyes, 'stop this drama or I will tell him what you're really like.'

She lit up and pushed him playfully, 'Shut up, Musty. Okay fine, just don't tell him I asked you anything or I will kill you. Why do you all like cricket so much though?'

'With Kabir it's a bit more than that. It's like a religion for him.'

Sahiba sighed wearily. 'Anyway, what did Mian Qadir want with you?'

'I don't really know, he asked me to come into the bakery so that he could talk to me. Sounded serious.' He shrugged his shoulders.

~

Sareen stuffed his keys and wallet into multi-pocketed camouflage cargos. He pulled on a red, full-sleeved Reebok t-shirt tight enough to hug the contours forming on his shoulders and arms. Taking a cue from his new gang, he had built up his workout routine to almost a hundred push-ups a day. Although the results were modest, he would spend several minutes in front of the mirror reveling in the shape his body was taking.

Mrs Geeta Amil, his mother, was in the sitting room, intently watching a rerun of the previous day's soap opera. She was spread out on a large furry sofa, dressed comfortably in a pista green salwar kameez. Having been widowed early in life, she now lavished all her maternal energies on her only son. In her eyes, Sareen was the adolescent incarnate of Buddha, Krishna and Hanuman, all rolled into one. His mischief was charming, and his virtue unblemished.

After her husband's death, she moved into her brother's palatial home. Their Sindhi family were jewellers and her brother, Vivek Chachlani, was instrumental in expanding the business from one store to two. He extended his penchant for shiny things into his home through a liberal use of marble, glass and golden metal. A few years ago, he had enhanced the façade of their home by installing four large ornamental Doric pillars overlooking the road outside.

Sareen was unused to the atmosphere in this mercantile environment. He didn't think his uncle was a bad man, but Vivek Chachlani only cared for things that fell neatly within the confines of his perspective of life. He was not a curious man and his relationship with Sareen's father, Himmat, was destined to be fraught. Sareen's father was an intellectual and a public servant. His philosophy and motivations did not make sense to Vivek, who did not see the point of 'intellectualizing' everything. Himmat Amil's lack of interest in Mercedes cars and his general sense of contentment as a public servant was seen as a character flaw, a lack of ambition and manliness.

Sareen's father had been a gentle man of books and culture, devoid of lofty ambition for riches or materiality. Contented with his government job at the railway department, his great passion was music and he played vinyl records of old movie tunes all day long. When the weather was good, he would take Sareen to Dargah Yousufain with Mian Qadir for Thursday night qawwali.

Sareen had happy recollections of narrow streets fragrant with freshly grilled kebab and the excitement of entering tinsel strewn archways to the shrine. Sitting mouth agape on his father's lap as the troupe of singers swayed their audience to the rhythm of these folk songs.

Geeta was matched with the Amil family who were well respected in the larger Sindhi community. She had led a happy life with her kind husband, but at times she wished for additional creature comforts. She would chide him occasionally, 'Would it be so bad to have a foreign holiday for a change? All we do is ride the railway'. But Himmat Amil had a lot to discover in India before setting off to the European mountains – it was one of the reasons he took the railway job. He dragged his family across the great Indian landscape from the palaces of central India to the forests of the Western Ghats. It was a great help that the rail travel was free.

Sareen's teenage truculence confused his uncle. The boy had been provided everything he could need. If only Sareen could be more like his cousins.

Vivek Chachlani had twin sons who worked in the jewellry store. Both breached the bastion of amateur obesity early in life. Tweedledee and Tweedledum had children by the time they were twenty-five and were providing a sedentary and velvety life for their families. Vivek Chachlani had offered Sareen a job at the store but the thought of spending the day around his cousins made Sareen completely uncooperative.

'Sareen is going through a phase... leave him, he will be okay,' Geeta would implore her brother, who was affronted by the slight. Sareen was used to the regular jibes aimed at his father but now these were slanted towards him – the son of the accused. It became so ingrained in everyday chitchat that Vivek Chachlani would not even notice this constant derision. He liked lecturing his captive audience about himself but always began by proclaiming that he did not like talking about himself. Naturally, Sareen had fostered an aversion towards him; when he was younger, he would absorb the little digs about his adored late father. But, it had gnawed away at him and as he grew older it manifested in him 'acting out'. On the other hand, in Sareen's mother's eye's, her brother was kind and angelic for taking them in and providing for them.

'Ma, I'm going out. I'm meeting some friends.'

'Beta, what about dinner?'

'I will eat out, don't worry about me.'

'But your uncle has asked for all of us to eat together today. He just got back from his trip; it would be nice if we could all sit together.'

Sareen would rather have spent the evening strapped to a dentist's chair than listen to the corpulent Chachlani brood talk about themselves. He felt a tinge of guilt because he knew it pained his mother, but it was easily obscured by the resentment he felt towards her for not standing up for him and his father.

Mother and son lived in a small extension to the house, which thankfully had a back door. He made his way silently across the garden, taking care to avoid the main house. The family German Shepherd half-barked when he saw his darkened figure creeping across the garden. Recognizing Sareen, his tail wagged and he trotted up, his head bowed in greeting. Sareen was Simba's favourite human and he usually followed him around the house. He scratched behind Simba's ears and made his way out of the gate.

Waiting across the road were three men in an open topped Mahindra jeep. As Sareen approached, the man in the front seat got out. Dressed in a kurta with a waistcoat. His strong features were framed by a lavish, well-tended beard. Sareen only knew this older man as Sardar and never cared to ask what went before or after the name. Sardar hugged Sareen warmly and gestured for him to get into the backseat. He did not recognize the driver but beside him, he recognized one of the students handing out the flyers earlier that day. All settled in, they set off for an AVP meeting.

CHAPTER TEN

Appraising himself in his mirror, Kabir cocked his head from side to side. A natural curl fell on his forehead which he was trying to adjust to the right spot. Today, he had planned to accidentally bump into Sahiba.

In preparation he had showered, cut his nails, combed his hair and now thought he looked like a dork. The clean job-interview look wasn't going to cut it. He ran his hands through his hair to tousle it. What he would give for a rough sandpaper stubble; sadly, the hair on his face was of the downy variety, so best to shave.

He had four shirts. Two of these were foisted upon him for formal occasions. Of the other two, he reckoned one would fit the bill. It was a black, cotton poplin, round-collared shirt with snap buttons. Modelling it, he turned sideways, three quarters and front on, all the while squinting his eyes and looking disinterested. The jeans were from a recently opened Pepe jeans store down the road, with a rip above the left knee. It was perfect.

Kabir had left his door ajar and found Sakshi standing there, wide-eyed with curiosity. She had never seen Kabir preen before.

'Who are you going to meet?' she asked with a shy smile. Sakshi had never been an annoying sibling. She was a self-sufficient girl who was the more likely of the two to graduate with a law degree. Kabir took her to piano lessons, athletics practice and friends' birthdays. In turn she doted on him.

'I'm just going to see Mustafa. We are hanging out with some friends.'

Prem walked past the door and the situation didn't take long to dawn on him; he had never seen his son voluntarily clean up before going to meet friends. A pang of paternal instinct came over him and he returned with two pairs of his leather shoes. He couldn't imagine anyone making a good impression in his son's blue Reeboks, which had been worn doggedly since the day they were purchased. Kabir, on the other hand, looked on in horror at a pair of black leather loafers and tan lace ups. They looked like they belonged to a funeral director at a wedding. The Reeboks prevailed; all he was missing was a few sprays of his father's Drakkar Noir cologne. He liberally coated himself with the woody citrus fragrance, creating an olfactory halo around him, which heralded his announcement into every room for the rest of the day. As he left, his father stood by the door watching him with a strange look on his face. A sentimental Mr Menon was pulled away by his wife who wished Kabir a good night.

Sahiba was also appraising herself in the mirror. Kajal and a hint of blush was all she could manage if she were to sneak out without too many questions asked. Having spent the last couple of minutes hopping around, pulling herself into new white denims, she contemplated her choice of a navy-blue blouse with a little tone on tone embroidery or a little printed tank top. After turning to check out her bum in the mirror, she chose the blouse. She grabbed a scarf to wrap around her head to hide the make up as best as she could. Not that she was doing anything wrong but she desperately wanted to avoid the multi-pronged inquisition. This required her to walk through the courtyard and out the door unnoticed.

She breezed past her mother and Fatima who were sitting in the courtyard.

'Wait wait, where are you going?' Zia called out. She had that suspicious motherly look about her.

So near and yet so far. Sahiba resignedly turned back. 'I am going to meet Mustafa and some friends. We have plans to hang out... maybe, go for a movie later.'

'Are those new?' Zia asked pointing at the jeans.

'No, you have seen them before.'

This was a lie but better smoke and mirrors than have a long conversation about it. All hopes of a quiet exit were dashed as her grandmother came out of her room with Ruksana.

'I'm not sure I like them, why don't you change into something else, it looks a little...'

Bade Ammi now chimed in, 'Why did you change out of your kurta beta? You were looking so lovely.'

'So who all are going to be there?' This question was a staple but it baffled Sahiba because her mother never remembered her friends despite having met several of them.

Fatima saw an opening to have a little fun of her own, 'What film are you going to see, Sahiba? Maybe I will come along too.'

Sahiba flashed a 'don't you start' look at Fatima. Knowing that she was dangerously close to getting pulled into a family discussion, Sahiba needed to take swift action.

'Ammi, I like these jeans and I am getting really late. They must be waiting for me, I need to go now. Love you.'

'Arrey, at least have a bite to eat before you go.'

Another baffling custom. Why did she need to eat something every time she left the house?

Hastily turning away she bumped into her father at the front door. Masood Baig was just returning from work and encountered a whirlwind for a daughter who gave him a quick hug before running off.

~

67

It was that time of day just beyond the afternoon but too early for evening. The time when birds start becoming more vocal right before their daily ritual of frenzied panic as darkness approaches. A pleasant breeze had blown away the warm afternoon and patchy clouds intermittently blocked slanted rays. Mustafa and Kabir stood by the ticket counter at the entrance of the Golkonda Fort. As he pointed his camera up the battlements of this impressive citadel, Kabir tried to recall his last visit. It had been almost four years ago.

Mustafa spotted Sahiba and Priya as they got out of their auto rickshaw and Kabir started getting that nervous sensation in his stomach. Tickets in hand, Mustafa led them all to the gate and into the sprawling fort. For a while they all explored the place together. Mustafa's calm, settling nature allowed an easy natural conversation between them all. They talked about college and their homework. The girls were both studying biological sciences and wanted to pursue careers in pharmaceuticals. Their stories about dissections and lab experiments had the boys engrossed. As they walked through large courtyards, Mustafa held sway with his knowledge of architectural elements and the history of the place.

Kabir was unable to focus on the details of 'weight bearing innovations in ornamental doorways,' but the girls seemed very interested. They kept asking intelligent questions, so Kabir had to go along with it. He needed to find a way to be alone with Sahiba. As time went on, his courage thinned and he almost abandoned the attempt. She was friendly but offered no signs of her complicity, there were no extra glances towards him nor any attempts to walk next to him. He looked up at hawks circling high above the citadel searching for their last quarry of the day. He couldn't help cursing them for how easy they had it, just happily swooping around, never having to be in this position. They had reached the end of a series of interconnected courtyards; one path led to the royal palaces, but there was also a way to climb up the ramparts to the top of the hill.

Mustafa suggested the climb up for the view, this presented a sliver of an opportunity

'I want to take some pictures of the palace. I haven't been here for a while. Sahiba, do you want to come? We will catch up with these guys after.'

The pause felt like minutes.

'Yeah sure,' she smiled evenly at Kabir and added to the others, 'we will see you guys up there.'

Relief flooded through him; now all he had to do was not be himself for a few minutes. Priya gave Sahiba a knowing look and headed away with Mustafa.

Sahiba seemed to have the confidence that Kabir so badly needed. 'So how come I have never met you before? Mustafa tells me you went to school together and have been at their home plenty of times.'

'I don't know. Had I known you were around, I would have come more often.' A bold opening. Would this corny flirtation result in the desired effect or boomerang in his face? As they were walking alongside each other, he couldn't see her reaction. There was no immediate response either.

'Mustafa tells me you are not sure what you want to do after college. What are the options you are considering?'

Damn Mustafa... what else has he told her? He would have to tell him to keep his mouth shut.

'Oh yeah, I am looking at various options, you know? I have already got offers to join lots of companies. But I might decide to play cricket seriously, you know, to turn professional...'

These were half-truths at best, but he wanted to impress as best as he could.

'Really? Wow that sounds like you have it all figured out.' Kabir detected a hint of frostiness. 'My brother had a friend who tried to play cricket professionally. It's really tough to make it, you know. Very, very few people actually succeed. But it sounds like you are totally sure about it. Don't lose those offers from the "lots of companies" though. You may need them as back-up.'

Perhaps he shouldn't be showing off – it wasn't going too well. He was terrible at posturing and envied the guys at college who could talk a big game.

'I'm just kidding. I have zero job options in reality but plenty in theory.'

'Well, at least you have cricket.'

'Oh no, you're also right about the cricket thing. We have trials in a week, but I am only the fourth best batsman in the team, forget about the city.'

'How many batsmen in the team?'

'Four. Five if you count the guy who can bowl as well. Six if you count the wicket keeper. Seven if you count the one guy who's not permanent in the team.'

She turned and smiled.

'I don't understand how you all get so wrapped up in cricket. It's just a game and it takes hours, if not days, to finish. You guys get so emotional about it.'

Kabir winced.

'Have you noticed anything different when interacting with people the last couple of days? Did the auto rickshaw guy seem cheerful? Or did a shopkeeper seem upbeat? Were the people on the street smiling a little more than normal? It's because yesterday Azharuddin scored one of the best centuries of his life. The entire city is "mast" because he is one of us. He probably walked the same path as you and I just did with his friends. He ate at the same dhabas, heard the same namaaz, dodged the same traffic. Yesterday he showed the world his magic.

'His innings was savage and beautiful at the same time. He handed out a thrashing that will take the Australians years to recover from. This is what entranced the city. What else can give people joy and hope the way cricket can? It elevated all of us because he is one of us. It was as if we were all battling the Australians.'

Sahiba, quietly charmed by this impassioned description, did not respond immediately.

'You know who he is, right?'

With an exaggerated head roll, she shot back, 'Of course, even I know who he is!'

Kabir noticed the ageing caretaker sitting on a little stool, wearing a white turban. His thin frame supported itself at acute angles. His crossed knees propped up his folded elbows, which in turn supported his shoulders. He was smoking a beedi under the looming, crumbling edifice of the palace. Moving quickly to capture the moment, Kabir took a couple of steps to his left, dropped to his knees and took a series of pictures before the man shifted.

The two of them continued exploring the ruins and looked for compositions together. Kabir handed her the camera and as he explained its functions, she came up by his side and leaned on him. Taking turns with the camera, they poked around the palace, its adjoining courtyards and the mosque. Sahiba drew up next to him a few times to try and understand the workings of aperture and shutter speed. When she did, there was leaning and contact. Kabir had been trying to figure out whether it had been accidental the first time but now it was definitely intentional. Almost certainly.

They talked effortlessly, enjoying each other's humour. Sahiba spoke about becoming a teacher one day. Then they naturally fell into more intimate stories about themselves and their families. Sahiba mentioned the afternoon episode with the jeans and her mother's reaction. Kabir gently teased her about it. He told her about his father's shoes and she chided him playfully for not wearing them.

The evening light was adding a warm tint to the black granite as they made the steep climb up the ramparts to the top of the hill. The wind was blustery, pushing them back a little. Kabir had a couple buttons undone and his shirt was fluttering against his chest. He imagined he looked a bit like a matinee idol. Sahiba had tied her scarf to her head to protect her hair from flying wildly and as she tried to hold it in place, her balance shifted against the wind. They laughed at their attempt to push themselves against the gusts and she held his arm to steady herself. The climb was beautiful, with the city laid out below them. The fading sunlight dispersed through little wisps of cloud, turning them yellow and then orange.

At the top was a modest white-columned building with arched doorways. It was easy to imagine why this hilltop was of such strategic importance. From this vantage you were perched as though on top of a needle in a bowl, you could see advancing armies from all directions. Chirpy families and amorous couples now held the fort in place of the watching sentinels. They sat in a row, gazing out at the setting sun. Kabir took a picture of the lined-up sunset watchers. He couldn't spot his friends in any of them.

Kabir ventured, 'I guess we should go back down to find them.'

'No, let's stay up here for a bit and watch the sunset. It's so beautiful, we can get some pictures.'

Not needing to be asked twice, Kabir looked for a place where they could be a little removed from the others. Unable to find a secluded spot on the ledge, they clambered up the rocks and found a spot where they would be facing each other.

For the first time Kabir sat looking directly at Sahiba. She smiled and he was whacked by the full-frontal blast of her gorgeousness. Her beauty was in the softness of her features; an oval face with large warm eyes, full lips and a small, slightly upturned nose. She smiled, all dimples and perfect teeth, and turned to look out at the view. He watched transfixed by her wisps of hair fluttering in the breeze, at a loss of what to do next.

They stayed up there for a little while longer, not saying much. An intimacy began without words and when the sun dipped behind the horizon they made their way down, holding hands.

72

DAVID VS GOLIATH
Bangalore 1996, Jadeja vs Waqar

If there ever was a David vs Goliath cricket equivalent, it occurred on this crucial quarter-final world cup match. Matches versus Pakistan were grudges. Even purists, who would applaud a good performance, irrespective of their affiliation, abandoned their even-handed magnanimity and turned into baying partisans. Perhaps it's because the countries were partitioned fifty years ago and the wounds never healed. Perhaps it's because we fought wars and there remained the question of Kashmir. Perhaps it's because we look the same, talk the same, dress the same, eat the same – it makes the rivalry more personal.

In truth, the Indian fan came off as insecure, while the Pakistani seemed self-assured. At the time we overemphasized our national virtues to outsiders as though we weren't entirely convinced by them ourselves. This tournament was held in India under lights. It was glitzy, the team had superstars and endorsements came thick and fast. The sensory overload rendered the crowds schizophrenic. One moment an Indian batsman would hit a boundary, they were delirious with joy. The next moment, when an Indian batsman was declared out, dejectedly they fell into a collective bereavement. The opposition fielders could be forgiven for feeling less than confident standing at the boundary, for any minute a missile could hasten their chances of re-incarnation.

Kabir felt none of the animosity when thinking of Pakistan. What he felt was a nagging dread considering the mercurial talent in the opposition ranks. In those days the Pakistani team seemed to toy with the Indians. A frequent topic of anguish was their ability to produce strapping, tall, dangerous, long-haired fast bowlers whose singular purpose seemed to terrorize batsmen. India never produced that quality of fast bowlers.

73

Instead, we produced thin, bespectacled spin bowlers with guile who could outfox batsmen but not intimidate them. While it was quite certain the Indian bowlers could have been successful engineers or accountants and definitely had better alternative job prospects than the Pakistanis, Kabir and the Indian fan would have given a bucket of spinners for a threatening Goliath or two.

The toppling of that very Goliath is chronicled in the Indian cricket equivalent of a Biblical story. Towards the end of India's batting innings stood Ajay Jadeja, a fidgety gangly lad from Delhi, whose technique resembled a professional fly swatter. All wrists and flap, he had somehow managed to avoid every correct habit of batsmanship. Facing him at the end of his run up was the muscular Sultan of Swing, the Toe Crusher, Waqar Younis, a man fresh from vanquishing the English in their backyard. All the other recognized batsmen had been dismissed and the Indians did not have a competitive score on the board yet.

Kabir was on a stupid class trip to a stupid wildlife reserve on this critical day of his life. Honestly what was the point of sitting in this forest rest house, cut off from an event capable of changing the course of history? Luckily, in the kitchen a cook had a transistor radio and some friends were sitting around the now-defunct-fireplace trying to discern the commentary through a crackling transmission.

'...Waqar to Jadeja, oh he's smashed it... that could be six, it IS six, that's gone miles over the top, what a little beauty...' Tony Grieg's breathless commentary sent the boys into raptures. It was a practical demonstration of sacred texts, the morals from Aesop, the lessons from the battlefield of the Gita. The impossible was happening – David was slaying Goliath.

CHAPTER ELEVEN

Sareen awoke with a metallic taste in his mouth. His eyes took a few beats to focus. The left side of his jaw and lip felt sore as he pulled his legs off the bed. Sitting up was perilous; as his head swam, he propped up his arms on either side to steady himself.

'What the hell happened to me?'

As the cloud of disorientation gradually cleared, his hunched figure registered the detritus on his bedroom floor. In amongst his discarded shoes and clothing were streamers with bright tinsel flags, a signboard written in Urdu and what looked like the hubcap from a car.

The night had begun without portent. Sardar had picked him up and they drove to an internet café fifteen minutes away. On the first floor, they were ushered into a room with small chairs lined up in front of a single computer screen, a little like a classroom. It was a large, empty, tube-lit space, devoid of any pretentions of decoration or design, with the exception of a clock mounted on a picture of a racing car on the wall facing them. As they entered, there were already ten, maybe twelve, people milling around the room. Sareen did not know many of them, but they all seemed friendly and keen to get to know him.

Sardar was the eldest and the central figure in the room. He personally introduced everyone. He spoke as though he had known them all for years and was generous in praise of each of them. After a few minutes they were ushered to sit and some of the lights were put off and a CD was inserted into a battered CPU connected to the screen. The film started up with a song. Lofty patriotic swells piped through two small speakers plugged into the back of the screen – its tinny, electro-mechanical sound belied the song's lofty emotion. When the song ended, the black screen made way for familiar news reels of the demolition of the Babri Masjid in Ayodhya. The narrator of the film lauded the Hindu heroes for reclaiming their fundamental rights. For the next twenty minutes, it listed out a series of injustices heaped on the long-suffering Hindu. Reservations of college seats, jobs and a fundamental right to practice their faith were the mainstays. Sareen was getting more and more uncomfortable. He had found himself in completely the wrong place; he didn't care about any of this. Squirming in his seat, he was gathering up the courage to bolt out of the door. Just as he was about to make a run for it, the video ended and the lights came back on.

Sardar thanked everyone for being there and announced that now it was time for fun. An ice bucket with beers suddenly appeared as did some bottles of Signature whiskey – maybe he would stay just a little longer after all… to see where this all ended. The mood turned festive.

Sareen was talking to some people who were complaining about not having got into Sikandra University due to the biases that existed there. They were making an argument against the Muslim families which ran the city and sponsored the university with Muslim-only scholarships. Sareen kept his mouth shut, he had never heard of such a thing. In the back of his mind he wondered whether this chap may not be the sharpest tack in the box.

Sardar was lurking, listening over his shoulder. He made a few sympathetic noises and interrupted the ongoing tirade. Making a big show of it, he reintroduced Sareen to the group as 'Sareen Dada,' a tribute to how tough Sareen was. Sareen liked being called dada. He felt chuffed as the honeyed effects of liquor began to flow through his veins. Sardar narrated Sareen's story to the group, drawing upon the misfortunes that had befallen the family when his father died. In particular, the fact that his mother and he were thrown out of the house they had lived in for twenty years.

'Without care or compassion to their plight, they were thrown out into the street with their possessions, not even allowed time to resolve their matters... and who was this heartless, money-minded Muslim landlord who would throw a mother and child out into the street?'

This was confusing, how did Sardar know about any of this? His mother had never mentioned being evicted to Sareen, let alone due to a Muslim. Sareen never spoke about his father and to have his life exposed to a group of strangers was unsettling.

Now as he hunched over the side of the bed, recounting the night, Sareen knew that this had been the critical moment. He should have excused himself and left right then, right before it became a rallying cry, right before he was painted with the brush of victimhood. But while it was happening, he couldn't claw himself out of it. By that time, Sareen was under the charge of an intoxicated aggression, which lifted his spirits. The undercurrent of the room had turned belligerent. There were proclamations being made and calls to action.

His memory of the rest of the evening was patchy at best. He recalled a mad rush into the jeeps, a skirmish in a market, breaking things and finally fleeing. He had a vivid recollection of men advancing and him swinging at them. His slurred vision was creating neon tails on the lit storefront signs. He remembered the angry bearded face of a man in a white cap right before he saw a flash of overhead lamps. He was punched and knocked to the floor but could not piece together details. All he knew was that he had been part of something – something vile, something he couldn't undo.

Burying his head in his hands eased his headache somewhat, but it didn't help assuage his feeling of being overwhelmed. Recollections suffocated him with remorse and anger. He felt alien to himself. He needed to be somewhere familiar, somewhere more innocent, somewhere that felt like home. He stuffed his things from the floor into a bag and set off to see Kabir.

~

Time, far from being a precise, constant dimension, sometimes had an elastic quality. Occasionally it would move at its predicted metronomic consistency, other times it seemed to take twice as long. This afternoon, Kabir was daydreaming, and time whistled along at speed. The thought came to him as he realized that the two hours he had allotted to study had flown by. Like the ebbs and flows in a test match. At times it would be turgid and then suddenly it hurtled forward, and outcomes would be decided in an instant.

Kabir tended to overestimate the use of cricket metaphors and used them to explain most goings-on in life. He would also use them liberally in interactions and invariably took it too far. On occasion, he admitted to suffering friends and family that perhaps losing one's virginity, price of auto rickshaw rides and India's nuclear tests had little similarity to cricketing analogies.

A phone ring snapped him out of his thoughts and propelled him into action. In a couple of bounds he was in the hallway and at the table by the front door where the home phone sat. He allowed it to ring once more before answering with a busy sounding 'Yes, hello'. It was for his mother. His twitching muscle fibers dropped into a state of sloth as he wrote down the message. Back in his room, he tried to concentrate on the monetary policy rule equation but his mind was restless.

He was expecting Sahiba to come over later today. They could hang out in his room, listen to music and maybe more. Looking around, he thought that perhaps he should rid the place of the excessive cricket paraphernalia.

Since that day at the fort, they had seen each other almost every day. Their time together resembled a tour itinerary of Hyderabad's monuments. These large, landscaped public spaces provided just the right amount of privacy while having a distraction. They met under the pretext of taking pictures, but now without their friends in tow. Soon they outgrew the need for pretentions. Their trysts shifted to cafés where they would sit on the same side and lock fingers under the table.

Kabir stood at his bedroom door, critically evaluating its first impressions. Other than his desk and chair, there was no furniture. All other furnishings and finery were on the floor in the form of cushions, floor lamps and bolsters. Even his bed had been eschewed in favour of a small platform. A large tie-dye throw was slung from the corner above the bed. The walls had the odd cricket poster, Indian team jersey, Pink Floyd print and a bookshelf. The room was small; its relatively large window opened out into the upper branches of a large peepul tree. When leaning back on the bolsters you had the distinct impression of sitting in a tree.

The elasticity of time now stretched the other way. Having made last-minute adjustments, the final minutes were slowed by the weight of waiting. He was looking at the clock constantly. The doorbell gave him a start. Sahiba stood, head slightly askew, smiling up at him. Every time he saw her, his chest would tighten and his pulse would quicken. It still took him a beat to stop staring at her bright-eyed loveliness. She broke the silence by grabbing his arm and pulling him in for a lingering hug.

They started with a quick tour of the apartment. The blinds in the living room were pulled down to keep the harsh afternoon sun at bay, giving it a deserted, forgotten-in-time air. Kabir rolled up one of the blinds. A flash of slanted light from the gap picked up little flecks of lint as they floated in slow motion. Light gave the room its colour back; the upholstery warmed, the marble floors brightened and wooden almirahs regained their stateliness.

Their home in Hyderabad carried much of how they had lived in Calcutta. The potted palms and jute blinds, all belonged to a particular post-colonial aesthetic. A large wall clock from Chowringee, an ornamental chair upholstered with block printed raw silk from Bhagalpur, a teak table and paintings from the Bengal school – it felt like the house had a story to tell.

Sahiba seemed curious about Calcutta, in particular old photos of the family. She asked Kabir about the people in every other photo, where it was taken, the story behind them. He took a little creative license in embellishing his version.

Sahiba bent down to look at a picture frame on a side table. 'Wow. What a striking woman!'

Kabir acknowledged that the picture of his late grandmother – in her sari and pearls, grabbing the reins of a race pony flanked by some Englishman in a topee – was reasonably exotic.

'Yeah, she was quite something. She would have needed to be to keep my Dada in line.'

Sahiba turned her head arching an eyebrow

'So, her claim to fame is her ability to handle her man? Your grandfather, who I'm sure was some superhero.'

'No, no, that's not what I meant,' Kabir hadn't seen that coming. 'It's just that Dada was a bit of a rogue, always getting into trouble, and she was the only one to put him in his place.'

Sahiba let it pass and smiled quietly to herself.

Kabir leaned in conspiratorially

'Dada did some crazy stuff in his day.'

'Did they have a happy marriage?'

He had never even thought of this. His grandparents were… his grandparents – they were like the protagonists in stories you were told as kids, virtuous and wholesome. Marital problems, feminism, taxes, cooking, children, smart casual dressing were topics outside his purview.

'Sure, they did, super happy.'

Sahiba's worldliness intimidated him. The last time they met she decried society's double standards in their depiction of women. Words were strung together in a sequence that was altogether novel to him. He staved off that line of thought with empathetic noises and a visit to the loo. He had heard of this topic, but it was the first time someone was including him in a dialogue. Her certitude made him feel a touch inadequate to comment. So, he dutifully nodded along.

However, the confidence that intimidated Kabir was not altogether Sahiba's own point of view. She herself borrowed it from overheard conversations. Her posited positions came from experiences she had not yet had. As the junior member of the Baig courtyard, she soaked in the dialogues of a life to be lived. With her friends, she was experimenting with her personality as a woman, no longer a girl. Mostly she wanted to seem mature and reactionary.

Kabir had turned out quite differently from what Sahiba had imagined. He had a lanky casual handsomeness, and his disarming smile was always at hand. Despite the strange clannishness to cricket, she found he was able to make her laugh. Walking around the fort with him was one of the best days she had had in a long time. She wanted to be close to him, to grab his arm, to have adventures together.

Peering at the old Menon family photographs was fascinating to her. Images of Calcutta – of men in summer suits, women in pearls and chiffon, hair coiffured, looked urbane and otherworldly to her. So very different to the old photos of her family where men wore white kurtas with silk waistcoats and skullcaps. Women in both households wore sarees, but the sarees in her family pictures were of a crisper, diaphanous quality with specks of gold and silver. The common themes in both were the starched poses, raised foreheads and the three-quarter-turn to the camera. Both families looked as if they all needed to be frozen for posterity as paragons of uprightness, almost afraid of the camera capturing their true fallible selves.

Soon, they found themselves draped on the cushions on Kabir's bedroom floor. A stereo with owl-eyed speakers sat between them. Choosing from a stack of CDs on his desk, Kabir rattled off a bunch of names that Sahiba had never heard of. He settled on Pink Floyd's 'Dark Side of the Moon' and was at pains to explain the history of this album and why it was so damned important. Sahiba could not understand the excitement over an album made twenty years ago, but was willing to go along. As he put it on, she moved over and lay next to him. There wasn't all that much to talk about, so they leaned in and gradually twisted towards one another. After a little while he asked if she liked the music. She said it sounded like a bunch of mechanical whoops and crashes and not music in the sense she understood it.

This made them giggle in unison. Now laying there, facing each other, their eyes met and the remnants of their laugh faded. Kabir took a deep breath and was just about to... Suddenly the doorbell rang. Then again... and again. Kabir jumped up. He had ensured that he had the house to himself.

The first thing he thought of when he saw Sareen standing at the front door, with a cut lip, was an expression his mother sometimes used – 'His face looked so small'. Cowed and shrunken, Sareen resembled a kicked puppy. Before Kabir could say anything, Sareen pushed the door open and let himself into the kitchen. Kabir followed. After helping himself to a lemon barley drink from the fridge and some ice for his lip, he fell into a sofa in the living room.

'What happened to you?!'

'Long story, man. I had a really strange night...' Sareen hunched over the edge of the sofa, elbows on knees, staring at the carpet; he sat still, not offering any further explanation.

'Did you get into a fight or did you fall on your face?'

Sareen looked up wearily, unamused and turned back to stare at a spot on the carpet. He was conflicted. He wanted badly to confide in his closest friend but was afraid to own up to what he had been part of. Having come to a safe place, he needed an arm around his shoulder, a confidant, someone to tell him it was okay. His emotions were sitting on top of a thin layer of caramelized surliness. All it needed was a gentle tap to crack and let in a flood of relief.

Kabir was far too distracted to see the signs. Although he was itching to know what had happened, having a girl in his room was such a novelty. He did not have the patience to coax anything out of Sareen. Not getting any more information, Kabir went to what he knew best.

'Well look on the bright side, at least it's an improvement to your face. Buddy, sorry but I need you to leave right now. Why don't you come back for dinner tonight? The folks haven't seen you for ages. It will be fun, I think we are having meat curry.'

Sareen had never asked for permission to hang around here before.

'Tell me, did you think it a little strange the way we moved into my uncle's house so soon after Papa died? And we never went back home. Did you ever hear about the landlord throwing us out?'

'What? What are you talking about? No, I never heard anything like that.'

Sareen showed no signs of having heard him. Kabir was fidgety – he skulked around the room inspecting an ashtray, looking at a book, hoping the penny would drop soon. His awkward, annoying lurking finally got the message across.

'What's going on? Why do you want me to go?'

'Well, there is someone here. Just come back later, okay?'

Sareen quizzically looked around and then nodded towards the corridor which led to the bedrooms. He made towards the rooms. Kabir stepped in his way.

'Why are you being weird? Who's here?'

Kabir whispered, and gestured for Sareen to keep it down.

'Sahiba is here!'

'Sahiba? Sahiba from college?'

'Yeah. We have been hanging out a bit over the last few weeks.'

'Have you? How come you didn't ask me?'

'Ask you what?'

'I mean, how come you didn't tell me?'

'I don't know, it just happened. Musty and I met her and her friend Priya the other day and we just started hanging.'

Sareen's face hardened. He picked up his bag and slung it across his chest.

'Fine, I will go.'

Without looking at Kabir, he moved towards the front door.

'Come back for dinner though, okay? Around eight?'

Sareen ignored him. He opened the front door and descended down the stairs leading down from Kabir's first floor apartment. As he got to the landing, Kabir called out, 'Sareen… come on, man. Are you okay? Will you come?'

Sareen turned to glower at him, and then was gone.

Kabir remained standing at the top of the stairs. He never did find out what happened to Sareen's cut lip. He felt guilty about sending his friend away and also a little deceitful. Perhaps he could have handled things better.

But the pressing matter of Sahiba in his room quickly flushed away other thoughts.

Back in the room, he found her sitting upright. Wide eyes made her look nervous, as though caught in the middle of a heist.

'Who was that?'

'It was my friend, Sareen'

'Oh, are you guys hanging out?'

'No, no he just comes by whenever, but I sent him away.'

'You told him to leave?'

'It's fine, it's fine. He's always here. He will come back later.'

'Oh okay, did he know I was here?'

'I had to tell him, otherwise he would have walked into the room.'

There was an awkward acknowledgement of being discovered. Nothing to do but let the moment pass.

After the exertions of the intrusion, Kabir lay back in his spot and Sahiba turned to her side and put her arm over his chest. They lay there for a moment, their faces inches from each other. Looking up at the ceiling, Kabir could feel her breath on his cheek. He turned to face her and putting his hand on her hip, their bodies pushed against one another and their legs tangled. They kissed gently at first, but it quickly grew more passionate. As their mouths opened, he felt the warm wetness of her tongue against his. Their shapes shifted and fitted into each curve and corner as though wheels inside a clock. The afternoon was spent in that delicious stupor, kissing and clinging. All of it happened so naturally, akin to batting when you time the ball sweetly without effort and it flies off the bat. Before they knew it, the afternoon had given way to twilight, and it was time for Sahiba to head home. They held on for a last hurried kiss and he dropped her to a taxi.

DESERT STORM
Sharjah 1998, Tendulkar becomes a god

This script was written in the heavens. It had been a decade since the international debut of five-foot-nothing, sixteen-year-old Sachin Tendulkar. He had already done enough to be christened a savior, a genius, a freak of natural talent – the opposition knew that if you beat Tendulkar, the rest of the team folded.

But over two April nights out on the edge of the Arabian desert, out strode this diminutive colossus to play out his destiny. It was the performance, the rite of passage that a player must make to gild his legend into immortality. It was the anecdote, which would hang by their name in the history of the sport.

It wasn't just a 'great' innings – it was savagery, as if angry gods possessed him to smite the opposing forces. That night the stadium was engulfed with a storm of swirling desert sand as Sachin Tendulkar single-handedly defeated an Australian team of supermen.

Back home, the country was left wide-eyed in disbelief. Kabir walked around in a tingling daze as if the applause were for his own conquest. There was electricity in the air. Kabir had just kissed Sahiba and the world held wonderment and a promise of possibility.

CHAPTER TWELVE

Barman climbed up to the terrace of the Sheer Mahal Restaurant and Bar. Large bolsters covered by Turkish textiles pushed up alongside rattan chairs and Kashmiri carpets softened the floor. It wasn't a luxurious space, but the attention to detail was evident. In the summer months, small cups of jasmine flowers were placed on the tables, rendering a light fragrance to the passing breeze. This lasted until the large tandoor ovens were fired up and the wholesome wafts of freshly fluffed naan and marinated mutton punctuated the terrace.

Barman had been frequenting the spot since his early professorial days and although the kebabs were very good, he preferred coming in before the dinner service began. He liked the quiet time before the tandoors were lit. The bar opened at six in the evening and it was the best time to sip on a frosty Kingfisher beer. Dusk approached and the warm orange residue of the day seemed to rise up from the city floor. The buildings around had acquired a uniform patina and just then, the first strains of the evening prayer pierced the air. One after the other, mosques and minarets across the old city took up the word of God and the terrace was engulfed in its haunting echo.

Sitting across from Barman on the table was a purposeful man in his forties, formally dressed in a shirt and Nehru-collared waistcoat. He had a sharp jaw, perfectly parted hair and a trimmed moustache. Amar Rathore's visiting card proclaimed that he was in the real estate and import/export business. As the muezzin calls reverberated, they could no longer hear each other. To avoid looking at each other, both turned their chairs slightly to gaze out over the rooftops at the setting sun. It was a respite for Barman who would have preferred being in any number of places, doing any number of things over having this conversation. But his hands were tied – the VC of the college, Harshad Bhosle, had tried urging, cajoling, reasoning, and eventually downright demanding, that he take this meeting.

They had begun with small talk, which was at the best of times taxing for Barman's fickle attention span. His patience survived enquiries about health and favourite foods but once it took a turn towards the unseasonal rains, he cut in.

'Mr Rathore, you seem to be a busy man. What are we doing here?'

Amar Rathore seemed mildly amused at the directness of this fidgety professor. He was used to people who danced around the point for a little while.

'You see, Mr Choksi, I am a businessman but also a man of my community...'

This opening led to a loose description of myriad businesses, important people he knew and who he interacted with. Barman was aware that this was an attempt to impress him or at the very least impress upon him the important connections Rathore wielded. The names came thick and fast, but only one or two rang distant bells. Barman was trying to piece together why any of this should matter to him and again – why was he here? A prickle of irritation prompted Barman's condescension.

'You seem to know a lot of important people, Mr Rathore. I'm sure they are far better equipped to help you in whatever task you may have than I am.'

Rathore paused and registered the sarcasm. His soft-spoken demeanor loosely masked an underlying mettle. Here was a man who seemed accustomed to getting things done his way.

In a low voice, he said, 'Okay Professor, I'll come to the point and you'll see how you can help me. I wanted to talk to you about one of the students standing for elections, Samrat Singh. Now, I know the boy has failed exams and some such, plus he has been a little mischievous, but his heart is in the right place.'

'Yes, Mr Bhosle asked me to look into this, but he isn't a student at the university anymore, so he is no longer eligible. His records show that he stopped attending two years ago after failing the finals exams.'

'Well, yes, but technically he could still be considered – there has not been any official expulsion, you see. Just to ensure that no one goes digging into it, we were hoping that you could include him in your cricket team. A sports scholarship, you see. He wouldn't have to play of course, but as long as he is in the squad... You understand, it would make things much easier. People wouldn't need to enquire about his academics. We will take care of the past records, not to worry.'

'I'm sorry but why is this of any interest to you, Mr Rathore?'

'Let's just say I am keen to share my successes with the younger generations. It's important to give back to your community. We must all understand our duty and the position we have been given in life, don't you think, Professor?'

This newfound interest in small Sikandra University's elections baffled Barman. Up to this point elections had been the bastion of thick-rimmed political science students who would have gladly traded any student body office for a steady girlfriend. The nature of Sikandra University was more academic, scholarly even, and it prided itself for being sheltered from the forces of the outside world. It's what attracted Barman to tenure in the first place.

'I'm sorry I cannot help you, Mr Rathore. The rules require the student to be enrolled at the university and it's quite clear that this boy no longer attends. As for the cricket team, there is absolutely no question about him being selected. The boys work very hard to be a part of that team and it's a prestigious position. It's not something that can be gifted.'

'Mr Choksi, please understand that we must all adjust a little bit for the greater good. I understand that you will be going out of your way to do me this favour and of course you must be compensated for it. It'll be the beginning of our friendship and you will see that I know how to take care of my friends.'

Rathore put a hand in his jacket and placed an unmarked white envelope on the table between them.

Barman had already started to bristle with indignation at the suggestion of sullying his cricket team but this envelope, this suggestion of a price, this implication of his complicity nearly manifested itself in physical agitation. Thankfully, right at this point, the evening prayer interrupted them. It provided the respite that Barman badly needed to put his thoughts in order and keep the reddening rage at bay. Teeth clenched and working hard to maintain steadiness in his voice, he turned to Rathore.

'Listen, Rathore. You have the wrong guy. This conversation is over, I can't help you.'

Without looking at it, Barman flicked the envelope off the table. As he did this, he also twisted his body away from the table in dismissal.

Amar Rathore sat unmoved for a moment. He smiled, but the curling of his lips was unaccompanied by any softening of expression.

'You know, Mr Choksi, we must all make choices in life. Sometimes we make good ones, sometimes bad. Since you do not know me and this is the first time we have met, I am willing to allow

a certain leeway for misunderstanding or maybe what I mean is…
'misjudgment'. I will let you think about this conversation and soon
I will present my offer again. By then, I trust you would have come
around to thinking differently.'

'You don't understand. I have no interest in your envelopes or
your illusion of importance. There are higher purposes in life, and
I would not sully the reputation of my office, the university or the
team. Keep yourself and all your pretentions far away from me.'

Rathore rose from his seat, picked up the envelope from
the floor and tucked it back into his waistcoat. Barman noticed
two men in dark clothing sitting at a table at the entrance rising
simultaneously; he didn't realize there was an entourage.

Rathore started straightening his appearance, paying attention
to his sleeve and then his waistcoat.

'You have some notion that you matter in all of this? I came
here to try and reason with you out of courtesy for your reputation
but believe me, I did not need to. You may think we come from
different worlds, and, in a way, we do. But my world, Mr Choksi,
has a longer reach. We are like the roots of a tree – you don't notice,
but we spread underground far beyond where we appear to stand.'

He looked at Barman menacingly. 'I will give you one more
opportunity. I suggest you do the smart thing.'

Barman watched him leave, flanked by his two hangers-on.
When he had left home, he anticipated meeting someone, an alumni
perhaps, who wanted to contribute for the honor of having a bench
or a tree or a building named after them. At worst, he imagined a
parent trying to gain admission for a ward. This was something
else entirely. There was little left to do but try and push it out of
his mind.

~

It was not like Sareen to be unreachable; usually he would err on the more underfoot end of the reachability spectrum. But, six days had passed since that afternoon when Sareen had come to the house unannounced. He did not return for dinner later that night. Kabir called his home a couple of times but ended up speaking to Geeta Aunty who smothered him with syrupy affection through the phone line.

Surprisingly, Sareen showed up right on time. He seemed a little frosty, but they fell into their usual repartee.

They bought the same cell phones and headed to a park bench nearby to activate their new windows to the world. Their first call was to each other. The only other interesting thing on the phone was a game where a worm inched around the screen at accelerating speed and the player had to prevent it from hitting the edges. Uncertain how to broach the subject of Sareen's split lip, Kabir simply asked if everything was okay.

Sareen recounted the events of the night in question, which had Kabir enthralled. As the retelling got to the stupor and collective vandalism, Sareen thought he sensed disapproval.

Afterwards they both fell into a heavy silence. Kabir pictured a drunken, staggering Sareen, trying to fight. Although amusing, it was a disturbing picture. But he felt guilty about pushing Sareen out of the apartment. So he was careful at the tone he took, preferring to make light of things. Kabir had never seen that look on Sareen's face and he was keen to put it behind them.

'Wow that's a crazy story. Do you know where exactly you went and who punched you?'

'No. No idea.'

'Thankfully it sounds like no one you know saw you. You probably got away with it.'

'Yeah, probably.'

'What about these guys you were with, what do they say about all of this?'

'I don't know. I haven't spoken to them about it.'

'I would have loved to have seen that. Do you shout slogans before you punch someone? Or after you have punched them?'

Kabir couldn't let this opportunity pass to tease Sareen. It was too much fun.

Acknowledging his leg being pulled, Sareen smiled for the first time that day.

Emboldened, Kabir continued, 'I think this is probably the stupidest, most idiotic thing you have ever done. When did you learn to fight anyway? You're lucky you got out of there when you did.'

As these words were spoken, Sareen's face darkened. Kabir couldn't quite understand it. Sareen was always the jokester. He had often been called a fool – in jest, in earnest, with love and in passing, and it never really bothered him. But today, he looked resentful.

'It's not all bullshit, you know. There is a lot that needs to be answered for.'

'Answered for? What are you talking about?'

Sareen flared up, 'They are not like us, okay? They don't want to be integrated. They hate us. They smile to your face and can't wait to stab you in the back and twist the blade. Never mind, you won't understand anyway.'

Kabir looked at Sareen and shook his head in disbelief. 'What are you talking about? What don't I understand, huh? You realize that Mustafa is Muslim, you asshole? You forgot about him, did you?'

Sareen didn't respond. Surely Kabir had just served the coup de grâce and Sareen would be aptly chastened. But all this was very uncomfortable, and it needed some good old-fashioned distraction. Kabir got up into a stretch as if indicating that he had brushed off the entire episode; it was done and dusted. Sareen remained sitting.

'Don't say anything to Mustafa. I will tell him myself. Just say I got into a fight, that's all.'

'Well, your lip is almost healed anyway. Shame about your face, you're looking like you used to again.'

He picked up his bag from the bench and made a motion to move. They were supposed to meet Mustafa later to smoke a joint. Sareen lingered, gazing out unfocussed, contemplative.

'Come on man. Don't worry about it. It's done. Let's go get stoned. It will all be forgotten soon.'

Kabir offered his hand and Sareen grabbed it and lifted himself. It was the nature of these relationships. Nothing pulled them away from their natural center of gravity for very long.

Sareen seemed lighter from unburdening himself, but Kabir sensed that things were not quite resolved. But his mind did not linger. He was already planning the mixed CD he was going to make for Sahiba.

CHAPTER THIRTEEN

It was the night of Eid and as promised Kabir was chaperoning the TV crew through the bazaar.

Sunset kite-flying battles heralded evening celebrations in the old city. The sky was littered with chits of square kites. Combatants stood on terraces trying to entangle their opponent's string. A flick of the wrist would cut the line and victory was savored watching the untethered kite flap aimlessly to its inevitable fall to earth. As darkness descended, the crew made their way to the street.

A thin crescent moon now sat above the rooftops. The street was lit in the ubiquitous neon of the Indian cityscape. A festive atmosphere pervaded the market. Eateries were spilling out on to the street. The aroma of grilled meat intermingled with smoke from the coals. On offer were mutton and chicken of various marinades, but the specialties were goat softened by cream and steeped with cashew, cardamom and spices, cooked on a hot slab of granite – a remnant of the nawab's table.

Kabir closely observed the shooting and watched playbacks on the little screen. He had to restrain himself to keep from asking too many questions of the crew.

Small, gentle palms cupped his eyes. The familiar scent she used spun him around more excitedly than the mild surprise warranted.

'You came! How?'

'I snuck out.'

'Isn't Eid a big deal at your house?'

'It is.'

'Won't you get caught?'

'There were guests over. Hopefully no one will notice I'm gone early. Anyway, everyone will come down to the bazaar later, so I will find them.'

Kabir's looked incredulous. She couldn't help laughing.

'If they ask I will say I was with Priya. Now stop looking so worried. What's happening with the shooting?'

'It's almost done.'

'Okay good, now we can go see the shops.'

'I'm supposed to wait for Mustafa'

'Oh, come on, we will find him around eventually.'

Kabir said his goodbyes to the crew who smiled knowingly at the new priority holding on to his arm.

They poked their heads into little stores and joked with familiar street vendors. Sahiba found a stall with little necklaces and trinkets. She tried them on and asked Kabir's opinion. He stood around watching her, talking to strangers, content in the sway of things. Everywhere seemed to have a haloed glow. The dense mist of their coupling had settled on everything in his life – even cricket took on a supporting role (but not by much).

'Kabir!'

Mustafa had spotted him from across the street and trotted over.

'Where were you?'

'Oye. Looking for you.'

'Where? We were supposed to meet at… oh.' Mustafa spotted Sahiba.

'Hi Musty,' she smiled.

'Hi Sahiba. So you're the reason I have been looking for this idiot for the last hour.'

'No, no, we were looking for you,' she pleaded.

'I just saw Khaled with his friends.'

'Where?'

Mustafa jerked his head behind him. Kabir looked on questioningly.

'Khaled…' Mustafa said with an arched eyebrow.

Sahiba bit her lip. 'Yikes. We should avoid my brother. Let's go this way,' and tugged Kabir in the other direction. 'Mustafa, you coming?'

Mustafa took this as his cue to bow out. 'No, I'm heading home. Have fun, you guys.'

The courtship between Kabir and Sahiba had been slow and restrained at first. But of late they were constantly petting and holding on to each other. Mustafa gladly left them alone and headed home.

Kabir and Sahiba spent a little time in a quiet café where they could be alone and then they both drifted home in their honeyed happiness.

At home, their change in behaviour did not go unnoticed. At the Menons,' Prem was baffled at how Kabir managed to become even more disconnected and distracted than before. Even the slimmest cord of awareness to the outside world seemed to have snapped, debate hour was a distant memory and the permanently attached headphones were likely to be muddling that brain further. Radha Menon recognized the telltale signs and gently corralled Prem who was left staring open mouthed after Kabir had slunk in past the front door, not having heard his father's enquiry due to the volume on his Discman.

At the Baigs, Sahiba walked into the courtyard to find her mother and Alya. The others were all still at the bazaar. Zia noticed the faraway glaze in Sahiba's eyes. Over the previous few weeks, Sahiba's participation in the courtyard chatter had waned and she seemed to be in her own world. Zia had also noted her daughter's frequent glances at the clock earlier that evening. The little alarm bell in a mother's head chimed caution – it knew that this friendship with the Menon boy was something more and it could lead to trouble.

Physically, things had moved quite quickly and to Kabir's surprise, it was Sahiba who took the initiative. He found himself the other night in a small pharmacy pretending to browse at a glass shelf of featureless cardboard packets of pills. The silver haired proprietor behind the store length counter – who in this tiny space was barely ten feet away – looked like an uncle who was likely to call his dad. Luckily another customer diverted his attention and Kabir surreptitiously moved over to the young assistant who was stacking boxes. 'Hey buddy, do you have condoms?'

They were each other's firsts and once they got started, they moved to finding empty homes, rooms, friends' homes, restaurant bathrooms and behind trees after dark. Kabir was in love and he knew she loved him too. They had said it to each other plenty of times. She told him that when they parted she would watch him leave longingly till she couldn't see him anymore. Intimacy was a wonderland.

~

Exams were around the corner and that meant everyone saw less of each other these days. Kabir and Sahiba managed a daily meeting, usually in the evenings, sometimes twice a day. They had tried to study together but that just didn't work.

Once examinations began, time flew by. The economics tests were clustered together and ended quickly. Now all attention had turned to cricket practice – the HCA trials were close.

The remnants of spring were wilting under the mid-afternoon

heat. Practice was pushed till early evening and they would play as late as the light allowed.

Kabir packed up the kit and loaded it onto the back of the scooter to drop it off at Barman's. The boys lingered after practice to exchange notes. To his relief, he wasn't the only one undecided about the next step. Like others, he had dispatched applications to software companies, banks and other sundry businesses that left pamphlets at the career center.

It was dark by the time Kabir pulled into Barman's house. He parked the scooter at the back and slung the heavy kit bag over his shoulder. He paused under the drawing room window; light coming through the beveled slats formed three stripes on the ground in front him. Hearing voices inside, he gingerly set the kit bag down and lifted himself onto the ledge using the windowsill to hoist himself up.

'...is an important man in these parts, it is a benefit that he wants to participate... way things are done.'

It was Bhosle's voice.

Barman's reply was barely audible as he paced around the room. '...letting a snake in the door...'

Bhosle's default expression rarely deviated from a disingenuous, syrupy smirk. He sported a generous shock of rust orange hair combed over the top, the result of traditional henna hair dye remedies. Back and sides remained unadorned in an older man's more-salt-than-pepper. A man of the system, his great talent was endearing himself to people who mattered. It had enabled his rise through the system without any distinguishing academic abilities.

Kabir couldn't quite make out what was going on, except Barman sounded agitated. He ducked around the front to better eavesdrop.

'Choksi, this needs to happen. It's for the sake of progress – we must embrace the way things work at other larger colleges.'

'That's what we must NOT do. Sikandra University has always

retained its independence; it is one of our greatest strengths. If it becomes political like the other universities, it will kill its character.'

Bhosle chuckled mirthlessly. 'For a young man you are certainly caught up in the past. I thought you were a progressive. You talk in a grandiose manner about academic reform, but when it comes to cultural reform, you become orthodox.'

Kabir heard the soft shingle of ice in glass and peered into the crack of the door. It all looked perfectly civil – Barman was handing Bhosle what looked like a refill of his whiskey. Bhosle took it with both hands and sipped generously.

He continued, '…the donations as well as the enhanced profile of the university would have hugely beneficial effects. A professor like you need not worry about the day-to-day challenges of running a university. There are bills to pay, Choksi. Where do you think the money for the enhancement of cricket facilities will come from? Or the research grants you have been asking for?'

There was a light pomposity in his tone, a patronizing flicker in his pasted smile.

'Where it always comes from, Mr Bhosle – from college fees, from donors who want their names on buildings. We are not political and I, for one, will not stand by allowing it to become so. If Rathore wants to contribute to the university, let him donate legitimately. But he doesn't want to leave a paper trail, does he? Where do these funds really go? I doubt they will be spent making any research facilities.'

The tone of the exchange had turned brittle.

'Oh God, Choksi. Your sanctimony is tiresome. I have already wasted too much time with you. This is going to happen – Samrat will be given a ticket, whether you like it or not. We don't want to draw unnecessary attention, so we are asking you to co-operate and in turn, we will make it worth your while. Do not drag this any further than needed.'

'Bhosle, I won't do it. If you and your cronies try anything underhanded, I will expose this entire stinking affair.'

'No, that's not how this is going to go. I would be careful about making threats. Everyone has skeletons in their cupboard, everyone!'

Bhosle presented Barman with a paper folder and rose to leave. As Barman read through it, his jaw tightened.

'Is this a joke? What do you get out of all of this Bhosle? How much are they paying you?'

'Be careful, Choksi – don't stretch further than your reach.'

Barman stood glowering at Bhosle, who strode towards the door.

Kabir quickly moved away and hid around the back. He watched Bhosle's receding figure walk outside the compound and slip into the backseat of a waiting Ambassador car, which Kabir hadn't noticed before. There was another figure in the back seat. The crunching sound of gravel faded as the car drove off.

After a couple of minutes, Kabir crept into Barman's house to find his slender form sprawled on a rattan armchair. A warm orange lampshade lit the centre of the room and left the edges dark and brooding. The curl of smoke from a half-finished cigarette loped upwards to the lamp, extinguishing itself in a haze around the yellow bulb. Barman's shirt buttons were undone, a whiskey glass dangled from the edges of his fingers and the faraway stare made him look hazardous. Kabir remained unacknowledged as he perched on the sofa. After a couple of minutes, Barman poured himself another drink.

'Everything okay, sir?'

'How long were you listening?'

Kabir looked away, unsure of how much he should leave out.

Barman scratched his chin wistfully. 'The winds are shifting, Kabir. It's a good thing you are graduating. This place is going to change. Maybe it's the end of the road for me here...'

'Sir, what's going on? It's about the election, right?'

'It's about the team as well. They will take me away because I won't let their candidate stand.'

'What do you mean, sir?'

'They want me to put someone on the team, an ex-student. They want me to give him a sports scholarship.'

'They want him to play for college?'

'No, no. Only so that he can legitimately stand as a candidate in the student election.'

Kabir couldn't fathom why anyone would go through all the trouble for student body president. But not wanting to seem uninitiated, he nodded.

'Won't there be old records of this student?'

'They have changed the transcripts, I have the originals.' Barman half-nodded towards his room as though the secrets lay within.

'Who's doing this, sir?'

Kabir's wide-eyed concern snapped Barman out of his despondency. A little drunk, it took him a bit of effort to clear the fog.

'Look, I shouldn't have told you all this. Don't talk about what you heard today. Keep it to yourself... for both our sake.'

'We can fight them, sir, don't worry.'

'We don't even know who to fight and anyway, I think we are playing a different sport from them.'

Kabir's genre of life at university had been more young-adult satire than political drama. These machinations were like storylines from a matinee production.

'What are they going to do, sir?'

'I think they are going to accuse me of having done the very thing I refuse to do. Look, I want you to promise me you will steer clear of all this. Don't be a hero – stay out of trouble, alright? Now get out of here, I have things to do.'

Kabir nodded mutely. As he rose to leave, a manila folder caught his eye. It was the one that Bhosle had handed over and the catalyst which drove Barman's stance from combative to defeated. Barman noticed his gaze and put his arm over the boy's shoulder and walked him out the door. Whatever was in that envelope was important.

~

Kabir and Mustafa were biding their time at Sunshine Bakery. Mustafa sat back, rocking on the hind legs of his wooden chair. On the linoleum table was a plate of flaky chicken puffs, a Sunshine Bakery staple. Kabir was tense; he slurped noisily at a frothy cold-coffee concoction. His leg was tapping rapidly while Mustafa yawned, stretched and gazed blandly around the room. This half-asleep, belly scratching, disinterested dope was hardly the rousing musketeer that Kabir needed to galvanize his passion and focus his fire for the HCC trials today.

The minute hand of the wall clock seemed not to be moving at all and he couldn't take it anymore. Kabir jumped up.

'Okay come on, let's go.'

Mian Qadir waved away Mustafa as he reached into his pocket to pay and went up to Kabir.

'Good luck, son. Try not to think about it too much and just enjoy it. Play freely.'

Kabir grinned nervously and nodded. He piled into Mustafa's father's car and they drove over to the ground. Sareen awaited them at the gate and broke into an exaggerated jig. He seemed to be his old self again. At the ground, they wished him luck and stood a distance away from the nets where the trials were on.

Sareen spotted Rana warming up in the distance and shouted, 'Oye mountain… Stop shaving your legs! My granny wants her razor back!'

Rana came up to Kabir who was padding up to bat and grumbled, 'Why did you bring that idiot?'

'Just ignore him and concentrate on your game. Good luck, Rana!'

Kabir's trials lasted about an hour. There were students from across the city, each striving to get noticed. Quality was abundant and they all looked skillful and confident. The coach, dressed in a red tracksuit, was active and animated. There was none of the traditionally stoic, squinty-eyed, disparaging taskmaster. Here was a bouncy, encouraging, kneel-with-the-players, supportive-touch-on-the-shoulder type of interaction. It was from the hand-on-heart, modern age coaching manual. It looked bloody professional.

Kabir batted twice. The first time, the ball seemed to zip off the pitch as though it gathered momentum after the bounce. He struggled with these superior bowlers but managed to hang in there. It felt like a different game to what he played at the college nets. The second time he was better, more assured. His feet started moving instinctually, he started finding the middle of the bat and towards the end, he even played quite well. But was it good enough?

After all these years, it was difficult to imagine that his life's greatest desire would be determined by a passing glance and a few minutes inside a cricket net. Would the coach look at you when you played the best stroke of the day or when the opposing bowler felt it coming out of his hand just right? The fundamental randomness of that instant and the circumstances surrounding it would determine selection; how you felt earlier that morning, a passing gust, a distracting car horn, a conversation with a lover lingering on your mind – the pure chance of it all weighed heavily on Kabir.

The coach took the time to speak with each player individually – some at length, others only briefly; some with a smile on his face, others without. He chatted with Kabir about where he played and what he was studying but didn't call him back for another session.

Kabir sat on the grass, his kit spread out around him. He began to feel like the nets were moving further away; he was now a spectator. As he walked back to his friends and out of the stadium, he took a last look at the sliver of green turf. He knew there was going to be no callback. An extinguished dream felt like the loss of a companion, one who knew your frailties intimately; it left him mourning for something that never was.

The posse headed back to campus. There they sat on the field, chewing on fresh long stalks that grow between the grass. They talked of nothing much, without much else to do. They just spent time with the ease afforded to those unpressed by it.

Kabir was trying to unglue himself from the sticky realization that his cricketing career was now resigned to being a competitive amateur. He had told Sahiba that he would call her after it was done, so he peeled himself away from the group. Kabir hoped some sweet nothings would help balm his mood.

Sahiba was busy helping her family prepare for the arrival of some distant relations to their home the next day. She was distracted and to her, it was just cricket.

'...you told me that it was a long shot anyway. So it didn't happen, its okay. You will be fine.'

Kabir felt a flicker of irritation. This matter of fact, point-out-the-obvious response was not what he was hoping for.

His pause was long, born from a sulk.

Clearly preoccupied, she hung up with a quick, 'Babe, we will meet later okay? I need to go now.'

Kabir looked over at his gang sitting in a circle, laughing about something. The rest of that day was like old times – even Sareen had come out from under his dark cloud.

Towards the end of the night, they found themselves standing around a late-night canteen, awaiting their order of chicken rolls to soak up the excesses. A TV on the counter was showing the India vs Pakistan series being played in Canada (of all places), and Pakistan was in the ascendency. A group on the table next to them seemed a little stewed and in the mood for a skirmish.

These late-night college rumbles had a predictable sequence. It would commence with a snide quip or an undirected expletive, tempting players to engage.

Ears pricked at the occasional phrase spoken a little louder.

Sniggers. Sareen sneered, '...are you idiots talking about us?'

Kabir quickly tried to mitigate the situation with a quiet 'forget it, yaar'. By then, one of the boys from the other table stood up and made for them and Sareen jumped to his feet, eyes blazing. Mustafa stood quickly beside him.

Once the object of attention was baited, a circular movement began around each other. Each combatant was allowed darts towards the other but he mustn't ever come too close. Then some swing-and-miss bravado. Finally, the 'friends' make a two-step interception and pull the matador back and away. Right now, Sareen was being pulled away by his friends as was the fighting party from the other table.

At this point, the fighter is at his most vigorous; straining, pushing himself against the seemingly impermeable barrier of his friends to strike his opponent, make his point, teach a lesson. Usually both sides leave with pride intact, a scratch for the retelling and punches that never connected but air.

So it was when it played out this night until something unexpected happened. As the two sides separated and the opposing numbers were walking away, one of them shouted at Mustafa, 'Go back to Pakistan, you fucking mullah bastard!'

The otherwise mild-mannered Mustafa became enraged and charged after them. He caught up with the offender and flailed at his head and body with wild, unpracticed swings – a few blows landed but did no real damage. The boys bolted behind him and pulled him away. Mustafa's face was contorted into a frustrated, tearful rage. Their opponents had turned tail and fled, and Mustafa sank quietly to the floor. There he sat breathing heavily, face stained, shaking and staring straight ahead.

Kabir was concerned. He had never seen Mustafa react like that. 'Are you okay?'

Sareen returned from the chase, hitching up his jeans and laughing.

'You scared the shit out of those guys, man. Mustafa, what a dark horse you turned out to be! We should have you fight all our battles – Mustafa for president!'

He grabbed Mustafa's hand to raise it in victory, but Mustafa snatched it away and got up.

He snarled, 'Why Sareen? Don't you also think I should go to Pakistan? Those guys must be friends of yours.'

'Take it easy, Musty.'

'Why? Does it make you want to beat me up? Huh? Is that what you want?' Mustafa was practically yelling.

'I will, if you don't shut up.'

Kabir stepped in. 'Whoa, whoa! Nobody is beating up anybody.'

'Fuck you Sareen. You want so badly to be a big shot that you joined a gang who beat up old men. It's sick. You're sick.'

Fighting back tears, Mustafa grabbed his bag and took off.

Kabir and Sareen watched him leave. Kabir turned to Sareen, 'What was he talking about? Did you guys have a fight or something?'

'Fuck it,' the words were spat out almost to himself. He headed off in the other direction, leaving Kabir standing there.

THE WEST INDIES

There was a swagger about the West Indians. Any kid learning about the game was introduced to them with hushed tones and wide eyes. They held sway over world cricket for over a decade and were downright intimidating. For instance, every schoolboy batsman idolized Vivian Richards but very few dared to impersonate him; it was almost blasphemous. He was too cool, too damn good.

The islands and their way of life were so very far away for a boy from Hyderabad. When cricket was televized, Kabir would catch glimpses of impossible blues and verdant greens. He learnt that the islands were separate countries with their own political structures. But they came together for the noble pursuit of cricket under the maroon West Indian flag. It sparked a lust for exploration, a desire to travel and see these wonderments firsthand.

Paradoxically, these lands of 'take it easy maaan!' were also the most hazardous place to play cricket. Athletic, black, sand-dusted, beach physiques, wide smiles, slow baritone drawls and dangerous bowlers. The mettle of a player was measured on their performance in the West Indies; Sunil Gavaskar, the pint-sized Mumbai batsman, faced up without a helmet and became a legend. Mike Gattings' battered face and flattened nose (thanks to a fearsome Marshall bouncer) was the image that always made you flinch. Australia's triumph against them in 1995 was akin to the Greeks conquering Troy, the cymbals turned from calypso to a mournful Harry Belafonte lament. After all, it heralded the passing of an era.

~

Except for a few, more esoteric courses, final exams across the university had ended. It was that magical time of nothingness – results were awaited and there was little else to do. Kabir liked the calm around campus without the bustle of classes and schedules. Students hung around to meet friends and to find out where next to hang out.

From a distance, a white notice was attracting attention on the bulletin board. Kabir loped towards the action, his arm slung over Sahiba's shoulder.

From the Office of the Vice Chancellor

It is hereby notified that Professor Barman Choksi is under administrative review. All offices held by him will be managed through the VC's office till further notice. The History Department will publish the interim schedule of lectures and office hours.

The notice was highly irregular. Students were never allowed a peek into the machinations of the university administration. Teacher common rooms were protected by large wooden doors and were out of bounds. This proclamation had the makings of scandal – this sense was only exacerbated by the lack of detail and caused a wildfire of insinuation and conjecture. Students formed salacious clusters around campus. As the enigmatic bachelor on campus and the cricket coach, Barman aroused a lot of interest.

'I heard Barman slept with another professor's wife who then killed her husband.'

'I heard he was secretly running a gambling racket.'

'… not just a gambling racket, he is part of the underworld.'

'That's rubbish, it's just some stupid formality.'

Kabir, with Sahiba in tow, rushed to Barman's home to find a group of men rifling through his documents. Upon enquiry, he was told Barman was meeting with the board and it was none of their business who they were. They went off to the offices hoping to encounter Barman there.

Normally the chatter of university folk would bounce off the cool polished stone. Today there was a strange, sinister stillness in these central halls. Meetings were underway behind closed doors and the administrative offices were visited and exited by older, important looking men. Kabir and Sahiba stood in the first-floor gallery hoping to discover what was going on, but they had no chance of gaining access to the impenetrable administrative offices.

Kabir, inflamed by a crusader's zeal, felt it his duty to set the facts straight and did the very thing Barman asked him not to. Kabir went full sermon-on-the-hill to whoever would listen.

Most of the cricket team was loitering around the ground and he tried galvanizing them to help spread the good word, but some were skeptical. It was one thing to stand by the coach but implicating the senior administrators could get them into the kind of trouble they could do without.

'Guys, isn't it crazy?' Kabir would begin.

'Yeah, no way can this guy be on the team.'

'Not just the team man. They want him standing for elections!'

'Yeah, it's unbelievable.'

'So we should do something, right?'

'We definitely should. What do you have in mind?'

'We can all go to Bhosle.'

'Nothing will happen. He won't even listen to you.'

'We should definitely do some kind of protest. We can even put it in the press.'

'I'm not getting involved in that, Kabir. I just want to graduate peacefully.'

'Come on guys, this is important! We need to do something.'

'Are you mad? I'm not fighting the university administration. They could expel me!'

Adding to Kabir's frustration was the fact that he was unable to locate Sareen whose bluster would have been an invaluable asset in this time of need.

The day softened into early evening and the college canteen started emptying. Kabir watched students walk away from campus and a melancholy came over him. His days of belonging to this world were almost done and this affair with Barman had a foreboding sense about it. Sahiba had gone home, and he seemed to be the only person left on campus. As darkness fell, he grudgingly made his way home with a disconcerting sensation in the pit of his stomach.

That evening, Prem Menon came home as usual, showered and slipped into his white kurta-pyjama. He was sipping on Black Label with ice and soda when Kabir skulked in through the front door, his face betraying the anxiety disquieting him. Prem followed his son to his room and found a surprisingly responsive, headphone-free, young adult in the erstwhile body of his son. Later, they sat in the living room and Prem had a rare heart to heart with his boy. Radha kept to the fringes for a while, acknowledging that her presence may inhibit this father-son chat, but she soon joined them. Prem was grateful for her softer perspective.

Kabir felt an unburdening as he narrated the events of the past few days. His parents listened patiently. Their expressions were attentive to implication. Only the tight pressing of their hands betrayed their unease. For Prem and Radha, any ethics around this matter were clouded by concern for their son.

'He shouldn't have told you in the first place,' Radha murmured.

'But Mama, he trusts me!'

'It's not your fight, son; its Barman's. You are not in a position to do anything. You shouldn't have said anything,' Prem Menon seconded his wife.

'But he's doing the right thing… if not for him, we would have anyone just put into the team or as president and it would ruin the university.'

'Look, there are usually two sides to every story, we don't know the other side so we can't jump to…'

'He has evidence!! What other side is there?!'

'I know you mean well, Kabir, but you need to distance yourself. I'm afraid that the administration will hear what you have been saying and it will turn out bad for you.'

'I can't believe you guys! I'm going to go to the press.'

'Kabir, enough! We don't know what part Barman has had in all this.'

Kabir couldn't imagine he would need to be defending Barman

rather than reproving his detractors. He needed help to extricate Barman from the situation; instead, he was being told to distance himself. It was agonizing. He expected his parents, the paragons of fair play, to galvanize to this cause. Instead, they were more concerned that his graduation may become compromised. No resolution was found, and that night Kabir stayed up, tossing and turning. It was the first time in his life that his parents did not have the right answer, the first time he disagreed with them on a substantive matter.

Prem had been around long enough to know when to fight battles and when to lie low. Kabir needn't fight one now. Contrivances took time and haste was usually detrimental. He grappled with how to get through to his young son, how to explain that only fools rush in. But what unsettled him most was not the goings-on at the university but the insidious atmosphere around it. Sareen had been a part of their home for years. Kabir had just told them about the boy's slide towards these new sinister friends. Prem could smell trouble brewing. As a boy he remembered the riots in Calcutta and recalled the poison spreading like blotting paper – it had wrenched the future from the young. The thought of Kabir being swept up into all of this made him breathless with dread.

CHAPTER FOURTEEN

It's the sound which first lifts the spirit; a light patter followed by drumming on tin, splatter on stone. Initially sharp and scattered, then rising, reverberating, thudding.

The earthy smell of moistened dust punctuated the air as the first monsoon rains hit dry parched earth. The busy market street emptied almost immediately, leaving only a cow on the road, languid and impervious to the drenching. The rain sweetened all things.

Mian Qadir's black umbrella matched his black shoes, which otherwise contrasted against his white clothes. He hopped along the edges of the storefronts to avoid the wet splatters falling from awnings onto the street and ducked into his shop.

Mustafa was caught in the sudden downpour. He hurdled over puddles towards the warm safety of Sunshine Bakery. His hair dripping, shirt clinging, he shook himself off once inside – much like a mutt would – and perched opposite the long suffering Mianji who handed him a towel to prevent puddles forming on the tabletop.

Shuffling nervously in his seat, Mustafa knew that this request to meet, more like an instruction, had a serious import, but he had not the slightest clue what it concerned. Mian Qadir removed his glasses slowly, deliberately.

Taking a deep breath, he began, 'Son, have you thought at all about taking a role in serving your community? We need young men such as you to lead us into the future. To represent our interest and protect what we stand for.'

Mustafa stared back blankly. Mianji continued, 'Well, you should. You are a sensible young man with a bright future. You are a credit to your parents and your community. Maybe you can spend time with me, and I can start showing you the ropes.'

This made Mustafa uncomfortable; he preferred being the quiet, studious boy in the corner. The prospect of community engagement gave him visions of starched politicians, public speaking and a lot of hand pressing. This was much too far from his comfort zone.

'I don't know, Mianji. It's not really my kind of thing. I just want to be an architect.' Wilting under Qadir's stern look, he added imploringly, 'Maybe I can help build something for the community when I am a certified architect?'

'Your generation is fortunate not to have seen the violence that we saw. Mobs claimed the right to our homes, you know. To this day, there are those who call us foreigners in our own land. But if we look to revenge, spite and anger, then we are lost. That's why we need intelligent, sensible young men... men like you.'

Mustafa had heard this tome, but it was someone else's story. There was no time for religions narrowing identity today. Who cared anymore? Y2K, gaudy liberalism, American TV and beauty queens defined his generation. He, for one, was not going to spend his life, his youth, hankering after an identity, a religion, which didn't define him. But Mian Qadir was an elder and Mustafa would not dare argue or try and prove him wrong with constructed factualism. It was not done. He nodded obediently and promised to think about it.

~

Khaled Baig had driven Sahiba, Ruksana and Fatima to a forested park on the outskirts of the city. It was a beautiful overcast afternoon and a firm, fresh breeze heralded the onset of monsoon. The girls giggled as their scarves swept across their faces and they walked on the red clay paths around the forest.

Later, Sahiba sat with Fatima on the low-walled embankment of a lake, their legs dangling off the edge. They watched the layers of lashing clouds advance from a distance. Ruksana's quest for ice-cream had pulled Khaled away, giving Fatima the opening she needed to be alone with Sahiba.

'How're things going with Kabir?'

'Good. Actually, really good! He's so sweet!'

Fatima had met Kabir a couple of times, albeit briefly, and found him markedly different from the other 'Sahiba suitors'. Initially nervous about meeting someone from the family, Kabir soon warmed to Fatima and charmed her with his easygoing disposition. To Fatima, he felt like a safe and nice boy but she wasn't sure about how involved her younger sister was.

'That's great, but where is this going? Is it serious?'

'I don't know, didi. I mean it's great but I don't know where it's going. It's still early for it to be serious, I'm just...' She checked herself as she turned to Fatima, who looked quite serious.

'Why? Why do you ask?'

'At home everyone speaks as though we are open-minded and worldly but in reality we are still a pretty conventional family. Your parents seem liberal – they drink, speak English, travel the world, but they come from a different era. For them these are all things that happen to others'

'What things?'

'Oh, I don't know. Independence, love, sex. I mean sometimes I think they themselves are confused about what they believe in...'

Fatima sighed wistfully, speaking to a distant audience. She continued, 'When push comes to shove, in my experience, we fall back into convention, fearful of what our forefathers would say, what other people will say.'

There was a pause. Sahiba put her hand on Fatima's. 'Is that why they don't talk about your "friend"?'

'Yes, I suppose. And it's why you need to be realistic about yours and the reaction it will trigger. Your dreaminess has not gone unnoticed and there has been gossip. The other day the neighbours came over and mentioned it.'

Sahiba was put out, 'I wish people would mind their own business... What did Ammi say?'

Fatima laughed, 'If people minded their own business, what would we have to talk about? Anyway, I wouldn't worry about your mother. She's cool. For some reason, it was our young *shehzada* (princeling),' Fatima jerked her head towards the direction Khaled had just gone, 'who seemed a little put out. All I am saying is that don't expect people at home to think like you do. They are likely to be less open-minded than you think... and please, no surprises. You are being careful, right?'

Sahiba nodded and sat pensively for a little while. 'You know, I think Khaled is the one that really needs a girlfriend,' she said in mock annoyance.

'He DEFINITELY needs a girlfriend!'

They laughed just as the clouds burst above them.

~

Kabir loved getting drenched in the downpour. The city cooled but the rain itself was warm and inviting. Cricket practice was cut short, but he stayed back with some of the boys. They were busy launching themselves into running slides on the submerged outfield when he spotted an animated Janardhan Seth standing at the equipment shed. He was marshaling his groundsmen who ran around covering the pitch and putting away equipment.

'Sethji, how are you?'

Not one for cheerful greetings, Janardhan continued stacking the heavy rope from the outfield. He took his time to acknowledge Kabir, 'Not so good', he said brusquely.

'Sethji, have you met Mr Choksi? I have not seen him since the notice went up.'

'I have met him. He is staying away from campus at the moment.'

'But what has happened? Why is he suspended?'

Janardhan paused, apparently considering the question. 'He has been accused of taking a kickback. They say he was enabling sports scholarships for students by putting them on the school team.'

It was a sacrilegious suggestion. The team was sacred, and nobody held the torch higher than Barman.

'WHAT?! That can't be true. There must be some mistake, right? There is no one on the team who doesn't deserve to be there, and Professor Choksi would never!'

Janardhan replied emphatically, 'Of course, it can't be true! It's those new bastards in the office – they are the ones behind this dirty business.'

'What can we do? We must do something right? Should we go speak to Bhosle?'

'He's not going to listen to you, boy. We will do something, but we need to wait for a while till things settle down. I'm talking to some people. We will make something happen.'

Janardhan's confidence was reassuring. He knew how to get things done. The thought of Barman not being the coach, of him having to leave the university, was all too unreal. These absurd allegations all pointed to a giant misunderstanding. Kabir was relieved. It would all sort itself out in the end.

~

Things at home had been awkward since the big talk about Barman.

Everyone was walking on eggshells except Sakshi who didn't care for the laden atmosphere. She barreled into the pregnant silences with her customary cheek, 'Why is everyone being so weird?'

Cavorting in the rain had lifted Kabir's mood and he required a change of clothes. Hoping he could slip in and out unnoticed, he crept up the stairs to the apartment. As soon as he opened the door, he found his father looking somber with an officious looking manila envelope in his hand.

An academic show-cause notice: *Due to false allegations propagated by him and for disturbing the harmony between students and teachers* – whatever that meant.

Prem had received a phone call from the university administrative office telling him that Kabir was the ringleader and would face severe scrutiny.

'Kabir, we are worried about you.'

These words always rankled Kabir because it bestowed on its speaker a carte blanche to berate, opine or instruct without bearing any responsibility for what is said next. After all, they are worried about you – it's about you, not them.

'It's all a big mess. Barman has been caught taking kickbacks for giving out sports scholarships – this complicates everything.'

'Papa, they are lying. There isn't anyone like that on the team.'

'If you are found guilty, you will be expelled. You don't graduate and you get no degree.' The tone barely masked Prem's rising anger. 'They want you to come over to the office and sign a letter admitting you made false allegations. You will do it, you hear? No more of this vigilantism.'

Radha sat next to her boy and gently took his hand in hers. 'It's the best way to sort all this out, beta.'

The injustice of it all was infuriating. This pandering by his parents was tinder to the simmering cynicism of a twenty-one-year-old boy. He asked through gritted teeth, 'What will happen to Barman?'

Prem, anxious and exasperated, barked back, 'It DOESN'T MATTER what happens to Barman, damn it. You are not to see him again.'

Kabir was now glowering. A lump formed in his throat and with a shaking voice, he screamed back.

'IT DOES MATTER. You're only principled when it suits you. When I stand up for something, you don't have the guts to back me up.'

'KABIR!' Prem's eyes blazed in fury. 'Don't you dare talk to me like that!'

Radha tried to pacify her son and put an arm around him, but he jumped up and headed out of the apartment. He caught Sakshi behind the wall, listening in – her wide eyes looked afraid, as if something seismic had shifted the world.

Out on the street, he caught his breath. He had never raised his voice to his father before. Flooded with shame and torment, he started running.

Kabir ran almost all the way to Sahiba's home and told her everything. He found solace in her arms, but his mind remained prickly. He needed resolution, he needed to talk to Barman and figure out what to do. Knowing Barman spent many evenings at Sheer Mahal, they decided to try and find him there. Kabir called the cavalry for assistance. As was usual these days, there was no sign of Sareen, but Mustafa promised to join them later.

The rain had cleared; the air was still and moist. Up on the terrace of Sheer Mahal, an intermittent light breeze gave erratic relief from the stickiness. Kabir wrestled with a heavy wrought iron standing fan, aiming it towards where they were sitting. The loud gusts from its forceful rotor made it pleasant to sit outdoors. There was no sign of Barman, so they decided to order something and wait it out.

On the table sat a plate of roasted peanuts drizzled with lime juice and ground spices. Next to it was a perspiring beer and two glasses. Sahiba took only a few sips – it wasn't her favourite drink and she needed to be home soon for dinner. Conversation turned to the world outside, the lives they were destined for, where they would like to live, where they wanted to travel together. Kabir wanted to move to Australia or South Africa, pursuing the appeal of sun-kissed beaches and cricket grounds. Sahiba was happy to spend a few years in the US but in the end, Hyderabad was home.

While they chatted lightly about weighty matters, they felt closer, allied. The steady rhythm of their lives was changing rapidly. They were graduating soon. Events of the past few weeks had created a fair amount of uncertainty and as they held hands, they were glad to have each other as constants.

In that moment of sweetened daze, Kabir blurted, 'We should just run away together.'

Sahiba turned to him with a sparkling grin, 'We should, we really should. Where would we go?'

They made epic plans and traced itineraries that made Vasco de Gama look like a comfort class traveler. It was as if they were the only two people in the world, time slipping away – till Sahiba looked at her watch. She had to run home for dinner. Snapping out of their reverie, they considered that Barman was likely to be a no-show. She got up to leave and they hugged intimately, lingering. Kabir stayed behind to wait for Mustafa.

Alone now, he looked out at the view and rested his arms on the balcony wall. Talking about running away made him think about the excitement of that night in the bazaar with the TV crew. He was beginning to seriously consider options away from the traditional drudgery of law or banking. But the idea of a career in TV was so far removed from anything he knew, it felt almost irresponsible. His mother's cousin was in the film business, but he wasn't sure what she did and that was the closest he came to having a film connection. He had imagined that he would get a graduate degree at some point, so there was no need to settle into anything permanent yet, surely? As he contemplated these avenues, he heard a noise in the street below.

Although the sun had set, there was still an hour or so of light before the streets changed to pools of phosphorescence. The area was a warren of connecting alleyways, barely wide enough for a car to pass through. This made for a limited line of sight. Pushing his weight slightly atop the wall, he tried discerning what had caught his attention. People milled about, no more or less urgently than usual. Suddenly, there it was again, an unmistakable sound of breakage. A pause, then shattering glass, the noises coming in intervals. Gradually, voices became audible in the distance. They grew closer and more voices added themselves into the mix, their tones betraying alarm and confrontation. Other heads started to pop out of windows to see what was going on.

From the small patch of street visible to him, Kabir first saw a couple of men running, looking over their shoulders. Then some more men came through and turned to see what was coming behind them. The voices were now shouts. Sloganeering mixed with battle cries and the pitch of individual skirmishes. Then came the body of the disturbance, a group of men, maybe eight or ten, armed with sticks and what looked like machetes. Haphazardly they set themselves on the odd shop or street stall. Their unpracticed clumsiness would have been amusing if not for its sinister intent. More shouting and suddenly another body of men came rushing behind them, scattering them. This devolved quickly into individual combat.

Kabir gawped at the scene, as did others from the safety of balconies and windows. Something familiar caught his attention. He recognized the gait and manner of one of the assailants. He had his back to Kabir and was quite a distance away but as he turned, it was unmistakable – Sareen, holding a stick, trying to get away from a combatant. Kabir panicked as another fighter rounded on Sareen. He bolted down the stairs.

Street level was chaotic with people running here and there without any clear definition to the violence. Sareen was bent over and pulling himself away from the two assailants, one had a hold on his shirt, which was pulled almost up to his shoulders, and the other was trying to land an upper cut to his face. Kabir barreled into them – his momentum caused their grip to come free, and he now stood next to a disheveled Sareen, facing the other two.

Knees slightly bent, arms outstretched, Kabir tried to assuage the situation, 'Let's all just calm down, shall we?' He stared back into bloodshot, unforgiving eyes. Before he could put his thoughts in order, Sareen came out of his blind-spot with a hockey stick and swung it knee-high. Kabir watched with horror as the opposing number buckled. His partner backed away from the swinging weapon and as the stick finished its arc, he timed his lunge. Kabir intercepted Sareen's attacker with a swing to his face as hard as he could and connected with a crunch.

In that instant, time slowed down. He saw other combatants take note and move menacingly towards them. Now there was no question of pacification. He was all in. Kabir figured that the first crumpled adversary wouldn't be able to chase them. The blow had landed on the side of the knee. His own punch had splattered blood, with the sickening sensation of skin and bone on tooth. But most of all, he noted the acrid stench of disorder in the air – it smelled of charred wood and burning plastic. All this was inferred in a fraction of a second, until Sareen grabbed his arm and shouted, 'Run!'

As they spun around, Kabir was pushed and felt a punch glance his cheek. It did not land well but it still caused his head to spin. At close quarters, the scuffle was more grabbing and pushing. In the jerkiness, rush, and desperation to extricate himself, Kabir was punched once more in the ribs. Suddenly, he was free and in a wide-eyed sprint away from the scene. Running alongside Sareen, he heard sounds of people giving chase from behind but dared not turn. 'Here!' Sareen pointed, and they gathered their pumping legs into short rapid steps to pivot into another alley. The edges of their feet skidded as they leaned sharply to take the turn. The terror of being caught and the adrenalin spurring them on. At times, their pursuers seemed to be an arm's length away and any second, Kabir expected a sickening thud from behind.

After another couple of sharp turns, Kabir saw a door ajar in a recessed doorway. He grabbed Sareen and ducked into it. In the dark, they stayed quiet, holding their breath, their senses on edge. The scuttle of running feet was interspersed by an occasional yell. They waited, hidden inside the doorway, for what felt like a few hours, and then it became silent. Darkness had descended, aiding their concealment. Eventually, they gathered the courage to peek out. They found themselves in a deserted alleyway, away from the shops and the bustle. This was a lane of small offices and traders and there was no sign that anything untoward had occurred.

Stepping out, Kabir was in shock. He had never been in a fight before. Adrenalin still hurried in his veins.

'What the hell was that, Sareen? Who were those guys?' His voice was louder than he had intended.

'I don't know, we were attacked!'

'Who's we? And what the hell were you doing there anyway?'

'I was with some friends, and we were attacked. We split up and then I saw you.'

'So, some guys just came up to you and started attacking you without any reason?' Kabir was shouting now.

'Yeah, I mean I was with friends, and they ran after us. It was mad!'

Unconvincing and slippery, Sareen twisted the question to evade a straight answer. Kabir knew this to be classic Sareen. It had never bothered him before. But at this moment, it was downright unbearable.

'Fuck you, man. I don't know who you are anymore.'

'Relax, Kabir. It's okay. It's not a problem. Nothing happened, right? We are fine, right? Stop stressing about it.'

'What did you do, Sareen?'

'Nothing! We were only doing what someone should have done ages ago. Let's just get out of here, they may come back.'

'Why should I? I haven't done anything wrong, I just prevented you from getting beaten shitless.'

'Come on, man. Let's just go.'

Sareen reached for Kabir's arm, but he snatched it away.

'I don't know what you have been doing but I have nothing to do with it.'

'I just don't think it's safe to head back that way right now, okay?'

'You go on Sareen, get out. I don't want to look at you right now.'

Sareen opened his mouth as if in protest, but changed his mind. Eventually he just said, 'Suit yourself,' spun around and trotted off in the opposite direction.

The streets had swallowed the chaos – like they always did. The colours of conflict mixed into their character. Kabir walked with trepidation through the lanes where the noises had come from. He noticed shopfronts wrecked, cracked glass, street vendors with overturned carts. Tobacco stores were smashed, their anatomy spilled out as cigarettes littered the road. A butcher's store was vandalized, the blood from a recently slaughtered goat splattered across its walls in a fiendish drizzle. Smudged footprints of blood trailed onto the street.

The shopkeepers were silently cleaning up the detritus. Their entire lives were invested in the shards they now swept away and the debris they collected off the ground. It was heart-wrenching watching them work silently, mournfully.

Something Sareen had said came back to Kabir, 'Someone should have done this ages ago'. This was a Muslim area and the dawning comprehension of what had transpired made him sick. These were folks he had grown up with – his uncles, his friends, his people.

Yet they looked at him differently – their faces hardened as he walked by. The hair at the back of his neck stood up as he took stock of himself. His shirt was ripped, his arms scratched. He caught a brief reflection of his face, which was muddied and slightly bruised, and began to worry. He wanted to help and lend a hand. He wanted to tell them it wasn't him, tell them he wasn't like that. But he could feel an uneasy static in the air. He needed to get out of there. He slipped into an alley as quietly as he could and gathered pace till he started running.

~

He sat on the cinema hall rooftop. There was never anyone up here – it was where they got stoned before watching a film. At this height, the glow from the hoardings waned, unwilling to go higher. A cacophonic orchestra of horns, cars and hawkers drifted lightly upwards, echoing the animation of the street below.

Kabir felt soiled. He wished he could wash it off; he wished he could turn back time; he wished he hadn't seen Sareen when he did.

Sareen was his best friend. It was impossible not to have seen this coming. Did that make him responsible? He racked his brain for signs he may have missed, clues he may have ignored.

His phone chimed with a text message:

Hey im really sorry where r u I rlly need to talk

It was from Sareen. He ignored it.

A few seconds later:

I have been an idiot I feel really bad

and then:

Im just really confused right now lets meet please

Texts came rapidly; then the phone rang – it was Sareen. Kabir disconnected and typed back furiously:

don't message me don't call me

He felt soiled and culpable. Kabir needed to free himself of this burden. He called the only one he could trust to understand all of it.

Mustafa came immediately. As Kabir paced and seethed, Mustafa just sat there, nodding his head sagely. He didn't lash out at Sareen as Kabir expected, he just took it all in and stayed solid, constant.

Slowly Mustafa shifted the topic, gently drawing Kabir away from the gnashing. He didn't think anything good would come from dissecting it over and over again.

~

As the men of the recently vandalized bazaar shuffled in, they were met with suspicious looks from the constabulary. Traditionally, the languorous ease inside the police station repelled any urgent pleas from inconvenient victims, but their sheer numbers right now created consternation.

Petty pickpockets waiting on the benches tried to blend into the background for fear of being recognized. The body of men moved into the Superintendent of Police's (SP) office to file their complaint. Mian Qadir led the delegation.

Sitting behind a large, file-laden desk, SP Singh was younger than many of the inspectorate lurking in the halls outside. Here was a man who had rapidly risen through the ranks as a high achiever. He felt a sense of déjà vu, watching these men line the back walls as their representatives took the chairs opposite him. Having been posted in multiple districts, SP Singh had seen a version of this at every posting. Clan, caste, class, religion dotted the graph of his experience and skirmishes differed in name but remained the same. Thankfully, he was not faced with men baying for blood. Like the streets that nurtured them, these men understood the eternal nature of conflict. Resignedly, they filed into the secretary's office to document their individual grievances.

The discussions around next steps were circumspect. Something needed to be done before more vandalism incited a retaliatory response. SP Singh understood that this was what the perpetrators sought; it was essential to move quickly.

There had been little forewarning of this recent flare up. It pointed towards a single political individual, looking to make his mark. The easiest path to notoriety was to prey on disaffected youth. It was that heady instant charge, the opioid of statecraft.

The conversation between SP Singh and the elders lasted for forty-five minutes. Mian Qadir was duly impressed by the maturity and intelligence displayed by this young policeman. The task of gathering names of the miscreants was shared within the community.

Outside the station, Mian Qadir stood to acknowledge each person who came. They gently touched their hearts and whispered their greetings and thanks. As the last of them dispersed one of the younger members of the congregation, Qadir's nephew Moin, took him aside for a word – he had a black eye.

'Mianji, I recognized some of the boys from that night. A couple of them are well known to you. That boy Kabir, who is always in your shop, was there along with his friend. I don't know if Kabir was part of it from the beginning or if he got involved along the way. But his friend was one of the guys who…'

'Sareen.'

'Sorry?'

Qadir sighed.

'His friend's name is Sareen. I knew his father well. In fact, both their fathers are close friends of mine. Look Moin, keep this to yourself for now.'

'I will, Mianji, but someone else may have recognized him.'

'Yes, thank you for telling me, son. I will look into it.' He patted the boy's arm affectionately and walked away, his lips pursed in concern.

∼

Things moved quickly. News travelled fast and events crashed into one another. Murmurs of politics replaced the market gossip; suspicions and distrust between communities grew and the institutions seemed implicit in it all.

A few days after the trouble in the bazaar, the police assaulted a young Muslim leader in the old city, who was campaigning for the opposition. Rumours abounded that it was done at the behest of the ruling political dispensation. Resulting suspicion of the police led to hardened hearts within the community and Mian Qadir's moderation was questioned.

The usual free gaiety of the streets was replaced by a sullen purposefulness. Vendors, traders and customers went about their business with little time for conversation.

Prem Menon sat drinking tea with his old friend Qadir. The last few minutes had been spent discussing the atmosphere in town.

Qadir turned to the topic at hand. 'Prem, I think the boy was in the wrong place at the wrong time, that's all. But things are not good right now. There could be people who may have recognized him. After the news of the police action the other day, there is a mood for retribution.'

'I can't believe it, Qadir, it's so unlike him. It has been difficult to get through to him. He's in his own world these days.'

'He's of the age, Prem – don't be too tough on him. I heard about events at the college, they must be taking a toll.'

'Yes, yes, but he's being a fool. We didn't have the luxuries to gallivant and play at things we didn't understand. In our time, we had to buckle down and listen to what we were told.'

Qadir smiled reflectively. 'Maybe your memory isn't what it used to be, my friend. We all had our times when we strayed. But Kabir needs to be kept out of this neighbourhood for a little while till things calm down. The vandalism has enraged people and God forbid, he is caught by the wrong sort. Also, someone needs to talk to that Sareen boy.'

'I tried speaking to his uncle – that man is a damned fool. It's no surprise that Sareen stays out of the house. As for his mother, she can't fathom her son is anything other than that sweet twelve-year-old boy. Anyway, I will try and speak to Kabir, but he may not listen to me.'

'Yes, you might be right. I will call the boy and lay it out for him. *Ya Allah,* what a mess all of this is. He shouldn't have to skulk around. But leave it to me. I will let you know how it goes.'

'Can't you reason with the police and just nip this in the bud? A few arrests and we should have things back in order. Once they cut off the head of the snake.'

'The trouble with the police is that you don't know which side they are batting for.'

The two men smiled ruefully and sipped their tea.

~

Sahiba entered the courtyard of her home to find the women of the house gathered around her brother. Missing was the usual tinkle of conversation, instead their faces wore masks of censure. Something was amiss. Fatima's face was knitted with concern. Her mother led her to sit with the others. Holding Sahiba's hand in hers, Zia narrated what Khaled had just told them all.

He had come to learn that Kabir was in a gang, which led to the vandalism in Jaffar Ali market the other day. He had been spotted beating up Muslims and destroying shops.

Her mother ventured conciliatorily, 'We know he is a… good friend of yours from college and you spend a lot of time together.'

'Yes Ammi, but there must be some kind of mistake. He's not like that at all. There isn't any violence in him. I don't think he has even been in a fight in his life!'

Khaled cut in curtly, 'It was definitely him, Sahiba. You know there is a gang now with some boys from Sikandra University, running around being thugs? There are those flyers pasted all around campus –'

'Yes, but no one takes them seriously and also Kabir has nothing to do with that. He's very anti- –'

'Sahiba, he's not someone we can trust. How do you know what he gets up to outside of university?'

Khaled sounded aggressive and Sahiba didn't like it.

'I know better than you do, Khaled. And anyway, where have you heard all of this from?'

'We have business in that market, and I have been keeping an eye on that guy. I don't trust him.'

'Keeping an eye on him?! What the hell are you doing keeping an eye on him? You don't know what you are talking about!'

Sahiba looked around imploringly to the women for some support. She was surprised that this home of matriarchs stayed silent.

Her mother ventured in a placating tone, 'Beta, we are concerned. It would be better to keep your distance for a little while. We don't know all that much about this boy and things are tense at the moment.'

'But Ammi, he isn't like that! Really! Ask Fatima, she has met him. She'll tell you.'

Fatima let out a slight squeak as if to speak but no-one seemed interested in her opinion.

Sahiba grew more animated in defense, 'Ammi there must be some mistake. Kabir is not involved in any –'

Khaled cut her off. 'Enough, Sahiba! You are not to see him anymore. We can't have someone from this home being seen with those thugs.'

This enraged Sahiba. Khaled was only a year older than her and they had grown up as equals. Ever since he started working in the family trade, he had started throwing his weight around. It was largely ignored and put down to his growing phase. But today he was speaking as though he wielded some authority over her.

She yelled, 'Who are you to tell me who I can see and who I can't? Why don't you mind your own business?'

A hush fell across the courtyard. Her outburst had sounded a little hysterical and she knew it. Tears welled up in her eyes as she saw the futility of this exchange and she ran into her room. Fatima ran in after her.

AVARICE

Ever since the 1996 World Cup, the slot machine of sponsors and day/night matches accelerated the avariciousness of cricket organizers. Meaningless tournaments with no antecedents popped up in the service of multi-national companies salivating at the potential of a billion customers. Whichever team had a spot of time between doing better things turned up. There were a lot of matches against Zimbabwe.

The transmission was dusty, sepia toned and without aesthetic. Featherbed pitches bred some bits-and-pieces talent. Even the comforting crack of ball striking bat was replaced by a damp sounding thud.

For the fixated, it remained essential to watch, live and breathe these one-day travesties, but they yearned for the test match – where real legends were made.

India hardly won anything in those days. On overseas tours, they were particularly poor. There was however, the odd bright spark. Of special mention was the debut test match for Saurav Ganguly and Rahul Dravid. On a gloomy, chilly afternoon at Lords, both youngsters caressed the ball repeatedly to the boundary. Ganguly wore an air of entitlement and had the kind of gumption that gets under the skin of the opposition. Was this the sign of things to come?

~

Prem left his son alone. Had he tried engaging with him, he would probably sound insensitive, aggressive, or simply not know how to say what he needed to say. This would lead to another brawl. But tomorrow morning was the academic hearing and he needed to ensure Kabir showed up.

In turn, Kabir had avoided being home as much as he could. He had spent a couple of nights at Mustafa's and when he did come home, he tried to slip in and out unnoticed.

Radha kept tabs on him and reassured Prem that everything was fine. In fact, he was with Mustafa when his phone rang and 'Papa' flashed on the screen.

'Uh… Hello?'

'I hope you are coming home tonight. Tomorrow is the review and you should be there early. It's important. I'm sure you understand that.'

Even when trying to be accommodative, Prem couldn't keep the rebuke from his voice. Perhaps Radha should be doing this. Kabir was silent for a moment.

'Kabir?'

'Yes, papa.'

Prem heard the reluctance in Kabir's voice. He was unsure whether to tell him that Barman had called twice or to wait till Kabir got home. Hoping it would soften his son's affront, he ventured uncertainly. 'Listen, Barman called for you a couple of times. I don't think he knows you have a mobile.'

'Oh. What did he say?'

'I didn't speak to him, your mother did.'

'Okay, I will be home later. I'm with Mustafa right now.'

'Okay, not too late.' He paused and added, 'Please' before he hung up.

Kabir turned to Mustafa, 'I don't know what to do, Musty.'

'I don't think there is much you can do. It's not a smart idea trying to fight this battle yourself. I don't think Bhosle will think twice before kicking you out.'

'But what have I done wrong? They can't prove I said anything. It will be the committee and not just him alone, they might listen.'

Mustafa was getting impatient by his friend's lack of sense. It was obvious what he should be doing. 'Why are you trying to be such a hero? Listen, you don't even know what happened. Just do what you need to graduate. Later on, we can figure out what to do. Just get your degree first.'

'I didn't think they would come after me like that.'

'Obviously they were going to come after you – you went around telling people that the VC was a fraud. Just do the smart thing, okay? Also, Barman will probably just agree to do what they want, and all of this will blow over. He may not be sacked, after all.'

'He won't do that – I know he won't.'

'Well, it's not on you to save him all on your own. Anyway, you can't do anything in this case, so why be stupid? Just tell them you got that information from Barman and apologise.'

'But I'm not alone, I told you Janardhan will...'

Now Mustafa was really exasperated. 'So where is he, huh? Where is Janardhan and his army? If he was going to do something, don't you think he would have done it by now? It's as if everyone is seeing the light except you!'

Kabir couldn't argue with that. It had been all-quiet on the western front – there was no sign of Janardhan's cavalry. He saw the rationale, but when he imagined himself standing in front of the committee and physically mouthing the words, it felt like betrayal.

He needed to speak to Barman – it was the only way to solve this.

'Come on, Musty. Let's go talk to the Prof. He might be home and we need to drop the scooter back at some point.'

Reluctant at first, Mustafa eventually came around and off they went. As they rode out towards the campus, the busy streets eased into empty, leafy roads. The wind whizzed past their ears. Kabir tried to find a cricket analogy to parallel this injustice and it came to him almost immediately.

The injustice of Darrell Hair vs Muralitharan. A few years ago, the Sri Lankan team was touring Australia. In their ranks was a short, spindly, weird looking kid – with big eyes and a crooked elbow. Muttiah Muralitharan with his dark skin could have been the poster boy for the dollar-a-week, bleeding heart brochure of the third world. Darrell Hair was umpiring that game and stood a foot taller – a large, white, stock-of-the-Empire type man. If there were ever polar opposites in humankind, it was these two.

Kabir recalled watching in confusion as Darrell Hair repeatedly no-balled Murali for no apparent reason. The world cricket authorities had legitimized the unusual bowling action as an accident of birth. But here was this white-man-authority-figure who appeared to be making an example out of him. As though the Sri Lankans with their unorthodox quirks needed to be schooled in this game of Empire. It was an insult to these proud cricketers. He could never reconcile that despite this high-handedness, no action was taken against this pompous man. The incident dented his faith in the assumed fairness of cricket (and life). In Kabir's world, it just didn't make sense that the wrong was not righted when the evidence was so clear.

The boys pulled up to Barman's house and saw the windows open. They found him standing in the middle of his study looking at a stack of files scattered on the floor. It seemed they hadn't been cleared since the ransacking from a week ago.

'What happened, sir? We tried to find you when we heard the news. What did they do? We have been talking to the students. Most are behind you, sir, don't worry. We will create a demonstration on –'

'Kabir, I have been trying to get hold of you. I heard what you did and I know you think this is helping me but its not. You need to stop all this, I told you to stay out of it. They will expel you – so don't be a fool.'

'But, sir, we can't let them do this!'

'It's already done. I have resigned. I will finish the term and leave.'

'But sir –,' Kabir implored. 'They are making it out as if you accepted bribes for allowing boys into the team. If you resign, everyone will believe the lies. It will ruin your reputation.'

Silence passed without the need to punctuate it. Each of them needed a moment to process what was happening.

With a slowly drawn breath, Barman looked up at Kabir.

'It's not a lie. I did do it. It was many years ago when I first took on the team.'

Kabir stopped short. 'Sir, what are you saying?'

'I'm saying that it did happen. Not in the way they are portraying it happened, but it did happen. I helped a couple of students get scholarships by giving them spots on the team.'

Kabir couldn't believe what he had just heard. He glanced at Mustafa whose face betrayed what he was thinking – 'I told you so'. As the sequence of implication formed in Kabir's mind, he ventured timidly, 'Did you take… money?'

The boys shifted forward, imperceptibly.

'No, not exactly. But there were favours done for me. It was a different time then – the concept of buying seats did not exist. It was different.'

So far Mustafa had been respectfully quiet, but Barman's reply was too vague for his diagnostic mind.

'What favours?' he blurted out, sounding fractionally impertinent.

Barman sighed. 'Well, small things… I was living off campus at the time – one of the parents made furniture, so I got a couple of chairs. Someone bought me a bicycle. That kind of thing.'

Kabir was less concerned about the monetary value of the gifts and more with the sanctity of the cricket team.

'Were they substitutes? They would be good enough to play at least one –'

'No. They were never actually in the squad. They didn't play a single game.'

'But then why sir?'

'I was just starting up here. Their parents couldn't afford the fees, so I thought I was doing the right thing. I stopped doing it because people started turning up for a free ride.'

Mustafa still hadn't closed the loop. 'So how did they find out all these years later?'

'It wasn't a secret. It was during Professor Ramaswamy's time. I had discussed it with him when it got out of hand. I was officially reprimanded but as I said, it was a different time. It's probably documented deep in my file somewhere. What surprised me was that someone would bother going through all that to dig it up.'

'Sir, it was a long time ago. We should still fight them back.'

Barman smiled mildly. 'I don't think I can carry on here, Kabir. It's time for me.'

'But what about the team? What will happen to them? What will happen to our rankings if you leave?'

'They will find someone else.'

Barman's attitude was grating. After all, the team meant something – it went beyond a job or a vocation; it was about loyalty and their tribe. Kabir couldn't understand how Barman was so dispassionate, so blasé about this when he was the one who drilled these virtues into the team. He was meant to maintain the tradition, irrespective of graduating classes and real-world jobs. Once you were in the team, you were always in the team, right?

They shuffled out without a parting salutation – there was nothing left to say. Kabir felt unmoored. It was as though the essence of Barman had left behind a body, a prop, which looked like his coach – but wasn't. Was there something he had missed?

Kabir saw himself as the gullible, naïve, teacher's pet who proclaimed the coach's innocence all over campus. But he was not dwelling on the act itself. The money or the favours did not cut him as very important. What bothered him was the easy surrender. Somehow the 'having done' was part of life, but the 'not continuing, not doing' confused him.

As he plodded home, his conflict with his father was forgotten. The meeting with Barman overshadowed any scuffle worth carry on.

CHAPTER FIFTEEN

The academic review was distasteful. Reprimanded and shamed into signing an apology, Kabir left the offices cowed. The featureless academics in the room, those slaves to filing in triplicate, lacked any sense of the abstract. As if there could be no nuance, no circumstantial properties to things – Barman had committed the sin and in the way of binary morality, it was unforgivable.

Kabir's enforced penitence left him hollow. The spartan logic of it all didn't ease the feeling of disloyalty. Stabbing fingers apprised him of the committee's charity – 'You are lucky, young man!' He was not expelled; he would graduate and get on with his life. The punishment meted out was in line with this awful narrative – Kabir was off the team and could no longer finish his last season for the university.

Once he was out of the room, he carried with him the weight of betrayal. His mind kept repeating his damning words of apology, not able to fight the feeling that he had directly implicated Barman somehow.

Usually, before he left campus, he would walk past the canteen to catch up on goings-on. Today he walked straight out. He pulled out his phone. Texts to Sahiba had gone unanswered. They had not spoken for a couple of days. He called her again and her phone rang until it didn't. She may be 'talking' to someone else. It was the first time Kabir felt possessive. An involuntary knot of jealousy drew like a weight in the pit of his stomach. He tried reasoning it away, but couldn't help his mind careening through possible scenarios. He shook off the feeling as best he could. Just as he was thinking of turning up at her house, his phone rang. It was Mian Qadir.

Half an hour later, Kabir found himself at Mian Qadir's home. His visits here were rare. Usually, it was with the family on a religious holiday or a formal occasion. Memories of the place were clothed in a clean white kurta, sitting on clean white bolsters on the floor. Today, dressed in several-days-worn-jeans, he felt unsure of leaning on the spotless low-seated platforms.

He would normally meet with Mianji at the bakery, but he was firmly instructed not to go to the bazaar and come here instead. Something was awry.

Mian Qadir sat cross-legged opposite Kabir, looking down, reading some sort of official circular.

'Son, I heard about the trouble in Jaffer market the other night. Do you know anything about it?'

Kabir tried suppressing his rising panic, 'I don't know what exactly you are talking about.'

Mian Qadir folded up the circular slowly. He took off his thin-rimmed glasses, placed them by his side and shifted to face Kabir. Looking him straight in the eye, 'I know you were there, Kabir. I know what happened, so you can drop the act.'

Kabir's heart sank. He did not want Mianji to think of him as one of those people. Worst of all, Kabir had tried to keep it hidden. A confession's restorative properties were no longer open to him.

His mind was unable to formulate a response that could explain why he had become involved. He couldn't pin it all on Sareen either.

'Mianji, I... it wasn't my fault, I just...'

As though reading his mind Qadir asked, 'Why didn't you tell someone? You could have told your father or me! And why did you lie to me just now?'

'It was not me, Mianji. I was waiting for Barman, and I saw something happening. Then I saw Sareen getting attacked so I tried to stop it. But then I don't know how we got into a fight and ran.'

'Didn't you see what was going on? I really don't understand you kids. You think this is some sort of game that you play and then you move on to the next thing? This has serious implications, Kabir.'

Qadir's voice did not rise but his words were spoken through gritted teeth. Kabir had never seen anything resembling anger on Qadir before.

'But what was I supposed to do?'

'You shouldn't have been involved in the first place. It's a real mess – you were seen that night and recognized. There is a lot of anger towards those who did this. You need to stay away from those areas – it's dangerous right now. In fact, better to lie low altogether. I told your father to move you away somewhere, but he insists that he can watch over you at home. Now listen to me, boy; go straight home and don't show your face around till all this blows over.'

Now Kabir was terrified in earnest. This meant his father knew.

'But Mianji, I didn't do anything! Can't we explain that it was a misunderstanding or something?'

'Don't be an idiot, boy. No one wants to hear that right now. Angry people cannot be reasoned with. I will do my best to smooth things over and put your case forward but you need to be away and out of sight.'

'Where will I go, Mianji? What am I supposed to do?'

Staring into his lap, he couldn't think of what to say next. His head throbbed, completely at a loss for how he could sort this out – this royal mess, not even his own. Kabir's body slowly slumped.

Mianji looked pitifully at his dejected figure. He rose and put a hand on Kabir's shoulder.

'I know this is not your doing, son. You would never be tied up in something like this, but there is mischief afoot. I don't want you getting caught in the crossfire like your friend Sareen has been.'

'He's not my friend. I'm nothing like him.'

'But he *was* just like you. That boy needs help too. I want you to tell him to come and see me. Maybe I can reason with him…'

'I'm not speaking to that guy.'

'You will speak to him because I'm asking you to. Now go straight home, your parents are worried sick and I don't blame them.'

Kabir left Mian Qadir's home, incredulous at the day's events – and it wasn't even lunchtime. Although Mianji's prophetic warnings were concerning, they seemed exaggerated. Hiding and skipping town happened in movies, not in Hyderabad, and certainly not to him.

Despite a morning when he lost his place in his beloved university cricket team and was potentially exiled from his home, what bothered him most in that moment was that Sahiba hadn't called back. Sitting in front of Mianji, he had to restrain himself from checking his phone, but now that he was outside, he whipped it out immediately. Relief coursed through him as he saw a missed call from her and a text:

sorry something came up, I tried calling you back

It was a little less emphatic than he would have liked but he was glad for it all the same. He dialed her immediately and she answered on the second ring.

'Where have you been? I have been calling and texting! You won't believe the day I have just had, and I really wanted to talk to you about it. You should have called me back.'

'Relax, I was busy, okay?'

He didn't intend to sound demanding, and he didn't think he did, but Sahiba's tone was brittle. It threw him off a little.

'Umm okay, sure. I… it's just that a lot of strange stuff has happened, which I need to tell you about.'

'I heard.'

'You did? What have you heard?'

'Why don't you tell me what happened?'

Kabir launched into a blow-by-blow account of what had transpired, starting from the time she left him waiting for Mustafa at Sheer Mahal. He told her about the fight on the street and then of Barman's confession. Then he told her about the morning he had just had – the university committee and Mian Qadir's warning.

When he tried engaging her in the substantive bits, she sounded a little bored.

He felt like he betrayed Barman was met with a disengaged 'it's okay'.

He couldn't believe that he wouldn't play for the team again, should he appeal to the committee to allow him to? 'You could, I guess... Up to you.'

Kabir paused. Why was she being so distant?

'Sahiba, what's the matter? Is something wrong?'

'Tell me what happened that night after I left you.'

'I just did...'

'You're sure you didn't start anything yourself?'

'Of course not. You know what Sareen is like. I saw him getting beaten up, so I went to help. Then they started running after me. I only figured out what it was all about later.'

Sahiba sighed heavily.

'I wish you had told me immediately so that I had known.'

'Everyone is saying that. Mianji scolded me for not telling him as well. But what's the matter? What happened?'

Sahiba described the incident at home with Khaled. It had become a regular topic for the women of the house who discussed it like gossip. Comparisons were made, unrelated analogies were stitched together and usually the beginning had nothing to do with where the narrative ended. They would talk as if Sahiba was not even in the room. Hearing outlandish theories was frustrating and embarrassing but she knew better than to object – it would be futile. She had to let it pass.

'But you don't believe that I would actually do something like that, do you?'

'No… No, I don't. But what am I to do? Nobody is listening to me!'

'What should we do?'

'I don't know, Kabir. I think we need to stop seeing each other right now.'

'Why?! I haven't done anything wrong. Let me come over and speak to your family, I'm sure they will understand.'

'No, no, please don't, this is not a good time – it will only make things worse.'

'Sahiba, what are you saying? Do you want to break up with me?'

'Of course I don't, but I don't know what else to do –'

Her voice cracked. The effort it had taken her to keep her composure was telling. Kabir's outrage softened instantly. He was relieved that she was emotional. It meant that she cared.

'Sahiba, I love you, I can't imagine not being with you.'

Sniffling on the other side of the line and then a reassuring 'I love you too.'

Now spurts of giggles in between bubbling tears.

They spent the next hour on the phone clawing back the few days they had lost. New promises were made, and declarations assigned. They hadn't discussed the new realities of Kabir's life, but he didn't care. She loved him. The lightness returned and all was right side-up again.

The issue of her family was left unresolved. Kabir did not place too much emphasis on it primarily because he wished the unpleasantness away. He assumed that in time it would all sort itself out. He would speak to Khaled and try to reason with him. Till then they would meet clandestinely, which suited him just fine.

~

The next morning had stillness about it. Missing were the routine morning calls of fruit vendors and newspaper delivery. Something was amiss. It was as though unseen forces were swirling outside the walls and the best thing to do was to hunker down.

Kabir tried Sareen's number – it went unanswered. He still resented Sareen, but had been instructed by Mian to sort things out. Anyway, he figured at some point things would resolve themselves and Sareen would come to his senses. A little while after that Prem received a call from Sareen's mother.

Geeta Amil was in pieces – the police had shown up at their door and taken Sareen to the police station for questioning. Unused to dealing with the machinations of the outside world, Geeta was in great distress. Prem spent a long time on the phone trying to calm her down. The Menon family sat around him, intently listening to his side of the conversation. He promised to make some calls and get back to her as soon as he could.

Mian Qadir was on the way to the police station himself when he received Prem's call. The night had been restive and there was news of fresh skirmishes. Vandalism had been reported in several areas and Qadir had been called in to help make sense of it all. He himself had only recently become aware of the trouble and he had very few details. Prem told him about the call he had received from Geeta. Their conversation was rushed – there seemed to be people pressing Qadir on the other side of the line. He promised to call back soon and warned Prem to stay indoors.

Prem locked the front door and called his offices and instructed them to close. Sakshi and Kabir couldn't remember their father taking a day off. Whatever was said over that call, it had the omens of something Prem feared. The sound of latching the front door lent gravitas to the room.

Prem turned to Kabir. 'Now son, tell me exactly what happened the other night.'

Once again, Kabir narrated the events at Jaffar market, expecting to be admonished. Instead, he was heard patiently, and the family closed ranks around him. The trivialities of any earlier conflict were extinguished. They discussed the sinister developments. What worried them most was the fact that Kabir was implicated. Would the police come for him too? Would there be retaliation?

Prem looked out of the windows of the living room, one at a time, reviewing the street below. He latched them as he went around. Suddenly a forceful knock rattled the front door. It startled the Menons. Prem held his arms out as though to instruct everyone to stay still. Then again, a heavy knock.

A voice muffled through the door, '...Kabir?'

Kabir knew that voice – he opened the door to find Mustafa looking quizzical.

'Hi! Your bell isn't working,' Mustafa said brightly.

The oblivious, bespectacled, floppy-haired Mustafa was comic relief to the mounting suspense. Radha laughed and hugged the boy. They set upon him with questions on what was going on.

He had not noticed anything irregular. He travelled by auto rickshaw as per usual and had his nose buried in *Batman – Legends of the Dark Knight* (book 12). Come to think of it, there were fewer people on the road and maybe some of the stores were closed. But there were no signs of rampaging mobs or anything like that. The atmosphere in the Menon household caught him by surprise.

Kabir explained the events that had transpired over the morning and Mustafa's face fell – 'I should go home'. But Prem Menon wouldn't let him leave. He called Salim Reza – Mustafa's father. Prem left the room as the two men fell into a lengthy conversation.

The phone at home rang and Kabir answered. It was Geeta Amil again. She sounded a little unmoored. As usual, she gushed at Kabir about how much Sareen loved him. For a few minutes, she reminisced about the early days when the boys used to get up to so much mischief.

'But now things are different and Sareen means well, he really does – it's just that he is impetuous sometimes, you know what he's like. Just like when he was a boy. He doesn't mean anything by it,' she offered helplessly.

Geeta slurred a little as she repeated herself, 'You know, you are like a brother to him. He needs you, you should speak to him, little Kabeeroo, hmmm?'

She clearly had little idea of what her cherubic son had been up to. Kabir wanted to get away from this conversation. He did not want to become Sareen's conscience. At the moment, he found it hard to think of him as anything other than the villain of the piece. Thankfully, Prem strode back into the room and took the receiver.

The rest of the morning followed a strange pattern. Prem spent all his time on the phone, trying to pick up signals from the outside world. There was nothing on the news and whatever little information there was, dripped in sparingly. Everyone sat around, waiting for a sign of what to do next. Then Kabir's phone rang – it was Sareen.

'Hello... Sareen?'

'Yeah hi...'

'Are you okay? We heard you were taken by the police. What did they ask you?'

'It's fine, they asked me a few questions about that night and about the elections and stuff. Don't worry about it, Sardar has connections – they can't do much to us.'

Kabir didn't know who Sardar was and was not interested in finding out.

'Did they ask about me?'

'I didn't tell them about you. They aren't looking for you.'

'Were you alone? Did they beat you up or anything?'

'Nope, they wouldn't dare – there were a whole lot of us there. Also, there isn't any evidence. It's just those damn shopkeepers who complained, so they had to round up some people.'

Kabir had expected Sareen to be a little cowed. He imagined

that being hauled in by the law would be a wakeup call. Instead, Sareen sounded arrogant and almost spoiling for a fight.

'Listen, your mother has been calling – she's worried and you should call her. Also, Mian Qadir wants you to call him. He wants to help you get out of this mess.'

'Qadir? I don't need help from that old goat. He's as bad as the rest of them.'

This infuriated Kabir. 'Again with this "us" and "them" nonsense. Who do you think you are, all of a sudden? Qadir has known you your whole life – he was a friend of your father's. You need to get your act together, man. What's with all this posturing? We are all just trying to help you.'

Sareen sneered icily, 'Thanks for the advice, Menon…You don't have a fucking clue as to what's going on. Just mind your own business and stay out of it or you might get hurt.'

One testosterone slight begets another – so Kabir snapped back, 'Oh, you think you are some kind of gangster now? You're full of shit, Sareen.'

'Whatever. Bye.'

Sareen hung up, leaving a smouldering Kabir, who could not get the last word in. Mustafa sat next to him, shaking his head philosophically.

~

The afternoon calm revealed none of the portents of the night to come. Prem slipped out of the house to investigate. Streets were eerily quiet and the market near the house was shrouded in an ominous silence. Shop shutters were pulled down and traffic was limited to the lonely bicycle and the odd taxi.

The only other movement was a pamphlet softly sailing on eddies of the breeze. Prem picked it up and noticed several strewn around the place. Large black writing smeared these fragile squares of paper. They looked hastily drawn up as though printed by a hand shaking in anger. Two colours of paper – pink and green, written in Urdu and Hindi, pitched one side against the other. Ironically the message was the same. It was a rallying cry to protect their kin from the forces that would harm them. Religious debate was intrinsic in the tapestry of this multi-plural city, so it was not uncommon to see declarations of community. But the venom in these little flyers of hate was exceptional. These were calls to arms.

~

Mian Qadir was walking through industrial back alleys – he had only been to this district once before and was unfamiliar with it. Warehousing sheds and metal shops dominated a drab brown cityscape, rendering the air acrid with the smell of soldering metal. Qadir's nephew Moin, had received news of some Muslim youth gathering with intention.

Entering through the backdoor of a large shed, Qadir walked into a cavernous space. He came upon a group of twenty or thirty young men, many of whom he recognized. Clearly his presence surprised them. Bloodshot eyes and fatigued faces were hardened by purpose. He felt great sorrow. His hand involuntarily went to his heart in traditional salutation. Many of the boys reciprocated the greeting, looking sheepishly at this elder who had caught them in the act.

Sizing up the temperature in the room, Qadir knew better than to exhort the group. In amongst these men were those who used such opportunity to galvanize power. He gently went around the room, occasionally touching the arm of boys whom he recognized.

Addressing the group, he asked for their loyalty. He reminded them of their families and the impact violence could have. Mostly, he feared for the consequences this would have on their youthful lives.

The boys listened quietly, obediently. Some faces barely masked a snarl but most just looked exhausted. They heard him out without interruption as a sign of respect. When he had spoken his piece, one of the boys stepped forward, 'We need to protect ourselves, Mianji. If they come again, we will not turn the other cheek. Now you must go.'

All Qadir could do was look at them beseechingly. Debate was futile. He nodded and made to leave. On his way out, he noticed a pile of rudimentary implements in the corner – makeshift clubs and axes with sharp metal edges. They looked flimsy and jerrybuilt as though made by an unpracticed hand. But they bore a devilish aspect, and seeing them piled in the corner made Qadir picture their sickening intent. He thought of crushed bone, sliced skin and gnawed flesh. He was afraid.

~

Barman was in his new first floor apartment overlooking a leafy street. The dappled light filtering through the leaves swayed up and down the room. He was fairly contented with the new lodgings except the limited space for his books and reference material. Not having found storage for all the papers, they remained in piles on the floor.

Listening to the rustle of wind through the trees outside, he imagined himself the protagonist in exile. Over the years, he had made great efforts not to become emotionally invested in his students. He justified it with ideals of 'correctness'. He thought of how many times he attributed events to the 'way-of-things,' thereby avoiding active participation. He recalled his supercilious superiority towards his colleagues and peers.

Flashbacks from his youth illuminated the tributaries of cause and effect. An early, lonely childhood in a boarding school. Surrounded yet isolated. An expectation of a stiff upper lip and to get on with it. A good education and a firm hand. Role models found in libraries and pages, but not in life and people. It had seeded an aversion for sentiment. Getting close to people made him anxious for fear of not being good at intimacy.

He contemplated the cowardice of his own cynicism. Unwilling to lower himself to the level of those he felt beneath him, he had become a parody of the very same armchair intellectuals he derided. He had refused to explain himself, brushing off the investigations of lesser men. Affronted by the slight on his character, he had chosen the high road and resigned. Now, here he was, pride somewhat intact but toothless and unable to affect anything but his own principals.

He could feel himself becoming forgotten.

As he chastised his own foolish conceit, he felt a burgeoning resolve – a feeling he had not had for years. If he did not stand up and fight, then what was he worth?

Barman decided to go and speak to whoever would listen. But first he needed to make amends – invigorated, he called Kabir to meet him on campus.

~

Sareen pulled on the chillum and the sticky smoke filled his throat. Exhaling slowly, he watched one of the guys tie a cloth strap to his head like in karate films. 'I bet he thinks he looks dangerous in that', he sneered to himself. A group of men sat around the same room where he was first inducted into this gang. They were awaiting instructions.

He didn't know why he was there exactly, but he didn't mind being there either. Things had happened and now he was part of them. The seeming lack of consequence over the past few weeks had emboldened him. Cocksure and confident, he felt bullet proof. Untouchable. This heady, coursing, testosterone was reason enough. It was a purpose in itself.

Today was a pivotal day. The antagonism after the Jaffar market incident and the pamphlets had caused the desired backlash. It was also Election Day at university and their group was expected to turn up and 'show solidarity'. This was code for intimidation.

Sareen considered those around the room. He saw no common ground other than their lust to fight. These men brought with them independent frustrations, but here they were galvanized into a single force. It was their path to belonging.

~

With Janardhan's help, Barman managed to cobble together a small platform and microphone outside the central building where votes were being cast. There he gathered the candidates standing against Samrat and propped them up to speak. News of his appearance had caused a stir and students flocked to see the spectacle. A polite, lethargic applause followed candidate speeches, with each making the requisite promises of timely repairs and better canteen food. But the crowd had gathered to hear Barman.

Sensing the restlessness of the collected youth, Barman stood up to speak. He began with a full confession and then went on to lay bare the events which had led to his ouster. He steered clear of lofty ideals and principles, sticking to the facts of the case. Once he was done, he paused. As he gazed out at the faces of the crowd, he felt an ownership of the moment. He realized he was looking out at what really mattered in his life's work. Right there in that moment, he could fashion the very narrative that he had spent his life proselytizing and teaching.

He continued, painting a vivid picture of what was happening to their beloved university. His clipped accent, trusting eyes and evocative timbre made for moving oratory. Gathering momentum and emotion, he beseeched the students to vote with their conscience and hearts. He implored them to shed the fear that came wrapped in the menace of 'these outsiders'. He held his audience captive in the palm of his hands. The cheers punctuating his declarations were getting louder.

Kabir and Mustafa had used the opportunity of Prem's absence to sneak out of the house. Having received Barman's text, despite whatever was going on in the world outside, they had to be on campus. They arrived just as the fervour was picking up and watched transfixed as Barman spoke.

It was then that things began to deteriorate. At first, no one paid attention to the odd squeals. The occasional shouts were undecipherable and were mistaken for declarations of support. But soon the shouts became screams. Barman looked out from his vantage point. He saw the edges of the crowd crumble and caught the first glimpse of the swinging rods.

Pandemonium descended rapidly. The attackers looked like swarthy and battle-hardened men as they scythed through the students towards the podium. Indiscriminate cracks resounded as bamboo and metal hit bone and muscle. Boys and girls were beaten and kicked, hair was pulled, and clothes were ripped.

As the crowd stampeded, many were caught under friendly feet panicking to get away. The ground began to show the first splatters of blood. The students stood no chance against this organized attack. Unarmed and unprepared, they fled, and were pursued by what seemed like a burgeoning number of assailants.

Mustafa and Kabir were both knocked down to their knees but managed to crawl away with minor bruises. As they got up, they looked over to the podium. Barman stood his ground as attackers rounded towards him. Students who looked prepared to fight flanked him and the boys lost sight of what was going on in the crush of bodies around them. Kabir pulled Mustafa away, but as soon as they reached open space, they were spotted and chased. They ran away from the madness as fast as their legs could carry them.

Kabir knew to go behind the equipment shed – they could hide there. It was a fair distance off and they did not look back or slow down. By the time they slid behind the shed, they were heaving and it took them a long while to catch their breath. This was the second time in his life that he was evading a gang, and both times within a week of each other.

'What the hell is going on???'

'It must be the same guys from Jaffar market,' Mustafa spat.

'Did you see what happened to Barman?'

'No...'

'We have got to go back.'

'Are you crazy?'

'But we can't leave him, Musty,' Kabir pleaded.

'Okay, let's see what's going on, but we have to do it carefully.'

Using hedges and trees to hide themselves, they cautiously made their way back to the center of campus. A couple of students came running from the direction of the main building. Mustafa jumped out from behind a tree, startling them. He asked them for an update. In their version, the men swinging rods and clubs were local goons. The police were now on the scene, and everybody had scattered. The cops came out swinging themselves and anyone they got their hands on was being arrested. In fact, if they knew what was good for them, they would get off campus. Rumours had already started that there was serious trouble in the city and a curfew was imminent.

Kabir suddenly broke into a sprint. Mustafa took a moment to register and went haring after his friend.

The normally quiet front lawns wore the air of a spent battlefield. Beige-clad police stood around a blue metal van with bars on the windows. Some men sat scattered on the ground, but otherwise the place was deserted. The constables, at first, did not notice Kabir as he dashed out from behind a cluster of trees. By the time they did, Kabir dodged and flatfooted them. He jumped up on the back door of the van as it slowly lurched forward and peered through the bars. Barman sat right at the other end, facing him. He was handcuffed and flanked by what looked like friend and foe. Shirt and hair disheveled, his eyes widened as he saw Kabir. Shaking his head in alarm, he mouthed something. Kabir felt an arm pull him off the van and throw him on the ground. He watched the metal box raise dust and gather pace away from him.

~

Mustafa's kindly demeanour had negotiated Kabir's release from the hairy arms of the inspector. They were cautioned to go straight home. Taking a longer route, the boys avoided hotspots, but they could smell burning rubber in the air. Running around the bend into Kabir's street, they came upon a large group of his neighbours huddled together. Harried faces were teaming up to keep the neighbourhood safe.

A roster of watch duty was being drawn up. In case trouble found its way into their streets, plans were drawn up to protect the women and children. The veteran general who lived two buildings down asked the group if they had weapons. A few hands went up – these men were automatically chosen as the guard. Doors were bolted urgently and windows were boarded up.

Thus far Kabir had managed the series of calamitous events without dwelling on them. He had dealt with things by putting one foot ahead of the other. Proceedings had seemed removed from his real life – until this moment. Here it stood brazenly as his gentle neighbours banded into a middle-aged militia. The sight created a physical revulsion and the sensation of unsteady ground beneath his feet. The world, taken for granted, was coming unstuck. Just a few weeks ago the things he had held to be unshakeable now seemed like a fragile chimera. His neighbours, whom he called uncle and aunty, were collecting kitchen knives to drive into the flesh of trespassers.

And who were these rioters? Boys and men clustered around TV sets in the market, watching Sachin Tendulkar. Together they would chuckle at a choice description of the portly opposition captain. Together they drank tea and offered up their last cigarette.

Involuntarily he edged away, wanting to distance himself from all of this. Mustafa noticed that Kabir was no longer by his side. He turned and saw a faraway look in his friend's eyes.

'Kabir... what are you doing?'

Kabir continued walking backward.

'Hey! Where are you going? Don't do anything stupid, it's not safe.'

Kabir ran to his cycle parked at the back of the buildings. He jumped on and pedaled furiously. As he swung a left away from his street, he heard the shouts of Mustafa and some of his neighbours calling out to him. It only made him pedal faster.

CHAPTER SIXTEEN

Street lights were flickering on as the fading light cast a dusky patina. There was an expectant air over the largely deserted streets. It felt like the quiet before the first notes of a recital.

He waited for Sahiba around the corner from her home. They would often meet at this small, ruined mausoleum. The entrance was padlocked but they knew an easy way up over a wall. It was secluded and they could be alone. He had called her in agitation, and she agreed to come at once.

They clung to each other, having not met in a while. The look of desperation on Kabir's face concerned her. He told her about Barman's arrest and the trouble on their side of town. The news had spread, and her family too was staying indoors, locking doors and waiting for the tumult to pass.

'How did we get to this? There are people we know in the middle of it. I always thought things like this happened to other people. I had never imagined it would come so close to our lives.'

'People are taking sides, Kabir. Even my friends in college have strong opinions.'

'Everything seems to have gone crazy. People think I have something to do with this. I have been advised to leave the city and

I'm beginning to think that it may be a good idea to start afresh somewhere.'

'That may not be such a bad idea, Kabir. Where would you go? Bombay?'

It was not what he wanted to hear. Kabir had hoped that Sahiba would be opposed to him going away. He had hoped she would convince him to stay. He wanted to hear that they would find a way to work it out.

Feeling more dejected than he had thought possible, he mumbled, 'Yeah, I have an uncle there and it would be easier to get a job there to start with...'

'Hmm.'

Kabir mustered up the courage to say what he needed to say. He felt a mixture of excited nerve ends and dread. 'Sahiba, that's the reason I came here. Let's go together. We have talked about it before, why don't we just start afresh? We can move there and figure out whatever we need to. It will be an adventure and we can build our lives together – won't it be cool?'

Sahiba remained quiet. After what seemed an age, she murmured, 'That's sweet.' She smiled, as though playing along.

'I'm not joking, babe. I mean, life here has turned so sour. It's better to start somewhere new. Plus in Bombay there are so many more options. We can get into the TV world maybe – who knows?'

She continued smiling but didn't respond.

'Sahiba, I need you. I can't do this on my own. We said that we would run away together and now is our chance! Let's just do it.'

'Kabir, I can't just run away with you. My home is here. You're very sweet but you can't be serious!'

He was being completely serious. Sahiba was the one silver lining. With her by his side, he felt strong enough to start a new life. Even though this ask had seemed like a long shot, deep down he believed that she would go with him. He had convinced himself of it. But she was barely considering it.

157

'But then what? Maybe you need not come immediately... I can set things up and you can come in a month or two, maybe –'

'Kabir, I needed to talk to you anyway. Look, right now is not a good time. The family is being paranoid, plus there was that thing with you getting into a fight. It's all too much and it's creating problems.'

'I don't understand. What do you mean problems? I told you I had nothing to do with...'

'I know, I know. Look, our lives are going to drift apart now, you may leave the city and I need to get on with my life. To be honest, my family is already talking about suitors for me. They may have even started looking...'

'Wait, wait, wait. What?! Who are you and what have you done with Sahiba? Suitors??' He looked at her, half-hoping this was all a badly-timed joke.

'I'm serious, Kabir. It's not like I am doing it, it's just that, you know, these things are happening. I can't help but feel like things are changing.'

'What are you saying, Sahiba? What about us? I thought you and I...I mean, you always said that you didn't care what others said and you would rather be alone than give in to conventions. What happened to all of that?'

'Look, we need to think of the future. Maybe you and I want different things.'

'But we want the same things! We talk about them all the time! You said you saw us together forever and all that.'

'And I meant it, Kabir!'

'So then what happened? What changed? Babe, we were supposed to be together regardless.'

'Those were fun things Kabir, but don't be so childish.'

Kabir recoiled at that word. He felt like he had been called 'childish' a lot over the past few days.

She continued, 'Seriously, we come from different places and you want to see the world. I love it here in my home and I don't want to prevent you from things.'

'Listen, you are the most important thing. I will do what you want. I mean we could even get married... should we?'

Sahiba giggled, charmed by his impetuousness.

'No, don't be silly. We can't get married so soon.'

'You said you loved me!' He was painfully aware of how petulant he sounded.

'I do...'

'So then why can't we find a way?'

'My family is involved and things are really complicated.'

'But I can come and speak to them.'

'No, it's not possible right now.'

Kabir's tone hardened. 'If your family is so complicated then how come we got together in the first place? Maybe you don't actually love me. Maybe it was all just...'

'All just what?'

'I don't know. All I know is that I don't say things that I don't mean.'

'Well, some of us have to think of others.'

And so it continued for a while. Declarations of love and fealty turned into frustrated accusations. They began to lightly wound each other; each trying to balm the hurt by soliciting little flatteries along the way. The dance continued back and forth, neither able to wrench themselves away.

For the second time that day, Kabir felt like he was standing on quicksand. Doubt turned into a sinking sensation. At first, unable to understand her meaning, it dawned on him that she was not coming. In fact, she seemed to be breaking up with him. Finally, when he could stand it no more, he flatly asked, 'Are we breaking up?'

'I think so, at least for now.'

'But Sahiba, we were meant to be together.'

'Maybe we were, maybe we weren't. Maybe we will eventually find our way back to each other. But for now, I think this is best.'

She got up to leave. Blood rushed to Kabir's cheeks, his skin tingled, breath shortened. He felt panic welling up but was frozen to the ground. He couldn't move.

'Sahiba, don't.'

She looked at him, her eyes moistening. She smiled sadly and was gone.

CHAPTER SEVENTEEN

His phone was heavy with missed calls and messages from his family. They must be worried sick. He texted saying he was alright and on his way back.

He cycled home cautiously, keeping an eye out for any clusters of people. The roads remained empty but from time to time he could hear the unmistakable sound of breakage in the distance. As he drew closer to the bazaars on the route home, the streets were littered with broken things.

He suddenly came upon that universal symbol of unrest – a burning tyre in the middle of the street. Kabir slipped off the cycle and moved silently, ducking behind walls and traffic police posts. A drone of collected beings grew louder until finally he came upon it. Down a perpendicular street, he saw makeshift barriers behind which an angry mass of people glowed with flaming torches. A policeman in a helmet grabbed him. He looked Kabir up and down and deduced him harmless. Reprimanding Kabir for being caught in the wrong place, he shoved him towards the best route out. Kabir looked back to see the gang behind the barrier heaving, preparing to make a rush for it. The shopfronts around them were destroyed and a few were ablaze. On his side of the barrier, a rally of other helmet-clad policemen made their stand behind shields made of cane. The cries of destruction from the masses were terrifying and Kabir pedaled home as fast as he could.

Men stood outside the buildings of his street like sentinels. A mob had been through here already, evidenced by the litter they shed in their wake – the odd tyre, metal screws, pamphlets and indecipherable rags. There was no sign of other destruction. Seemingly the men of the neighbourhood had managed to keep them out of their homes.

Kabir came upon the shape of Prem Menon standing outside their building. The light from the streetlamp cast a glow over him so you could only make out his silhouette holding a pistol. Kabir recognized it as the service Beretta his grandfather had. Many years ago, his Dada had taken him target practicing. He hadn't seen it since then and did not even realize his father had it.

Prem saw the bereft look on his son's face. Wordlessly he strode up to him and hugged him. Kabir couldn't hold back tears streaming down his face, wetting his father's shoulder. As they broke their embrace, Kabir saw splatters of angry black ink thrown on their letterbox and across the entrance. Their home had been branded the enemy – because of him.

In that instance, he was engulfed by the ripping, agitated, adrenalized sensation of hate. For the first time in his life, he understood its consuming companionship.

CHAPTER EIGHTEEN

Almost as though it were orchestrated by some divine mischief, the newspapers carried news of the greatest betrayal that same week. The Menons had locked up their apartment and holed up at a friend's house for a few days. When they returned home, they were relieved to find that other than the ink stains, no further damage had been done. The neighbours had kept their home safe. Something caught Kabir's eye as he picked out a newspaper from the uncollected pile outside their door.

At first, he couldn't comprehend what he was reading. A 'match fixing' scam – a term so unfamiliar he thought it had something to do with scheduling. As he read further, the contents, the implications and the protagonists sounded unreal. He stood rooted to the spot, reading about an undercover sting operation. Journalists claimed to have discovered a nexus of gambling cartels, which had paid players to 'fix' games.

Only a few weeks ago, Kabir's life was inextricably linked with university and his childhood. Their goings-on were the most important things in the world. The cricket team was his brotherhood, and he was secure and confident of his place in this world. He was in the deep sway of his first love; the loveliest girl in college was smitten with him.

Today he stood as though discarded, questioning linkages he had placed so much importance upon. Was he so easily forgotten? Was his world and its kinships all a figment of his own imagination? A fantasy he had constructed?

And then came this final straw. The gust that blew down the house of his personal truths.

Over the next few days, the media cackle was brimming with seedy, paunchy bookmakers and gangsters. Testifying to their links with players. They claimed that match results had been manipulated in exchange for suitcases of cash. Amongst the accused were Azhar and Cronje – the captains of the team, the heroes of their nations.

Poor quality, handheld camera footage of sting operations, carried out on boastful fixers and their supplicants, was broadcast on repeat. Those loops with scratchy sound needed subtitles for the viewer to understand what was going on. Fist-thumping, bombastic, breathless news anchors demanded answers. Repeated clips of bookies were shown on a loop. These nondescript short, paunchy men were led in cuffs in and out of investigations all day, their entries and exits made for breaking news. Every day, a new accused would come forth. They were unbelievable names. Paragons of Indian cricket, men whose herculean efforts were the bedrock of cricket parables.

On the street, people spat their opinions about this match and that. They sneered at the men who not so long ago they idolized and feted. A betrayal of this magnitude was difficult to cope with for a cricket-crazy nation. These virulent fans, who would leave their birthing wives to watch India win, now sat shell shocked, disbelieving.

Perhaps the old Kabir would have been more skeptical. He would have pointed to holes in the investigation. He would have found flaws in the logic. But today he didn't have the heart. Every time he saw a newspaper or switched on the news, there it was.

A few days later came the moment, which broke whatever little hope he had of all this being a bad dream. The breaking news showed a scratchy hidden camera film taken by an ex-Indian cricketer. The footage showed this man visiting homes of his teammates. He tried getting them to admit to something or implicate someone. This slithering act of manipulation had the stench of greed and spinelessness. It was a sign that the daggers were out, teammate turned on teammate, gods turned lecherous and all that was good turned into farce.

~

A couple of weeks had passed. It had become clear to the authorities that the trouble in the streets was connected to the university elections. It was less clear who was involved. That bloody night had claimed four lives, two on each side. There were numerous broken bones, bloodied faces and opened gashes. Hospital beds continued to treat victims. Gangs had settled their scores, but it was more than the thugs who took to the streets. Regular men and women had participated and now everyone looked upon each other with suspicion.

Kabir was unmoored and wanted an escape – he made up his mind to leave Hyderabad. The family tried to reason with him to stay but did not push him too hard. His parents saw the merit in a new start, but both wished it had not come under these forced circumstances. Preparations were made for Kabir to move to his uncle's home in Bombay. He would interview for jobs and start a new life there. Radha and Prem did their best to encourage their son, telling him what a great adventure this was all going to be. Little Sakshi didn't like the thought of her resident chaperone leaving and she made no bones about it.

Kabir had quietly muttered acceptance to all this. He had embraced the notion that this was the practical thing to do.

Secretly he stared at his phone, yearning for it to ring. For a message to flicker – an apology, she didn't mean it, she wants to come, of course she will come. But it remained lifeless.

He had tried contacting Barman but could not find him. Mustafa told him that Barman had been released after a day in jail. He had no idea where he was now. Kabir felt slighted. After the loyalty he had shown, shouldn't Barman be concerned where he was? Whether he was okay?

Now the family stood on platform 5. The railway station was thick and old with stories of journeys embarked here. The milieu of passengers and the rush of red-clad coolies felt historic. The present mingled with the past; those who had stood here left behind something – you could sense their presence somehow.

To Kabir, everything about it was just sad. The clatter of travelers hauling their trunks into the compartments. The inexorable time spent waiting for the train to start moving when all you could do was look at your loved ones. Nothing to say, just look at each other, living the tug of the moment.

Prem Menon was unable to express his feelings, so he hopped in and out of Kabir's compartment instead and busied himself adjusting the luggage. Occasionally, he muttered banal bits of practical advice.

Radha Menon held on to her son's arm, less perturbed than her husband. She smiled reassuringly, as though willing her son not to dwell on the moment.

The large metallic over-bridge disgorged and swallowed people through connecting metal tubes on every platform. Kabir scanned these repeatedly. He clutched hope that he would catch a glimpse of Sahiba coming down the stairs to see him go. He knew that word had got to her about him leaving.

Mustafa was there to see him off. He didn't want his friend to leave but given the circumstances, he was trying to be cheerful, making jokes. Mustafa, seeing the pained look on his face, took Kabir aside.

'I thought she would come, at least to say bye, or something.'

'Don't think about it, Kabir.'

'But Musty, we had something special, you know?'

'If it was that special, she would have been here.'

This wounded him.

'Look Kabir, you are starting a new life, it will be painful for a while but eventually you will move on.'

People standing on the edge of the train were beginning to board. Kabir hugged Mustafa. 'It feels wrong not having Sareen here, Musty.'

'Forget him, yaar. He wouldn't have come anyway, he's changed.'

'I don't think he has, Musty. I'm sure if he knew he would have come.'

Mustafa grew impatient.

'He knows you're going, his ma would have told him. He doesn't care, don't you understand? Now don't worry about this stuff. Go to the big city, have fun!'

Kabir turned to his family. Little Sakshi had tears rolling down her face. Prem's brows were knit, Radha continued smiling and pulled her son into her arms. There was so much to say but Kabir couldn't think of a thing.

The bored voice of a station inspector loudly crackled through the air, heralding his departure. Just as Kabir grabbed the handle to pull himself up to the train, he heard his name called out. To his great surprise, he swung around to find Barman jogging up the platform. The long wiry frame sporting tweed trousers and a white shirt made him look ever the intellectual. Relief flooded through Kabir.

Barman came up a little short of breath, nodded to the others and went straight to Kabir.

'So, you're off, eh?'

'Sir, where have you been? I have been trying to speak to you, I wanted to say that... that –'

The train started its imperceptible initial roll forward. Kabir fumbled to get his words out.

'Sir, I'm really sorry. I shouldn't have admitted anything, it's wrong what happened to you.'

'Nonsense, boy. All this will pass, it will be okay, it's time to move on.'

Seeing Barman had made things better and worse. His forbearing, melancholic, angular form stirred up a jumble of feelings. His last words were unsatisfying, irritating even.

There was no time left. Barman shook his hand. Prem Menon pushed Kabir towards the door and he clambered aboard. The wheels gathered speed. He watched his people on the platform, staring back at him, receding, waving. Sahiba never came.

BOOK 2

The room looked like it ought to have a damp musky scent, but it didn't smell of anything. It felt vintage due to the lack of natural light and its gloomy choice of upholstery, all approximating brown. There were bars on the windows, stone slab counters and the bulbs barely illuminated the place. It was an older couple's apartment, scarcely visited but familiar nonetheless.

Kabir stood behind his senior colleague, Prashant Mehra, who sat at the linoleum dining table next to a grey-haired man. They hunched over a snappy presentation, replete with arrows and graphics. Prashant was laying out the parroted sequence of words in excited elocution. They were selling units of a mutual fund. The objective was to make the listener feel like a dullard for not having already put his money into this 'foolproof' scheme. It was working. The older man sat unspeaking, trying to absorb all this information. This only caused Prashant to speak faster. More examples were thrown in with jargon this poor man had never heard before. *The state of the market, the bull run, the guaranteed stock splits, the middleclass dividend, the IT soft power, the Infosys effect... it's now, now, now BOSS!*

Behind the elderly man, stood his wife. Nervously twisting the end of her saree, she looked concernedly at her husband and the incomprehensible papers on the table. Her expression induced a lurch of tenderness in Kabir. He wanted to reassure her – it was going to be okay – but he himself was at a bit of a loss as to what all this meant.

It had been a little over a year since he moved to Bombay. He found a job at a bank and was thrown into tasks without much training of any sort. On the job learning, he was told. A large part of his day consisted of accompanying his reporting boss, Prashant, to acquire people's money. They did this by selling dreams of wealth via mutual funds, advisory services, stocks and so on. All around him there was chatter about the markets and its great opportunities. The word 'software' came up in every second sentence. Not really knowing how these things worked, Kabir conjectured and guessed his way through most conversations. Standing in front of this kindly, elderly couple, his moral certitude was wobbly at best. On Prashant's cue, he presented the mutual fund application form for multiple signatures. Even the application form looked conspiratorial. The size of print seemed to become smaller as you went down the page. It was as though the authors were hiding its true scheme within the miniscule lettering.

To be fair, everything Kabir had seen in his short-lived career pointed only one way – stocks seemed to go up all the time and people seemed to be making a lot of money. Everyone said that there was a dotcom boom underway and that the world had changed. This was going to last forever.

After getting the requisite signatures, they helped the man write out a sizeable check. Prashant's toothy congratulatory smile was accompanied by his limp handshake, and they were off, back to the office.

HFCI Securities was a newly hatched wing of a traditional bank. Its offices seemed to be in a constant state of flapping-fish-out-of-water energy. It was rapidly dealing with the new workload, which explained Kabir's gunshot hiring and subsequent lack of induction.

Kabir sat opposite the trading room. The tiny area and sullen energy of this 'trading room' belied its dynamic-sounding purpose. Screens monopolized the space and facing these screens were three chairs, each belonging to a trader. The room was only wide enough to walk in sideways. The screens were littered with tables and graphs blocked in different colours, resembling a poorly played game of Tetris. Kabir would loiter in there from time to time and try and make some sense of it all. He quizzed the prematurely greying traders who sometimes indulged him. They seemed to spend their time hedging moves, guessing what other traders may be doing – it sounded like gambling.

In this new world, the language of money was the one coherence to all of life's pursuits. Everything else became subservient. But it wasn't simply greed, although greed was implied. Money was spoken of as a token of score rather than the benefit it was able to buy. All human endeavor aligned towards maximizations, efficiencies, stripping away and exponentials.

He had a visiting card with a logo above his name. It carried an implied competence whenever he walked into a room. In the rush of moving cities, living with his cousins, finding an apartment and the mundanity of phone connections, work shoes, presswala, shopwala and safaiwali – he barely paid heed to the heavy stone in his gut. But it didn't take long for the new sheen to rub off. Routine soon trampled the sparkle of it all.

Having initially sniffed around him, curious co-workers had stopped trotting over to ask nosy questions. Kabir was no longer distracted from the heartbreak and homesickness. Now the reality of being alone and making his way in the world became fully apparent.

By day, he felt lost in a machinery in which he would never be seen. His imagination and individuality had no value here. Yet he saw around him smiling faces, high fives and the thrill of accomplishment. Was there something wrong with him? His father had once warned him against becoming a dilettante. He had had to look up the meaning of the word and did not like what he read. He dared not complain for fear of fulfilling that prophecy. In his mind he heard his father saying words like 'commitment' and 'perseverance'.

When the day ended, his attention would wholly be turned to that pestilent sinking feeling. Lying in bed, he would imagine scenarios and hypothecate about home. Mostly these thoughts were about Sahiba. Sometimes in these stories she would turn up at his door, teary-eyed, unable to live without him. But of late, he would imagine more and more that she had met someone else. Perhaps someone more acceptable to her family. Walking around the same monuments, she was smiling at this new (taller) person, having forgotten Kabir. These thoughts would pull his features into a grimace and he would look up at the front door of his barely furnished apartment, almost willing her to knock.

At that moment, Kabir was copying numbers from physical forms onto another form on the computer. He would then open another form in which he would add the file number of the current form he was filling, thereby recording all the forms filled thus far and their numbers. A third form required tabulating the number of leads pursued and their statuses and these were to be linked to the number on the first form. It was important to get the numbers right otherwise the first form would need to be filled in again as would the second form and so on. After all the filling and all the forms, he would be responsible for putting together a memo setting out the total number of sales made – forms filled, reasons for aforementioned successes or underperformance and recommendations for improvement. This report would be passed up, one rank at a time, for monitoring and reviewing. Kabir had long since eschewed the brutal honesty he exhibited in the first few memos he wrote. These reports went up the chain after all and the hierarchies did not appreciate a junior officer's insight. They now bore a light, dull, company-line optimism.

Kabir stared into his screen, lost in this mundanity, when Ranjit jumped up to his desk with a cheerful chirp.

'Mr Kabir, what's up yaar?'

Ranjit was the closest approximation to a friend Kabir had at work. They shared a table in the lunchroom in Kabir's first week. Ranjit was from Calcutta, and they got talking about Kabir's visits to his grandfather's home. A gregarious, garrulous type, Ranjit was the kind of person who seemed grateful for every moment. Slightly chubby, with a dark complexion and big glasses, he carried a handkerchief at all times. He used the 'hanky' to dab at a thin layer of perspiration, which always accompanied him. Every time he chuckled, which he did often, his eyes would squint and his shoulders would roll. Like almost everybody else at the bank, Ranjit had studied engineering, but unlike the others, he seemed less dorky and more urbane. Kabir felt like he could be himself around him.

Kabir leaned back and drew in a long-suffering breath.

'Oh, you know... same stuff. We went on a sales call today. Managed to get some old couple to write out a pretty big check.'

'That sounds cool!'

'I guess, but I wish I knew more about what I was talking about. Most of the time I'm just repeating the same stuff Prashant says.'

A couple of the younger guys, not wanting to leave an opportunity to loiter unmissed, came up to join them. Kabir knew one of them was called Anil and the other one's name he could never remember – something with an S? Sunil? Subeer? Whatever.

Anil inserted himself in the conversation, beady-eyed, 'What's up guys? What are you talking about?'

'Oh, our friend Kabir was just saying that he didn't know what the hell he is selling. He just takes peoples hard-earned savings,' Ranjit giggled. Kabir smiled, slightly tilting his head back to his computer screen.

'Shuuuuut up yaar. You don't know that stuff or what?' piped Sunil, Subeer, Sagar or whatever. It was said with relish.

He ignored it. 'Anyway, guys you better get out of here before Prashant sees you. I'm supposed to finish up a report for him and today he's very stressed out...'

Anil and the other one slunk off, snickering and looking pleased with themselves.

'What's with those guys, man?'

'They are weird, don't worry about them. Anyway, listen, a friend is having drinks at his house this weekend. He knows lots of girls... you know what-a-mean?' Ranjit did an impression of a cowboy – bowed feet, finger pistols by his hip, shooting them. 'Tshew, Tshew'.

'I don't know, man. I might be busy'.

'Come on, Kabir. We almost never hang out after work. Only once did I get you a little drunk and I have to tell you, drunk Kabir is a much cooler guy than sober Kabir. Come on, it will be fun!'

'Okay, okay. Fine.'

'Good man and keep it hush-hush. I don't want your best friend Sagar showing up.'

Sagar. That's his name. Ranjit now stood around in that undetermined way of filling up a pocket of time. It was almost lunch hour and he had intentionally come over twenty minutes earlier. After surveying the tops of the cubicles a couple of times, Ranjit ventured, 'Should we go for lunch then?'

'You go, Ranjit. I need to finish some of this stuff. I can't step out now.'

'Okay boss.'

On his way out, Ranjit greeted people, jostled and laughed. His friendliness was infectious. It reminded Kabir of something, someone, back home. Turning back to his computer screen, he waited for enough time to pass till he could get lunch without being spotted. He preferred eating alone.

A revelation of his time in Bombay had been his discovery of a street food vendor selling vada pav – a deep-fried potato dumpling in a bun. Lathered with sweet and spicy chutney and sprinkled with rough salt, it was served with a tiny, hair-raising green chili. The wholesomeness of the first bite mingled with the crunchiness of the salt and the tangy afterburner left a light perspiration on top of his scalp. He ate a couple of them before dragging himself back towards the office. On the way, he sidestepped a small gathering of people outside the BPL TV showroom. As he walked around them, he looked over at the wall of TVs in the window. All of them were tuned to a cricket match, which obviously had some import given the eagerness of the crowd. Kabir grimaced and quickened his step, ignoring the cheers behind him.

~

He would sometimes carpool back home with someone or the other, but today he left later than usual. Prashant had asked him to finish a pile of paperwork. He flagged down a taxi outside the office and sunk into its hard, barely-cushioned bench seat.

Gazing out of the window, Kabir noted that the buildings rarely looked new or unblemished. The lashes of monsoon and salted air would stain the exterior and give the edges a greenish quality. Roads would pass through denseness and then come upon a patch of open sea. Just when you think that the teeming was left behind another would swamp you. In this city, the ivory towers nestled within sparrows' nests.

In the first few months, Kabir had struggled to come to terms with Bombay. He thought it a miracle that the teeming chaos didn't devolve and disintegrate. But slowly he started to understand its rhythm. He began to comprehend its wheels within wheels. The interconnectedness of the city made it strong and almost staid. Its massive machinery seemed implacable and immovable.

Over the past couple of weeks, the weather had mercifully

changed. After the monsoon, the lashing winds had given way to bright stillness and with it came the sensation of walking in hot clear broth. After surviving a few months of shirt-sticking, lung-pressing assault of humidity, thankfully the breeze had picked up towards the end of October.

Another alien experience to Kabir had been the assailing, eye-watering stench of drying fish from the coastal villages. It punctuated the evening breeze into the city and for the uninitiated, this required some girding of loins. Even though he had grown used to it, the initial onslaught always took him by surprise.

Since the weather had improved, Kabir preferred jumping out of the taxi to walk the remaining kilometer or so to his apartment. He enjoyed walking home along the seafront, accompanied by swaying coconut trees. Halfway down, he took a couple of turns off the promenade and left behind the crackling onslaught of the bustling city and walked through narrow, quiet, old lanes. Dotted along its sides were small, sloped-roof buildings, each soldiering on against the thick richness of the tropics. Interspersed within these gullies were little chapels and crosses. Portuguese names were chiseled on house fronts. These little streets whispered stories of a genteel past. The area felt older than the encroaching, chest-beating city right on its fringes.

Then out of nowhere came an open space, a maidan, dotted with groups of kids playing some sort of organized cricket. There seemed to be no clear demarcation of one game from the other. Players playing different matches would overlap and yet it all seemed to work. The playing areas were large, red-earthed patches interspersed with spots of grass valiantly holding on for survival. The richness of the land willed little green shoots to appear wherever they could. Players were leaving the ground as dusk approached. Their clean white trousers now rendered an ombre brown up to the knees. Diminutive kids, with oversized caps and kit bags as tall as they were, shuffled into buses heading back to their homes. Kabir paused here, but he soon moved on. It was impossible to avoid the game in this city.

After living with his uncle for a couple of months, he had moved into a small one-bedroom apartment in a six-storey building. He unlocked his front door to find his Maharashtrian bai in the kitchen cooking him his evening meal. She would come in once a day, clean the place and leave him tiffin for the evening. Usually, she would be gone by the time he got home. He greeted her with a grunting noise. Pleased to see him, she proudly stuck a spoon of prawn curry under his nose for approval. Everyone likes their cooking to be appreciated.

After dispensing with her, Kabir poured himself a shot of Royal Challenge whiskey. A glug of water broke its sinister spirit, and it was a cheap way to get the job done. Kabir's unfocussed stare out of his window would take him close enough to the end of another day.

Some days he would find himself wanting the reassurance of a familiar voice, someone who could make him feel lighter and safe. When he called home, he put on a false bravado, a blusteriness about his new life. He didn't like the slightly high-pitched pretense in his voice. He didn't want to complain about things – it would seem inadequate, weak.

In the first few days in Bombay, he called Sahiba often. She wouldn't always answer and when she did, she was casual. Banalities of her small talk pierced him sharply. He would get anxious during the conversation and afterwards agonize about her words, tone and meaning. She became more distant and his affront no longer held her attention. Jealousy gnashed his insides when they spoke, its coils heavy and sinking. Eventually, he had to restrain himself from calling her – he hated the way he sounded. She never called him. It had been months since he had heard her voice, yet her lingering weight remained. As he took a large gulp of his drink, his eyes squinted from the forcefulness of the spirit in his mouth. He wondered when the passage of time would salve the acute tear of Sahiba's absence.

~

Dear Kabir,   12th April 2000

I hope you are well. I am sure you're doing great things at your new job. You always were an intelligent and creative boy. I am proud of you for taking your life in your own hands and starting afresh in Bombay. I'll admit I was a little concerned about this sudden decision to leave home. I did not want to say anything at the time, as it was difficult enough for you with whatever was going on. I heard about your fight with Sahiba. These were challenging things to deal with and I wish we could have helped you more. But you are living your life, as you should – I suppose, as your mother, I would always want you close by.

Your father is getting more melodramatic every day. Sometimes he tells me I should have convinced you to stay. Other times he pats himself on the back for this brave decision you have taken to leave. I think he misses you most. He hardly watches cricket anymore, since there is no one to watch it with. I tried to fill in for you, but he got irritated with me.

The house feels quite empty without you. Sakshi's new dog has developed a fondness for your father's chair in the living room. He has virtually chewed off all the cushioning at the arm. We are glad to have him, and Sakshi says it reminds her of you as it keeps the house cheerful.

Son, I know that you are grown up and I can no longer tell you what to do. But as your mother, I feel like you are hurting. We receive the occasional call from you, but we hardly know anything about your life other than you saying that you are well and we shouldn't worry. I do wish we could chat more often. I know your father would like that.

Love you,
Ma

The paper rustled as he folded the page and slipped it back into the envelope. Its intent was to uplift his spirits, but instead it created weight. He couldn't pinpoint why he had become reluctant to communicate with his family back home, but he rarely did. When he did, he sounded wooden and closed.

He would talk to Mustafa occasionally, but chatting about nothings with a friend after a few drinks was different from the sober concerns of a parent on the other end of the line. He just didn't want to answer questions about whether he was eating properly or if he was okay. He didn't want to engage with his father who would most likely foist some life lesson upon him.

He loved talking to Sakshi. He would tease her and she would giggle. But those conversations were short, she was still at the age where her opinions were secondhand and green. He couldn't confide in her as a fully-baked person.

He wished he didn't feel shackled. But the longer it went on, the unsaid things just became heavier.

Not wanting to get pulled in to talking about it, he preferred avoiding it all together.

CHAPTER TWO

Kabir pulled the door till he heard the satisfying click of bolts fastening in place. He hid one of the keys behind the mailbox for the maid. As he turned, a boy hustling down the stairwell pushed him back into the wall. The boy was carrying a kit bag, which looked twice his size. Kabir had seen this kid playing cricket in the driveway. He was dressed in cricket whites and looked purposeful. Kabir followed him down the stairs, out of the building and towards the cricket ground. Taxis seldom drove past their building, so a short walk would be necessary to a busier thoroughfare. Kabir would normally hail one from the same ground he would pass on the way home. It wasn't necessary to go that far, but he would.

As they walked, Kabir inadvertently fell in step with the boy. The boy looked up at him. 'What's your name?'

'Kabir.'

'You live on the third floor, na?'

'Yeah.'

'I'm Arjun. Do you play cricket?'

'I used to.'

'Are you a batsman or bowler?'

'Batsman.'

Arjun nodded in approval and continued his determined march towards the ground. At the ground, Arjun hastened to a trot and joined a cluster of boys surrounding what looked like a coach. Kabir leaned on the short grill separating the pavement from the grass. He watched for a while as the boys did a warm-up lap. Arjun pulled out a blue felt cap from his bag that looked a little large for his head and padded up to bat. Kabir watched the other matches for a little while and eventually flagged down a black and yellow taxi.

By the time he got to his destination, the sun had set. He called Ranjit from the street, who came downstairs to get him.

'So, you came. I wasn't sure you would.'

'Well, you did tell me to come a hundred times.'

Ranjit chuckled, 'Yeah I did, didn't I? Anyway, good. I'm happy you're here early but I warn you, many of the guys from work are here.'

Kabir groaned. Ranjit pushed him playfully to the elevator.

The host couple played clichés – the wife's effusiveness was tempered by the husband's gradualness. Her postbox-red lips shone stridently against her oak brown complexion. She wore an equally striking cerulean dress, which left her rather stocky shoulders bare. After a few awkward seconds of conversation, her friendly eyes darted towards another distraction. Her husband stood in his nondescript, half-sleeved blue linen shirt, his droopy eyes shielded by large rimmed spectacles. His frame looked like it could once have been athletic but now the muscle was slack from its structure for lack of use. He seemed to be a nice but plain man who obediently placed himself behind his wife's bright chirp. Once she had hopped away, he looked bereft of purpose, shifting his weight from one foot to the other.

Kabir slunk off to get himself a drink. He was spotted by some guys from his office with whom he exchanged perfunctory, polite conversation. They wanted to talk about the markets and the cars they were thinking of buying. They spoke of their managers at work and their careers. One of them even boasted about smoking weed sometimes. Kabir thought to himself how lame this evening was. He spotted Ranjit out in the balcony and made his way out to him.

'Hey Kabir, how you doing, my man?'

'Yeah, okay really, I was trying to get away from the nerd patrol over there.'

Ranjit looked over his shoulder smiling. 'Oh, they're okay. Nice guys. Not as cool as you, of course,' he sniggered again.

'I guess.'

'They're better than those dudes I was speaking to. They kept droning on about cricket. I mean I like watching it sometimes. But man, I hate these guys who are all statistics and argue about which South African is a better batsman than some Englishman because his elbow is straighter or his pants are tighter. I mean, come on... it's a party. Are you into cricket?'

'Not really.'

'Do you want another drink?'

'Yeah, sure, I guess.'

'Okay, wait right here.'

As Ranjit left, Kabir saw a girl leaning on the balcony, smoking. He noticed her bare slim pointed shoulder as she propped up her elbows on the railing. She acknowledged him with a smile and turned to look out at the view. Kabir came up to the balcony next to her and introduced himself. She too was new to the city, and they chatted about the strange peculiarities of Bombay life. Ranjit got him his drink, then he had another and another. They remained moored on the balcony, each reluctant to be displaced from their newfound connection. Loosened by alcohol, they chatted freely; she touched his arm a couple of times. At some point, she excused herself to go to the restroom.

Kabir looked back into the apartment through the glass doors. Returning to the party felt like an ordeal. He stayed outside, waiting for this girl to come back. Alone with his thoughts, Kabir felt reluctant to commit to the moment, to these people, to this life. The alcohol was making him irritable. Abruptly, he put his drink down, headed for the door and walked out without saying anything to anyone.

On his way home, he felt annoyed with himself. Why did he leave the girl on the balcony? He didn't even remember her name. He picked up the phone and dialed Mustafa, who answered in a hushed, somber tone.

'Hi Kabir, I'm at Mian Qadir's house. I will call you back.'

'MUSTY! What's up, what's aaaaaap. What are you doing there?'

Kabir came off a little too boisterous, his voice a little too loud. The whiskey coupled with Mustafa's voice lifted his spirit.

'The elders are here – the meeting is about to begin. I better go in before he sees me on my phone. You know what he's like, he hates people talking on the phone at these serious things. I will call you, okay?'

'What rubbish, man. Mianji will be cool with me. Just give him the phone, let me speak to him.'

Kabir was enjoying the liquid spurt of bravado.

'Are you mad? He will kill me. I got to go.'

'Shut up, Musty, its fine. You're getting serious about these community things, huh? Are you standing there in a clean kurta with the little topee on your head?'

'Yeah man. Is everything alright?'

'Everything is GREAT, I'm just calling to chit chat.'

Mustafa scoffed playfully, 'Yeah it sounds like everything is great. Your night seems to be going well. Kabir bye, I have to go now, okay? I will tell you all about it later.'

'What's going on over there? It sounds like you guys are doing lots of meetings.'

'It's been like this since election time. Things are not like they used to be. Anyway, look I really need to go now; they are calling me in, bye.'

'Wait wait…'

Mustafa had already hung up. Kabir really wanted to talk more. He wanted to admit that his new life wasn't great and thrilling; he wanted to admit that he was lonely; he wanted to say that he felt like he let people down back home; he wanted to say that he was homesick. He wanted to talk about Sahiba. Mostly, he wanted to be himself.

Instead, the liquor flared up in a petulant spurt of anger. 'Fuck it,' he muttered, feeling sorry for himself. A sinking longing for the familiar grew into resentment – a reaction particular to young men.

There were a couple of messages from Ranjit:

hey where are you dude

did you leave?

He wrote back:

yes will see you Monday

~

Much of the alcohol's effects had abated by the time he trudged up the floors to his apartment. Inserting keys inside his door, he paused before pushing it open. There was an unmistakable familiar, friendly waft in the air. Quietly he removed the key and crept up the stairs. The small stairwell folded back around the elevator shaft and had hidden landings halfway up the floors. Kabir climbed one floor and the smell got stronger. He suddenly came upon a woman sitting on the stairs above him, giving him a bit of a start. She remained unmoved. Hidden between two floors, she could not be seen, which is why she picked this spot to smoke her joint.

'Um… sorry,' Kabir blurted.

'It's okay.' She looked at him glassy-eyed.

He lifted his head to look at her. The first thing he noticed were long, dusky limbs and slim, high cheek bones. She was wearing shorts, with her bare legs extending down a few steps, crossed at the ankles. Her arms pushed up against the step she sat on, limber and thin. Her body looked languorous and natural as though it draped well.

'I… I moved in downstairs.'

'Third floor, right?'

'Yeah, I thought I smelt something, so I came to check it out…'

She smiled, took a long drag of the joint and extended her arm towards him. He took it and sat below her, resting his back against the wall.

'You met my son?'

Her son? Kabir racked his brain. That kid with the cricket bag? She was clearly older than Kabir, but he would never have imagined she had a son.

'Oh yeah, Arjun?'

'Mmhmm, he said you walked him to cricket practice.'

'He kind of walked himself there.'

She smiled wistfully, 'Yeah, he's crazy about his cricket, that kid. So, what's your story?' she asked, arching her eyebrow. Damn, she was cool.

Kabir cobbled together a disjointed series of events, leading him to the present. It sounded lame. She told him that she had moved to Bombay for college and stayed ever since. She came from a small hill station in the south and she now lived with her son. No further details were offered. Intimidated and now a little stoned, the best Kabir could manage was, '…Cool…'

'Okay, well, nice meeting you.' She stood, half smiled and turned to walk up. Kabir staggered to his feet.

'I'm Kabir…' he called out.

'Natasha.' She waved and disappeared behind the wall.

CHAPTER THREE

Prem Menon pulled the sliding door shut. His ears adjusted with a thump to the thrum of air conditioning. The cool filtered climate indoors was a marked difference to the dry heat he had just walked in from. Sheltered from the sounds of the outside world, the insides of the office felt like a cocoon.

Prem walked past the rows of glass-topped tables, accumulating nods and 'good-morning-sir's on the way to his corner office. Akhtar's table was outside the door and the man balefully looked up from his new typewriter. Not one for much fluctuation of expression, Akhtar nodded scarcely to acknowledge his employer of twenty-five years. Once Prem had settled in, Akhtar rose gracefully, his head remaining unnaturally still as he glided into the room with the day's correspondence. The move to computerization was a bridge too far for this man of shorthand and ninety words per minute. Prem Menon recognized the inevitable displacement of his secretary to the modern world, but for now he retained this unflappable assistant of many years. As Akhtar's paan-stained mouth related upcoming appointments, Prem Menon's mind wandered to that fateful day in Calcutta.

It was the mid 1970s and industrial unions had enveloped

Prem's fledgling factory with their political militancy. The work had stopped and the workforce had put a seal on the gate, so that no one could go in until their demands were met. Disruption was more politically useful than resolution; so, during discussions, whenever a grievance was resolved, a new demand would take its place, each more impractical, more onerous and more impossible to resolve than the last. The doors of his business remained sealed for many weeks. It was nerve-racking for Prem to see the bustling shop floor he had built so painstakingly go quiet.

One day, Prem had snuck into the shuttered offices to fetch some belongings. News had got out that he was in the premises and a restive crowd of men, wearing red scarves and armed with sticks, surrounded the entrance. Luckily, Akhtar was with him. Through some (since unseen) resourcefulness, Akhtar got some help and snuck him out of the back of the building. That was the breaking point for Prem; shaken and disillusioned, he couldn't help imagining the fatal outcome had he faced the mob. That was the day he decided to leave Calcutta.

After a few months of setting himself up in Hyderabad, despite being scarcely able to afford an assistant, he called Akhtar to join him. Since then, the most sentiment he had ever received from this man was a slight raising of eyebrows.

Prem glanced at a promotional mailer from a new stock broking company.

'You know Kabir has moved to Bombay, Akhtar?'

'Yes, sir.'

'Oh yes, of course you do. He has joined a stock broking company. Like this one, but bigger.' Prem waved the envelope with a plastic window.

Akhtar looked on, unmoved. You would think that this studious-looking man had never met the boy, let alone watched him grow from a paperweight prodding toddler to a stationary-thieving boy and finally to the young man who pestered him to draft flyers for his cricket team. Prem let a pause hang, hoping for a response of some kind. After a moment of peering disdainfully over his glasses, Akhtar turned and saw himself back to his typewriter.

It was the start of the workday and he would have normally waited till evening, but Prem picked up the phone to call Kabir.

~

That morning Kabir had woken with a flutter in his stomach. Over the last few weeks, a gnawing, growing dread of stagnation had been pestering him. The novelty of working at HFCI had been replaced by fear of what the rest of his life might look like. Convinced that every moment he remained in this existence would take him deeper into an irreversible quagmire, he became filled with a low level panic.

Seeing his father's number flashing on his phone felt as though fate was intervening. Prem had scarcely uttered a greeting before Kabir launched into his existential crisis. He spoke quickly, barely pausing for breath, leaving no room for Prem to interject with correction or censure. Kabir wanted to quit the bank and try his hand at something else. When he had run out of things to say, he paused for breath. The momentary silence on the phone line felt loud and laden.

Prem was cautious. Conscious of the need to be gentle, he restrained himself from reacting immediately. The strain in Kabir's voice was troubling. Coupled with the difficulties leading to him leaving home, Prem wanted to be understanding and supportive.

To Prem what seemed like an instant, a required motion of time, felt to his son like an eternity – an ominous finality of a passing era. How could Prem explain to someone whose fully grown physical form had barely existed a couple of years that time ensures that this too shall pass? Life stretches around things. But to his son, a month was equivalent to a highly divisible proportion of his adult life.

Prem advised Kabir to stick with it for a little bit longer and if things didn't change, then perhaps they could talk about it after a couple of months. Kabir left it there – it was enough that he had been spoken to as an adult. Pushing the topic wasn't going to change anything. Besides, he had already made up his mind. The next few days were spent trying to figure out where he wanted to go, what he wanted to become. His father's conditioning of a steady job and income created walls and moats. But the thought of continuing down his current path filled him with a dread strong enough to galvanize his thoughts into action.

Kabir had thought of reaching out to Prakash Gawde – the TV producer he had met and showed around in Hyderabad. But his courage deserted him every time he reached for Gawde's number, convinced that he would not remember him. When he finally did call him, Gawde answered the phone on the second ring and miraculously did remember Kabir. Gawde monopolized the conversation. He seemed pleased to hear that Kabir had moved to Bombay and boisterously invited him over to his office.

The next day, Kabir went to a glitzy, glass-clad tower. Gawde made a great show of welcoming him. He introduced him around the place as a natural 'TV guy' as though he had known him for years. This unexpected bonhomie was disconcerting and flattering in equal parts.

He barely started to tell Gawde about his job at the bank, when Gawde interrupted – 'What rubbish yaar. You don't belong in a bloody bank. You're a natural. Come on, work for me. I am always looking for smart young guys. Its boom time boy, time to get things done. There is a lot of action out there. You start next week. Okay?'

Gawde grabbed his phone and barked at someone to get into his office.

'Sir, that's very kind of you but I can't start so soon. Can I think about –'

'Look I don't have time for you to think. There is a line outside the door waiting for a job like this. I can give you a week to figure it out. After that, the offer is gone…'

He sounded menacing, but recognizing that he may not get another opportunity, Kabir's mind cleared.

'I will take the role. But I have a notice period of one month from the bank. I need to complete that. I know that you would want me to do the right thing.'

Gawde smiled. 'You have three weeks. Figure it out. Now go, I have things to do.'

On his way out, Kabir noticed things he hadn't on the way in. Much like the bank, there were rows of chest-high cubicles. The floor layout looked like a DNA diagram of corporate productivity. But, unlike the bank, posters and bright colours twinkled through the openings of these little cubbies.

Gazing over the tops of these small walls, he saw a large sign in the corner of the room – STUDIO 1. Like bees to the hive, all activity headed towards the studio. Groups of men marched through the aisles with lights, black panels, cables and stands of all sizes. Intrigued, Kabir followed these men. Falling in step with them, he walked through two double doors into a darkened room. In the middle of the cavernous space was the familiar news set he had seen on TV. It was lit up by a multitude of lights on stands and had three large cameras pointing at it. Kabir was most taken by the cables on the floors like a thick mangle of black snakes with cautionary symbols pinned on them.

Everyone seemed to be in motion, and nobody paid any attention to him. Mouth agape he wafted over to the frenetic pathway leading directly from the door to the stage. He was knocked sideways by something short and travelling at speed. Spinning around, he found himself staring at a woman with a familiar face. She was a shade above five foot and slightly stocky in a feminine way. Attractive, she could be characterized as cute or pretty but not beautiful. The impact had been forceful, and it had pushed her back a few feet, resulting in her dropping some files and her phone. Her eyes blazed as she rounded on Kabir.

'What the fuck?! What do you think you're doing? Who is this guy? Who the hell are you?'

Her flash of fury came so suddenly, Kabir froze.

'Are you a complete idiot? Walking into me like that?'

'I'm really sorry, I was ju–'

She seemed to be gathering fury, her voice a shade below an all out scream.

'Who are you? Will someone tell me who this guy is?!'

'I… I came to meet Mr Gawde.'

There were some supplicants hovering around her, picking up her dropped objects, pressing their hands, fear writ across their face. She looked over her shoulder and yelled to no one in particular, 'MAYKE UUUUP!'

Turning back to Kabir, 'Gawde doesn't produce my show. Why is one of Gawde's guys here?'

Again, this was barked at no one in particular.

'Yes, sorry… I just meant I came to see him.'

She looked at Kabir incredulously, condescendingly. Her expression was making Kabir prickle.

'Are you a complete moron? Do you have a name? What rubbish is this? Tell me your name.'

Kabir replied icily, 'You didn't ask me my name. Had you asked nicely, I would have given it to you.'

A hush descended around them. The clucking supplicants stared at him with wide-eyed disbelief. A couple of black-clad security personnel grabbed his arm and pulled him towards the door. The woman stood speechless at his temerity as she watched him marched out. His last image of that room was two flapping men, armed with a belt bag of brushes, sponges and a hand mirror.

Kabir walked out into the lobby of the building. There she was again, on a poster, smiling sideways.

193

Neha Singh, the spunky prime time news anchor, a strong woman's voice in a chauvinistic world. Standing shoulder to shoulder with any man. Her guts earned her their respect and her looks kept them tuning in.

Kabir felt like something was reaching into his chest and squeezing. He had blown his chance. A voice called out to him. It was Prakash Gawde, walking out of the elevator, heading towards him. Gawde seemed to oscillate between two facial expressions – glowering menace and teeth-baring mirth. At the moment, his bushy knitted eyebrows, thick moustache and his curly hair made him look like an angry South Indian film villain.

'You are here one hour and already you are making trouble, huh, boy?'

'Sir, I'm sorry I didn't know who she was and I –'

Gawde stared into Kabir's eyes for an instant before throwing his head back and laughing heartily. Putting his arm on Kabir's shoulder, he swung him towards the door and whispered conspiratorially, 'I'm glad you did. That stupid girl needed to be cut to size... haha, I love that you did that. Well done boy, we are going to have some fun.'

And with that, he got into a waiting car and sped off. Kabir stood outside the building, thrilled and relieved. He flagged down a taxi and headed to the bank.

CHAPTER FOUR

Mustafa called Kabir after a couple of days, and they fell back into their natural rhythm of boys who had grown up together. Mustafa seemed weighed, slower to gather into their boyhood banter. Other than his continuing architectural study, he was now interning with a small firm. But his new gravitas came from the bi-weekly meetings held in Mian Qadir's home. What had been a society of neighbours, with grievances no more serious than street parking or stray dogs, now encompassed a more communal gathering of Muslim men from further afield. Their discussions delved into the status of the youth, their marginalization in local politics and even their safety.

Kabir listened incredulously. He could scarcely believe his gentle, bookish friend, was now participating in the affairs of his community. It was difficult to picture Mustafa in a white kurta-pyjama, sitting on his knees on a floor laid out with white mattresses, among bearded old men, talking somberly.

'Musty, you sound so grown up. How did you get into all this?'

'It just happened. I don't know how. After the trouble around college, Abba made me go to some of these meetings with Mian Qadir.'

'And then?'

'It was really boring at first. I didn't know what I was supposed to do. But then Mian Qadir made me follow-up on little things.'

'What things?'

'Little things, yaar. Like someone needed a letter written to the electricity company because their bill was too high, that kind of thing. I can't say no to Mianji, you know that, plus Abba insisted. It's not much work but now I'm expected to be in the meetings. Sometimes it gets quite serious – they talk about politics and stuff. Honestly, I don't want to be there. Now that I'm in an internship, I won't go for a few weeks and then hopefully they will forget me.'

'Do you think that will happen? How can anyone forget that nose?'

'Oh, that's not a problem. A lot of them have noses bigger than mine and beards also, they will forget me easy.'

'What about Sareen? Have you seen him?'

'I saw him once after that. He's cut his hair really short – you can see his bald head. He thinks he is a gangster or something. But he doesn't meet me anymore. I hear about him getting into fights sometimes. That guy has lost it man. Have you spoken to him?'

'I tried calling him once or twice but no answer. He hasn't reached out to me. But forget it, I don't want to speak to that guy anyway.'

Kabir felt a twinge of guilt even as he said it. Relationships forged in childhood take on a familial nature and you didn't say things like that about family.

Mustafa talking about the world back in Hyderabad made Kabir feel left out. A melancholy, a feeling of unbelonging. His neighbourhood, a place he felt he felt he knew so well, had sides to it that he had never seen.

Yet paradoxically and unwittingly, the yearning of those first months to return home had dissipated. Bombay had enveloped him and was now showing itself. The thrill of the unknown had become stronger than the lure of returning to the familiar. Hyderabad had begun to seem… small.

'What's going on with your job, Kabir?'

Kabir told him about the new job, but his mood had dampened. He couldn't evoke the excitement that he had wanted to.

'Are you okay otherwise, K?'

Fine. Of course. He was fine. No worries. Thumbs up. These days he wore nonchalance as a layer, cynicism as a charm.

'Yeah, I'm fine; all good.'

After they were done talking, Kabir's thoughts fell silent. Home felt distant and something told him that he would no longer find his solace back there.

~

Cutting ties at HFCI Securities was more complicated than Kabir had imagined. Given that he had worked hard at remaining unseen, he had assumed that nobody would register his exit. However, once he told his boss of his intentions to quit, he was sent to HR under a cloud of disapproval. Human Resources wanted rationale and explanations. His reasons for leaving were considered suspiciously, as though wanting to try another vocation was not a real explanation. He had injured the ego of a faceless corporate organism, which wanted answers and apologies. But he couldn't care less. Kabir felt like he was doing something right, for a change.

Through his time at the bank, he had made himself the outsider. These suited, booted, pen-in-top-pocket, ironed-chinos, career sorts were the archetype of what his father wanted for him and he dreaded becoming. Not wanting to get too close for fear of them rubbing off on him.

So, when he left, he left. He packed his meagre possessions and walked out, not lingering for farewells and handshakes. He did not even see Ranjit before he left. Instead, they spoke on the phone. Ranjit was surprised at the suddenness – he tried lobbying for a good-bye night out, which Kabir side-stepped. He had acted callously towards Ranjit, but it was done. He was out.

~

At Indiworld TV, days never seemed to end. People would chat about events and scandal well beyond office hours. Kabir was thrown in at the bottom rung, the junior assistant of all things. From photocopying to proofreading newsreels, logistics and always the back-ups – the constant shuttling of data drives. Mostly his time was spent handling the logistical burden of getting people and equipment from one spot to another. But sprinkled into it all was the fairy dust of being in the center of the universe. The outside world fed off the buzz created here. The headiness instilled a sense of righteous importance and the network had its fair share of pointed opinions and inflated egos.

Post-office drinks at the local bar were ritualized. Large pegs were consumed with a wholesome, habituated thirst. Loosened tongues wagged their laments, and all was forgotten by the morning's twisted hangover. Wit and banter was often directed at one of the participants and you needed a thick skin and the ability to take a joke.

A feature of these gatherings was the preponderance of men. Much of the clumsy, bawdy humour involved women and sexuality. Occasionally, a woman from the office would join but, if anything, the jokes became coarser. The girls never flinched or objected. Kabir played along, it seemed the thing to do.

On one of these nights, the seductive taunt of revelry took them beyond the bar on their street. It had rained; red brake lights, yellow streetlamps and fluorescent storefronts bounced off the black wetness. City streets merged into its walls and into the sky.

At night, the metropolis was welcoming to its enthusiasts. Little gullies leading off the main drag, each had the allure of secrets, the thrill of the illicit and the multitude of lives being lived. It was easy to slip from one bar to the next; to jump into clunky neon lit taxis and stagger into a roadside eatery, presenting a new incident, a new stimulus every minute.

The group had whittled down to five by then. Gawde rarely stayed long, and the rest of the guys were less inhibited without his presence. Tonight's attention was turned towards Chayan, one of the junior guys from Kerala. Chayan had moved to Bombay with his mother's idli press and his father's English-bending Malayalam accent. The liquor had turned his quirky turn of phrase into a one-man variety performance. A mild-mannered, innocent sort, Chayan played along without being aware he was doing it. After a few drinks, he was 'fit ayee' and explained his father's illness a few years ago as 'faaather serious'.

The early buzz of the night made for good-natured ribbing at Chayan's expense. But as the evening grew longer, the gathering's intoxication grew sharper elbows. Kabir began to feel uneasy. He recalled an unpleasant odorous memory. The 'he's this and they are that'. One person's religion, another person's tribe.

Don't trust Mallus, they are damn smart.

Loud, exaggerated laughs peppered over things said as though the cackling sound gave them license. With some of the senior guys, the ribbing turned into something sinister. Gaming Chayan for their amusement, they were trying to get him to say something incriminating. Something inopportune to be whispered about later.

Soon they staggered out of the bar and Chayan went into the restroom. Everyone piled into a taxi. Kabir left the car door open. Sameer Sirohi, the senior guy in the group sat in front. He turned drunkenly, 'Let's go, come on!'

Kabir replied timidly, 'Just waiting for Chayan.'

'Screw him yaar, let's go.'

The others joined in. 'Come on,' 'let's go'.

'But we should wait, he will be out soon.'
'Shut the damn door, it will be funny, leave him.'
Kabir uncertainly pulled the door shut and they sped off.

CHAPTER FIVE

Natasha absent-mindedly gazed out of her window. Her study table overlooked the entrance to the building, and she watched the security guard yawn at the world going past. Her focus sharpened as Kabir walked out of the gate, looked to either side and strode away. She took note of her own interest in him. The meandering moment was abruptly interrupted by a clatter of fallen objects. She turned to find that Arjun's swinging kit bag had knocked over a stack of her stationary equipment. The look of surprise on his face made her laugh.

'Arjun, I told you not to wear it inside the house, you will knock things over and now you have.'

'I was just checking something.'

'No, you weren't. You just like wearing that thing around. I have seen you looking at yourself in the mirror.'

Arjun really did like his new kit bag. It looked professional with the big logo and the bat handle sticking out. He would put on his cricket cap and transform into a serious, mercurial cricketer.

'Did you finish your essay?'

Responding to the tone, Arjun's head fell back and he dropped his bag. The chest out, broad shouldered cricketer now slouched and dragged his feet back to his room.

'It's almost done.'

'You didn't finish it? We talked about this, Arjun. You promised you would before you went to the ground yesterday.'

'I will finish it on the bus, Mama, promise.'

'You will do no such thing. Get it over here now. Sit here and finish it. I told you if you didn't do it… no more cricket.'

Panic bred a previously unseen productivity. Natasha sat over Arjun, watching his knitted brow scan his history textbook, occasionally pausing and sticking his pen in his mouth in concentration. Then resolving the thoughts in his head, he would dive into the empty page, writing in a loopy cursive. She didn't leave his side, afraid that her broken gaze would cause another drifting of Arjun's attention away from medieval Indian history to some obscure cricket statistic.

She stared at the floor, her vision resting on tiny pebbles speckling the grey stone tiles. She found it unnatural to be a disciplinarian and knew she was not good at it. Arjun's father did not live with them and most of the time she was guess-working on how to play both roles. Arjun's interest in cricket and his boyhood-isms were alien to her. She wanted desperately to manage well, terrified of screwing him up. A great tenderness passed over her as she watched him sit cross-legged, his expression fierce in concentration.

An industrious half hour passed till it was time for his bus. She read the couple of pages he had written – it was not bad. No time now, a pat on the bum as a light rebuke, followed by a wholesome hug which may have been a little too tight. Arjun wriggled out of her arms and looked up with large, pleading doe eyes.

'Can I go to practice after school?'

She was never really going to resist.

Arjun bounded off, and she returned to her design work. But the distraction made it difficult to click back into gear. Her mind wandered to the past. After art school, Natasha cut her teeth at

Bombay advertising agencies. Hundreds of hours of resizing logos, sticking cartoon mascots on every surface, brightening colours to gaudiness and phosphorescence. *You have to catch the customer's eye, that's advertising!*

Her creator's heart grew weary – years had been spent making things which were the diametrical opposite of what she believed to be beautiful. She wanted her hands to fashion something she would be proud off.

Timidly, she struck out on her own. Her reputation grew and the demand for her work grew proportionately. Soon she hired a small team and rented a small office down the road. Her work was boutique – it wasn't the large names selling large volumes to gluttonous millions who came to her; it was the smaller la-di-das and the brands selling to the imported set that sought her out. This was a limited pool, and it suited her fine.

Friends urged her to think bigger and she even received some offers of investment, but something held her back. Her time was constantly torn between being a single mother and an entrepreneur.

Arjun had been unplanned. She had met a man in the big city in her early twenties. Pramod was kind, sweet and handsome. Lacking the airs of her snooty, creative friends, she was drawn to him. They had barely dated a few months when she became pregnant and in a whirlwind, they had decided to get married.

Natasha herself had grown up in a single-parent home – her father chose not to be a part of their lives. Although she exuded independence, the what-ifs of the lives not lived left her yearning for a more traditional nuclear household. Pramod seemed perfect and she was in love. He provided a wholesome anchor.

The first few years went by in a flash. She moved into his family home. He worked in a sprawling family business, replete with uncles, aunts and cousins. The business was in manufacturing of some description of chemicals for plastics. Natasha stopped working for a bit and played the role of a dutiful housewife.

After Arjun was born, things began to change. Natasha swung into an unfamiliar loop. She bore it for a while but once Arjun had outgrown his infancy, she began to itch for an independent life.

She prodded Pramod to get a separate house for them. She wanted to get back to work and spend long evenings with friends. She wanted her son to be brought up in a casual bohemian style and not in this safe, cloistered environment. Pramod wanted to give her what she wanted but he did not fully recognize her struggle. Promising to find an apartment for them soon, he would brush it off, expecting her to get over 'the phase'.

Resentment crept in. Instead of being charmed by his innocence, she now saw him as gutless and spoilt. Their home felt like a prison, and she began spending more time alone, in her corner.

Her coolness caused the drift between them to grow insurmountable. Pramod's concern for her changed to feelings of hurt, which then hardened into bitterness. Each played out their resentment with a quiet, polite fortitude.

Soon she felt like she couldn't breathe. Doubts created chasms from little cracks. Perhaps she married too quickly; she should never have agreed to move in; she didn't know him all that well; when she became pregnant, should she have taken care of it immediately? That last one singed her; she pushed it away from her thoughts.

And then one day, the fear of taking the leap, the aloneness, no longer scared her. She yearned for it. She left Pramod, got her own apartment and started putting her life together again. Her mother, who had done the same in her time, came to live with her for a while. Slowly, she stopped crying herself to sleep.

Natasha caught herself reminiscing and pulled herself back into reality. Grateful for her life's sedate tempo, she felt like she could do without any further excitement for a little bit longer.

~

There was something hypnotic about the man. His deep baritone muffled through the scarf tied around the lower half of his face. He spoke deliberately, calmly, never falling prey to Neha Singh's goading. But it was his eyes which seized attention. Blue with speckles of green and copper, they held the untamed sparkle of mountain people.

Cradling a machine gun, he spoke about his murdered kinsmen. The betrayal of the pretend-guardians and the compulsion of young men to take to arms, to fight for their destiny. Eloquent and magnetic, you couldn't help but feel a kinship to this man.

He spoke about vengeance, about the necessary acts of rectitude. Descriptions were delivered in a leaden, murderous monotone, triggering an inadvertent shiver up the spine. This was television gold dust.

The short interview raised ratings to previously unseen levels. An impromptu celebration was held at the studio in honor of Neha Singh. She was the toast of the town. Over the last few weeks, she had determinedly carried her microphone into situations where few others dared.

Gawde and the other production heads fawned and raised their glasses. They laughed at her jokes and listening ingratiatingly to her stories. Kabir had kept his distance, hoping she would not see him, but it was an intimate space and at some point, he was introduced to her. Under the cinematic lights in the studio, glass of whiskey in hand, the adulation and libation had cast her in a dreamy glow. She shook his hand and appraised him somewhat lecherously – she didn't seem to remember him and he was quickly dismissed.

Kabir rejoined his team who were huddled around Gawde. She was looking at them. Gawde gave her a wide smile and raised his glass. 'God, now that woman is going to become insufferable.' She nodded back, half-smiling.

~

A week or so later, Kabir was in a taxi, heading home in a slow river of honking cars and motorcycles; his taxi lurched forward in step with the mass of metal. They were passing a rare stretch of road where the speedometer made a brief looping-upward curve. Sandwiched between a harbor and a mangrove swamp, this artery connected the islands of the city. A welcoming breeze came off the water. The sea had turned into a warm rust colour of early evening. The biggest, shiniest hoardings of the city loomed over this stretch. The largest one in the center was Indiworld TV and their star – Neha Singh smiling heroically, arms folded. Kabir couldn't help feeling admiration for this woman.

He got out of the taxi at the cricket maidan. Since leaving Hyderabad, he had stopped following the Indian team. After the match fixing scandal, the sport had become sullied – he found it preferable to avoid it altogether. But watching the game being played in a maidan was different.

Back in Hyderabad, Kabir was accustomed to the natural isolation of cricket where the batsman stood alone to face the opposition in a large field. In the Bombay version, you were never alone; the challenge here was to stand firm against a swarm of distractions.

A batsman had flicked uppishly towards the outfield. A gangly fielder on the boundary jerked in acknowledgement at his newly pivotal role and belatedly loped towards the looping ball. Kabir watched in anticipation, willing the fielder to catch it. As it happened, the ball bounced out of outstretched palms. Kabir sympathetically watched the teammates adopt hands on hips and shaking heads. The guilty fielder made a show of the extenuating circumstances. He disbelievingly shook his head at the sun and kicked the uneven turf.

The sounds of cricket in this tropical metropolis were different from back home. Bombay's ochre earth swallowed the sharp fizzing sounds and gave them a thudding, springy quality.

Kabir ambled behind some practice nets. The whooshing sound of ball on netting awoke a muscle memory. Elbow up, wrists through the ball, Kabir instinctually shadow batted and didn't notice Arjun come up next to him. For a moment or two the boy looked up at Kabir's expression, taut with concentration.

'Should we go home now?'

Arjun had an unsentimental, slightly unnerving directness about him. Unaccustomed to mentoring a younger relationship, Kabir would find himself floundering at the brutal certitude and probing questions.

Walking home they talked about Arjun's game. He should try and shift his weight forward while driving the ball. Both nodded sagely.

Kabir walked him up to his apartment, hoping to 'inadvertently' find Natasha. The apartment door was ajar and Arjun rushed in, squealing, 'Hi Papa!'

'Hi son!'

Kabir's first reaction was to flee as though his imaginations about Natasha were admission enough of guilt. He did not want to interact with the ex.

But before he could act on his flighty impulses, 'Papa, this is Kabir he lives downstairs and he used to play cricket and now he is showing me some stuff and he seems quite good and he was also a batsman.'

This was rattled off without pause or inflection and now Kabir stood marooned.

'Er hi, I was just walking him up.'

Natasha popped out, hearing his voice.

'Oh hi, what's up? Pramod, this is Kabir.'

She had an undecipherable hollow look in her eyes as she went around the room, putting things in a bag.

Pramod stood in the centre of the room. His clean-shaven, spectacled face was expressionless. He scarcely acknowledged

Kabir and had the look of someone with other things on his mind.

Kabir started edging towards the door, hoping to melt away. Natasha looked pointedly at Pramod, who then turned and offered his hand.

'Hi, I'm Pramod. I believe you recently moved in downstairs? Natasha told me.'

She had been talking about him.

'Er, yeah – a few months ago.'

An awkward moment passed. Pramod seemed not to care that they stood in a room as strangers devoid of conversation. Kabir froze, unable to recall how to speak or move.

Would someone else please engage with this man so he could dive out unseen?

To Kabir's great relief, Arjun appeared. Pramod gathered him into his arms and took the bag from Natasha.

'I will speak to you later,' he added solemnly and walked purposefully past Kabir to the stairs.

Now alone with Natasha, Kabir remained standing silently.

'You know, in the first few years, watching them leave would always make me so sad.' She looked up and smiled. 'You want a drink?'

'Yeah.'

Kabir perched on a generously cushioned yellow futon.

'Sit back, be comfortable.'

It required him to remove a couple of smaller bolsters from behind him as he scooted back. Natasha pulled open an old-looking wooden desk revealing a small, neat bar. She busied herself with glasses, orange slices and aromatics to produce a red drink with several cubes of ice.

Handing it to him, she said affably, 'Negroni. Have you had one of these before?'

Kabir shrugged indeterminately. Not wanting to seem uninitiated, he changed the topic, 'It's a really nice apartment.'

'Yes, it's home. We have been here for two years now. You won't believe the trouble we had finding this place. First, the landlords only want corporate leases or embassy leases. If you can get around that then you need to belong to the right religion. Around here you need to be "mac".'

'What's mac?'

'Oh, it's what they call Catholics here.'

'Right...'

'But the real deal breaker is a young single woman with a kid. Wowee, you really are the peddler of sin then. Nobody wants a girl with loose morals living in their apartment. I got lucky with this place – the landlord lives across the road, and they are a sweet old couple. Did you find it difficult to find yours?'

'Oh, well, my cousin knew my landlord, so I barely had to look.'

'You're lucky. So, tell me more about yourself, Kabir. What are you doing alone in this big, bad city?'

Natasha sat sideways, her arm resting on the backrest, her body turned towards him. He looked straight ahead, feeling her gaze on his side. She coaxed his story from him, letting him talk. Once he began opening up, he couldn't stop, surprising himself. He had not spoken about home to anyone since moving to the city. Largely sticking to the facts, he tried his best to keep from expressing any real emotion. But they slipped out here and there when he spoke about Sareen and Barman. He didn't mention Sahiba.

At the end of the retelling, he stopped and there was silence. He stared down at the table. Natasha had listened thoughtfully and seldom interjected. She was the audience he had been craving. Slowly she unfolded herself, shuffled over to him and wrapped him in a friendly hug. Kabir smiled.

'So how come you guys split up?'

The words felt bold. Natasha straightened herself and didn't respond. Kabir felt like he had misread the moment.

'Well, it's a long story. I guess, in the end, we didn't really understand each other. Or maybe we didn't understand ourselves when we met.'

Kabir had no idea what this meant. 'Hmm' was his considered response.

'I met him when I first came to Bombay. Pramod made me feel safe. You know, I didn't have a big family when I grew up. My father left us when I was very young, so in a way, the idea of living in a big family seemed so great.'

'So what happened?'

'I suppose what always happens. We started to change as people. Or maybe I started to change. I wanted a different life, but he didn't. Maybe he did as well, who knows? We became unkind to each other and eventually we just ended up drifting apart.' She trailed off for a few moments. 'Oh god, I don't know why I am boring you with this stuff. I have only just met you and here I am, talking about my ex. If you want to run away, I won't blame you.' She laughed and fixed him with a dazzling smile. Kabir didn't want to be anywhere else.

'No, it's fine, really.'

'Let's talk about other things.'

'Okay. What do you do?'

After that the conversation turned to their stories of living in Mumbai. They now sat closer, facing each other. She spoke about things in life that Kabir had never experienced. She sounded urbane and worldly; he wanted to hug her again.

Natasha thought he was a great listener.

Having shared what they shared, kinship developed and the mood lightened. They rolled a joint. Natasha lit a large square candle and threw some fabric over the lamp shade; a woody vanilla scent wafted around the room. Kabir gazed up at poignant black and white photographs interspersed with the occasional art poster – Klimt's golden coupled entwined in a kiss, soldiers returning home, a girl staring pensively out of a window. He teased her about all the strangers she had on her walls.

The alchemy of things made the atmosphere silken and liquid. Kabir found his arm folded into hers and her face inches away. Suddenly, yet gently, Natasha moved forward and kissed him. He kissed her back and felt her weight pressing upon him. Hands furtively ran under clothes and soon bare skin rubbed and wrapped into each other. This was nothing like Kabir had experienced before. There was no hurried shyness of his first few times – this was languid and bold. Natasha led the way and he fell in step.

When they were done, they lay naked and breathless upon each other. After a few quiet minutes, Natasha stood up to fetch the paraphernalia for another joint and Kabir watched her move across the room, unconcerned about her nakedness. This was the first time he had truly gazed upon a woman this way. As they smoked, they covered themselves in a thin blanket. Kabir felt a delicious wooziness as they settled in and fell asleep.

He woke up in the pitch black not knowing what time it was. Carefully he got out of bed, dressed and went down to his apartment. She remained asleep.

CHAPTER SIX

That day was spent in a room with two white boards. Gawde had had an idea to develop a show covering the parties, fashion shows and celebrities of the city. He wanted sexy girls and glittering nights. Although this was an old trope, Indiworld TV had the reach and access, which would pull advertisers away from the smaller channels. Four members of the marketing team had gathered for a brainstorming session to launch the series.

Opinions within the upper echelons of the network were divided. Amongst the more vociferous voices of opposition was Neha Singh, who decried this type of content. She argued that it diminished the channel's reputation as a serious banner of journalism. Two opposing camps had formed on the issue.

Gawde was bullheaded in his pursuit of TRPs – that golden covenant of ratings, which governed the ability to pull in advertisers. He stubbornly pushed on and this meeting was a step towards planning the launch. It was no secret to those in the room that this was a cloak and dagger affair. Gawde's team relished their subversive intent, while the marketing team whimpered at being caught in the crossfire.

Gawde was missing from the room; he never went into early-stage meetings. The results from this room were to be presented to him so that he could tear down the first proposal along with the unfortunate soul who had the task of presenting it to him.

Placed in front of Kabir were three thick ring-bound volumes of 'consumer studies'. Buckets of prospective viewers were created based on age, sex, electronics at home, employment, neighbourhood, and disposable income down to their meal preferences. Then, multiple pages of multiple-choice questions asked the faceless people in these buckets questions they had never asked themselves. For instance – 'If your TV was a person, who would it be?'

An elaborate hypothesis then placed each person in a neatly defined box. Once this was done, the research people would sink into their chairs with relief at having resolved the unsettling vagueness of individual taste and preference. These marketing men and women, with slightly stylish button-down shirts, would roll up their charts, shake hands and prepare a long colorful presentation for it all.

Kabir pored through the material with interest. Emboldened by having been asked to join the discussion, he cockily tried his hand at exposing holes in their research. It was what Gawde would do. Encouraging looks from his team goaded him further. The marketing team, suitably bullied by Gawde's 'gang', left the room chastened. They promised to work on it again.

For the umpteenth time, Kabir secretly pulled his phone out of his pocket to check for any messages. There was nothing. He had not seen Natasha since 'that' night and it was coming up to a week. After sneaking out of her apartment, it took Kabir a couple of days to message her. He wanted to reach out sooner but was at a bit of a loss of what to say. Was it too early to call her? Should he just go up to her apartment and say hi? Should he give it a day? What would she think if he reached out immediately? He should just relax and play it cool. Right? Finally, he settled on sending a text. But what should it say?

He pored over it for a while and settled on:
hey how are you? All good?
He regretted sending it as soon as he hit the button. It sounded asinine and distant. He berated himself; after all those hours, that's the best he could come up with? Could he not have been just a little more intimate? Maybe:
hey thanks for the other night
or
im sorry I haven't seen you in a bit, lets catch up soon
Literally anything else.

Kabir could scarcely believe he had slept with a divorced woman who had a son! He desperately wanted to share the story but couldn't think of anyone to call.

His thoughts scampered back to that night. The light from the street creeping through a split in the curtains revealing her in small slivers – the curve of her bare hip, the light sweat where their skin lay on each other. It had a deliciously illicit flavour.

He was thinking of her constantly.

Natasha did eventually respond to his text:
hello you I have been busy but im good. How you?

'Busy' – that indeterminately, irritatingly, vague word. Why is it that when someone says they are busy, it never feels like they are actually busy? Its appearance on glowing pixels was akin to an electronic shrug of indifference. That one word turned his feelings from cautious curiosity to an anxious pining.

Now it felt like she was distancing him, which made him even keener.

~

It was an unfamiliar room without a roof, with several doors. Sareen, Barman, Mian Qadir and some others were huddled in a corner. Although he could not hear them, he knew that they were talking unfavorably. Mian Qadir was irritated and dismissive of counsel from the others. Kabir stood on the other end of this strange room as though waiting for a verdict. A deep sinking feeling. They asked him to leave; they said he had no place here.

He ran out of the building and down a path. His mother stood up ahead and she moved towards him. He dodged her and came upon a field. At the far side he noticed some girls – Sahiba may have been amongst them. They looked over their shoulder at him and giggled conspiratorially.

When he woke, the feeling of dread lingered like a bad smell.

Disoriented and cloudy, his eyes slowly grew accustomed to the light. It was the in-between time between day and dusk. The cawing cacophony of crows heralded the day's end. He hated this sloth borne from afternoon naps. The ebbing light made his spirit sink.

He looked up to see Natasha sitting on her study desk. Her hair formed a glowing halo from the lit table lamp. She was working on something. Her bed was low slung, and he gradually swung his legs off the end.

'Oh, hi sleepy.'

'Why didn't you wake me?'

'You were so tired, I didn't have the heart.'

'Ugh... I hate waking up at this time.'

'Yeah, I know what you mean. Let me get you some tea.'

Earlier that afternoon, Kabir dragged himself up the stairwell of his building. He had not slept for thirty-six hours and instead of stopping at his apartment, he had clambered an extra couple of floors. He was exhausted, but he did not want to be alone. The fatigue had him craving company and Natasha's apartment was nicer than his. She fixed him a sandwich and he decided to put his head down for a minute.

215

Natasha handed him tea.

'You look half-asleep.'

Kabir hadn't been able to shake the fog that seemed to have settled in his head. She sat back in her chair and continued sketching. Kabir stared at the floor, listening to the scratching of her pencil.

'I had a bad dream.'

'What about?'

'I'm beginning to forget the details, but it was about home. And you know when you wake up feeling like you did in the dream?'

'Yes.'

She turned to look at him. Putting her pencil down, she came and sat beside him and kissed him on the cheek. She didn't ask him more questions; they just sat there. Kabir liked that about her.

'Where is Arjun?'

'He's at a friend's place.'

'Can we turn the lights on? It's getting a little depressing in here.'

Natasha rose to turn on the lights. 'So, what happened last night?'

'It's been totally crazy. We were on a location shoot. Just waiting for something to happen.'

'Is this all related to the attack on parliament yesterday?'

'Yeah…'

Twenty-four hours. Only yesterday, but to Kabir it seemed much farther than that. News had filtered in about a terrorist attack on the parliament in Delhi. Pictures of men in white Indian formal against the stately red sandstone. Men of power, cowering, ducking for cover, stiff from indolence. They looked like ungainly caricatures. The popping of gunfire sounded innocuous on TV, like little firecrackers. The same footage played on repeat, disjointed and giving no indication of the sequence of events.

At office, people rushed around purposefully. Equipment was hauled into vans. Everyone was deeply attentive, fully focused on how to get the right picture, find the right interviewee, write the eyeball-grabbing relentless ticker at the bottom of the screen. It was simultaneously intimidating and exciting. Kabir stayed close to his team, not wanting to get in the way of the rest. Even he, the new kid, got front row access. All he needed to do was stay out of the way, do as he was told, and 'God forbid, don't opine on anything'.

Tags of 'jihadi', 'separatist', 'Pakistanis', 'mullahs' were smeared from the moment it all started. Bad blood could easily spread to the streets. In the late afternoon, the news team was dispatched to a Muslim neighbourhood where, Kabir was told, riots had claimed many lives ten years ago.

When they got there, they found quiet streets and shuttered doors. The place looked like an empty movie set, a pastiche of the everyday hustle-bustle where objects were bought and sold, livelihoods made and lives led. But today, there was barely a soul on the street. Signs on shop fronts painted in Urdu were the only marker of what this place was. The weighty silence felt ominous.

A nagging, prickling memory – flickers of those broken streets back home. But unlike Hyderabad, he didn't recognize this place. It didn't feel like it was happening to him, he was only an observer. Hours were spent expectantly, waiting for something to happen. But nothing did.

Finally, a call came in from Gawde to the head of the unit. Instructions were nodded and the van lurched through the narrow lanes. Suddenly, they stopped. A police jeep stood in the middle of an otherwise empty street. Constables were rounding up men and pushing them into the back of a van. Cameras rolled; the 'on-ground' presenter barked into the mic and interviewed bearded men proclaiming innocence.

Kabir marvelled at how they had happened upon this action deep within this labyrinth. Gawde had a knack of knowing where to find things. It was unclear who these men were and what they had done. The inspector in-charge seemed accustomed to the cameras. He had received a tip-off. Something about organized crime syndicates.

Back at the studio, there was much back-slapping. Indiworld was the only news channel with new footage. All other networks had been playing the same clips on loop since morning. It was all very exciting.

'Hey Kabir, are you okay?'

Natasha's voice brought him back to the present.

'Yeah. Yeah sorry, I'm still a bit dazed.'

'Wow. Do we know who did it? Or what's happening?'

'I don't think anyone knows exactly what's going on. As soon as it happened, Neha Singh rushed to Delhi to cover it – obviously.'

Natasha tilted her head and smiled in censure. She liked the plucky Neha Singh and had previously chided Kabir about his insinuations. To Kabir, Neha's behaviour was pompous, her ego brittle. He didn't understand how difficult it was for a woman to achieve what Neha had.

Their entanglement was at a stage where neither of them pushed their point of view too strongly – disagreements were excused with a smile.

'The news has been on the same loop since yesterday. Fourteen people and five terrorists killed. They are talking about war!'

'Yeah, the atmosphere in the studio was tense. They expected violence and sent us out on the streets. But mostly it was quiet. We did see the cops arrest a group of guys. They were gangsters or something.'

'Did they have something to do with the attack this morning?'

'I'm not sure… I don't know really.'

Kabir had started spending more time around Natasha. It was rare for him to be alone with her in her apartment. Usually it was a few minutes after dropping Arjun back from practice, the occasional meal and one Sunday afternoon. Mostly they went out or she would come to his apartment for a few hours before sneaking back upstairs.

Kabir's nights were consumed. Gawde took him to multiple industry events, and late-night meetings were common. He began exploring the after-dark allure of the city with a traveler's thirst. Metallic, heady, rushing. In this intoxicating, sparkly throb, the world was aglow with possibility. Kabir was rubbing shoulders with TV personalities, with impossibly beautiful women and with people of power and influence. They didn't know who he was. Yet. He quickly became party to the aspiration that someday they would know who he was and soon 'he' would be 'them'.

He was becoming habituated to being out and staggering home late. Some nights he came home to an empty echo. Sometimes when surrounded by all the new people, he felt the most alone. But mostly he yearned for it. It helped fill a void.

Natasha provided a gentle panacea. Kabir called her whenever he grew weary of the excitement. She provided a much needed, quiet balance. He would listen to her talk, eat her cooking and feel something akin to home.

Natasha, for her part, was unfazed by his sporadic calls. She found it charming when he flopped onto her futon in a daze, ready for a quiet evening at home. It provided a glimpse into a life she no longer had.

Sometimes it prickled Kabir that she never seemed put out with him. She never even tried to make plans with him.

Both avoided thinking about it too much. It was not a predictable choice for either of them, so they pushed those thoughts away. Perhaps it imbued a light touch – without expectations, without fear, without questions.

Kabir turned to Natasha and they kissed. After a few minutes of twisting and caressing, they broke off. He stirred from the bed and pulled himself into a long languid stretch.

'I need to go and meet the team for dinner. Gawde just called us out to discuss work.'

'Okay, good luck. I will see you later.'

'Will you be up late?'

'Nope – it's a school night. Why don't you come out and meet some of my friends this weekend? Arjun will be at his father's, so we can have a night out.'

'That… would be great. Let's do it.'

Kabir walked downstairs, pleased with himself.

Natasha watched him leave, biting her lip. Bringing him in to meet her friends implied a level of intimacy and acknowledgement of his place in her life. It made her nervous.

CHAPTER SEVEN

The clattering of plates and spoons, the soundtrack of the famed
Krishna restaurant, were amplified in the small space. It implied
serious eating and serious food. As a child, in his landlocked
hometown, Kabir rarely ate seafood. Freshwater fish was one
of his least favourite things, what with the bones and the smell.
Tonight was his first time at 'the Krishna' which specialized in
local seafood; Gawde was particularly partial to its fare. Like
other patrons, seven of them were squeezed onto a single table
that would have struggled to hold five. Elbows jostled and dishes
tilted up to each other but no one seemed to mind. As one table
vacated, another was readied in seconds for the next set of patrons.
Dishes, glasses and crumbs were whisked into an awaiting bucket
manned by a crew-cut-lowest-in-the-pecking-order apprentice.
The tablecloth was whipped off while another wafted like a sail
and settled on the table.

Waiters, clad in an incongruous livery of purple waistcoats and
ties, worked with practiced hustle. Beer glasses were filled before
you read the third line of the menu. Patrons were allowed about
five minutes to ponder their choices before these hyper efficient
conductors swept in to rattle off the specials.

Gawde ordered with an experienced wave of the hand. First, an inspection of crabs, tentacles slowly clawing the air.

What followed was a meal the memory of which remains embedded on your palette. A smear of gustation to be recalled in vivid detail for months, if not years, to come.

Crab was cooked in garlic, butter and fresh pepper, served with naan still rising from the clay oven. The shell-on succulents required fingers and cracking; the tender flavoured meat juicy and dripping. This was followed by the first pomfret Kabir had ever loved. A full fish stuffed with green herbs, aromatics, fresh spices and grilled to a char. The fish fell off the bone and tasted fresh and moist. Accompanying everything was the yellow daal retaining the character of the earthen pot of a seaside village. Tangy yet wholesome, spicy yet smooth. The table also included deep fried little bits of squid and prawn.

Sameer Sirohi took the lead.

'The story is limited to Delhi. Enough resources have been sent over there, and there is little for us to do but play support on this end. We need to look for something else.'

Gawde looked up from his plate and surveyed the people on the table.

'We should support as best as we can. Any requirement from Neha's team needs to be dealt with urgently. Okay?'

His declaration was confusing because it was unnecessary. Heads around the table stayed quiet. A point was being made, but they were unsure what it was. Gawde had a way of throwing people off.

'Something else has come to light though. It is still unconfirmed and therefore we need utmost secrecy. Nobody here opens their mouth for fear of death by my hand. Is that understood?'

Being threatened by Gawde was also not new for any of these men, but this time it did not sound like the everyday, throwaway promise of castration.

'You all know of the famous interview with the terrorist last month. We were told that our local handlers had reached out and they agreed to speak to Neha. Well, it seems it may not have gone down that way.'

Gawde paused to let it sink in.

'It seems that someone may have staged the whole thing.'

Immediately the table erupted in urgent questions.

'What!?' 'What do you mean staged?' 'Did they know?' 'Staged by whom?'

'Hang on, hang on. Firstly, and most importantly, in a time like this we work as a team. Forget your personal feelings about Neha and her people. This reflects on us all and we must rally together. So, no shooting off! No throwing accusations around. Is that clear?'

There was silence.

Gawde growled, 'Is that clear?'

Heads nodded vigorously.

'Okay, good. So, what we know currently is that the person on camera may not have been a terrorist. We don't know who he was. I mean, he could be an actor, for all I know.'

He paused again thoughtfully.

'Also, we don't know if any of our team was in on it. The handlers we use in Kashmir could have set it up and Neha may have known nothing about it.'

Sameer Sirohi harrumphed, 'Well they could have checked their sources.'

Gawde replied impatiently, 'Don't be a fool. It doesn't work like that. What are you going to do? Ask them for their terrorist ID? In this situation, you trust the handlers. They have been working with us for years.'

Sameer, unhappy at being cut to size amongst the juniors on the table, defended himself, 'They shouldn't have taken it live without doing more background work. We have others we know in Kashmir; they should have cross-checked with them.'

'I suppose they did run it as soon as they got the footage. Perhaps they should have been more careful.'

'Who gave you this information? Is it certain that the guy's a fake?'

'As I said, we don't know if anyone is complicit at our end. I pray that it's all just a big misunderstanding but for now keep it under your hat.'

Gawde paid and rose to leave. Outside the restaurant, a couple of the guys lit up cigarettes and started peeling off. Kabir hailed a taxi, but Gawde waved the cab away.

'Come with me, I will give you a ride. It will give us time to catch up. I want to hear about your adventures. We are heading in the same direction.'

It was more a directive than an offer.

They rolled down the windows and enjoyed the cool evening breeze blowing through the car. At this hour, the colonial part of town looked romantic and quiet. Gawde's anecdotes about the city had a storyteller's rhythm. Casually, he asked Kabir about his life and in particular the people he had been meeting. He listened intently as Kabir narrated inconsequential bits and pieces.

'How are you liking the job?'

'It's very interesting, sir. I am learning a lot.'

'Good, good. I think it's time you started getting more involved with things, eh? Tell you what, why don't you come over to my place after work on Monday? I have a little work and I need someone I can trust with it.'

The car rolled up to Gawde's building, he got out and tapped on the roof of the car in a parting 'good night'.

～

Natasha climbed the stairs ahead of him. A fluorescent blue tube light lit the stairwell and cast sharp shadows on the chalk white walls. Ajanta building bore the traits of so many other buildings in this neighbourhood, sharing their brutal practicality of unadorned blocky space. Exteriors were papered over with a bright lick of paint or hidden under a shadowy canopy of trees.

This felt like their first night as a couple. They had spent the evening with Natasha's friends – artists, aesthetes, creative, worldly people. Nervous at first, Kabir had said little. He noticed a couple of loaded glances towards Natasha but the 'friends' were otherwise kind to him. It felt grown up, like a world he would like to belong to at some point.

It occurred to him that women developed idiosyncrasies and individuality much earlier than men did. They read Russian literature; they were moved by their chosen contemporary artist; and had moral positions on women in Bollywood. Girls liked laments of warbling singer-songwriters and slow, moody films. At the same stage in life, men reverted to obsessions and clannish passions. Sports and action movies were standard initiations, and any eclecticism was limited to passed down rock albums, comic book heroes and posters of cars. There were exceptions of course, but by and large, men seemed to band together and choose their individuality in clumpy groups.

To Kabir, Natasha seemed self-assured and experienced. But sometimes chinks would appear and betray her fragility – momentarily raised eyebrows or her hands gripping a little too tightly, a little too long. Tonight, on the way home she talked of how she knew so many people, yet she barely felt close to anyone.

Kabir had found comfort with her. She held his attention in a way that Sahiba never had. It made him wary, intimidated. He told himself it was just a fling, it must be. But his attempts at indifference belied his growing attachment to her. He tried to not let his thoughts linger on her for too long or imagine a more lasting connection between them.

For her part, Natasha had begun to think less and worry less.

She pushed away thoughts about what she was doing with a boy almost ten years younger than her. He felt wholesome and innocent, almost like a refuge. But as she grew fonder, she grew more cautious.

The will of things had surreptitiously started to create permanence for both of them.

Natasha opened the door to her apartment. They slipped in as though habituated to this ritual of returning home. Her friends had liked him, and the question of their ages became inconsequential. Relief flooded through her and made her want him even more. As soon as the door closed, she pushed against him and slipped her tongue into his mouth. Each pushed and grabbed more urgently than before. Their lovemaking was less inhibited. Ravishing and quenching, it felt more expressive. Kabir slept over that night.

CHAPTER EIGHT

Gawde perched forward and placed his whiskey on the ample space the armrest provided. The curved seat of his favourite planter's chair looked like a cat's arching stretch. Fragrant wafts of coconut and spice drifted out from the kitchen.

Although they had help in the house, Mrs Simli Gawde preferred handling the cooking herself. This large marbled apartment was a long way from her ancestral village of thick palm fronds and waterways. She felt most at home in the kitchen amongst the earthen jars and soaking rice.

No matter how far they came, the Gawdes would carry the simple aesthetic of what felt like home. The apartment was sparse, and the few bits of furniture were crafted from thick teak. The soft white upholstery and rattan carpets made it look like a stately coastal home. As a boy, these were the symbols of taste Prakash Gawde aspired to.

Simli Gawde threw in a fistful of curry leaves and left her pot to simmer. As was their routine, she came into the living room to spend a customary hour with her husband before dinner. Wrapping the ends of her sari around her ample waist, she sat on the small sofa beside Gawde. He briefly looked up from the newspaper to acknowledge her. Over the years, these hours had become quieter. When first married they would use this time to talk wide-eyed about the world they were discovering together. They were each other's rafts in an uncertain tide.

Sitting in silence, she thought back to their wedding. The entire village had attended; people sat on the floor and ate on banana leaves. The young Prakash Gawde had secured a job in the nearby town's vernacular daily and they left home to start a new life. Gawde's tenacity and intellect led them from town to big town, from city to metropolis. He worked excruciating hours in order to lift them from the dead-end backwater from which they came. Over time, he grew in stature and wealth, and their life became unrecognizable. When they bought their first colour TV, it was garlanded. She recalled how they fell into peals of laughter at the absurdity of their first washing machine. Neither could have imagined a machine would thump the stains out of their clothes.

From the written word Gawde had jumped into video in the 90s when the airwaves opened up. It paved the way for his move to Bombay. By the time they got to the big city, they had spent two decades together. Prakash took to his new life like a fish to water – he thrived in the cut and thrust. Simli had long stopped agonizing about the change in this sweet, simple boy from her village. They would still exchange glances of comprehension, off and on about where they came from. But by and large, she avoided his office parties, social engagements and colleagues – she just didn't belong.

Gawde got up to pour himself another drink.

'Did you see Neha Singh's interview?'

Simli raised a questioning eyebrow. 'With the terrorist? Of course. Everyone has seen it.'

'What do you think?'

'What is there to think?'

Gawde paused momentarily before dropping a cube of ice into his glass.

'Come on… I'm asking because I want your opinion.'

'Really? That hasn't happened in a while.' Simli let this hang in the air. When they were alone, he had no pretense – she was his equal. 'Is she being celebrated at the network? Is that what's bothering you? You have been muttering around the house for a few weeks now.'

'Yes, she is quite the flavour.'

'It was powerful, you know. She certainly has a way with the viewer. Especially women – they look up to her.'

'Yes, well. That she does.' Gawde sat back down in his spot and gazed into the glass.

Simli turned to him and cocked her head, 'So what have you got planned for her?'

'What do you mean?'

'If there is anything I know about you, it is that you won't allow a threat to linger, and I know you see her as a threat.'

He pursed his lips in a wry smile, 'Maybe I have changed.'

Simli Gawde pulled her head back and leaned on the bolster. It was a skeptic's gesture and she left it alone.

The doorbell rang.

'Oh, I forgot, one of the boys from the office is coming over. Won't be too long. You eat if you like.'

Simli rose with an accustomed sigh. She preferred not sitting around trying to make conversation. Gawde turned down the hall to open the front door. His voice changed into bombastic exclamation.

～

'KABIR my boy! Come come.'

The first thing Kabir noticed was Gawde's starched white lungi wrapped in the fashion of men from the coast. A woman came out behind Gawde, looked at Kabir and turned away down the corridor and into a room. Gawde did not seem to notice her as he ushered him in. Kabir handed over a pile of documents and Gawde sat at the dining table to study and sign some pages. As he waited, Kabir looked around at a cluster of framed photographs on the walls. All were black and white portraits of groups of people staring stiffly into the camera, shot in archival style. The backdrops looked important – large wrought iron gates, exterior of a cinema hall, long curving staircase – and the people looked somber and dressed in their best. Men wore all white and were largely in lungis similar to what Gawde had on; some had small Mohammedan caps on their heads. Women were all in sarees draped over their heads. Each picture a little jewel of time.

Gawde noticed Kabir's gaze. 'Those are all from my village. I found them in a secondhand store. They would have been thrown away if I had not seen them.'

'They look old. Do you know these people?'

'Some of them I remember from my childhood, but some of them are quite ancient.'

'When were they taken?'

'A few are dated from before Independence, but most are unknown. We had a photography shop in the village where everyone would come and get their annual family picture taken. The owner was third generation when I was growing up. They were the official photographers of our district for many, many years.'

'What happened to the shop?'

'The same old story. The generations spawned more generations, people didn't need to travel to get their picture taken, alcoholism, kids wanted to do something else and so on. I hung on to these. They have a great style.'

'They are quite amazing, sir.'

'Well, Mr Menon, can I get you a drink?'

'Er, sure sir.'

'Whiskey?'

'Yes sir, thank you.'

Gawde motioned for Kabir to sit and went to fix him a drink. They settled in and talked about Gawde's upbringing and his arrival to Bombay. It was impossible not to be rapt by the story of a high school dropout who became one of the most powerful producers in news television.

Gawde had played this hand before. His story of humble roots told in his brotherliness; it disarmed and charmed. He poured Kabir another drink.

'So, anything new going on? What are the boys saying about the Neha Singh issue?'

'I… I don't really know, I have not–'

'Don't worry, I respect that you would not want to betray their trust.'

Gawde walked over to an antique-looking teak desk and from the drawer, pulled out a thick rectangular parcel the size of a large envelope. He handed it to Kabir. The contents were tightly wrapped in sellotape.

'I want you to deliver this for me tonight. My car will take you to Dadar station. Once you are there, call the number on this card. A man called Pandit will take it from you. Hand it to him and him only. Clear?'

Kabir nodded

'Can I trust you to do this?'

'Yes, sir. Of course.'

'Good. Now don't let it out of your sight.'

It made Kabir feel important – he was in the inner circle.

'Sir, what are you going to do about Neha Singh?'

'I will keep it hidden. Hopefully it will blow over.'

It seemed the honorable thing to do.

~

231

Dadar station wore a desolate look. The rows of vegetable-sellers who laid out their wares in the day had disappeared. In the dark, it was unrecognizably peaceful. Kabir got off the car and called the number. The other end of the line was gruff and monosyllabic. A boy appeared, about his own age, and motioned for Kabir to follow him into a warren of gullies.

Kabir bleated questions while trying to keep up with the boy. Where they were going? How far? Where is Pandit? An unease crept up over him as they went deeper into the dense shanties. Humanity lived in close quarters and eyes were watching everything.

Suddenly the boy ducked into a narrow stairwell and loped upstairs. Kabir hesitated as he looked up at the looming tenement wall. Locally these were called 'chawls'. A deep breath later, he dutifully followed him to the first floor and through a couple of corridors. An inner landing opened into a large courtyard. People loitered on the shared balconies.

Finally, they came upon a blue door. Irregular peeling revealed layers of paint-overs. Inside the small room, two men sat on low cane stools. Kabir was motioned to sit. The boy went into an adjoining room behind a curtain. The men looked at Kabir briefly before resuming their card game. One of them had a gash on his cheek. A moment later the curtain parted and in swaggered a man in a white vest. His paunch stretched the cotton around his midriff; his chest and shoulders were thin in comparison.

'Gawde sent you?' A direct, loutish tone.

'Yes. Are you Pandit?'

Kabir thought better than to push for a reply. He handed over the package to the outstretched hand and left.

Making his way back through the gullies, Kabir had the nagging sense that the man's face seemed familiar. Where had he seen him before?

～

Footsteps clattered on the vast marble floors. The three of them, huddled in a cubicle, waited for the steps to recede towards the swinging door and disappear. Silence returned in the large, cavernous bathroom of the luxury hotel. Kabir sniggered with the other two, and they cut more white powder on the ledge above the toilet.

Kabir had become accustomed to these parties and these people. His new friends were frequenters of the night. There were no lunches, or movies, or meeting up for daytime activities – he saw them often, but only after dark. Kabir snatched a rolled up five-hundred-rupee note and snorted a line. A euphoric rush filled the hollow.

The boys fell out of the toilet and straightened themselves up in the mirror. The narcotic awakened every pore in Kabir's body. His mind trilling with energy, he rolled into the party cocksure and supreme. It was a glitzy affair at a rooftop bar. Frenetic camera flashes captured the rich and famous as they went around rubbing shoulders. The next day's daily would have double page coverage of the event, tens of little pictures elbowing for attention.

Tonight a trio of socialites was hosting a fundraiser. Their cause was the marginalised women of Bombay, those exploited who worked in menial jobs. Large, glamorous, black and white posters of famous models and actresses were placed around the room, many of whom were present that evening. Emblazoned on each of them was a tagline – 'I am Sarita' or 'I am Vineeta', names that sounded to these twinkling hosts as appropriately marginalised. The pouting, lascivious photos sat incongruous to the message at hand. In his heightened state, Kabir scoffed at the absurdity. To him it sounded like these well-meaning, diamond-dripping ladies had each co-opted their maids' names. He mentioned this to his friend who laughed at the observation and immediately contradicted himself by exclaiming how great the campaign was. One of the organizers was a very, very dear friend, you see.

It didn't take much for these nocturnalists to dissolve into cackles of laughter. Kabir had noted this trait when he first spent time with these people but soon became habituated to it – he had become a cackler himself. Floating around the room, Kabir darted in and out of conversations. The social set was beginning to recognize him; it gave him a swagger to be known by some of these celebrities. In this heady state, he was unable to hold dialogue for too long. After effusive greetings, followed by exaggerated laughter, his nerves started to jangle, and he shifted away.

On his third lap around the room, he spotted Natasha. A deep-necked black dress draped on her chest, her collarbone caught the light, accentuating her slender form. Ravishing, she seemed to stand out in the room – as though under a shaft of light designed singularly for her. She was laughing, seemingly enjoying herself with a group of people unknown to him. A jealous ache pulled at Kabir. A rush, an emboldened bravado made him want to possess her from others. Her eyes lit up as she saw Kabir approach. Bumbling into their conversation, he barely registered what was being said to him. The women talking to Natasha became visibly uncomfortable and drifted off.

Natasha was caught off guard by his charge. Her expression shifted from incomprehension to annoyance. Wanting to be alone with her, he grabbed her arm a little more forcefully than he intended. They walked into a corner.

She whispered, 'What's wrong with you?'

'What do you mean? I'm fine. What are you doing here?'

'What do you mean, what am I doing here? I know people in the city, you know. I have lived here a long time.'

'I know, I know. That's not what I meant.'

A silence followed.

'Let's go dance.' He was trying to break the awkwardness but his attempt at casual friendliness came out rough.

'No, I'm fine. Listen, I want to catch up with some of my friends. Let's find each other later, okay?'

A flash of anger came over him.

'What's the matter with you?'

'What's the matter with YOU? Why are you being so weird?'

Unable to formulate the correct response, Kabir kept shaking his head.

'Whatever Natasha – go do what you want!'

'Kabir, this is not like you. You are trying to fit into some idea of something. Please believe me, this isn't you.'

She looked around the room before continuing.

'Also, these new friends of yours – don't become like them. I honestly don't know what you see in them.'

She sounded condescending.

'What makes you think you know me so well? You are so judgmental. You don't even know who I hang out with!'

'I know enough to know that those guys are not really your friends.'

It may have been the effects of the drugs or the fact that her observation furrowed a gnawing suspicion that Kabir had chosen to ignore. Either way, he felt assaulted and wanted to wound her back.

'What would you know? Where are your "true" friends? I don't know where you get this superior attitude of yours. It's probably the reason your marriage didn't work out and you're now alone with a child.'

Natasha recoiled. She held his gaze momentarily and spun away.

Kabir took his feelings back to the cackling friends. They went on to another bar and then a house party somewhere. Kabir carried around a stone in his gut. He had done something bad. All he wanted to do now was to wash it away. The rest of the night was spent chasing a rush – elusive and momentary.

CHAPTER NINE

Kabir came in early that morning as he had for most of that week. The bottom of the rung was required to attend to numerous tasks, each varying in mundanity, and he had put them aside for too long.

He hadn't seen Natasha since the other night. It had been almost a week. Twice his calls to her had gone unanswered. He yearned to be around her, to nestle in that hollow of her neck. He wanted to run up to her apartment and lay himself bare. But recollections of those miserable weeks spent pining after Sahiba held him in check. He remembered the razor-edged longing, the affront mingling with despair. Unable to understand the whys. Jealous simulations, things held and not said.

So, he held himself to himself. Resisting the urge to appear too needy. Sometimes, rarely, his feelings swung away from thoughts of her, and he felt unweighted. But mostly his heart waded through treacle, heavy and sunken. He preferred being away from his empty apartment. These early mornings at the office had become regular.

As he stepped in through the double doors, something was amiss. The office was quiet, yet there was an urgency to scurrying feet in the halls. The few people in the office at the time sat in huddles; the atmosphere was conspiratorial.

Walking towards his cubicle, he came upon two 'editing guys'. Video editors were ghosts of the office – always around but only seen at invisible hours. They would live in darkened, screen-infested dens, emerging only occasionally. Round, bespectacled and unshaven, editors tended to look like they needed sleep; fresh air, sunshine and fewer cigarettes wouldn't hurt.

Due to their access to everything that flowed into the network – in equal parts content and chatter – they knew what was going on, where it was going on and most importantly, who was carrying on the goings-on. Smug with their superior access to other peoples' business, they carried a disdainful indifference.

'What's going on around here guys? It feels quiet.'

One of them looked at Kabir condescendingly.

'Nothing a child like you needs to know.'

'Oh, come on, guys. Tell me!'

The editors exchanged glances. Should they let this upstart in on their worldly pulse of things?

Another defining trait of editors was that they loved to gossip. Once they got started, they spared no detail. So much so that their initial contemptuousness seemed a ploy to get you to speak to them in the first place.

'That interview with the terrorist? Arrey, Neha's one… Yeah, that was fake.'

'The guy wasn't really a terrorist.'

'Staged.'

They played off one another, whispering breathlessly into their hands. A cloak and dagger pantomime.

'I always knew something was fishy about that.'

'No you didn't, you never said anything like that.'

'I never said it because it was obvious. You remember when we were cutting the piece, we were both suspicious!'

'That's true, we were.'

'Anyway, the producer in her team fucked up.'

'Or it was planned all along?'

'But Kabir, keep it quiet. We are the only people who know right now. We don't want the news to spread. Better to handle it internally.'

Kabir had listened unmoved. After revealing this choicest scandal, the portly editors stared at him with injured expressions at his lack of excitement.

'What?' Kabir asked the two staring faces.

'Do you have any idea what this means?'

'Relax guys, I have known for a while. It's an old story.'

Kabir smirked as he walked away. He could feel their bewildered gaze on his back – they were not the first to know and it must be killing them.

'Wait, come back here Kabir, what do you know…?'

Kabir trotted off; there was too much to get done. Budgets and filing expense receipts had to be completed before they set out on any story leads for the day, otherwise he would have to stay back late again. In the thick of the paperwork, Kabir barely noticed the morning slip away and the office fill up.

Chayan sat in the cubicle next to him and had slipped in without Kabir noticing. He too was a member of the bottom rung and was doing much the same as Kabir.

'Hey Chayan, what's going on?'

Chayan stared and did a little hop in his seat.

'Heyyy Kabir men. The news is out men.'

'I heard, I heard. How did it get out? I thought we were the only ones to know.' Chayan shrugged in a polite sort of way.

'I need a break, you want some coffee?'

Fifty meters outside the office and into a small gully was a coffee stall, cigarette shop, snack counter, all rolled into one. Frequented by the staff at the network, the proprietor would serve coffee in tiny metal cups with protruding lips. To cool the piping hot drink, a balletic performance would ensue every few minutes

– sweet south Indian coffee poured from one receptacle to another from great heights with extended arms. Left, then right, then left again. Watching the pouring routine was half the joy of coming to this place.

Kabir recognized many of the patrons from the office. He did not know what most of them did or the departments they belonged to. Kabir and Chayan pretended to speak amongst themselves but in earnest were focused on eavesdropping.

'...She must have known boss, look how much publicity it got her...'

'It's a mistake, it could happen to anyone.'

'Don't be stupid–'

As with all good gossip, every scenario had a patron. Conspiracies, sympathies, personalities were each given air to burn.

And then a new thread picked up.

'...it's a setup, someone planted it.'

'I bet that Gawde had something to do with it. He's too clever, he's not going to let Neha get too powerful.'

'He definitely has his reasons to do it. I wouldn't put it past him.'

Chayan and Kabir exchanged a look – they would never have considered this.

Nobody contradicted the direction this chatter had turned towards. Insinuations became more sinister and the conjectures more damning.

An indignant flush compelled Kabir to blurt, 'You guys don't know what you are saying. Gawde knew about it, but he didn't want to tell anyone. I know for a fact that he's really supportive of Neha and why would he do it anyw–'

Conversation stopped. A row of guarded faces stared back at him. Chayan, wide-eyed, was trying his best to blend into the wall. Nobody responded; they peeled away wordlessly.

Kabir had blundered. He recalled a similar indignation when he spoke up for Barman. But college was a much smaller world, the

239

students were known to him. There was an innocence about it. Here the stakes were unclear; there was no shelter, no implied forbearance of elders. Nobody cared for the purity of your intentions.

Back upstairs at the office, the atmosphere was expectant.

The door of the large boardroom remained closed for the most part. Occasionally a greying, manicured, suited type would walk out, speak on his phone for a few minutes and walk back in. Lawyers.

Just then, a soft rustling of whispers flowed through the office. Kabir looked up to see Neha Singh marching towards the boardroom. She looked unbowed, her chin defiant as she pushed open the glass door.

After some hours, the boardroom emptied out. Participants strode away as though to put distance between themselves and what had transpired there. Gawde, however, stood outside the door talking, taking representations, placating those who needed soothing.

Many hands rested on his shoulder while he nodded somberly, repeatedly. A seeming tilt of fortunes dripped favorably towards him. It was masterful.

Across the sea of cubicles, Kabir watched Neha Singh collect her belongings from her office. Her people loitered around her in support; others gawped at the spectacle, unable to look away. Neha was asked to 'unofficially', 'temporarily', stay out of the office. A cooling off period while 'we can figure all this out'.

Up until yesterday, Neha's team had preened and strutted. Today, bereft, they were the subjects of slanted whispers. Meanwhile Gawde's team watched with self-contented smirks. Loyalties, for the most part, turned and flowed in the eddies of opinion. The swiftness of change was unsettling and confusing for Kabir.

News hit the stands the next morning. Coverage of the scandal spanned from salacious innuendo to measured editorial commentary. Staccato images of Neha Singh and screen grabs of the masked terrorist were everywhere. Politicians, opinion makers, generals, and even the odd film star, shared space on live television's little opinion boxes. Debates raged for days. Gawde represented the network – making statements about mistakes being made and the need for transparency. He was being recognized; he was becoming a household name.

CHAPTER TEN

It was early evening. Kabir had just enough time to return home to shower. Life was now a swirl of Indiworld and the Bombay nightlife.

Twice more he had made a trip to the chawl to meet Pandit. An underlying menace continued to punctuate these trips. Fear induced excitement accompanied him every time he went. But he now knew his way into the tenement – the men in the room had stopped sizing him up and Pandit deemed him worthy enough to ask his name.

Kabir had remembered Pandit as the police inspector who was in charge of the arrests they had filmed in the Muslim area. The packets he carried were wads of banknotes. Kabir figured they were exchanged for information and assumed it must be how things were done.

Something about the whole affair made him think of Sareen. They hadn't spoken since he left Hyderabad. It made Kabir feel strangely culpable. For so long he had wanted to be angry and indignant. But at this moment, he didn't feel quite so righteous. He picked up his phone and dialed his old friend.

Several rings went unanswered. Kabir was about to hang up when a voice, small yet familiar, gently proposed a 'hello'.

'Sareen? Hey… It's Kabir.'

'Hi Kabir baba, how are you?'

'I… I'm good, I'm in Bombay. How are you? What's going on?'

'Yes, I heard you were there.'

Kabir had not known what to expect. He was prepared to counter Sareen's bolshiness. But instead Sareen spoke politely, formally. His diction was slow and deliberate. It wasn't a formality borne from contrition. In fact, there was no hint of affront at all.

'What are you doing now?'

'I am working with my uncle in his shop.'

'Really? And you are okay with that?'

'Yeah, it's going good.'

Sareen was known to brandish his heart on his sleeve. Yet here he was, seemingly living a life he had dreaded, showing no emotion at all.

'So, what about your new "gang", are you still doing that?'

Silence.

'Did you get into trouble?'

'Leave it, it doesn't matter. What are you doing now Kabir?'

'I left my job at the bank. I joined Indiworld TV.'

'The news channel?'

'Yeah.'

'That's good, you were always into stuff like that.'

'I guess.'

'Well, good to talk to you. I need to go now.'

'Err, okay.'

'Bye, Kabir, take care.'

They both hung up. The conversation felt wooden and unnerving, like talking to a stranger.

All that carried-over resentment remained unsated.

Kabir's thoughts lingered on the call as he walked down to hail a taxi. He saw Arjun across the road, kit bag slung across a shoulder, the bat handle sticking up and to the left. After his row with Natasha, Kabir felt certain that she wanted nothing to do with him and he had chosen to avoid Arjun altogether.

Their eyes met and Arjun's face lit up. He crossed the road and the boy's pace quickened towards Kabir, his kit bag jiggling behind him. A taxi pulled up and Kabir got in without waiting. Arjun's confused expression fell into a wounded sump. Mouth slightly ajar, the look followed Kabir as he sped past.

~

Late evening, the bustle outside Dadar station had yet to scatter into its nightly slumber. More eyes around at this time, yet the jumble allowed for anonymity. Kabir made it to the usual door, and was let in by the lanky boy who had fetched him the first time he came here. Uncharacteristically, the room was empty. Pandit wasn't there. 'Lanky boy' told him to wait as he disappeared behind the curtain separating the room from the rest of it. Knowing better than to expect any more conversation than a well-timed grunt, Kabir chose not to ask questions.

Kabir sat on a small wicker stool and glanced around the sparse room. On the small table beside him a spread of papers caught his eye. Familiar names popped up, underlined. A thickly scribbled schedule – cricket matches and names of players. Here and there numbers were added to the margins.

'Lanky boy' re-entered the room. In a smooth practiced motion, the boy swung himself onto a stool opposite. Lanky looked like he had been written into that moment, in that setting. His teeth held a toothpick off one side, his hair tousled, ever the gangster's apprentice. In some moments he looked fourteen and then thirty-five but rarely his real age, which was somewhere in-between.

'You know what that is?' Lanky asked arrogantly.

Kabir shrugged.

'Half the city's betting runs through us.'

Kabir didn't know who 'us' was and didn't really want to ask. He stayed quiet.

'We run the games.'

He was bragging now.

'Run them how?'

Lanky threw his head back in a sneer. 'How do you think? You know how much money flows through here? All those players ask us permission if they as much as want to take a piss.'

'I heard a couple of players were involved.'

'Fully. They are all fixed. All these fuckers are handled.'

'Can't be all of them.'

Lanky pushed forward intimidatingly. 'What do you know, asshole? It's not just the Indian team. The Pakistanis have been in the pocket of the underworld for years and now it's the international teams also. Even the umpires are fixed. We run the whole system.'

Lanky was reveling in his sense of importance. He was the most gangster gangster in that room.

'Oh okay. I was told to collect some documents. Can I have them?'

'This betting is so much cleaner than other things...' Lanky seemed not to hear Kabir's attempts to get out of there, nor the discomfort in his voice. He stretched and continued, 'You only have to fix things here and there. There is no "forcing" required, nobody needs to get "tapkaoed," you understand? Only if someone doesn't pay up, a little push is required.'

The trill of a cheap phone called from a back room behind the curtain. Lanky jumped to answer. Kabir couldn't hear what was being said. Suddenly the boy rushed out and threw open the front door. Holding the frame, he leaned over and twisted left towards the urgent voices and shouts coming down the corridor. Kabir couldn't see anything from where he was sitting. Afraid to move, he sat rooted to his spot. Lanky jumped out into the corridor and for a moment, Kabir was alone in the room. Voices were getting closer along with sounds of feet scraping and shuffling.

Bodies burst through the open door and at first were undiscernible. Kabir pushed himself towards the corner. Three men, followed by Lanky, had dragged and lifted another man into the small room and laid him on the floor. The men, sweaty, heaving with effort, open shirt fronts, chest hair, gold amulets and there in the waistbands their mechanical, heavy instruments – pistol, knife; laying on the stone floor, a taller man, eyes barely open – then closing, breathing thin, clothes crumpled by hands looking for purchase. The man looked exhausted, spent.

Air filled with the smell of sweat and panic. Kabir looked down at the smooth stone floor – a red smear pulled from the doorway to the victim. The scene began to reveal its goriness. Blinking rapidly, Kabir saw the large sticky wound in the man's torso. In synchrony, his eyes met with one of the hunched men. Red eyes knitted in rage.

'Who the fuck is that?'

Kabir's ears tingled. His heel slipped on the blood as he pushed himself up off the floor. With a scamper of limbs he found himself upright and bolted out of the door. In a mad dash through the corridors of the building, down the stairwell and into the gullies – Kabir did not dare look back. He hurdled over people and objects. Behind him the noises were undefined. His heart pumped, afraid that at any moment footsteps would catch him. Scampering through the last alley, he made it to the station and dove into the first taxi he saw. Ducking under the seat, 'go, go, go'. After a lurch, the motor caught some momentum and whined itself into the clunk of changing gears. Kabir lifted his head slightly to look behind. In the mass of people, he couldn't discern if he had been chased.

Unsympathetically the taxi driver raised his drooping eyes to the rear-view mirror. 'Where to?' he drawled with a bored, practiced practicality. Kabir jerked back to look again through the rear windshield. Still no sign of pursuers, if indeed there had been any pursuers – his heart slowed.

Through the rest of the ride, he felt little shooting pricks of panic. What had he seen? Was he recognized? Would they come for him? And then the sequencing cause and effect, what was Gawde's role in all this? Was he complicit?

One overwhelming, nagging thought – It couldn't be! Was everything fixed?

$\sim$

Simli Gawde clutched her half empty glass of wine. She had nursed it for the better part of an hour. It was unlikely to ever be finished. Gawde rarely asked her to come to these things anymore, so it must have been important. Small talk and handshakes had been graciously offered. She had a practiced formal charm – always remembering something about everyone and never forgetting a name. Mrs Gawde was a mystery; some assumed she had been an academic, others thought she came from nobility.

Dinner was at the home of the industrialist owners of the network. 'A few friends' counted over fifty guests. The palatial apartment was accustomed to the numbers.

Gawde's presence seemed to be an audition. Did his jib cut the right way into the inner circle? Simli stood with a group of wives a few feet away. She watched her husband press flesh and play along. He had looked at his phone a few times in the last couple of minutes. Then his face turned stony – she knew that look. After a minute, he excused himself and went to the front door. Simli followed.

At the front door she saw a familiar-looking man. He had come to their house before, wearing a police uniform, but here he was in civvies. The man had the type of face that seemed to always be in shadow. He looked animated, speaking excitedly. Gawde stepped outside and took him away by the elbow. Simli stayed back at the party.

'Who was that?' she asked softly on their way home.

'Who?'

'You know who.'

'Nothing escapes you, does it?'

'Well?'

'It's a small thing – one of my boys was at the wrong place at the wrong time. He saw something he shouldn't have seen.'

'Is he okay?'

Gawde waved it off.

'The one at the party, I have seen him come home before. Is he one of your fixers?'

'We call them informers.'

'Whatever you call them. I don't like the look of him. Is he safe?'

'He's a bit of a loose cannon. But it should be okay.'

'Just be careful. You don't want any dirt on you right now. These chances don't come around all that often.'

~

Natasha marvelled at Arjun's defiant little look. A couple of days earlier he had come home from cricket teary eyed. It took her some time to coax him out of his room. He had grown quite attached to Kabir. She was angry at herself for putting them in that position.

Arjun remained withdrawn for a little while, but soon returned to normal. There was no more talk of what happened and any attempts at drawing it out were met with stern silence. He had an ability to shut things out. Natasha fretted that these were signs of a boy from a broken home. She couldn't share this with his father; God knows how that discussion would go.

So she tried talking about cricket, allowed him extra time in front of the TV and bought ice cream every day that week.

~

Kabir awoke from a thick, syrupy slumber. It was a violent type of sleep born from exhaustion. But his head soon cleared. Unsure about the reception he was likely to receive from Gawde, a nervousness twitched his fingers and feathered his stomach. As he drew closer to the studio, he became hesitant.

Hours had been spent turning over the incident in his mind. A tenacious seed of doubt had clamped down on him. Was he an imposter in this role? Would he be exposed as one? Was it cowardice that prompted his flight from that dank, stained room? Should he have stood his ground? But what if he had? Those men might have turned on him. He could be seriously hurt, if not worse. Why had Gawde not reached out to him afterwards? Did he know?

The news channel itself had become news. Reporters stalked the entrance of the building to get any glimpse of more scandal. Squirreling his way through accusatory lenses and flash bulbs added to his feeling of unease and guilt. Inside the offices, the atmosphere was strange. Kabir headed to his desk to stay hidden.

Gawde's cabin was a hive of activity. Overnight he had been entrusted to right the ship and had become the de facto leader of the news teams. People strode in and out purposefully.

Kabir's attempt at staying under the radar was quickly quashed as he was called in for an all-hands meeting. Gawde's room was filled with new faces. Chairs held at least two, one on the seat and the other on the armrest. The floor curried favour with the more junior staff and the rest found standing space by the wall. From production and anchors to the technicians and camera staff, all departments were there awaiting their next directive.

Animated voices threw around ideas, which were then set upon by the others. A common objective was the need to 'distract the viewer from the Neha story,' to 'shift the focus'. The atmosphere was barbed; there was prickliness between groups, in particular members of Neha's team. Gawde sat unmoved for a time but soon enough, impatience crept into his expression. He suddenly jumped up, interrupting the proceedings.

'No, no, no, no, no. It's as if none of you have any idea what profession you are in. When there is a hot story, you don't try and subdue it, damn it... you add fuel to it. We are the best placed station to cover this story. So let's cover the hell out of it. We aired the interview, right? Now use the opportunity to get exclusive interviews with the people no one else can get interviews with. Call the prime minister if you must, god damn it – get someone important to tell us off on our own channel. They are all dying to blame someone or something. Let them do it here! Exclusively! Now get on with it.'

It was a bold, exciting directive. People started peeling off. Gawde caught Kabir's eye and gestured for him to stay. Soon they were alone and Gawde looked dour.

'What happened yesterday?'

Kabir narrated the sequence up until the part he fled.

'What did you see?'

'I... I'm not sure, the guy was hurt. What happened to him, sir?'

'Nothing happened, okay? It's best you forget about it. Don't talk about it.'

Gawde paced, plotting versions of the next move with little shakes of his head and irritable, muttering breaths.

'Why the hell did you sit there for so long?'

'Sir I tried to get out but the guy didn't give me the package, what was I...'

'Then try harder, for god's sake, don't be so helpless. Do you know the mess you have made?'

Kabir's tone stiffened at the injustice. 'You never told me what I was supposed to do. You... you just sent me in there!'

Gawde's brows raised. The pause was laden.

'You're right. I should have known better than to send you there. It's my fault for trusting you with this.'

It was an insincere riposte. Chastened, Kabir felt a thrush of anxiety rushing up his chest.

'No sir, I just meant that –'

'It's fine. Get back to your work.'

'Those guys could have done something to me. I just didn't know –'

'That's why you don't hang around. Don't be an idiot, man. This is all part of the world we live in, you need to be able to handle yourself.'

'But sir…'

'Enough, enough. Go, I will handle it.'

Back to his desk, Kabir flopped on the chair. Gawde's dismissal stung sharply. What did this mean for him? Would he be off the team?

CHAPTER ELEVEN

He leaned back against a lamppost, bathed in its orange pool of light. The dark tar of the road seemed luminous and close. He couldn't quite remember how he got here. The last couple of weeks had been spent in the throes of intoxication and tonight was no different. He remembered getting into the car earlier, but things got hazy in that second place. He recalled bouncing slightly to the thumping hypnotic sound. Pull of powder, clink of ice and something greedily put into his mouth. Now he sat here, bereft, exhausted. Occasionally, a pleasant swell in his brain came and went, but these were becoming infrequent. Already two women had walked up and propositioned him, all tight fits and red lips. They offered him a good time, their voices harsh and incongruous to their hair and gait. Both had angular eyes. The first time they came to him, Kabir did not understand what they were saying. He could feel they were still around, under a shadow over there somewhere.

All he had on him was his phone – he couldn't find his wallet or keys. Staring into the glowing green, he scrolled down for the only name he could think of. The phone rang a few times before it was answered by a befuddled, groggy voice.

'Hello?'

'Ranjit… it's Kabir.'

'K-man! What's going on? What time is it?'

Relief flooded through Kabir upon hearing the friendliness in Ranjit's voice. Kabir took a taxi to Ranjit's building, who was standing on the road to pay the fare. Kabir stayed that night in his small one-bedroom apartment and slept through most of the next day as Ranjit left for work.

In the evening, they went for a walk. He briefly caught Ranjit up to speed with the events since they last met. Getting a job with Indiworld, Natasha, he spoke of the nights out and the people he met. Ranjit listened without interruption. At the end, Kabir turned to find a look of brazen fascination on Ranjit's face.

'Wow Mr K, you lead an interesting life… I'm still hanging with the guys from work.'

Ranjit chuckled spontaneously and Kabir joined in.

After ambling some more, they came upon the seaside. The beach was a warren of little eateries and juicers, each adorned with gaudy, hand painted typography and the brightest colours available at the paint shop. In the dusky hour, little, coloured lights were twinkling, and the scene looked like a chaotic fairy tale.

Ranjit pulled Kabir into the mesh of chaat shops and they sampled their way through them. They walked through the gaiety of balloon sellers and errant wards running between their legs. Mouths ablaze, they ricocheted from juices to tangy mouthfuls. Tamarind fizzled with the heat of green chillies on their tongues. Ranjit was in his element and his moist upper lip excitedly led Kabir to the best spots. Kabir felt a lightness he hadn't felt for a long time.

Darkness had fallen by the time they wandered back to the apartment. They didn't talk about how long Kabir expected to stay, but there was an unspoken understanding that he wasn't about to leave just yet.

They sat on wicker chairs in the whitewashed hallway. Ranjit opened the window as if to let out some of the fluorescent tube light stuffing the room. Kabir wordlessly turned on the single table lamp and turned off the bright tube. The room became softer, beiger, less alarmist. Ranjit looked around quizzically as if he had never considered this before.

Kabir had not parted on the best terms with Ranjit and since then, Kabir had made no attempts to reach out. He felt sheepish. But despite his callousness, Ranjit bore him no ill will. Watching him cheerily surfing channels made Kabir want to confide in him.

'Listen Ranjit, I haven't told you everything.'

Ranjit muted the TV, placed the remote on the table in front of him and turned to Kabir.

'I was wondering when you were going to get on with it.'

Relieved to find a trusting ear, Kabir's narrative was thick with detail. His flow jumped back and forth, voicing the jumble he had kept in his thoughts. Despite being singed and angry, he could barely mask his admiration for Gawde. He spoke of his new grudging respect for Neha and the politics behind her humiliation. Ranjit, wide-eyed, kept pulling the conversation back to the incident at the chawl. Kabir brushed it off, not wanting the story to become about that.

And then through the ramble, Kabir somehow found his way back to Natasha. How intimidating and exciting she was. He spoke of trying to play it cool but failing miserably. He opened up about how much he liked her but was completely adrift about dating a single mother. Could he even do that? What were the rules? In all likelihood, he had screwed it up already and it made him ache.

Eventually it was mostly all said and repeated and there was some quiet. Ranjit brought up the chawl again. 'What did you see? Was the guy shot or stabbed? What do you think? Do you think they will come after you? I can't believe your boss sent you in there.'

'It's how it works, Ranjit.'

'Are you mad? He can't just send you to a gangster "adda." It sounds fully extreme, boss.'

Ranjit continued dredging and Kabir began to realize how bizarre it all sounded.

'While you're at it, tell me about what happened last night.'

'It was a bit of a crazy one, wasn't it?'

As Kabir told Ranjit about his nights out on the town, he sounded alien to himself, like he was wearing a flashy costume. How he had met these new people, how he began to party with them, the first time he snorted cocaine. The thrill of discovery, the intimidation of moving in these new circles and the larger-than-life characters were so far removed from the Hyderabad kid whose parents would be horrified to hear all of this. But once having tasted it, he knew that he couldn't put the genie back in the bottle, nor did he want to.

Ranjit continued in his role as Kabir's dutiful audience. They sat for hours, propped up on the meager furniture, sharing cigarettes and a quart of Royal Challenge whiskey. Seeing his story through Ranjit's eyes made Kabir feel chuffed in some parts and cringe in others.

They laughed and got a little drunk. While they were chatting, the blueish green glow of the TV set pulsed in the background. Something distracted Kabir and as he turned to look, it was a cricket match. Ranjit reached out to turn it off.

'No hang on, leave it on. I want to see the score.'

~

Kabir had stayed the weekend and an additional couple of days. He hadn't called into the office to explain his absence. A lumpy couch and the mildewy odor emanating from his person eventually spurred his decision to leave Ranjit's apartment. The last few days had bolstered his confidence. Ranjit was a world away from his other life; and from that distance, things did not seem all that bad.

Chameleon-like, the city took on the mood he wore that morning. Kabir was filled with heady optimism – he wanted to knock everything into place right that minute. The absurdity of the city's chaotic milieu seemed funny, and it was a beautiful bright day. Kabir went home and ran up the stairs to Natasha's apartment. She wasn't home, so he jumped in a cab and headed to her office. She wasn't there either. He texted her, and after a couple of minutes, he texted her again. He said he was sorry and really wanted to explain.

By the time he got to the office, the workday was well underway. He slunk over to his desk unnoticed. The dynamic shuffle of the place, which had once felt exciting, at this moment felt oppressive.

Chayan noticed him first. 'Kabir men, where were you?'

'Hi Chayan, I got sick. So couldn't come into work.'

'Yeah, we called you also. You didn't answer.'

'I know, I know, I'm sorry. Anyway, what's been happening? Am I in trouble?'

'I don't know. Neha Singh is back.'

'What? Really? How come?'

'I think they need the ratings. You better see Gawde, he ask about you twice.'

Kabir took a deep breath to slow down his thumping heart. He threw himself into his tasks, hoping the day would slip by without any unpleasant interactions. Throughout that morning, he continuously peeked behind his cubicle towards Neha Singh's office. She looked her usual determined self, but her body language was missing its swagger. Kabir gathered up courage and made his way over to her. He stood outside her office, biting his lip and shifting his weight between legs. Finally, he walked in. Extending his hand and trying to keep his voice level, 'Hi Neha. I'm Kabir. I just wanted to say that I'm really glad you are back.'

She appraised him slowly and deliberately. After what seemed like an age, she shook his hand. 'Yes, I know who you are. Thank you.'

He shook her hand briskly and was walking himself out when she called out behind him.

'And thanks for not barging into me this time…'

Kabir spun around to see her standing behind her desk, reading something. There was a smirk on her lips as she looked up at him. He grinned and walked back. The levity didn't last long. He saw a note on his desk to meet with Gawde.

Gawde had moved into a larger office, and he now sat behind an ample table, which made him look smaller. Kabir's belligerence melted away as soon as he saw Gawde.

'Where were you?'

'Sorry, sir. I got sick.'

Gawde rose from his chair and stood closer.

'Did you tell anyone? Did anyone approach you?'

'No sir, I was just staying at a frien–'

'You're sure?'

Kabir nodded.

'Okay good. Listen. You need to be careful. Don't talk to anyone, alright? Even people at the network are not supposed to know.'

Now a hand on the shoulder, an encouraging pat. Back to the bonhomie of the jovial mentor.

'...I'm teaching you about the business. You need to keep your sources to yourself. Good?'

'Sir, what about that police guy? Are they asking about me?'

'You don't worry. I am looking out for you, nothing will happen to you, okay?'

'Sir, what's going on? Is everything okay?'

'It's fine, this is all part of the game. Part of the game.'

Gawde's voice trailed off and he turned back to his desk. Kabir left.

That week, a business-as-usual calm returned to the network. The drama of the earlier weeks was washed away with the latest titillation of Priyanka Chopra winning the Miss World title. International affirmation made public opinion giddy with excitement. News was a gushing stream of tribute to 'us as Indians' and her traditional values were touted as reasons for her success.

Glossies were hungry for the pictures of the swimsuit round, TV clamoured for her erudition in the personality round and the local garment traders pasted pictures from the traditional outfit round all over their shops.

Kabir could never have imagined that the scandal of Neha Singh would be so easily relegated to old news. At the time, it had seemed like the events would shake the foundation of the system. Politicians had berated the shoddy functioning of news channels; leaders had bemoaned the polarizing effect of these interviews; and intellectuals had rubbed their beards at the phenomenon of the celebrity news anchor. It felt like the discussion would last for months, if not years. But here was everyone, talking breathlessly about a beauty queen instead.

Walking the regular stretch home, a sharp familiar sound snapped him out of his thoughts. It was the hollow echo of a brand-new cricket ball being timed perfectly. He meandered up to the maidan. He lingered for a while, but there was no sign of Arjun. A reasonable period of time had elapsed for the two of them to pick up where they had left off, he thought. Now it would require a re-introduction of sorts – an apology, an explanation, the whole rigmarole.

Kabir remained agitated about Natasha. All his messages had gone unanswered. Should he try and meet her? Perhaps she would let him explain. But would that seem too confrontational? Should he let her respond to him? Perhaps he should write her a note and slip it under her door? Flowers? No, maybe that's too much. Exhausted by this mental ricocheting, he trudged back to his apartment. Fate's dark-humoured puppeteer seemed to mock him as he ran into Natasha at the gate. With thoughts of her twisted like a ball of wire, he stumbled and lurched till he found his voice.

'Uh… Hi.'

'Hi Kabir.'

She seemed unphased, as though greeting any old neighbour.

'I… I have been trying to reach you.'

'Yes, sorry. Been busy, what's up?'

What's up? What did she mean what's up? Unbalanced by her casualness, his response became reflexively blasé.

'Not much, I just wanted to, you know, catch up.'

'Catch up? Oh okay, sorry, I need to go now.'

She stepped around him and raised her arm to flag down an auto rickshaw. Kabir felt flustered, not wanting her to leave. He needed so say something. He blurted, 'How's Arjun? I haven't seen him in a while.'

She looked back at him as a rickshaw slowed and smiled slightly. 'He's good. You know.'

An expression briefly flitted across her face, a meaningful look. Kabir felt exasperated as she pulled away. A frustrating veneer of civility suppressed all the things that should have been said. He wished he had said more, but the moment didn't seem to have space to add anything. Watching her leave, he felt further away than strangers feel.

∼

Natasha exhaled slowly as she pulled away. She had not expected to run into Kabir. It had taken a mighty effort not to respond to his messages and she knew he had been looking for her. Reason made it clear that she needed to stop this now. There was no future in it. She really did not fancy spending months sniffling on the couch, pulling yarn from the balls of whys and what ifs when things inevitably disintegrated. It was better to nip this in the bud, like a Band-Aid, painful at the rip but necessary.

But the look on his face as she sped off, his large doe eyes, confused and appealing. She could see regret and guilt writ on his face. At that moment Natasha hoped this wasn't finished.

CHAPTER TWELVE

The high-pitched ring of the phone was amplified to his early morning, slumbering ears. Kabir reached out to find his screen glowing 'Dadu' and it was well before 7 a.m. Kabir cleared his throat and mustered his best attempt at sounding awake.

'Hello?'

'Hello son,' came the booming military man's riposte, 'Are you asleep?'

Kabir's spine stiffened hearing his grandfather's voice – a ward's ingrained reaction to a patriarch. The sensation felt so strange after all these months of living independently.

'Well good, I caught you before the day started. Now look here, I am coming to Bombay later today.'

'Really?'

'Well, you need not sound so excited on my account, son.'

Kabir smiled.

'But yes, I am coming and if you can temper that enthusiasm, perhaps we can calm you down enough to get a few hours together.'

'How long are you staying?'

'Oh, a couple of days. I have some business to attend to and many old acquaintances to meet. It will be a busy trip.'

'So, when do we meet Dadu?'

'Tomorrow, come meet me for lunch. I will be staying at the Officers Club. Come and see me and we can spend the day together. Okay? Good.'

As he turned over to snatch a few more minutes of sleep, a type of fidgetiness took hold in his joints. It was an old feeling but one he hadn't felt for some time. A gnawing, pestering yet exciting, lifting sensation. He turned over again but he couldn't sleep.

It had started a few days ago at the office. He couldn't avoid glancing repeatedly at a flickering sports segment. Australians were back in India and prospects looked bleak. The last time they toured India, it was a different world. Kabir was flooded by warm memories of college cricket grounds, of chasing around town in a scooter, of Sahiba; most of all, of Azharuddin and Tendulkar flaying the bowling.

But this team was different. His life in Bombay seemed to mirror the contrast from the previous test series. This time the series felt hard-nosed.

He watched a clip of Australia's warm-up game against the Mumbai XI. Justin Langer danced down the pitch and swung at a spinning leggie. The arc and motion of the stroke was crafted in the heavens. It was as though this diminutive Australian had been put on earth to sweetly time this lofted on-drive over, mid-wicket and into the stands. You couldn't help but admire the poetry of the accelerating bat swing. Ugh, it didn't look good for India. For the rest of that day, he wished he could un-see that stroke. He even managed to forget it for a little while but wherever he looked, there were hands rustling newspapers, little transistor radios pressed up against ears, kids playing on the street. The first test was to be played in Bombay and the city was thick with conjecture. As he went about his day, trying not to bother anyone, smatterings of players' names cut through the ambient city noise and stuck in his ears. Those lunch time commuters debating endlessly – did they not understand that he didn't want to know?

THE AUSTRALIAN RAMPAGE

In trying to correctly understand the Australians of 2000, you needed to get away from the statistics. The only appropriate marker was that they challenged the titanic West Indian goliaths of the 70s and 80s for the longest unbeaten run in test match wins.

Gum chewing, square jawed and sun-kissed, they were playground-bully-confident and smirked at the opposition's meek attempts at contest. Their gamesmanship was legendary and wherever they played, they did more than win; they humiliated their challengers. Almost half their team would be picked in any all-time dream eleven. Was this the best team the world had ever seen?

Expecting victory against this lot was impractical. The best that anyone hoped for was not to get skinned and try to draw out the contest a little. Their ranks included Shane Warne, already considered by some as the greatest cricketer ever. A tubby, shrewd, floppy, blonde leg-spin sensation who befuddled the greatest batsmen. Glen Mcgrath, arguably the greatest opening bowler of all time, would invariably wound the top order of your line up. The captain Steve Waugh, a tough-as-nails, salt-of-the-earth, man-of-few-words leader would demand death before surrender. Not that they ever came close to that choice. Ricky Ponting was one of the most talented batsmen to ever play the game; Gilchrist performed impossible feats at will; the list went on.

The only teams that came close were Pakistan who were fielding their potentially greatest ever side. Flying locks and rugged Pathan good looks had already been swatted into submission. The professional South Africans didn't stand a chance either. So, when these Aussies came to Indian shores in 2001, bar the mercurial Tendulkar, the rest of the team (and the country for that matter) looked woefully out of their depth.

~

In the colonial edifices of the old town, thin columned pillars curved into trellised plinths, punctuated by the odd gargoyle. Within the cluster of this once mercantile, imperial city were pleasure grounds for the sahibs to walk and amuse their passions for sport. The memsahibs would sit on the edges of the field, a strident gaggle of parasols valiantly shielding their lilywhite laces. Today those open parks continued their sporting traditions, but the colour and chaos would be unrecognizable to those erstwhile company administrators. The Officers Club abutted one of these parks.

Having stretched out on the white cane chair on the verandah, Mr Menon propped his stick and newspaper on the table in front of him. He crooked his neck ever so slightly so as to draw the attention of the bearer. A gin and tonic preceding lunch was protocol, one he had observed since his days in the Force. In those days it was par for course to mimic the white sahibs and their manners. 'Chotas' would soon turn into 'badas' before the remainder of the day turned to drunken administrative machinations of the Empire. Raj Menon smirked at the memory of how subservient they were to these moderately average Englishmen sent to India as glorified rubber stamps. His musings had turned towards his memories of Bombay city as a young cadet when Kabir popped up next to him.

'Hi Dadu!'

'Ah, hello young man. What's with this mop on your head? Did the city run out of barbers?'

The older man chuckled at his own joke as he hugged his grandson who took a seat across from him.

'I'm glad you're finally here. I am hungry enough to eat that waiter's arm off.'

Full of vigour and authority, Raj Menon waved over an intimidated waiting staff and ordered two portions of fried fish with chips and extra lashings of tartar sauce on the side.

Lunch was spent catching up with the goings-on. After a second gin and tonic, they moved over to chairs on the lawns. The older Menon tilted his head back and fell brazenly asleep, leaving Kabir to read the scraps of newspaper left on the table. It felt oddly comforting watching his grandfather's snoozing chest rise and drift, his mouth slightly ajar, emanating the hint of a rasping snore. For the first time in his life, Kabir noticed frailty in his grandfather's figure; muscle and bone looked slightly shrunken and aged. It was strange and faintly disconcerting to see this man, once so much larger than life, take on the hue of mortality. Slipping on to the grassy lawn, Kabir snatched one of the longer grasses and started chewing, the smell of the green was fresh and happy.

He looked at the newspaper and there it was – the sports page with analysis preceding the first test match in Mumbai starting tomorrow. Instead of turning the paper over, he continued reading. Bad portents got worse with confirmation that Kumble wasn't playing. They were exacerbated by Steve Waugh's form heading into the first test. Just as he began audibly grumbling, his grandfather's voice snapped him out of his thoughts.

'Okay come on then, let's stretch our legs.'

Kabir obediently followed his grandfather out of the club. They took a left outside the wrought iron gates and circled around the wall into the open maidan. Their route skirted the edges of the ground as Raj Menon described the city he had seen when he was a boy. There were far fewer people and far fewer buildings, but the gothic spires anchored the cityscape much as they did today. He recalled standing in the 'Indian' enclosure, watching polo, which was still played on this ground in those days. An occasionally errant whack of a mallet would send the weighty ball hurtling into the adjacent Parsi Cricket Club, holding up play. His tone barely masked the distaste as he reminisced of those times.

Today the field was a jumble of different club grounds with no discernable demarcation. Each club played their own cricket match. The mid-wicket fielder in one game looked equally likely to be in the covers for the game next to him. Raj Menon found a tree and they both stood under its shade for a few minutes, watching the organized chaos in front of them. Lightly swaying, impossibly tall palms framed the edges of the large flat field as though they were pillars holding up a big sky.

'So, Kabir. People back home seem concerned about you. I told them that I would check in on you and see what all the fuss was about. Now, I expect it's nothing more than a case of spreading your wings and sowing your oats and that sort of thing. I'm sure some girl has you wrapped around her finger and your eager hands are otherwise occupied.'

Raj Menon chuckled loudly at his own description of the situation. Even though he didn't share in his grandfather's levity, Kabir couldn't help smiling.

'But it's not that, is it, son?'

'What do you mean Dadu?'

'I can tell by the way your knuckles are dragging along the ground that something is bothering you. Your parents worry – when you speak to them you seem listless and distracted. My solution was to let you bump your head a few times and scrape your knees, but your mother insisted I check in on you. Talk to me boy, where is that annoying little pipsqueak I used to know?'

'I'm fine, Dadu. You really didn't need to come all this way.'

'That's quite enough of that feeling sorry for yourself routine, so unless you want me to thrash it out of you, start talking. You know I will do it right here!'

Both giggled happily as Raj put an arm around Kabir.

'I don't know where to start...'

'Well, then start at the beginning.'

Raj Menon swiveled on his heels as a sign to keep walking. They left the maidan behind and walked westwards through a leafy road, past a large, pastel yellow, art deco apartment building.

At first the words seemed perfunctory, their only purpose to act as vessels of incident and information. His grandfather expertly goaded him with open-ended questions and the words began to form patchworks of feeling and intrigue. Events in Hyderabad, just prior to his leaving, were stained with a feeling of bad faith. Bombay had turned from lonely to exciting. His experiences at the network were larger than life and in the center of it all, Gawde – laced with treachery and possibility.

They stepped off a pavement, crossed a busy road, yellow and black taxis whizzing around them as they did. This area was considered the quieter part of the city, but a din lurked behind the next building or around the corner. Passersby became more festive as they got closer to the ocean-front at Marine Drive. Office penguins shed their tucked shirts for a more unbuttoned matinee idol look. A giggling lilt of chattering girlfriends danced in the air as they headed towards the delights of seafront peanut sellers and ice cream trolleys. Apartment buildings on either side of the street created a tunnel for a joyful, whipping sea breeze, which hit the ambling Menons, picked up their collars and pressed their shirts to their chests as Kabir completed his story.

'And who is the girl?'

'What girl?'

'Come on, boy. I haven't come all this way to be bored by your stories of work colleagues. Confusions of this sort are rarely the result of anything else.'

Kabir remained quiet and Dadu didn't press any further.

Twenty silent minutes later, they found themselves sitting on cemented benches overlooking the Arabian Sea. Hoping to catch their last morsels, seagulls gathered and dove into the slanted, setting rays as the tide brought up tiny fish to the surface of the muddy ocean. Raj Menon broke the silence abruptly.

'Don't you get it, boy? His truth is different from yours. In his world, what he did defines his success.'

266

It took Kabir a moment to register that this was about Gawde.

'But it's wrong, isn't it?'

'Would you feel the same way if you were still in his inner circle?'

Kabir hesitated

'Yeah, I would. I mean, if he did what some people suspect. Also his link with the cops is strange, right?' he added unconvincingly. Raj Menon turned to look at the boy, a smirk returning to his face.

'Maybe, maybe not. That man hasn't had the luxury of high-minded ethics. In a scramble to get out of the weeds, you need to step on whatever takes your weight.'

'Are you taking his side?'

'It's not so simple, boy. People sometimes do what they must do.'

It surprised Kabir that his grandfather didn't agree. It sounded suspiciously like a conversation intended to build character.

Watching his grandson settle into a scowl, Raj Menon prodded him further.

'It's the same with what happened back home. Are you certain that if you were in your coach's shoes or your friend's, you would have done any different?'

'No Dadu, it's not the same. I would never have done what they did – there are some things you just don't do. What happened back home was wrong.' Kabir's tone turned brittle.

'You knew your friends so well, you looked up to your coach, so then why did they let you down?'

Raj Menon turned to look up at the curving promenade to allow some space in the conversation. Kabir, faced with a challenge to his certainties, became prickly. Shifting forward, he rested his elbows on his knees and stared out into the ocean, which was changing colour from brown to grey. On the horizon, rays of blue and orange light shot through gaps in the few wispy clouds scattered in the sky. It was getting late, and Kabir began to feel anxious. An uncomfortable realization had started gnawing at him. He didn't want to leave these thoughts unresolved.

'I suppose I understand what you are saying, Dadu. So, don't trust anybody, just do whatever it takes to get what you want. I'm not sure I understand because I know that's not what you believe.'

Raj Menon swiftly changed gears. 'I hear you have gone off cricket. How come?'

'After all that match fixing stuff, I just grew sick of it. They are all cheats.'

'Do you blame yourself for what happened back home?'

The rapidly changing directions were unbalancing Kabir who was inadvertently becoming short and terse. It felt like an interrogation.

'Blame myself? No. Why should I?'

'I don't know – maybe you could have been more involved? Maybe you blame yourself for leaving?'

Kabir's voice was now raised.

'I had no choice. Papa pushed me to go. Also, what was I going to do there anyway? They all deserted me. They behaved like –'

'They behaved like what?' Raj Menon yelled back.

'Like ASSHOLES!'

Kabir caught himself mid-shout. He expected Dadu to be angry at his outburst. You just did not scream at your elders, and you certainly watched what you said. But as he turned with a panicked look on his face, he caught his grandfather laughing lustily, the sparkle having returned to the old man's mischievous face.

'Good! Now that that's out of the way, let me give you a piece of advice, son. When you're a child, life has simple answers and that's wonderful. As you grow up, you can continue to be certain about things but now you have no excuses for your certainties. You become accountable. Nobody tells you when you pass from one phase into the other – but I'm here to tell you that now you have. You are now an adult. And as you mature, I hope you become even less certain, less sure about the answers.'

'Oookaaay... so what should I have done? What is the lesson you are giving me?'

'It's quite obvious, isn't it? The lesson is that people, like players, are imperfect. Life, like cricket, is imperfect and much of the time it is going to hurt you, but it's still a great game. It's still worth fighting for. As for what you should do, that bit is not so easy, is it?'

Kabir sighed loudly and buried his head in his hand somewhat comically. The gesture looked despairing but it was the opposite – it signaled a lightening of the mood. Raj Menon laughed and put his arm on Kabir's shoulder. The sun had dipped into the lightly swaying sea, leaving an orange afterglow. At the far end of the curving seafront, a prickle of lights showed the beach stalls coming to life. There were far fewer people where they sat and the whistling breeze had taken over from traffic noises. The wind off the waves felt warm but fresh.

'Just between us son, it's okay to stand up and give the occasional person the finger. Oh, and for god's sake, go and apologize to the girl, whoever she is, for whatever you have done. Women must be apologized to regularly and properly...' Raj Menon rose from the bench. '...Hopefully it will sort out that hangdog mope you are lugging around with you.'

Kabir stood as well and pushed himself into his grandfather, wrapping his arms around him.

On the way home, Kabir stared out of the window of the clattering taxi. Recollections flashed across his unfocussed gaze. They mingled with the taste of the conversation he had just had. Thoughts were throwing themselves in and out, unwilling to linger. Soon one image began to drown out the others. He pictured Natasha. It pulled him into a forceful, urgent longing. Kabir tried to push it away. He tried thinking about his grandfather's message and what it implied. But the more he tried, the more the thoughts of Natasha pestered him. Grabbing his phone, he punched in the only number that could resolve this.

'Hello?'
'Hey Ranjit, do you have a joint?'
'Yup.'
'Okay, I am coming over.'

CHAPTER THIRTEEN

Endeavouring to be positive, Kabir had decided to toe the line with Gawde and reclaim his lost confidence. Live to fight another day – he told himself. Riding up the elevator to work, uplifting strains of electric guitar in his headphones helped him piece together a plan towards his rapid promotion in the network. He would kick ass. The soaring choruses of the song made him believe that the universe was walking in step with him. As the mechanical doors parted, he was slightly disappointed that there wasn't a welcoming sequence of pirouetting, smiling co-workers, waiting to whisk him on their shoulders for the crescendo.

He was quickly brought down to earth with the realization that he mattered very little in the scheme of things. Gawde was unavailable and nobody else seemed to be aware, let alone care, that he had returned, resurrected, with a soaring soundtrack. People continued doing what they were doing and he was promptly handed the mundane drudgery of expense reports. Today was not the day Kabir Menon changed the world after all.

It started very badly. Pretty much the 'worst-case-scenario' type of start. Feeling immensely better about things, Kabir had timidly ventured to follow the match and now he wished he hadn't. Despite his best attempts at ignoring the score, he couldn't help walking past TVs telecasting the game. Every time he did, he chastised himself for being stupid and the clouds darkened. India was overawed and bundled out for under two hundred runs. The script was playing out as feared and events in his life began resembling the cricket once again – he should have known that everything was connected; he should have recognized the portents of doom.

Something was afoot. A mood akin to clanging of spears before a battle settled around the office. Rumours of Gawde's complicity in the scandal had thus far swirled on the edges. But on this day, the words were spoken out loud. Gawde's team was followed around with sideways glances and cold shoulders. Kabir found Chayan in a frantic state, not knowing what to do with his hands – he fidgeted, moved things around and wiped his sweaty palms on his trousers.

'Crazy men Kabir, everybody think we did this.'

'Who's everybody?'

'Yesterday night, HR call me on the phone. Today, everybody talking around.'

'Nobody called me.'

The morning took on a bizarre sequence. Small groups would form and scamper out of the office. There were several sorties around the back of the building or across the road. It was as though the words could not be spoken within the four walls for fear of combustion.

After a couple of hours at his desk, Kabir's extension phone rang. A voice he did not recognize summoned him to the upper floors where the executives sat, a place he had never been to before. He entered a meeting room with large glass windows on two sides and a view of the city below. He counted eight people, the only one he had spoken to before today was the head of human resources, Mrs Das. A green sari-clad lady in her sixties with sharp eyes and not a hair out of place, she had been a part of his induction at the network. He remembered his induction as a daylong exercise of sitting around a room with drones from human resources speaking slowly and condescendingly. Kabir's takeaway was the overwhelmingly hollow feeling of a whole day that he would never get back in his life.

At the head of the table sat a man he had only seen pictures of, Mr Puri, the president of the network. A slim, tall man, with a timbre which sounded like solid oak, Mr Puri personified something quite the opposite of Gawde. Silken and smooth, he spoke with an accented, clipped English and looked like he had slipped the knot of his old boy's tie after a round of golf this morning.

Kabir was low in the pecking order and the men in the room continued chatting amongst themselves, paying him no attention. Mrs Das asked him what he knew of the 'fake interview'. He said he knew nothing – he went on to narrate the sequence of events of how he had come to learn of it. As he spoke about the dinner at Krishna Restaurant, the room quietened and paid attention, and a hawkish man he did not know interrupted.

'So, you were at that dinner, were you?'

'Yes, sir.'

'Are you sure that's all he said? Because we have heard a different version from what you are telling us.'

'Yes sir, that's all I heard.'

'And you left after that?'

'No sir, I left with Mr Gawde and his driver dropped me home.'

'Really? You forgot to mention that earlier.'

'Yes sir, I didn't think about it earlier. But we never discussed anything in the car.'

Knowing glances bounced around the table.

'Has Gawde ever asked you to do anything for him beyond your job? Has he ever put you in an uncomfortable position?'

This line of questioning felt like quicksand. These were the people who, only a few weeks earlier, had lauded Gawde's resourcefulness. Sources of information and their antecedents were open secrets in the office. They had pulled him close for handshakes. With conspiratorial

273

winks and knowing grins, they pumped him up as being their man. What were they trying to do now? What did they know?

Kabir was caught off guard. His ears tingled.

'Don't worry, nothing will happen to you. You can tell us.'

'Err... No, sir.'

Two men jabbed simultaneously: 'You could get into real trouble'/'That's not what we heard from your team.'

'Sir, what do you mean?'

'It's better if you are straight with us now. Just tell us whatever you know.'

'About the interview?'

'Yes, and anything else you may want to tell us.'

Kabir's hesitation caused some shifting in chairs.

'I... I'm not sure. I have heard other people in the office talking about it, but I don't think Mr Gawde said anything else.'

The room descended on an opening. The prodding chorus came thick and fast now and it was more threatening.

'There is no point protecting him.'/ 'We know what actually happened.'/ 'You won't find another job after this if you're not being truthful.'

Kabir managed to stay firm and after a time the room paused.

Mrs Das now addressed him, 'We already know what happened, Kabir. When action is taken, it will be taken considering that you all worked under Gawde as a team.'

Mr Puri raised a hand, preventing unveiling the remainder of her threat. So far, he had sat impassively. Now he shifted forward and others around the room seemed to physically pull back. Training his strangely blue eyes on Kabir, he smiled, 'Kabir, I like you. You seem like a bright young man and surely an asset to this company, I can tell. I can also understand that you would have had no choice but to support your superior. I applaud your loyalty.'

Charm flowed through his baritone and enveloped the room. He paused, to let the compliment sink in.

'I was like you once, you know. I know how confusing these early years can be. But hard work isn't everything, we also need to make the right choices. I am sure you did not hear anything intentionally incriminating. But you and I know that there was always something going on. I want you to write a report with your version of events. Whatever comes to mind – even the smallest things. I can assure you that I will personally look into your position at the network and reward you for the hard work you have put in. We need smart guys like you in important positions here.'

With that, the president of the network stood up, strode over to him and shook his hand.

And there, just then, Kabir wanted it for himself. He wanted to belong on this floor, in this story. He wanted to have his voice heard. What would he call it? Ambition? Kabir began to see the virtue of it all.

'Mrs Das will walk out with you and brief you on what is to be done. Right, thanks, good to meet you. Oh, and if he made you do anything you were uncomfortable with – please make sure you let us know.'

Kabir stood in the lobby with Mrs Das. He wasn't sure what had just happened. It was done so glibly, so very velvet gloves – that he was drawn into Mr Puri's camaraderie.

Mrs Das' syrupy, dogmatic instructions snapped him out of this reverie. A version of things said about Neha on a casual day-to-day basis could easily be construed as mutinous and damning. In the little time he had spent in this business, everyone spoke shit about everyone else. It didn't mean anything and those in that room knew it. What worried him more was his own role in the chawl affair.

Kabir left the office confounded. A text on his phone from Mrs Das reminded him to get his report in to her as soon as possible.

CHAPTER FOURTEEN

Ranjit and Kabir were embarking on their second hour at the coffee shop. Iced, hazelnutted, creamed, sugared, frothed concoctions had long since been drunk. Their flat, milky brown remnants betrayed none of their former puffy glory. Dusk had turned to dark and the bright orange interiors of the zippy, youthful coffee chain shone brightly through the windows and spilled out on to the road.

Kabir had received calls from Gawde and a text message – 'call me back'. On the opposing side, human resources and others were also courting him. The fawning missives had dulled some of the awe of Indiworld TV. Larger than life characters now seemed human, flawed.

This attention made Kabir feel important; it was seductive.

Over the course of the past few months, he had come to appreciate Ranjit's steady, spartan logic. While he didn't always agree with him, Ranjit's jovial reasoning was annoyingly irrefutable. It was a process of sucking the emotion out of fact and event – something that didn't come naturally to Kabir.

Ranjit's views on happiness and achievement were not tied to notions of self-expression and individuality. Instead, he placed value in transcribed patterns of career and clans – possessions but not extravagance and investment, not flashiness. Maybe he aspired for a little flashiness but nothing outside of what his community would find youthful indulgence – a Mercedes, a Swiss watch, that type of thing.

So when Kabir came to him for advice, Ranjit had no hesitation in his prescription. Resolve it with the bosses, sell out Gawde. This was risk free and would save his job. As always, his logic was exasperatingly evident.

Kabir's counter argument was based on sentiment, emotion – something just didn't feel right. Frustratingly, he was unable to explain it.

Today, for once, Ranjit had his own dilemma. A dispatch had come from his family that it was time to settle down – they had met a few suitable candidates for Ranjit's marriage. Pictures had been sent and after some titillation, the boys had started dissecting the prospects. Kabir couldn't fathom how his friend could just pick (or have someone pick for him) and they went back and forth for some time about the benefits of this process of entanglement.

'Look, it's simple right? When you get a girlfriend, the first few years are great but then what? When the fun wears off it becomes a partnership and contract right? Kids, living together and you make a journey. In this way at least we know that the backgrounds are compatible, the families are similar, etc. It's much less messy this way man.'

'But what if you find that you don't like her?'

'Why won't I like her? I will meet her first. There will be some ups and down but in the long run you need to understand boss that this is a partnership.'

'I don't know man – it sounds very weird to suddenly marry someone you don't know. Someone you don't love.'

Ranjit flicked his wrist, dismissing the objection.

'Ha! Love grows boss. My parents love each other, and they didn't even meet till the wedding. Yaar it's not for guys like you.'

Kabir prickled slightly at that. Ranjit sometimes came off as sanctimonious.

It was time to go. Kabir's itchy confusion was not going to be cleared up by Ranjit today.

~

Time had passed – much water had flowed down many rivers, so when a knock on Natasha's door opened to Kabir, the sharp chafe had dulled. Arjun was asleep in his room and they sat on the stairwell where they first met.

To Natasha, Kabir seemed different somehow. He seemed more put together, more confident. She noticed a quirkier side to him as he played the fool. She liked it. Her gaze became attached to him, and a stubborn smile formed on her face. She checked herself – 'Careful Natasha' signs were flashing in her mind.

Kabir had spoken to her about his work before, but tonight he spoke breathlessly. It was as though he wasn't trying to dress it up for her anymore.

'That's why I really wanted to speak to you tonight. I wanted your opinion on what I should do,' Kabir finished.

'THAT'S why you wanted to speak to me?' Natasha teased. Careful Natasha, careful.

A grin wrapped around his face 'Well, that's the excuse I am using to get you to speak to me again.'

Damn – right answer.

'So, tell me what you wanted to talk about.'

Kabir told her about meeting with the top brass. He spoke of his suspicions.

Natasha bristled at Gawde's overreach. Men in power seemed to believe they had a right to trample upon a woman by whichever means they saw fit. Whatever her flaws, that woman was an icon. She deserved respect and fair play. Eyes blazing, Natasha interrupted him.

'Kabir, you MUST write that report for them. You must put this man in his place.'

It's what Kabir had expected her to say, but she hadn't really heard the whole story. He wasn't even sure if Gawde had done anything. There was only suspicion and rumour.

'Look Kabir, even if Gawde didn't directly set all this up, the fact that he often derided her behind her back is reason enough.'

'Yes, but everyone does that.'

'But they are all men who make all the decisions! Do you know how much harder it is for a woman?'

This was irritating – the question of women and their struggles wasn't the topic of conversation here. His inner scheming was not finding the reaffirmation he sought and he changed the topic.

Looking at Natasha directly, he shifted gears.

'What's happening between us? Are you still angry with me?'

'No. I'm not angry. But I don't think we should do that anymore. Look Kabir, the last time Arjun took it quite hard.'

'We had a fight. These things happen right?'

'Yes, but my life is more complicated than yours.'

Kabir had been pining for Natasha for so long that he expected to put up more of a fight. He didn't respond.

A flicker of disappointment came over Natasha's face and then it was gone. Kabir watched her slim, graceful limbs stretch out and stand. A familiar attraction tugged at him. They stood looking at each other and she quickly kissed him on the cheek.

'Good night, see you later.'

～

Kabir sat up in bed, his mind going over the alternatives. Hoping for an opinion to bolster his own, he called Mustafa. After hearing the entire episode, Mustafa didn't offer much of an opinion.

'My friends are advising me to write the letter and tell the

279

bosses what Gawde did. What do you think Musty?'

'I don't know Kabir… Just remember what happened in university. Just stay out of it. Better to remain quiet.'

Recollections of the large room with wooden desks and slow squeak of rotating fans, of professors and academics and the smell of ink. So inconsequential compared to the real world he was in now. Thinking back, his old self seemed childish.

Mustafa's response didn't seem to factor in the appropriate immenseness; his advice lacked the required boldness. Back home, they wouldn't understand.

Kabir's thoughts turned to Barman. When Kabir first moved to Bombay, he had written a few letters. Barman replied once – a brief collection of strung together pleasantries. Kabir wrote a couple more times, but life moved too fast for the sedate writing of cursive and eventually he stopped.

Back in college, Barman seemed so worldly and larger than life. Today, Kabir's circumstances were so alien. His old mentor seemed inadequate; he would have little to offer Kabir.

Kabir also thought of Sareen.

'Musty, what's going on with Sareen? You know I spoke to him, it was quite weird. He seemed like he was, I don't know, not himself. Quiet. I couldn't get much out of him.'

Mustafa usually avoided the topic, but tonight he told Kabir about what he knew. For a few tumultuous months after Kabir left Hyderabad, Sareen was often seen bruised and heavy eyed. He had also become entangled with the police, but all that had ended a year or so ago when it became too much. Since then, Sareen had left the gang and embarked on a rehabilitation of sorts. Mustafa barely saw him anymore. Sareen had tried patching things up but Mustafa had still carried the weight of who Sareen had become in those months.

Kabir felt like he already knew all this. It was a strange déjà vu.

Kabir was relieved to be removed from all of it. Lives lived back home felt limited, without possibilities.

Normally their conversations would have some catching up over the neighbourhood, the gossip, the who, what and wherefores. But these chats had become increasingly rare. Kabir was less interested now. Soon they wrapped up and Mustafa, in his gentle manner, wished him well.

A loud thundering sound woke Kabir – it felt like it was coming from the ground and the walls. Then he saw the world reverberating with brutality. Disoriented, it took him time to realize that this was an earthquake. He bounded out of bed and ran up the stairs to Natasha's apartment. The shaking had stopped by the time he got there. When she opened the door, he could see the fright on her face. He hugged her and for a moment they sat together with Arjun. Little else compares to the raw guttural fear of a natural event and even after they knew it had passed, Natasha and Arjun clung on for what seemed like minutes. After the shaking ended, there was absolute silence. Slowly, the world awoke with shouts, doors opening and bewildered people rushing to open spaces.

Natasha looked up at Kabir and then nestled back into his chest.

~

An eerie pall had blanketed the normal din of the streets. The city appeared undamaged, but there was an undercurrent of shock. Something awful must have happened somewhere and little snippets of news were beginning to seep from radios into anxious ears. The aftermath of the Gujrat earthquake was devastating. Images streamed into the control room and the destruction beggared belief.

It didn't take long for the impatient crackle of the network to resume. Given the magnitude of the earthquake, Neha Singh would have customarily jumped on the first moving vehicle in order to proclaim her 'breaking story', but today she was rooted in the office. Her absence may adversely affect the events afoot.

Kabir avoided calls from Mrs Das who was now pestering him to submit his report. Chayan and the others kept to themselves, unwilling to discuss anything with him or anyone else – the atmosphere was tense. Every so often, someone or the other would come to have a word with him and it was becoming difficult to fend them all off. The longer he vacillated the more threatening and suspicious the atmosphere became. Kabir decided to get out of there and just as he gathered his things, Gawde spotted him and beckoned him over. Kabir's heart sank – if only he had crept out a couple of minutes earlier.

Gawde asked him to close the door.

'I know they called you in, what did they say? Did they tell you that the others have confessed, and you should as well?'

Kabir looked at a tired, flustered man.

'Yes, sir. They asked me to submit a report.'

'I know they did. I also know you haven't done it yet. You know they might kick you out if you don't send them something? I don't know if I can protect you.'

Kabir nodded.

'Well? Are you going to ask me if I did it?'

Kabir had been staring at his shoelaces. His head snapped up to find an amused Gawde.

'No – you're not going to ask, are you? Well, I didn't do it, I'm not that stupid.'

'I don't think that's what this is about anymore, sir. They want to know if you asked me to do anything improper. It's turned into something else.'

Gawde spun around slowly in his seat and looked out of the window.

'I know, I know. It's a witch-hunt now. They need to keep Neha Singh and now that she's accused me, it has become about her being abused because she's a woman.'

After a moment of introspection, Gawde continued in a steady voice. 'She's the one who has had to struggle eh? I would have much preferred being a woman from the English-educated, intellectual elite club. All you people are connected, your parents know each other, you went to the same colleges, you have memberships to gymkhanas and members-only clubs and they think that they have had to struggle? My friend, you have no idea what struggle is. Being the wrong gender is far preferred to being the provincial native.'

'Sir, what are you going to do?'

'I'm going to fight them, of course.'

Kabir nodded and left Gawde's room. Chayan was waiting for him outside.

'Kabir, the team is meeting tonight to talk about what to do. Nine o' clock, I will tell you where, okay?'

Kabir nodded.

At the day's end, as he headed north up the artery of the city, he thought of another besieged leader. Saurav Ganguly was taking his beaten team to Calcutta. His form was woeful, and he was being branded as churlish by the Australian press. Ganguly had made the Australian captain wait a considerable time before coming down for the toss at the start of the match. It was written up as an intended snub – a childish man trying to score childish points. For not bowing to the niceties of the proper form, he was labelled the wrong man for the job.

Something Gawde said stuck with him. Or was it the way he said it? In this city you were surrounded by stories of sacrifices and paths chosen to get ahead. Kabir would need to make his own story because now he had a thirst for it too.

CHAPTER FIFTEEN

Familiarity doesn't just happen like the turn of a page. It creeps and seeps and kneads without the faintest suggestion. Then one day you look around and you just feel different. The bustling garment store on the corner, the eatery spilling out on the road had all once seemed mysterious and different. Now they are familiar because you have passed by enough times for them to assume permanence. They are now furrowed and mixed into memories of your life. And just like that you are no longer from out of town. You live here now; this is now home. Kabir pondered this as he stood waiting for his onions and tomatoes to be bagged in thin polythene that stuck to everything. Surveying his local market, he recollected how alien this three-way junction used to be with fresh fish vendors abutting the vegetable sellers and flanked by the more permanent general stores. Locals used the word 'naka' for a place where roads diverged and traffic gathered. It could be a market or a traffic light. Naka was a new word for him but now this naka had become his own.

Sauntering home, his flip-flops slapped up on his soles. He considered how casually people dressed here. When he first started the bank job, he would be the only one wearing a tie to the office.

He told himself that he would continue to wear a tie to stay unique and different but soon enough his uniqueness became routine.

Banter was another casualty of the city. Back home they would take pride in a turn of phrase and the orthodoxy of language. Bombay had more of a slapdash, theatrical approach with strange meaningless sounds taking the place of real words. Manner and language were martyred to humidity and universal comprehension.

Taking the stairs two at a time, he flew into his apartment. He had momentarily forgotten that the girl from last night was still there. Efforts at pleasantries were awkward; he had hoped she would leave when he was out. Thankfully it only took one cup of tea and some stunted conversation. It had been a bit of nothing really, someone who had shown interest but not someone who would be interesting. As he hurriedly walked her out, he glanced guiltily up to Natasha's window, but no one was looking.

Back in his empty apartment, it didn't take long for dark gloomy clouds to roll over him. Missives from the office had turned into threats and the thought of being thrown out lingered like a stone in his gut.

The team had met the previous night to discuss their fate. They remained loyal to Gawde. Despite his sharp tongue and occasional derision, Gawde had taught them everything they knew. He had helped each of them rise up the ranks.

Knowing that their safety lay in acting together, they decided that none of them would submit anything to human resources.

Kabir hadn't said much. This reminded him of game theory from second year economics. Prisoners' dilemma and the two thieves, each being interrogated in different rooms – both are given a choice to betray their counterpart, and they must choose. Perhaps he should have been paying more attention instead of admiring the parabola of the projected spitball.

But Kabir found himself in front of a blank sheet with a pen in his hand, about to commit an insinuation to record. Putting the pen down, he walked over to the window. He lit a cigarette to calm his nerves.

A flicker of an idea emerged. For a few minutes, he stared unfocussed in thought. From deep in his wallet, he pulled out a pressed, stained piece of paper with a number written on it. He thanked his stars for not having thrown it away. The number rang multiple times. Kabir almost disconnected before it was finally answered by a gruff ominous voice.

'Hello?'

'Pandit, it's Kabir.'

'Who?'

'Gawde sent me to you. Remember? I have met you a few times...'

Kabir sounded nervous. He was talking too fast.

There was a pause. This call was unexpected. The other end of the line was trying to comprehend its motive and implication. Kabir could hear breathing.

'What do you want?'

'I want to talk to you.'

'So talk.'

~

The two sides faced off across an irrationally long boardroom table. Neha Singh faced Gawde and around them sat the board and Mr Puri. The seconds hand of the clock was audible in the heavy silence. Neha restrained herself with great effort. She feared that if she made the opening salvo, a dam of accusation would burst uncontrollably, washing away any high ground or composure. Gawde sat implacably, looking respectful. This annoyed Neha even further, convinced as she was of his duplicity.

Finally, Gawde turned to the head of the table.

'Mr Puri sir, why are we here?'

Neha Singh, eyes blazing, shifted aggressively forward in her chair.

'Gawde, what do you know about the terrorist I interviewed in Kashmir?'

All gentle and honey-toned, Gawde fixed her with an even gaze.

'Neha ji, you tell me, you did the interview.'

'We all know that you have a racket with our handlers. This terrorist must have come through your connections, we know that'

'You keep referring to him as a terrorist, it seems he wasn't one.'

Neha was being expertly goaded. Her voice rose to a shout and hands began jabbing.

'Gawde, you planted that lead in my team – this whole thing has the stink of your doing. We can't even find that handler anymore.'

Gawde's tone remained saccharine, 'Let's be careful not to throw around accusations without proof…'

He now addressed the room, 'I do not appreciate my integrity being questioned. If there are others who feel this way, speak now.'

Neha's eyes darted around the room and fell pointedly on some, but no one spoke.

~

The sporadic, electric fizzle of the faulty streetlamp matched the staccatos of its blue light flashing on and off. Darkened walls in the alley looked wet as they flickered alight and then darkened. As he waited, Kabir imagined himself in a thriller film, waiting for something sinister to become. In a comedic twist, Chayan stumbled around the corner looking harried.

'Where have you been? I have been waiting ages.'

'Sorry man.'

'Did you get it?'

Chayan handed him a parcel the size of a thin brick.

287

'Did anyone ask you anything?'

'No man, but I need to put the money back by tomorrow otherwise it will be a big problem.'

'Don't worry, I will get it back to you.'

'I don't know Kabir, maybe this not a good idea.'

Chayan hovered nervously as Kabir stuffed the parcel in his bag.

Kabir punched a text message and snapped impatiently. 'Chayan, just go, alright?' Reluctantly, Chayan trudged off.

A few minutes later, 'Lanky boy' appeared.

'Why am I in the street? Why didn't you come up asshole?'

'It's better this way. Here I don't see anything I am not supposed to see.'

'Asshole.'

'Give me the file.'

'Mind your manners, otherwise I will need to teach you some.' Kabir's eyes bore into the boy's face. 'Either hand it over or I can let Pandit know that you didn't like my manners.'

Lanky handed over a thin paper envelope in exchange for the parcel and turned to leave.

As he tucked the envelope in his satchel, Kabir spoke to the turned back.

'Don't be such a hero the next time. Just do the job you're supposed to, okay?'

~

Natasha stared at the umpteenth iteration. Sometimes the frustration of client revisions was amusing, something to draw and moan about, an anecdote to regale her friends with about tastes of the 'corporate types'. Other times it was just the overcoming of drudgery as a necessary part of livelihood. Often it drew exasperation because the revisions rarely looked as good as the original. But today her mood was more vexatious than usual. Something else was pulling at her while she tackled the latest feedback on a logo. The P's and the B's were not curved enough, 'you know what I mean?', 'it just doesn't feel right, you know?' 'get where im coming from? You do na of course.' Of course she actually didn't. And god save her from another round of existential debate on whether there ought to be a period at the end of the logo – 'what will it mean?' 'what will it say about us?' 'how do we want people to feel?'

Ugh, all this for an incomprehensible bio-pharma-chemical-tech something company.

Earlier that day, her cleaning maid had made a comment about Kabir's 'lady friends' who come to see him. The comment seemed innocent enough, but given that it was completely out of context, it made Natasha bristle. The maids in the building were the purveyors of all the gossip. They had their game of planting seeds and nourishing them. Natasha was wise to their ways, and she tried ignoring it, but it had already gnawed its roots into her.

Her balance had been off ever since she heard it. Little pangs of loss tugged at her. Initially, after their fight, the thought of the added complication in her life kept her away but over the last few weeks, she had begun to miss Kabir. Perhaps she had been hasty, perhaps the problems were within her and not about him.

CHAPTER SIXTEEN

Waiting in the anteroom, Kabir plucked nervously at his sleeve. Security had guided him directly to the fifth floor, not allowing him a moment to set his things down on his desk.

News had got around that Gawde's ouster was proving to be difficult; having rejected a face-saving resignation, he had refused to go quietly.

A few moments later, Kabir stood in front of the same set of executives. These jowly, angry men looked like playground bullies, taking pleasure in plucking his feathers. They said it was too late for Kabir to save himself. He would be let go; he just didn't fit into the culture.

Kabir was dismissed, but he remained standing there, summoning courage to do what he must.

'If I write the report, can I keep my job?'

Someone responded, 'It depends on what you have to tell us. We cannot guarantee anything.'

'But will you remove the rest of the team?'

People in that room had spent many hours in deliberation and hand wringing. The mood was tired and impatient.

'Mr Kabir Menon, we don't need to explain ourselves to you.

Now, if you have something to say then get on with it.'

'Gawde has made me carry cash to pay off someone. I think he has something to do with the police. Also, I can tell you about what was discussed within the team about Neha, even though I don't have any information on the "interview" itself. If I submit this in a report, I need to know that I can keep my job.'

Nobody responded. Kabir willed himself to look directly at Mr Puri.

'Also, I have a big story. I have a list of important people, including some celebrities, placing illegal bets on cricket matches. I want to be the producer of the story.'

The resulting pause was thick and indecipherable. Kabir followed it up nervously. 'I have evidence.'

Puri was intrigued. 'Is this from Gawde's source?'

'It's now my source, isn't it?'

Kabir sensed a subtle shift of atmosphere in the room. Feeling bolder, he spluttered on, 'If you don't want me, I can take it to another channel.'

Puri shook his head, looking amused. 'Okay Kabir. We will keep you if you write the report. You can also take the lead on the story.'

'Also, I will need to pay my source. I need money today if you want the story.'

'Well, we cannot be officially involved with any such thing.' He pointed to a thin, bespectacled man, 'Mr Raja here works on our accounting and legal matters, he will help explain and sort things out.'

A door of some kind had opened and once again Kabir felt like he was being led into a private club.

'But Kabir, let's be clear. Gawde and the rest of your team will be let go. Will there be a problem with that?'

Kabir shook his head.

'No, sir.'

His newly acquired cubicle was small – but it was his. It allowed a table and squeezed in a couple of chairs. But it did not allow the luxury of standing room; you needed to be much more senior for that. Kabir was just pleased to have a door.

It felt odd to Kabir that Gawde's ouster wasn't more tremendous. Gawde was once such a centre of gravity that Kabir expected some version of disintegration or stunned aimlessness, but instead people went about and things carried on. Gawde seemed but a ghost, a rumour.

The old team had been disbanded, some had been asked to leave and others had been reassigned. Chayan had been let go and Kabir knew he had his part to play in that. He peered over at his empty table, surprising himself at how quickly he hurdled over the inconvenience of thinking about it.

A month had passed since Kabir had spearheaded the illegal betting story. When it broke, animated graphics bounced around a judgmental anchor, making it seem important and epoch-making. But it was gone and forgotten in a couple of days. No follow-up investigation, no shoving mics in faces. The 'important people' on the list ended up not being important enough or glamorous enough for another news cycle. Within forty-eight hours, something new garnered the animated graphics.

Since that story, Kabir hadn't brought in anything new. The spotlight had glinted briefly upon him and moved on. There was now an implied expectation on him to replicate, to perform, to stand out. It was a constant sense of discomfort like a misfitting pair of shoes.

That morning, weighed with these concerns, Kabir took his place in the back of the room. His first story had inducted him into the weekly editorial meeting, albeit as a silent observer. Mr Puri attended occasionally, and he was present that day. In these gatherings, stories were discussed for the week and plans were made. Today's stories included a politician inaugurating a new road, a farmer protest, trouble in a celebrity marriage and some communal unrest in Hyderabad.

Kabir's ears pricked up at the mention of Hyderabad. Meagre details spoke of some fighting in the city ignited by grassroot politics and spurred on by religious hardliners on both sides. Neha Singh and the senior editors debated the importance of this information.

'It's too small a story, these little flare ups happen all the time.'

'Yes, but it seems to be happening regularly.'

'I agree, there seems to be some planning behind these skirmishes as though they are building up to something.'

'What do you mean?'

'Doesn't it look like one side is goading the other to make a move?'

'Yes, all that's very well but we don't have a story here. We don't have a protagonist or a subject. By the time we get our resources there, the trouble could be all done and then there is nothing to report.'

Before he knew he was saying anything, 'I think I can get an interview subject – I know people in the city.'

Heads spun around to look at Kabir.

Without acknowledging him, Neha addressed the table, 'We need someone with more credibility. I don't think there is anything to this, let's move on.'

She made no attempt at concealing her grudges. The topic changed and the meeting continued. Kabir's cheeks flushed at the chastisement. It took a few minutes to collect himself. As he did, he became increasingly convinced that he needed to grab this opportunity.

He cleared his throat. 'Umm, I… I know someone who was part of these gangs, we can use him.'

'I already told you no,' Neha snapped back.

Mr Puri interjected, 'Hang on, Neha. Kabir, you know someone in these gangs personally?'

'Yes, sir.'

Kabir told them about Sareen and what he had witnessed in college. He left out details about their friendship. He also left out the fact that Sareen was no longer a part of that world – he would figure that out as they went along.

The idea was compelling enough to interest the people around the table. Mr Puri pointed and tapped at the table.

'This is good, it can work. We need a face to this thing and this guy seems perfect. Neha, this could be a good interview for you. Excellent work, Kabir – set it up.'

Kabir didn't mean for Sareen to be the subject, but the momentum of this thing had taken over the room. Copy was being discussed, logistics organized, and local stringers were being called. The machine was turning, and Kabir was central to it all – if done right, this would be big for his position at the network.

He lingered for a moment, half-wanting to correct the impression he had given. But then he decided against it and concluded that Sareen would, in fact, be perfect.

~

It was a long day at work and he got home late that evening to find Natasha waiting for him. She wanted to talk.

She spoke about herself – why she was the way she was and why she needed to separate and compartmentalize things. She spoke about Arjun and how she felt responsible for the consequences of her actions in his life. She spoke quickly, sometimes repeating herself. Then she spoke about 'us' and how he made her feel.

Unsure of what was going on, Kabir surmised that either he was being told off, or that this was a type of grown-up conversation he had never had before.

Gradually it dawned on him that Natasha was talking about getting back together.

He had imagined this moment many times over the last few months, willing it to materialize. He had missed her and he had ached for her. But something had shifted. Kabir was torn between wanting to pull her in close and stepping back. He wondered why he was now uncertain. Was it because his mind was diverted by the goings-on at work? Was it her exposed vulnerability which made him less keen?

He told her that he was going to be travelling on a story. They would talk when he returned. Things were hectic for him right now.

Soon they were in an embrace, but Natasha had noticed his momentary hesitance. As she turned to leave, she smiled at him quizzically. He hadn't asked her to stay and felt a little relieved when the door closed behind her.

Maybe she had left him standing alone a little too long. He had begun to become accustomed to it. Maybe he feared that it would happen again – the same agonizing lurch of things not working out, of being cast aside. But no, it wasn't that.

A clap of thunder snapped him out of his reverie and he went over to the window. An unseasonal storm was brewing outside. Its howling, whistling winds had a dramatic sense of foreboding and made Kabir think of Shakespeare's *Julius Caesar* at school – 'The ides of March'. He hadn't thought about home in sometime and as if by some divine providence, his phone rang. His father was calling.

CHAPTER SEVENTEEN

Cynicism spreads virus-like and can decay the bastions of the most bright-eyed optimists. An optimistic sports fan provides a warm, willing host to cynicism's parasitic coils. Years of dashed expectations have gradually yellowed any faith that they had of winning. Every game is now an agonizing, bitter experience of watching your team find ways to mock you and your juvenile hope.

However, even though cynicism finds purchase, it can never completely infect the mangled psyche of the obsessed sports fan; it can never truly infect something which is already so contaminated.

So it was with Kabir that despite the allegations and evidence of shady bookies and the story that he had produced, he couldn't help but watch the game. The first day of the Calcutta test match was deflating. Despite the mismatch in the two sides and evidence from the last defeat, Kabir held out eternal hope. But the muscular torment of Mathew Hayden flattened the Indian bowlers despite conditions tailor-made for the Indian team.

It was the first time Kabir was returning to Hyderabad. He had imagined his return so differently.

When Kabir saw Sareen – cowed, his hair shaved close to

his scalp, his eyes deep, the fire seemed doused. Despite Sareen's reluctance, Kabir had convinced him to come on camera - 'you owe me'. Sareen was pliant; he seemed grateful to speak to Kabir again and eager to please.

'What is this interview about?'

'It's a story about the local elections and stuff, nothing much. We need to speak to regular people – you are just one of the subjects. Since I am from the city, my job is to get some people for them to talk to.'

'You know I'm not into all of that anymore.'

'I know, I know, don't worry. You don't need to talk about that.'

Kabir had not informed anyone else. It had been less than thirty-six hours from the editorial meeting when they had decided to do the story in Hyderabad. Preparations had consumed all that time and he hadn't considered meeting anyone. In fact, had his father not fortuitously called the night before, he may not even have told his family he was coming.

Kabir carried a sense of guilt at the distance he had created with his family. He felt sheepish. Rather than address anything, he had left it vague. Prem Menon's stoic tone barely masked a hint of disappointment – Prem 'understood' of course, he would come by to the shoot location anyway, and hopefully they could meet.

On the way to Hyderabad, Kabir read the script. They would cast Sareen as the poster fanatic. Once cut with shots of broken detritus on the street, bloody heads, and a weeping relative of a victim – thin on detail, it will make for great TV.

This interview would be Neha's comeback and Kabir's big breakthrough.

They chose the alley by Mianji's bakery. The background of the old bazaar made for a compelling setting. It was to be broadcast live; the drama enhanced by large graphics – 'LIVE'. Repeated by anchors in the studio – 'Coming to you Live'.

A hand on Kabir's shoulder revealed Mian Qadir.

'Hello boy, you come back after so much time and not a word to your long-suffering uncle?'

'Mianji, I was just going to call you right after this shot.'

'Are your parents here? They didn't tell me you were in town.' Mianji looked over his shoulder expectantly.

'No, I... haven't seen them yet.'

'How long are you here for?'

'I leave tonight.'

'Oh, when will you see them?'

'I don't think I will on this trip, I'm quite busy.' Mianji's eyebrows knitted.

'And Mustafa? That boy doesn't stop talking about you, it's quite annoying.'

Noticing the activity behind him, he asked, 'Oh! What's all this going on here? Is that Sareen?'

'Yes, we are shooting about that riot trouble that happened a few days ago – we think it may have been another religious issue.'

'Nonsense, it was a criminal gang thing. Anyway, why here? That happened on the other side of town. What's Sareen to do with anything?'

'Don't worry about it, Mianji, it's just TV. We need to get some shots in different places around town.'

Mianji's face revealed that old no-nonsense look. He looked Kabir up and down as though having immediately sized up the situation. To Kabir's relief, someone from the crew called out to him but as he spun around, Mianji held him by his shoulder.

'Make sure my shop is not in your shooting, understood?'

His tone of disapproval made Kabir feel like an adolescent. Like a pup in fear of a pack elder. The reflex irritated Kabir. He wasn't a child anymore.

Sareen was being prepped by production. A presumptive hand up his kurta, a mic clipped to his lapel. Pushy crew asking him to repeat 1, 2, 3, a little irritated with his wide-eyed incomprehension of why he's being prodded so – he wasn't used to the brusque big city hustle. He asked Kabir whether he's going to get the ruler on his ass next, like in Mrs Mehta's math class, you know, the last time someone asked him to repeat numbers. That little chirp, that quip, that giggle – the old Sareen. Sareen bore the prodding studio-light in his face with the good-natured sunniness of his youth. He asked no questions.

Final preparations were underway; cameras rigged, cables laid and signals checked. Kabir played his part. He reassured Sareen that they will catch up after the shot, which will only take a few minutes.

He watched Sareen being led to the set like a lamb to the slaughter. Neha Singh sat with her face slightly upturned, eyes closed, to let the droplets of hair spray settle gently around her like a halo. In her hands, her notes had Sareen labelled. It wouldn't matter what he said. They would make him whatever they wanted to make him. She ignored Sareen's polite hello as he was placed in front of her.

Kabir noticed this. He had seen her postured arrogance many times but here it caused a flash of anger. But then he thought of Natasha; how she had explained Neha and the reasons behind things. That thought then flowed into other tributaries and soon he found himself reminiscing about all the times Natasha had been his raft through this confusing tide. The only mooring he had from getting washed into accepting that that's how things were done.

A passing crew bumped into him and broke his trance. Kabir shook away thoughts of her and moved back a few paces away from the set.

All that was left to do was wait out the minutes till they were cued in.

From the corner of his eye, Kabir was distracted by a waving figure. Mustafa stood with a bunch of onlookers who were being kept at bay, away from the shooting area. His face beaming excitedly, his arms waving. Mianji must have called him.

Kabir went over and spoke to Mustafa briefly who seemed thrilled to see him. Mustafa told him the score, India were fighting back – they should go watch it. Mustafa said he would wait for the shooting to finish.

Smiling teasingly, 'Big man you've become, Kabir.'

Again, this irritated Kabir. He didn't have time for this.

'Your parents are coming here too.'

Kabir felt uncomfortable – he saw other faces in the bazaar whom he recognized. His thoughts galloped – he wondered where Barman was right now. He imagined what it would feel like if he spent the night back home with his parents.

Just as the interview began, he thought he saw his father's face at the edge of the crowd.

This is a pivotal moment. The point of no return. This moment of television juice will be cut with visuals of the incident from a couple of days ago. It will be exclusive and live.

It will be Kabir's springboard, maybe it will set him up for a seat on that boardroom table someday.

Maybe Sareen will be okay after this. After all, memories are short.

But the screen is the screen, the opiate of opinion. Packaged and processed, everything becomes glossier, veneered and true. It's life, right?

The interview began and Neha, as scripted, smiled and began gently. Get the subject to like you, trust you. Kabir shifted position so he could see Sareen's face better. He looked intimidated but he had that impish charm, his eyes warm and trusting. Kabir couldn't stand there anymore. He walked away from it and followed the thick wires into the broadcast van. Only one operator sat in the van, his spectacles reflecting the green and blue of the screen, his fingers lightly placed on dials and knobs. Plenty of space behind him, Kabir would watch from here.

Then it began in earnest – the twist of the knife, the lead out of the interviewee to a place where they least expect. From which they don't come back. He heard Neha's voice '... so you are saying that it's okay to attack the Muslims because they are well off...'

'No, I, I didn't say that! I was just saying that...'

Just at that moment he thought of a mythological allegory. Something he had learned as a child. It wasn't clear if it came from a school play or a grandmother's tale. The story of the besieged king of the thousand brothers, sacrificing his kin to fulfill his ambition. Treacherous but justified to himself.

A hot dread, like dripping wax, came over Kabir. Being back in this place, seeing these faces, what seemed like a rational, evident set of choices now seemed duplicitous. There was a sense of finality in what was happening. Was this the rite of passage of becoming what you must become?

An avalanche of emotion caught the breath in his chest.

The lever just sat there, singular and away from all others. Simple in its function – on/off. Only the thickness of its handle betraying its pecking order in the myriad controls.

'Isn't it true, Sareen, that you have in the past been a part of these attacks on the Muslim community? We have evidence.'

'Who told you that? It was not like that, I–'

'Mr Sareen, did you attack Muslims two days ago?'

'No, I didn't.'

'But you know who did Sareen, so why won't you tell us who they were?'

Kabir couldn't get himself to look up at the live feed. The cricket was on one of the screens in the telecast van. His eyes sat unfocussed on the cricket match.

Kabir had to ensure that it went down, its weightiness mustn't resist his will. Blood pounded in his ears and panic welled up in his chest.

As though it was cued, Laxman pulled McGrath imperiously for four.

Kabir reached out and pushed down emphatically.

The lever was more pliable than it looked.

Everything went black. Broadcast switched to the studio in Mumbai. 'We seem to be having some technical difficulties'.

Urgent engineers bounded into the van to figure out what had gone wrong. Kabir squeezed between them and slipped out of the van. Reaching Sareen, he plucked the lapel mic off. In the confusion of voices and commands, nobody paid them too much attention.

Neha sat opposite, exasperated at one and all.

'Kabir, what are you doing?'

'I'm bringing him back in a second while we fix things.'

Neha spun back towards the van.

'Will someone tell me what's going on? Who the hell is in charge here?'

Kabir mumbled urgently to Sareen who looked on uncertainly, 'Get up idiot, quick!'

Yanking Sareen to his feet, Kabir pushed towards the crowd. He looked back over his shoulder at the van. The bespectacled operator stood at the door, his eyes trained accusingly on Kabir, his expression incredulous. He knew what Kabir had done and it was only a matter of time before everyone else did too.

No chance of folding into the confusion now. Bridges were well and truly detonated.

Kabir thought only of getting Sareen out of there. These were the same streets they were chased through a few years ago. This time Kabir ran to reclaim something. He ran because he had no idea what was going to happen next. Inexplicably they started laughing, and the more they laughed the faster they ran.

Sometimes, rarely though, the birth of something special can be pulled back to one incident or one moment. For Indian cricket, and indeed for much of the nation, you could argue that that spring day in 2001 was the harbinger of great change. A sense of rising belief and pride.

That morning the famed grounds at Eden Garden, Kolkata, drew smatterings of supporters. VVS Laxman (since christened Very Very Special) and Rahul Dravid took to the field. The best anyone expected was some good batting and polite applause. Perhaps they could balm the lacerations the Australians had already inflicted, make them a little less sore and sensitive. No one, absolutely no one (including the team), believed this match could be saved.

But then something strange happened. Only divine intervention could have produced the events of that day. Laxman, blessed with a very rare grace of batsmanship, played as though he was being controlled by his divine namesake. McGrath, the metronomic, fast terror, was caressed effortlessly, repeatedly, to the offside boundary. The ball seemed to ping twice as fast off Laxman's bat. Shane Warne's beguiling leg spin was smothered by dancing down the track and whipping wrists. The audacity of the strokes was mind boggling.

Slowly at first, but then steadily, the crowds started coming back in. Bengalis all over the city began to call in sick for their post-lunch shifts. The fabled echo of the Eden Gardens crowd began to thrum again.

And on the other side stood Dravid, strong and resolute. Having borne the taunts of the green-cap-loud-mouths, he unfurled a lesson of his own. Cracking and driving the opposition into the dust till he raised his century. Uncharacteristically, he gesticulated to the two-faced press cordon who had questioned *his spine all through that series.*

Ganguly stood in the pavilion, no longer the impudent, spoilt maharaja – but the shrewd, motivational captain.

It was glorious! It changed the fighting face of Indian cricket. India went on to win that match and the next one at Chennai. Even though there remained chinks in the armour, after that day, the Indians were no longer the polite also-rans. They were here to fight.

EPILOGUE

Something was strange. Every place was open for business and there were people around, but it still seemed deserted. There was almost no sound.

Sporadically the static cheers of a televized crowd piped through the gullies. Kabir and Sareen ducked into Sunshine Bakery. A TV was playing above the cash counter and the benches were filled with gawping customers. Kabir caught Mian Qadir's eye – he gestured them over. Mianji brushed away the occupant of the chair next to him who obediently shuffled towards the back. Kabir and Sareen sat down, smiling sheepishly.

Mian Qadir continued looking at the TV.

'I was wondering whether you had lost all your manners, Kabir. I heard you had decided to stay back for some days and you have only deemed your uncle worthy of your scruffy presence today. Hmmm?'

Qadir waved over some fluffy yellow cake.

'Sorry, Mianji.'

Mustafa showed up soon and squeezed in next to them. The place filled up over the course of the afternoon and into the early evening. Even Prem Menon and Barman had uncharacteristically eschewed their aversion to collective devotion. The two men sat beside Mian Qadir.

Every ball they watched, Kabir expected the story to end. One of the batsmen was bound to get out. But he didn't. Instead, over after over, the two Indians produced magical shots, dreamlike! It was unbelievable.

The ingrained superstition of the cricket fan ensured that workdays were missed, wives ignored and chores forgotten. The atmosphere in the bakery swelled. They all watched together like one tribe. Nobody was allowed to move from their spot for fear of displeasing the fickle goddess of fortune.

It was an afternoon every obsessed Indian fan could replay in vivid detail. They could tell you exactly where they were that day. They would tell you all the important tasks, errands, life's work they had ignored and at what point they began to believe.

At close of play the batsmen stood unbeaten. Kabir lurched out onto the street with the remaining occupants of the bakery.

Around him were family, his friends, his old gang.

He saw a text from Natasha:

are you watching the match? It's amazing.

It triggered a smile. He wished she was there with him.

'Mustafa, you know what this is like? You remember that last scene from *Return of the Jedi*?'

'The one where all the Jedi masters come back as ghosts and hang around with Luke Skywalker?'

'Yeah exactly. This is exactly like that.'

Sareen screwed his face up and looked back at them. 'What a bunch of nerds.'

ACKNOWLEDGMENTS

This idea probably germinated before the idea of this idea ever came to pass. I was in graduate school doing job interviews that didn't hold my heart, but left-brained their way into my psyche as the right thing to do. In those days of waiting rooms in shiny offices, in my one 'work' suit, I would occasionally (dreaming of another path) send my resume to a movie studio or a record label. Some of them humoured me, most changed their number due to the metronomic regularity of my over-eager phone calls. Clinging to a sliver of it-could-happen, I began to think of an idea for a movie. The story of a boy, at a place in time.

So a small scrap book was procured with one singular purpose. Half a story was conceived with arrows and thought bubbles. It was all done with hands and pens, no typing and saving of files. And then it was forgotten in the inevitable movement of life. Months passed, then years and even decades. Somehow this little scrap book made it unscathed through travels, new apartments and spring cleanings. It would always find itself at the top of the bookshelf, ready to be rediscovered. It was a sign.

Then Covid happened and like many others, I found myself locked down, staring out of a window. Much like the physical scrap book, the story of Kabir seemed to have a way of popping up. It found its way to fingers tapping on a keyboard. Suddenly the world had quietened and I figured I would try and write this movie in prose.

I never thought of writing or being a writer. To me authors belonged to an exclusive club, one in which membership or a rite of passage was required. So I called my dear friend, Priya Kapoor, who knows writers and writing (it's her day job). She told me to write a few pages and send them to her. She read them and encouraged me to keep going. This cycle repeated itself a few more times till I had a hundred pages. By then, to her great regret, my confidence had grown as had my gumption – 'Have you read it yet?', 'Yes, but what do you think about this (or that)?', 'What do you mean the ending doesn't make sense?' Thankfully she stayed firm and true, making me change the second half multiple times. I owe this book to her great patience and sense of humour. Without her it wouldn't have been written.

My mother read it during its formative period and with her surgical intellect, condensed the characters' motivations very early on, and it helped me think of them clearly. My father chanced upon the pages and he grumbled something about grammar, I think.

My mother-in-law, Lorrie Macgillivray, read the first draft diligently. She printed it out in large font, made copious notes on almost every page and couriered a large box all the way from a picturesque lake in Minnesota to Gurgaon. She made it through all the cricket references, which must have been as comprehensible as Chinese (she's not multi-lingual). She has an ability to analyse the rhythm of plot and her notes were essential in improving the manuscript. Most of all, it was her kindness and encouragement, which helped dispel my doubts on my ability to write a novel.

Christina, my wife, remained convinced that I could write this. She read it and made the right pointers at the right time. And thank you also to Vir and Kersi, who dabbled in some reading and nudged me along.

Finally, the thing was written and in came my editor, Isha Maniar. Her editorial eye was invaluable in getting us over the finish line. She was the first one who made me believe that this was a real book. Her humour remained unshakeable and attention to detail remained annoyingly steadfast. Even though she was sometimes exasperated at the 'boys' in the script and their foolishness (especially in matters of the heart) – I managed to convince her that we meant well. We got along swimmingly.

Manimanjari Sengupta, the smiling, brilliant, illustrator seemed to impart true emotion whenever her brush touched page. She indulged my concept for the cover art, improved it and changed it numerous times – all while chuckling through our phone calls and generally being all sunshine.

But I digress. The idea which came before the idea was conceived in an India of my youth. Looking back, we were but simpletons compared with teenagers today. Much like cricket, life's lessons from our elders were passed on as though they were yellowing paper and All India Radio. But at the same time, liberalization of the economy had thrown the gates open to the outside world. Foreign brands, TV shows, sponsorship, investments, opportunities and terrible advertising. Our morality was bound to be shaped by our youthful thirst to break away while clinging to what felt like home. Looking back, I feel like we gained more than we lost but we should have lost less. Today there is a danger of losing ourselves entirely and what it meant to be us. *Gods of Willow* is a work of fiction. Some underlying historical events in the book – the cricket, the attack on parliament, the beauty queens, however, were very real. To suit Kabir's story and portray the essence of the times he lived in, I condensed and rearranged some of these events into four years, which, in reality, played out around the time of this narrative but not quite. Hopefully this book will feel nostalgic for those who grew up in, and experienced, what was truly a changing time.